T0357633

"What a cracking start to a new se[ries]... peek behind the curtain of a writer'[s] misadventure between the Killer Que[en and the] police detective has something for everyone. Definitely worth diving into!"
—Carolyn Miller, best-selling author of the Regency Brides and Regency Wallflowers series

"Crystal Caudill has done it again! This enemies-to-lovers historical has it all—an endearing heroine, a protective officer, humor, intrigue, mystery, and redemption! Readers will be kept guessing, and will be eager for the next book after devouring this fantastic debut to Caudill's aptly named series, The Art of Love & Danger."
—Grace Hitchcock, speaker and award-winning author of *My Dear Miss Dupré* and *To Catch a Coronet*

"Danger, mystery, hidden identities, villains, heroes, and gallantry! Everything you would expect in a dime novel, but better! *Written in Secret* is a rollicking, fast-paced mystery with characters that pop off the page. The wit and intelligence of both the hero and heroine had me rooting for them from the first chapter!"
—Erica Vetsch, author of the Of Cloaks & Daggers series

"A rambunctious heroine and a stalwart, determined hero—my favorite combination! Toss in danger and loads of humor—not to mention a breath-stealing romance—and what do you have? *Written in Secret*, a fantastic new story by Crystal Caudill. This tale will leave you with a serious book hangover, making it hard to decide which character you miss most. For me, it's definitely the swoonworthy police officer, Abraham Hall. Truly an entertaining read!"
—Michelle Griep, Christy Award–winning author of the Blackfriars Lane series

"A pure delight! With a masterful artistic flair, Caudill seamlessly weaves faith and romance into a heart-pounding mystery. The witty and often humorous banter between the characters in *Written in Secret* lends a perfect balance to the riveting suspense. A must-read for anyone who enjoys a beautifully crafted romance with a deep faith and thrilling plot."

—Stephenia H. McGee, award-winning author of
The Cedar Key

"Crystal Caudill's *Written in Secret* is a twisty mystery that manages to be both a delightful caper and a serious exploration of justice and our responsibility to those around us."

—Janyre Tromp, best-selling author of *Darkness Calls the Tiger*

"Crystal Caudill continues to put a fresh spin on the Gilded Age with this brilliant first book in her new historical romantic suspense series. *Written in Secret* delights from beginning to end with a dashing policeman hero, a plucky dime-novel-author heroine, and a mysterious vigilante villain. The layered and amiable characters come alive under Caudill's skilled pen, and her engaging writing voice and clever plotting kept me solidly immersed in the story. This is another entertaining winner from Caudill, with meaningful, practical faith applications too. A must-read in every way!"

—Carrie Schmidt, ReadingIsMySuperPower.org

"An adventure novel with romance, depth, and intrigue! Fans of Michelle Griep and Erica Vetsch will delight in Crystal Caudill's newest release. What reader doesn't dream of books coming to life? They do in this story—only it leads to disaster! Caudill moves the plot along quickly with great tension and suspense while also weaving in a dramatic spiritual shift for the heroine."

—Joanna Davidson Politano, award-winning author of
The Elusive Truth of Lily Temple

WRITTEN IN SECRET

BOOKS BY CRYSTAL CAUDILL

Hidden Hearts of the Gilded Age
Counterfeit Love
Counterfeit Hope
Counterfeit Faith

The Art of Love & Danger
Written in Secret

WRITTEN IN SECRET

The Art of Love & Danger

BOOK ONE

CRYSTAL CAUDILL

KREGEL
PUBLICATIONS

Published by Kregel Publications, a division of Kregel Inc., 2450 Oak Industrial Dr. NE, Grand Rapids, MI 49505. www.kregel.com.

Crystal Caudill is represented by and *Written in Secret* is published in association with The Steve Laube Agency, LLC. www.stevelaube.com.

The persons and events portrayed in this work are the creations of the author or are used fictitiously, and any resemblance to persons living or dead is purely coincidental.

Scripture used in this book, whether quoted or paraphrased by the characters, is taken from the King James Version of the Bible, public domain.

Library of Congress Cataloging-in-Publication Data
Names: Caudill, Crystal, 1985– author.
Title: Written in secret / Crystal Caudill.
Description: Grand Rapids, MI : Kregel Publications, [2025] | Series: The art of love and danger ; book 1
Identifiers: LCCN 2024046926 (print) | LCCN 2024046927 (ebook)
Subjects: LCGFT: Detective and mystery fiction. | Christian fiction. | Historical fiction. | Novels.
Classification: LCC PS3603.A89866 W75 2025 (print) | LCC PS3603. A89866 (ebook) | DDC 813/.6—dc23/eng/20241106
LC record available at https://lccn.loc.gov/2024046926
LC ebook record available at https://lccn.loc.gov/2024046927

ISBN 978-0-8254-4907-9, print
ISBN 978-0-8254-4909-3, epub
ISBN 978-0-8254-4908-6, Kindle

Printed in the United States of America
25 26 27 28 29 30 31 32 33 34 / 5 4 3 2 1

To my mother-in-love, Linda Netherly.
We've walked through a lot of things together,
and always your love for God shines through.
Thank you for being that light . . . and sometimes
my unintended guinea pig for plot points.
I'll endeavor to never food poison you again.

He hath shewed thee, O man, what is good; and what doth the Lord require of thee, but to do justly, and to love mercy, and to walk humbly with thy God?

—Micah 6:8

CHAPTER 1

MANY DIME NOVELISTS EXPERIENCED CREATIVE blocks to their writing, but Lydia Pelton doubted any of them would stoop to impersonating a clown and rescuing a three-legged goat from the circus to overcome them. A wise decision on their part, no doubt. Letting Theresa convince her this was the best solution to both of their problems bordered on lunacy. Not only had they abandoned their corsets and skirts for—Lord, forgive them—oversized trousers and red shirtwaists, but they'd concocted the most ridiculous plan of extracting a bleating goat from the circus. At night. When everything was quiet and calm.

They were fools. The stench of the outhouses they hid behind only confirmed it.

Theresa tugged on Lydia's shirtsleeve and pointed between the wooden buildings toward the lantern light of the circus grounds' guard.

If he adhered to the same path as last time, he'd exit from between the colored tents, then meander toward the big tent—the opposite direction of the menagerie.

Lydia scratched at the tacky white paint on her face and watched the light grow brighter. *Please don't let this go like I'd write it.*

He exited and proceeded just as expected.

Good. Maybe tonight wouldn't be a catastrophe. After all, if she'd written this, the guard would have visited the necessary and discovered them. It was a perfect plot device for fiction. Not so much for real life.

Lydia leaned in toward Theresa to keep her voice low. "It's not too late. We should leave now before we're caught."

"Don't be such a coward. You're a Guardian, and Guardians do not leave the defenseless in the hands of such negligent brutes."

They might be Guardians, but half of their group were tucked in bed in their homes, like reasonable people. Besides, the oath they'd made during their school days to protect the defenseless hadn't been meant to extend to animals, but that was Theresa for you. She couldn't abide the abuse of man or beast—even if that beast were a three-legged goat owned by the Adam Beadle Circus. Lydia should have called on Nora and Flossie for help with her creative block. Maybe then she wouldn't be in this impossible position with Theresa.

"What if we're caught?"

Theresa readjusted the cone-shaped hat over the tight bun on top of her head. "With as often as I've evaded Grandfather's and Mrs. Hawking's supervision—tonight included—you have nothing to be concerned about. Just follow my lead. Now come on. Tipsy needs us."

She darted to the nearest tent, leaving Lydia to debate her next action in the shadows.

Just because you would pen this as a complete disaster doesn't mean that's how it will happen. Just pretend you're one of your heroines. Or better yet, Billy Poe.

The hero detective of her crime novels embodied bravery, determination, cunning, and strength. To accomplish this rescue mission, she'd take on his persona, not a damsel-in-distress heroine making stupid choices that placed her in danger. Granted, she was making a stupid decision now, but friends did stupid things for each other, right?

Lydia sprinted to Theresa's side.

The odor of the watchman's cigarette lingered in the air, but no one else wandered about. They dashed from one tent to the next, pausing at each one to ensure the path remained clear. Once they reached the menagerie tent, Lydia rubbed her palms over her coarse trousers and forced slow, quiet breaths. The next time she wrote a scene where someone sneaked around, she'd remember to include descriptions of sweaty palms, thumping heartbeats, and breaths held until dizzy for fear of being heard. No experience could go wasted. Not even something as absurd as rescuing a goat from the circus.

Theresa had better appreciate how much Lydia valued their friendship.

Muttered conversations and rumbling snores indicated they were close to the compact village of caravan wagons and sleeping tents. Much too close. Based on how many wagons she'd seen earlier, Adam Beadle must employ nearly one hundred people. It would take only one person to spot her or Theresa and sound the alarm.

This was their last chance to reconsider.

She crouched next to where Theresa struggled to lift the canvas bottom from between the tent pegs. "We should leave. It's too risky right now."

Her friend scowled. "The last show is tomorrow. It's tonight or never."

"Never sounds good."

Theresa dropped the canvas and planted her fists on her hips. "Neither the Guardians nor a Plane abandons a battle plan when a life is at stake. Tipsy will die if we don't rescue her."

"If we get caught—"

"They'll assume we're clowns."

No, they wouldn't. Clowns were *men*, and a blind person could see there was nothing masculine about either one of them. Theresa, with her small chest and petite features, might pull off the appearance of a young boy, but Lydia had curves that no amount of binding cloth could hide. Add her thick black mass of curly hair that couldn't be stuffed inside a muck bucket, much less the triangular little hat tilting to one side on her head, and no one could deny it. She was a woman.

With a coroner father and a healthy imagination, Lydia well knew the risks they faced should the largely male circus population discover them. But Theresa would never retreat. Her big heart outweighed reason.

Lydia sighed. She couldn't leave Theresa behind. If they worked together, they might make it out unscathed.

Maybe.

"Fine. But you know this is illegal, right?" Lydia wedged her hands between the hard-packed ground and rough canvas.

Theresa joined her. "Not when I'm paying for her. I'll slip a note and the outrageous sum Mr. Beadle demanded beneath the ringmaster's wagon door on our way out. I'm not giving the man a chance to raise his price *again*. I barely had enough from my painting commissions to pay this amount."

Unladylike grunts escaped as they pulled upward against the tension formed by two tent pegs and the weight of the canvas. They managed to raise an opening about a foot high.

Theresa dropped to her stomach and squirmed her way through. Once on the other side, she held the canvas for Lydia. "Be careful not to stand too quickly. I bumped my head on the underside of a wagon."

Lydia eyed the insufficient opening. *You can make it. Just think small.*

She thrust her arms and head through the hole, then clawed at the packed dirt. Filth and pebbles wedged painfully beneath her nails. With toes jammed into the ground, she wriggled until, finally, her bust cleared the opening.

At least Theresa had insisted on wearing trousers. With all the flailing she was doing with her legs, her thighs would surely have been exposed in skirts. Now to get her lower half through.

She glanced around. A few low-burning lanterns hung from wagon fronts and revealed there was nothing within reach. Theresa didn't weigh enough to hold down a sheaf of paper, but she was all Lydia had.

"On the count of three, pull me." She dug her toes deeper into the ground outside the tent and grabbed Theresa's arms at the elbow. "One. Two. Three!"

Theresa yanked. Her grip slipped, and she tumbled against the wagon.

Lydia didn't budge, but the commotion woke the wagon's occupant.

Yellow-and-black eyes flashed in the dim light.

A tiger's clawed paw shot out the cage bars toward Theresa.

Lydia grasped Theresa's legs and tugged them from beneath her.

Theresa yelped as she fell.

The tiger growled, clearly disgruntled at having missed out on a midnight snack. The paw disappeared, and padded feet paced the small confines of the cage.

Lydia fisted her hands to stop their trembling. Praise God for His protection.

"Thanks for the rescue. Now let's get you inside." Theresa crawled to the canvas stretched tight over Lydia's waist, and tugged.

Unfortunately, without standing and becoming prey for the tiger, her attempts were futile.

Lydia tapped her forehead against the cool ground. Of course she was pinned in place. It was exactly the thing she'd write to build excitement and anticipation for the reader. But this was not fiction, and the anticipation of being caught was making her nauseated.

Canvas bit into her as she twisted onto her side. "Find something to use as a wedge."

Theresa crawled beneath the tiger's wagon and disappeared from view.

Rummaging came from the other side of the tent, accompanied by the annoyed huffs, rumbles, and bleats of the other animals.

God, if we make it through this night without injury or detection,

I promise Theresa and I will never do something so foolish again. At least not until Theresa's next harebrained idea.

Maybe bargaining with God wasn't her most glorious moment, but at this point they needed a miracle.

Theresa came around the side of the wagon with a three-legged goat wobbling behind her on a rope lead. "Look who I found!"

Make that more than a miracle. How would they get a goat *out* if Lydia couldn't even get *in*?

At least the goat wasn't the only thing Theresa had brought. She set two small decorative wooden boxes in front of Lydia.

"This is the best I could find," Theresa said. "Will they help?"

Lydia pulled one closer. "It's not much, but I guess we'll see." She sucked in her stomach and jammed the box into the narrow space between herself and the canvas. With some effort, she forced it onto its tallest side. It only created a couple more inches, but every bit counted. After turning over carefully, she worked the other box into place.

Perfect. Now she just had to wiggle inside without her rear end knocking the boxes over. Maybe they'd get Tipsy out without being caught after all.

"Stop!" A man bellowed the order from outside the tent.

Of course. She should've known better than to even think they might succeed.

Well, if she was going to be caught, it wouldn't be with her body half outside. She rolled onto her stomach and kicked toward Theresa.

Before she could maneuver herself fully inside, a slippered foot landed on the back of her calf and rolled off. She winced, and the person who'd stepped on her grunted. Seconds later, the full weight of their body crashed atop her legs. Once again, she was pinned partially outside the tent.

Really, God? Was this punishment?

Unable to move, she listened as multiple sets of feet pounded closer.

"I've got this one, you grab the other," the same voice yelled.

The person on her legs scrambled to get up, and the pressure on her legs lifted. Using her elbows as leverage, Lydia attempted to pull the rest of herself through the tent's makeshift opening. She managed a couple of inches, but with a painful jolt, the weight on her legs returned, heavier this time, almost as if a second person had joined the first.

A scuffle ensued, and the weight shifted. "Don't be getting any funny ideas," the pursuer growled. "You're under arrest."

Great. Just what they needed. The police. But they hadn't been shouting at her. They were after someone else, and that person was now writhing around on her legs. Unfortunately, once the officer removed his quarry, he wasn't likely to miss her legs sticking out from the tent. If she and Theresa didn't disappear posthaste, Papa would hear of her escapade within the hour and make her a cadaver for the morgue's collection.

Lydia stretched her arms toward Theresa. "When I say *now*," she hissed, "pull!"

Theresa looped Tipsy's lead to a wheel's spoke on the next wagon over, then planted her feet and leaned forward enough to avoid the tiger's reach.

The clink of iron outside the tent indicated the application of handcuffs. A moment later the weight on Lydia's legs lifted.

"Now!"

She pushed with her feet. Theresa heaved.

Her hips cleared the opening, and Theresa tumbled backward.

Lydia jumped up, only remembering the tiger when its paw swiped at the hat still tied to her head. She shrieked. The hat came loose and flew through the air, bouncing off poor Tipsy's face. The goat scrambled awkwardly to the end of its lead and bleated with the volume of a fire bell. Then, as if that weren't enough, the tiger roared.

"By thunder! What was that?" the officer outside exclaimed.

Uh-oh. Time to make a swift exit.

Lydia bent to retrieve the borrowed hat. A man's face peered through the still-propped-open space at the base of the tent. The dome-shaped hat strapped to his head left no question that they'd just been caught by the police.

"Hey, you!" the officer called. "Stop right there!"

Theresa tugged Tipsy's lead free, grabbed Lydia's hand, and dragged them through the narrow space between the tent and wagon wheel.

"Hall! There's two more of 'em inside! Yount! Slide through and corral 'em."

And now there was to be a chase too? Had God decided to bring one of her books to life? She glanced back in time to see a twig of a man in an officer's uniform slide through the opening with far more ease than she.

Theresa took the lead, slowing only when her three-legged goat couldn't keep pace. Without any discernible logic, she cut between the wagons and temporary pens. Camels spat in their direction. Elephants trumpeted at them. A trio of black-and-white monkeys jumped and screeched inside their short red cage wagon like they were vicious and rabid. One reached out and tried to grab Lydia as she passed.

Enough was enough.

Only one real exit existed—through the tent's flap and out into the circus camp.

Two steps from freedom, she crashed full force into a man's short, lithe, muscular body. He took one wide-eyed look at her and then grinned.

Wasn't he one of the aerialists she'd watched at yesterday's show? Great. Now they were going to have the circus as well as the law after them. She should have known that if *she* wouldn't have allowed her characters an easy escape, God wouldn't either.

Before she knew what had happened or how, her feet left the ground and her body flew through the air like she was an aerialist herself.

Only her flight didn't include grabbing a trapeze.

Chapter 2

WHY DID HE ALWAYS GET the runners?

Officer Abraham Hall pushed faster in pursuit of the second member of the aerialist burglar duo. Officer Zimmerman had nabbed the first, but this second one was proving wilier. Lucian, Abraham's best friend and former partner, would be merciless in his circus jokes once he found out about tonight's chase.

Abraham pivoted around the corner and darted through the tent's still-swinging flap.

Only a few feet in front of him, his suspect heaved and flung something—no, someone—Abraham's direction.

The person slammed into his midsection before he could dodge.

Air exploded from Abraham's lungs. His feet went out from under him, and he landed on his back, a suffocating weight sprawled across his chest. He lifted his head, and brown trousers and a bright red shirt obscured his view. Dark eyes blinked owlishly at him from a white-painted face.

A clown.

Of course he'd been accosted by a clown. He hated clowns. With a shove, he freed himself, twisting to focus on the escaping burglar, now several yards away.

Another, much-smaller clown blocked the aerialist's path. Undeterred, the man shoved the obstacle aside only to be met with another in the form of . . . a three-legged goat? He tumbled over the goat's back.

That ought to slow—

But no. Somehow the cheat managed to tuck his body into a roll and pop back to his feet instead of landing face-first like a normal person.

This whole night was a farce. Vaudeville couldn't have come up with more buffoonery.

Abraham groaned as he pushed up from the ground. The mayor would have his head—and his job—if he didn't catch the fiends who'd been burglarizing the homes of the wealthy since the circus had arrived.

Shaking his head, he started after the aerialist again, but the smaller clown cut in front of him. He avoided the boy but collided with the goat.

Once again, he hit the ground—this time with the beast's only back leg bucking against his shoulder. Would this never end?

Elephants trumpeted as Officer Yount cut between them and the camels.

Abraham twisted away from the goat, and his foot slipped. Was that . . . excrement? His stomach lurched. By the size of the pile, it had to be an elephant's. He pulled his foot free and scraped it along the ground. He could just imagine Lucian's take on this.

Where was the good God he served? Of course, things could have been worse. He could have landed face-first in the vile stuff.

Yount angled toward the escaping aerialist, and Abraham charged to his feet to help corner the suspect against the wagons.

The aerialist ran faster, leaped against the side of the nearest wagon, and clasped a ring at the top. He swung and contorted to drop on top of the small red-and-gold wagon next to it. The force of his landing and the weight of his body tipped it over. The wagon cracked against the ground, and a side door swung open.

Three angry, screeching monkeys burst forth.

Two of them launched at Abraham. He ducked when he should have dodged, giving one the perfect perch on the back of his head. The other clambered up his front and dug into his pockets. Before he could grab the monkey on his front, the one on his head started jumping and slapping its tiny hands against him, all while screaming at a deafening pitch. Abraham reached behind him to fling it off, but the wretched beast gripped fistfuls of hair and swung around without letting go. Abraham would end up either bald or with a massive headache. Likely both.

"Get off him!" A female voice cut through the screeches. A thwack followed, and the monkey released its grip and flew through the air.

With one tormentor gone, Abraham wrapped his hands around the other, still busy picking his pockets, and hurled it.

A different shrieking started, and he twisted to find the monkey, intent on retribution, tangled in his rescuer's black curls. Since when were clowns female?

A shrill whistle cut through the chaos, and the monkeys froze.

"Come!" The command bellowed from the front of the tent.

Two of the monkeys scampered toward the gangly man standing in front of a growing crowd of circus workers. The third, however, remained thoroughly snarled in the clown's curls.

Between her screams and the monkey's screeching, Abraham's ears would ring for weeks. He snagged the rascal's hand and untwined it from her hair.

The ungrateful beast sank its teeth into his hand several times until, finally freed, it joined the others on the man's shoulders.

Abraham yanked a handkerchief from his pocket and wiped away the blood. It didn't appear the bites would need stitches, but that didn't lessen the sting.

A quick glance around confirmed the aerialist had escaped. So much for becoming this week's golden boy. Now he'd be the whipping boy.

His rescuer clown turned damsel in distress lifted wide brown eyes to his. Tears beaded unnaturally on the paint coating her face. Frizz and wild knots stuck out in all directions. The sight was enough to give grown men nightmares. Himself included.

"That is enough." The harsh words from the man with the monkeys cut off her shaky thank-you. "I am Adam Beadle, and this is my circus. I demand to know what is going on."

Abraham glanced at Officer Yount, who was brand-new to the Twelfth Ward and policing in general. So far, the man asserted his authority as successfully as a fish climbed a tree. Not something they needed in this already disastrous situation. That left Abraham to take the brunt of what was certain to be an unpleasant interaction.

"We're Officers Hall and Yount. We caught two of your aerialists burglarizing homes, and we pursued them here. Unfortunately, one escaped after releasing your monkeys, and your clowns interfered."

Mr. Beadle bristled visibly. "I do not hire crooks. The men you seek cannot be mine. Arrest those clowns if you wish to catch *real* thieves."

Abraham shook his head. He must have heard wrong. "You want me to arrest your clowns?"

"These are my monkeys, and this is my circus, but those"—he jabbed a finger in the direction of the two pests edging away with the goat—"are not my clowns."

At that accusation, the smaller figure holding the goat's lead stomped forward. "You couldn't pay me enough to be your clown. If you treat your animals this badly, how much worse must you treat those you employ?"

That was no young boy's voice. Two female clowns but neither one belonging to the circus? What was going on here?

"You!" Mr. Beadle stalked toward her amid a screeching monkey cacophony. "I told you, that goat is too valuable to sell."

"But not valuable enough to treat her wounds?"

Good grief. The petite woman crossed her arms and widened her stance as if she intended to go nose to nose with a man twice her size.

"Theresa!" The wild-haired clown snagged her friend's arm. "Don't antagonize the man."

"Officer Hall, I insist you arrest these two for thieving my goat."

"We didn't steal her. We're buying her!" The little clown—Theresa—

produced an envelope from somewhere within her shirt and tossed it to the ground near Mr. Beadle's feet. "The thirty dollars you required is there, just as we agreed."

Thirty dollars? This wasn't a carriage they bargained over. It was a goat. And a mangled one at that.

"Thirty dollars is no longer enough." The monkeys on Mr. Beadle jumped and screeched as if emphasizing his declaration.

Lord, help him. It appeared there was more to this supposed goat theft than first suggested. "Did you set thirty dollars as the price for this goat?"

"It was only a number I threw out, knowing she could not pay it."

But he did give it as an amount. Would that verbal dealing count as a binding contract? Abraham would let the lawyers decide. "Yount, take Miss Theresa, her companion, and the goat to the station. We'll sort it out later."

"This is preposterous! The goat is mine. She didn't even produce the money until after they'd been caught. I demand these women be charged with theft!"

The man had a point. "Charges will be determined at the station." Now back to the reason that brought Abraham here in the first place. "About your aerialists—"

"I do not employ crooks!"

Abraham clenched his jaw in an effort not to lose his temper. He'd personally caught the duo climbing out of the mayor's window and watched their acrobatics as they shinnied to the roof and jumped from house to house in an escape attempt.

Officer Zimmerman pushed his way through the crowd at the tent's entrance, pulling with him the first burglar. "I tried to grab the other one as he climbed through the opening in the tent's side, but he disappeared into the camp."

"Mr. Beadle, will you swear under oath that this man is not your aerialist? Mind you, I have evidence to the contrary, as he and his companion appear on an advertisement for your circus."

Mr. Beadle's nostrils flared, but he didn't speak.

"I'll take that as confirmation that he *is* your performer. I need your cooperation in apprehending the other aerialist."

"I don't know where he is. If you want him, get a warrant to search the premises. Until then, leave and take those clowns with you. The goat stays."

Abraham glanced at the pitiful creature. He wouldn't pay a quarter for the beast, but he wasn't above using it for his purposes. "The goat goes with us—unless you would like to exchange the goat for your man?"

Mr. Beadle spun away. "Jules, see these officers and clowns off our property."

The circus strongman, who was purported to have lifted an elephant, loped toward them from the crowd of observers. Abraham had no intention of physically opposing the man, but neither would he leave. Once he was off the property, Beadle could pack up his circus and be gone before Abraham returned with a warrant. Besides, he didn't need one.

"The circus grounds are city property, Mr. Beadle, and while you have a permit to use them, you do not have the right to remove officers searching for a fugitive."

Mr. Beadle flexed his fingers but did not turn around. After a prolonged silence, he acquiesced. "Escort Officer Hall through the grounds and assist in his search, but without a warrant, the tents are prohibited."

The man knew his rights. This was not his first experience with the police.

"Please, Theresa. Officer Yount can't carry the goat and escort us if you are uncooperative."

The anxious whisper drew Abraham's attention to the two clowns behind him. The damsel in distress wrung her hands as her gaze flitted between her scowling friend and a distinctly uncomfortable Officer Yount. If the little shrew decided to escape, Yount would be no match for her.

Better to amend his instructions than be reprimanded for allowing two criminals to escape in one night. "You two will stay and cooperate with Officer Yount until I return, is that understood?"

"No, I don't understand." The shrew—Theresa—aimed her scowl at him. "We haven't committed a crime. We should be free to go."

Abraham removed the handcuffs from beneath his coat. He hated to shackle a woman, but she left him no choice.

"That's not necessary, Officer Hall." Damsel in distress placed a hand on Theresa's arm. "We'll cooperate and go to the station to clear up this misunderstanding. You have my word."

"And why should I accept the word of a trespasser and thief?"

She winced. "Because I refuse to bring more shame upon my father's name."

Now she wanted to behave respectably? "And who would that be that it should matter to me?"

Her swallow was audible, but her words almost weren't. "Dr. George Pelton, a coroner for Cincinnati."

Pure fallacy. Dr. Pelton's upstanding reputation was known throughout the city, and the man was a personal friend of the recently appointed Superintendent Carson.

Abraham scrutinized the woman before him. He'd met Dr. Pelton on a number of occasions, but he'd only seen Mrs. Pelton with her daughters indirectly when they'd delivered baked goods. With black hair and thick curls, the woman before him undeniably resembled the impression the older daughter had left. However, the white paint on her face made it difficult to discern if anything else matched what he recalled.

The sinking feeling in his gut did far more than her appearance to confirm her identity.

"Please tell me you are not Lydia Pelton."

She offered a half smile and shrug. "I could tell you that, but I'd be lying."

Abraham scrubbed a hand over his face. Of all the people for him to arrest. The superintendent was going to have his head for not permitting her to walk away with naught but a warning. On the other hand, Mr. Beadle was demanding to press charges, and with the women's lack of payment before taking the goat, the man had grounds to demand it. Even if Abraham was willing to bow to the politics of his superiors, he could not release her. Perhaps if he kept her identity quiet and handled the paperwork himself, he could minimize the damage to both her and Dr. Pelton's reputations without compromising his ethics.

But he couldn't leave the search to Yount, and Zimmerman had his hands full with the other aerialist.

"Speak nothing more to anyone and do not allow your friend to cause problems. For Dr. Pelton's sake, we'll keep this quiet for as long as possible."

"I understand. Thank you."

He took one sweeping glance at her, from monkey-nested hair to her scandalously trousered legs, before pivoting away. She might be the criminal in this case, but he would be the one suffering the consequences. No matter how quiet he kept her initial arrest, the politics of its occurring meant, at best, a dressing-down. At worst? He didn't want to think about it.

Chapter 3

Lydia tucked her feet beneath the plush chair and adjusted the borrowed rubber coat tighter around her body as the booking clerk of the Oliver Street station house ogled her again. What had she been thinking when she agreed to wear trousers? As a novelist, she should've considered what would happen if they were arrested. Even with Officer Hall's attempt to conceal their appearance by borrowing raincoats, their scandalous apparel was still drawing the attention of everyone who passed.

It was either that or her red, hive-ridden face.

The clerk winced, then returned to processing paperwork.

She faced Theresa. "Please tell me it doesn't look as bad as it feels."

"I don't know how it feels, but it looks bad. Really bad."

Lydia dug her nails into a raised hive on her cheek. "Tell me again why we used oil paint instead of buying greasepaint."

"Stop picking at it." Theresa pulled Lydia's hand away before anything resembling relief could be had. "I already had plenty of white oil paint in my paint box, and I needed my money to purchase Tipsy. I didn't see the sense in buying something else when that would work as well. Although perhaps we should have stuck to removing it with soap instead of turpentine."

Only *perhaps*? Lydia's immediate reaction to the chemical ensured that hers was a face no one would forget, especially when displayed among the rogues gallery.

Officer Hall arrived with a rag in hand and a deep-set frown. "I'm afraid all I can offer is this. I didn't find anything that would help in our medical supplies."

The care in his molasses-colored eyes was as sweet as the cookies she often overindulged in. Too bad she couldn't give up the cookies and indulge in endless eye-gazing instead. It'd be better for her waist-line.

"Thank you." She took the proffered wet rag that fortunately appeared new, leaned her head back, and draped it over her face.

The coolness helped, but clawing off every agonizing welt would be better.

"Are you certain that you shouldn't go to a hospital or have a doctor sent for?"

She'd already assured him of that twice. "I'm having no trouble breathing or indications that I will. The only doctor I need is my father." As much as she didn't want Papa to know of her arrest and be disappointed in her, she trusted only him.

"I wish to notify him personally, but there's one more thing I must do before I can leave."

It seemed Officer Hall was intent on attending personally to everything connected to her arrest. She'd be surprised if anyone else knew she was Dr. Pelton's daughter. But he knew, and his preferential treatment of her and Theresa both disappointed and made her dreamy.

She'd never been on the criminal side of things. The experience of being treated like a common crook would do wonders for adding realistic details to her stories. Unfortunately she hadn't even seen what a holding cell looked, smelled, or felt like. Just imagine the information she could glean from actual criminals if placed in a cell! She'd ask where they socialized, if they had code words, and how they chose their targets.

But how could she hate the attention of a man with enough Mr. Darcy qualities to make her wish she were Elizabeth Bennet? At least the Elizabeth Bennet after visiting Pemberley.

"I'm fine." She removed the rag to make speaking easier. "Do what you need to, but are you certain you shouldn't put us in a holding cell so you don't get into trouble with your superiors?"

"I'm certain. Just do me the favor of keeping out of trouble from here forward. I don't wish to ever see you on the wrong side of my job again."

"But you wouldn't mind to see me on a proper one?"

Oh, that's a good line. If only she had a pencil to write it down for future use in a romance novel.

"I'm not sure there is a proper one. In my line of work, there are only victims and perpetrators." His gaze roved her face for a moment. "If your symptoms worsen, tell Officer Blythe immediately. He'll take you directly to the hospital. There is a pitcher and a bowl at the desk for you to refresh the rag as needed. I'll be back to check on you before I leave." He strode off with the perfect masculinity of every hero in every dime novel she'd ever read or written.

And just like her heroines, she sighed audibly with a touch of swoon. Oh yes, he needed to be the hero of a novel—sooner rather than later.

Theresa elbowed her side. "You like him, don't you? I've never heard you flirt so boldly before."

"I wasn't flirting. I was being witty and charming. I have to test, on occasion, what my heroines say, just so I know what a man's real reaction would be."

"So you're claiming research, are you?"

"Everything is research. Including flirting. The good news is that you were right. This experience has not only resurrected my creativity but also inspired a whole new story."

Theresa scooted closer. "Would that be a romance published under your own name or a crime novel published by our mutual friend?"

"I haven't decided."

"Mm-hmm. And should I expect the hero's initials to be A. H.?"

"Maybe." Lydia covered her face with the rag and smiled.

She could have a lot of fun with a hero like Officer Hall. First impressions weren't something to base a real romance on, but fiction only needed a spark, and, good gracious, did Officer Hall set off sparks. With a little encouragement, she could flame a whole series to life. She was unsure if Officer Hall's response to her flirting was discouragement, but she'd liked it all the same. Victims and perpetrators. It was such a police-like thing to say. Her publisher had asked E. A. Dupin—the pseudonym she used for her crime novels—to write more books a year. Perhaps she could start a new detective series in addition to her Billy Poe novels, one with a romantic interest who shared her name. She giggled. It wasn't like anyone but her closest friends knew *she* was E. A. Dupin. The hero could be named Detective Abe Darcy as a private joke.

"What have we here?" The unfamiliar male voice interrupted her musings.

Lydia tamped down a growl of frustration before it escaped. She much preferred imaginary characters to real people. Especially the nosy kind.

"The most interesting cases always come in during the night. Tell me, ladies"—the word *ladies* hinted at sarcasm—"what brings you here tonight in such attire?"

Lydia yanked the rag off her face.

Surprise lifted the brows of the man in front of her before they settled into curiosity.

The lack of uniform made it obvious he wasn't an officer, but she'd seen him around Papa's office enough to recognize his thin, determined face. A reporter. If she recalled correctly, one who behaved like he had something to prove. Ambition could be a great quality in a man, but not when it risked her identity.

Theresa stiffened in her seat next to Lydia, no doubt ready to launch into a defense that painted the circus as evil and them valiant.

Lydia clapped a hand over Theresa's mouth. "I don't believe that is your business, Mr.—"

"Eugene Clemens, from the *Cincinnati Commercial*. It's my job to report arrests for the sake of public awareness, so your story *is* my business. Unless you are the victims of a crime."

She knew better than to take the bait, but responding posed a challenge. Silence indicated guilt. Speaking up risked revealing too much.

"Your story's in cell two, Clemens." Officer Hall appeared with crossed arms.

Mr. Clemens glanced between them, and a smile edged its way up. "I assume you're referring to that aerialist you arrested for burglary. I've got what I need there, but I think the story sitting here will be of far more interest to my readers."

"Shouldn't you be heading to that murder scene just telephoned in?"

"Nice try, Hall, but I know a distraction tactic when I see one."

A pair of officers collected jackets, lanterns, and truncheons from the closet and rushed out the foyer door.

The confidence on Mr. Clemens's face faltered.

"Gilbert Avenue and Morris Street. Body's in the woods." Officer Hall nodded toward the door.

Mr. Clemens frowned and visually vacillated between his two options. Stay for a potential story or go after a certain one? His decision became apparent when he took off at a run.

"Did you really just give him the address of a murder scene?" Didn't that break some sort of investigation rule?

"No. If he isn't smart enough to tail the officers, he'll find himself at Eden Park on the opposite side of town." A mischievous grin appeared.

Gracious, that man's smile could make a heart stutter. Where was her fan when she needed it? Detective Darcy definitely needed his own story, and soon.

His heat-inducing smile died. "You didn't give him your names, did you?"

"Of course not."

"Good. I'm on my way to inform your father of your situation. Is there anything you need before I leave?"

"A promise that I'll see you again?" She batted her lashes like the ladies in novels and immediately felt foolish. Did women really behave this way, and did it really attract a man?

Next to her, Theresa giggled and then whispered, "More research?"

Officer Hall frowned. "That, I cannot give." Then he retreated out the door like Jonah avoiding his calling to Nineveh—with all haste.

Theresa burst into full-fledged laughter. "I think you've discovered how to make a man run away."

"At least an upstanding one."

Lydia refreshed the rag and endured an interested side-glance from Officer Blythe. Based on the hopeful gleam to his smile, he expected her to flirt with him too. The man would have to live with disappointment. She'd had enough uncomfortable interactions with men who took too much encouragement from her playful research. Officer Hall, however, had felt strangely safe from the moment she'd crashed into him. If a person could really determine such a thing in such a short time.

She settled onto her chair and under the rag. Perhaps she could finish plotting a Detective Darcy story by the time Papa arrived.

Unfortunately, plotting couldn't distract her from the intensity of her itching. By her dozenth trip to the bowl at Officer Blythe's desk, the water had warmed and failed to provide sufficient relief.

The foyer door rattled before opening. A thin woman in bedraggled clothes and reeking like she'd fallen into a keg staggered toward Officer Blythe.

Now *there* was a potential character for her books. Lydia discreetly held her breath as she lingered over the water bowl, repeatedly dipping the rag and then wringing it out.

"I demand"—the woman stumbled but caught herself—"I *demand* to sh-sh-shpeak to . . . to the de-de . . . officer in charge."

By the sounds of it, the woman hadn't just fallen into a keg, she'd drunk her way out of it as well.

To his credit, Officer Blythe didn't lean away when spittle flew at him. "Are you here to report a crime, ma'am?"

"Report it?" She slapped the desk and leaned forward so far, she almost lay down on it. "You've known 'bout it for weeks. Dupin killed my boy!"

Lydia dropped the rag. *Dupin?* But that was impossible. E. A. Dupin was just a pseudonym. *Her* pseudonym, and the only people she killed were fictional.

Officer Blythe straightened. "And you would be?"

"Mrs. Finn. My boy's Daniel Finn—"

"Daniel Finn?" Lydia's whole body turned to ice. "The same Daniel Finn who slaughtered a man for cheating at cards?" The one on whom she'd based an entire Billy Poe novel?

Mrs. Finn spun and tottered toward Lydia. "My boy weren't no murderer. He was tried and ex-ex . . . let go."

Yes, because of "missing" evidence and a key witness who refused to testify thanks to Mr. Finn's backdoor political connections. The entire city had been in an uproar. But what could the honest citizens of Cincinnati do? It was well-known that the city's leaders controlled the elections, regulated the police force, and manipulated judge and jury alike.

So Lydia had used the only means available to give the public what they desired—she'd written a story where Daniel Finn met an untimely end while under investigation by Detective Billy Poe. It was a poor consolation compared to real justice, but that didn't mean she wanted the *real* Mr. Finn dead.

This had to be a misunderstanding.

"And you're saying your son has been murdered by E. A. Dupin? The *author?*"

Officer Blythe cut around the desk and stepped between them. "I am afraid that is an ongoing investigation. Anything said is pure speculation."

"'Speculation,' my foot!" The woman jabbed a finger at his chest and lost her balance, landing on the floor. "Billy Poe himself left a letter claiming the deed, and Dupin wrote Billy Poe. Since Poe ain't real, it has to be Dupin. Why ain't he arrested yet?"

"I'm sorry for your loss, Mrs. Finn, but go home. You can visit Central tomorrow, when Detective Lawson is available to answer your questions."

She spat on his shoes before pushing to her unstable feet. "Forget it. I'll take care of Dupin myself." Threat after vile threat against Dupin spewed from Mrs. Finn as she weaved through the exit.

Heavens above! What would Mrs. Finn have done if she'd known the real E. A. Dupin stood next to her?

Lydia turned to Officer Blythe. "Is it wise to allow her to leave?"

He shrugged. "She couldn't find a hole in a ladder in her state. Besides, I'm not worried. If we can't find Dupin, she certainly can't."

"Then Dupin really is a suspect?"

He coughed and tapped a stack of papers together before nodding to the bowl. "Wet your rag and sit. I've work to do."

His avoidance was answer enough. What had happened that made Dupin a legitimate suspect in a murder case? The man didn't even exist. Edgar Auguste Dupin was merely a nod to her favorite author and detective. Even her character Billy Poe was a play on the name.

She dropped into her seat and stared at her empty hands.

Theresa leaned close and whispered, "Did she say E. A. Dupin murdered someone?"

Lydia could only nod.

"But that's impossible."

"You think I don't know that? What do I do? The police are pursuing a false lead, but I can't expose m— Dupin's identity. Word will get out."

And not just to the police department. The reporters would turn rabid over the chance to expose such a sensational story. Society barely tolerated women writing romances. For a woman to write crime novels went beyond the pale. E. A. Dupin's books were favorites among readers—yet they were penned by a woman. Her. And now she was wanted for murder.

Her reputation would be ruined. They'd equate her morals with that of a soiled dove. Worse, it would sully Papa's reputation.

His beloved job as coroner was an elected position. For better or worse, the Pelton name had an unblemished reputation to uphold. If her name was tied to murder—fictional or factual—he might not be reelected next May.

"I think I'm going to be sick."

Theresa jumped from her seat and dunked the rag Lydia had abandoned in the bowl of water. She rushed back and draped the rag over the back of Lydia's neck. "It'll be okay. Let's get through tonight, and then tomorrow we can figure out how to move forward."

"You say that like Colonel Plane isn't going to court-martial you and give you solitary confinement for a month."

"Okay, so not tomorrow, but I'm sure I'll be able to climb out my window and escape soon after. For now, tilt your head back and put the rag on your face. Your hives are getting worse."

The warm rag did little to ease the itching or the growing nausea. Despite Theresa's insistence they could figure everything out and all would be well, Lydia knew better.

What would Papa think if he discovered she'd been hiding her identity as Dupin from him?

She adored him, and he adored her back. How many other daughters had such wonderful relationships with their fathers?

If he discovered she was Dupin and the reason he lost his job, he'd never look at her the same again. What they had would be shattered.

But a man was dead, and the police were chasing a suspect who didn't exist. They'd never catch the real culprit if she didn't confess her pseudonym.

She gulped in air, trying to break through the panic gripping her lungs.

Risk her father's profession and their relationship or risk a murderer's escaping because of her silence—how could those be the choices she was stuck between? She wrote her crime novels so justice could be had for all, but could she really claim to be on the side of justice if she allowed a murderer to walk free just to preserve herself and her family?

"Miss, are you in distress?" Officer Blythe's voice came from the other side of the rag.

She was, but not because of her hives.

"I'll see to her needs, Officer Blythe." Papa's voice announced his arrival.

Normally the smooth baritone notes of his voice would relax her, but now they only added to her anxiety.

He removed the rag from her face, and his eyes widened. "They're coming with me. I'll inform Superintendent Carson in the morning."

"Yes, sir."

Papa pulled her to standing and directed Theresa to follow.

"Lydia Ruth Pelton, I don't know whether to hug you or throttle you. Are you certain you can breathe?"

She forced a deep, slow breath. "I can."

"Good, then when we get home, I want a full explanation. If what Officer Hall says is true, then we've got a big problem on our hands."

Hopefully he'd never have to know how big it really was.

CHAPTER 4

TENSION KNOTTED THE BACK OF Abraham's neck as he trudged home in the dark from Dr. Pelton's house. Informing the man that his daughter was at the station house wasn't nearly as bad as he'd imagined. Dr. Pelton fully understood the seriousness of the situation even though Abraham had whitewashed the details of the night. Then, instead of threatening to have Abraham fired for not releasing the women, Dr. Pelton had thanked him, insisted on treating his monkey bites, and promised to commend him to Superintendent Carson. Not that Dr. Pelton's influence would protect Abraham's job. His choice to arrest Miss Pelton and Miss Plane would still come with consequences.

So would the fact the second burglar had evaded capture along with his stolen goods.

Abraham massaged the tightening muscles. A headache threatened.

More than likely, the rogue's companions had aided him. Not that all circuses were spittoons of con artists and other criminals, but crime always increased whenever one rolled into town. Abraham just hadn't expected the circus to be the victim of crime instead of the perpetrator.

The image of Lydia Pelton's monkey-nested hair and wide, rich brown eyes set against a white-painted face flitted through his mind. What had possessed her to implement her friend's outlandish scheme? She obviously wasn't as zealous as her companion about saving the goat from "certain death." Miss Pelton was a puzzle of conflicting traits. She'd behaved like a criminal one moment, then turned into a model citizen the next. The flirtation had been an unexpected twist to her solemn behavior. Either the turpentine had affected her brain or the woman suffered from multiple personalities. If the latter were the case, that would explain much.

Still, he hoped that Dr. Pelton wouldn't commit Miss Pelton to Longview Insane Asylum after treating her hives. Abraham wasn't sure how to accomplish it, but he'd like to know which Lydia Pelton was the real one. The one who was deeply ashamed of what she and her friend had attempted to do or the flirty criminal who batted her puffy red eyes?

When Abraham finally turned the key to his family's home around three in the morning, all was dark inside. Mother, Father, and his younger brother and sister would have retired hours ago.

Or at least they should have.

A thin line of light shone from beneath his sister's door across from his bedroom.

Oh, Clara. Not again. He shook his head as he knocked their secret code on her door. She needed to marry a man who either worked nights or tolerated a wife who read through the night. As it was, Mother and Father were so frustrated with their sleep-deprived bookworm, they were considering confiscating her books and banning her from the public library. Not that Clara wouldn't sneak in visits whenever she could, but it would severely limit her reading time.

Clara opened the door and pulled him in with one hand. Her other hand stayed hidden behind her back, presumably holding her latest choice of adventure. She closed and leaned against the door. "Don't make me go to bed. The hero is swimming across a swollen river to rescue the heroine. If I stop reading now, he might drown!"

"I don't think your stopping will change how the story ends, Pages." He tugged on the dark braid draped over the shoulder of her wrapper.

"How do you know? It might."

At seventeen, she was too old to believe that, but he'd indulge her, just as he always did. "What's the title? More than likely, I can tell you if he survives or not." He tried to peek around her back, but she twisted away.

"But that will spoil the thrill!"

"Perhaps, but then you can go to bed and rest peacefully knowing that your hero will survive until morning, and that Mother and Father won't empty your room of books. If you oversleep and miss helping Mother with the bakery again, you know they will."

"But I won't this time. I'm only fifteen pages from the end."

"Sorry, Pages. You'll have to wait until tomorrow."

He reached around her back and grasped the book. Rather than a thick cloth-bound cover typical of the classics, a thin leaflet with a paper cover met his touch. Clara wouldn't, would she? He wrenched it away from her and frowned at the bright orange cover of a dime novel. There was a chance it was just a magazine that printed portions of treasured literature, but no Dickens, Austen, or Hawthorne graced the pages he thumbed through. It was one story, and—his attention caught on a passage describing a kiss—apparently a romance that no girl should be reading. When had Clara moved on from proper literature to this drivel?

"Where did you get this?"

Her chin jutted up. "From the newspaper stand while delivering bread to the Keppler Hotel."

"Do Mother and Father know you're reading this twaddle?"

"It's not twaddle. It's a moral tale of love, danger, and marriage."

"Are they married when they kiss here?" He held it open to the kiss midway through.

"Don't be prudish, Abraham. You've kissed a woman before, and you aren't married."

That was not the point. Putting false ideas of what romance and love entailed created unrealistic expectations for her future husband. "Men do not rescue their future wives from danger to prove their love or heroism. Nor do they have to be athletic, handsome, or secretly wealthy. If you keep reading that claptrap, it's going to compromise your morality."

Clara rolled her eyes before making a successful grab for the book. He held tight, but the front cover tore off, leaving him with a sheet of paper and Clara with pages of unwholesome subversion. He glanced down at the sheet, and his frowned deepened.

The Lady's Terrible Secret by Lydia R. Pelton.

Surely not.

"Abraham! That book cost me fifteen cents!"

He ignored Clara and continued to stare at the name printed along the bottom. It could not be the same Lydia Pelton he'd arrested tonight. Dr. Pelton was too respectable to allow his daughter to write such scintillating stories.

Except she did attempt to steal a goat from the circus.

And her flirtation? Was that a truer depiction of her character? He was tempted to grab the dime novel back and read exactly how detailed that kiss scene had been. And was it just kissing she'd included, or had she gone further? Danger to a woman's virtue inevitably came up in these stories, but Abraham had too much experience with his job to find entertainment in such depravity. And that was just one reason these books should be banned, especially from young, undiscerning readers.

"Give it back. She's my favorite author."

He released the cover but scowled at Clara. "You didn't answer me—do Mother and Father know you read this?"

"I don't hide it from them. Mother even likes Miss Pelton's books. She says as far as romance novels go, they're pretty tame."

As far as romance novels went? Did his own mother read this fire kindling? How else would she know how Miss Pelton's stories compared? "Hand over the book, Clara. I can't, in good conscience, allow you to continue reading it."

Clara backed up to her bed and sat on the thick leaflet. "No. If Mother gives me permission, you can't take it away. Once I finish, I'll gladly give you the opportunity to read it. Or if you are so impatient to know whether Miss Pelton's writing can be trusted, grab any copy of her works from that stack on my desk."

He glanced at the stack of dime novels she indicated. There must have been a dozen. "You've read all of those?"

"Multiple times." She arched a brow in defiance. "You cannot judge my reading choices without first having read them yourself. In fact, I dare you to. I bet when you're finished, you'll love her as much as I do."

Abraham considered shoving Clara over and stealing her current read, but with fifteen pages left, she'd probably fight him to the death. At least if he accepted her challenge, he could remove the rest of the perversion from the room and protect her.

"Fine, but I'm taking them now."

"As long as whatever you take, you read, and you finish them by the end of the month. After that, I'm calling your bluff and confiscating them back."

He snatched the stack and stalked to the door. "Go to bed, Pages. Your hero will survive until you next open the book."

She didn't turn off the light immediately, but by the time he'd changed into his nightclothes and checked the hallway again, the light was out. She'd probably just shoved a blanket against the base of the door to disguise the light. He grunted and climbed into bed. Clara was old enough to contend with her own consequences, and he needed to get what little sleep he could muster. It might be his day off, but he intended to attend the last circus show and catch his fugitive aerialist.

Well before it was time, someone knocked on his door.

"Wake up, Abe. Lucian's here and says they want you at Central." Jake's nine-year-old voice hollered through the door.

Grit bleared Abraham's vision as he checked the clock on his side table. Barely eight in the morning. He groaned. Word about last night's arrests must've already reached Superintendent Carson's ear. It'd been foolish to think the consequences would wait until tomorrow's shift to make themselves known.

"I'm up. Coffee, please?"

"Will do!" Jake's feet raced down the hall.

It was far too early for that much energy. Abraham crawled from bed and dressed in his last clean uniform. At least catching Clara last night meant she'd wash his clothes for the upcoming week in exchange for his silence.

She met him downstairs with a mug in hand. "Are you going to tell Mother and Father about my staying up last night?"

"Not if you agree to the usual payment."

She rolled her eyes. "Pile still in the corner of your room?"

"Of course." He kissed her cheek. "I assume you woke up on time?"

"Yes, I did, and they lived happily ever after."

"And here I'd hoped he'd drown."

Clara smacked his arm, splashing coffee on the floor.

"Quit teasing your sister. We need to get to the station posthaste." Lucian stepped forward, rigid as an iron gate. "Carson's in a mood, and you're the source of it."

Abraham took two large gulps before passing the mug back to Clara and following Lucian to where a hack waited.

"Is he so angry that you had to hire a cabbie?" Abraham settled inside next to Lucian.

"He's the one who ordered it. Said he'd have sent a patrol wagon if the city had one." Lucian tapped the roof and then placed his domed hat in the space between them. His mussed blond hair indicated he'd been fretting the whole way here. "What'd you do last night? Take his missus out on the town?"

"I arrested someone I'm sure he thinks I should've released."

"Awww, Hall. I know you're as straight as a die, but can't you bend to politics a little? I rather like having you around."

"I didn't have much choice in the matter. The circus owner wants to press charges."

"Circus owner? Friend, I don't know how you get all the fun chases, but I'm glad to have missed this one."

"You have no idea."

"So who was it?"

Abraham shook his head. He was no gossiping hen. Lucian was his best friend, but he wouldn't reveal Miss Pelton's identity or role in last night's escapades.

When they reached the City Building, instead of taking the basement stairs to Central Station, they joined the mix of bureaucrats and civilians entering through the main doors. Unlike the rest of the force, who were relegated to the basement stink hole, Superintendent Carson conducted his business aboveground, with a window all his own.

Unfortunately that blessing appeared to do little in lessening his ire this morning. Carson's rants carried to the tiled front foyer. Curious government officials and visiting citizens peeked from offices toward the noisy hall where the courtroom and superintendent's office were housed.

Rather than join Abraham in his walk to Carson's office, Lucian stopped beside the building directory board and doffed his hat to hold it over his heart. "Alas, poor Hall! I knew him, Horatio: a fellow of infinite nobility, of most excellent detective skills; and now, how I mourn his impending death."

Abraham punched him on the arm. "Your Shakespeare stinketh."

"Not as much as you will after you're done sweating it out with Carson."

Lucian dodged Abraham's next shot, then saluted before disappearing out the front door. His shift was long over, and the newlywed was not one to linger more than necessary.

Abraham straightened his uniform before making his execution walk to the superintendent's office. He'd done the right thing, but doing what was right didn't always guarantee a fair result.

Civilians waiting their turn in court filled the hallway, either engaged in lively chatter or sitting in grim silence.

He halted outside the superintendent's door and drew back his shoulders. Best to get this over with. He'd take his punishment and walk out with his head held high.

The door yanked open after his rap. The burly former butcher with a graying mustache as wide as a gun barrel shot a finger toward the punishment chair. The rickety thing had a split seat that pinched with blood-blistering force. Refusing to sit in it would only further incense Carson, so Abraham adjusted his jacket and sat as far back as possible.

"Did you arrest Lydia Pelton last night?"

"Yes, sir."

"And did you know that she is Dr. Pelton's daughter?"

"Yes, sir."

"Then why did you not release her at once?"

"Mr. Beadle is pressing charges for her part in stealing a goat from his menagerie."

"The circus owner? That man will be out of town in less than twelve hours. He won't be around to see those charges pressed."

"Even so, sir, it was the right thing to do."

"The right thing—" Carson ran a hand over his face and sat on the edge of the desk. "It's a wonder you've made it this long."

"I assume Dr. Pelton wants the charges dropped?"

"Of course not. You both have unyielding moral codes. Mayor Jacobs wants the charges dropped. Worse still, he wants the circus to surrender the escaped burglar. Fail, and he demands you be transferred to the Fifth Ward."

The muscles in Abraham's legs tightened as if he already stood on the dreaded Hunt Street and needed to run. Being transferred to the Fifth Ward, where the Deer Creek Gang reigned, was worse than being fired. The violent gang traveled in crowds of ten to forty. Almost nightly, the sharp crack of pistol shots and the curses and moans of wounded men filled the air. Officers patrolled in groups of four, revolvers ready and prepared to confront death. Being a patrol officer anywhere was a risk, but to be one in the Fifth Ward was a guaranteed fight for one's life.

All Carson's bluster died away, leaving behind a man in his late fifties, visibly exhausted by the political bureaucracy that plagued his job. Little could be done when the mayor held the power in who served as an officer—and superior—within the force. The failed attempt at a board of commissioners had ended in January, and police appointments were turned over to the mayor. It was a setback, but Abraham still prayed for a better system that would limit unscrupulous political influences. Even if he didn't live long enough to see it.

"You have one chance to make this right. The circus's last show ends around six, at which time Mr. Beadle will be brought in to formally press charges. Find a way to force him to hand over that aerialist and drop the charges against Miss Pelton and Miss Plane. I hate losing good officers to the whims of a politician."

"What do you propose I do, sir?"

"You've got the mind of a detective, Hall. I propose you use it. You're dismissed."

He'd issued a challenge, and Abraham wasn't one to back down.

Abraham strode from the office, formulating a plan as he went. He had two goals. First, convince Mr. Beadle to betray one of his own. To do that, he'd have to make the man more concerned about self-preservation than aiding and abetting a criminal. Mr. Beadle was a businessman, and if there was one thing Abraham understood about business, it was that money ruled. Circuses were notorious for breaking ordinances and incurring fines. If he found enough, it might shake Mr. Beadle's confidence.

He'd need more though.

If two criminals had been caught in Cincinnati, it was likely other crimes had occurred in previous show locations. Maybe Abraham could cripple Mr. Beadle's show by hauling in those with bench warrants. It was a long shot, but he had to try.

His second goal—getting Mr. Beadle to drop the charges against Miss Pelton and Miss Plane—would be near impossible.

One problem at a time, Abraham. God will see you through, no matter the outcome.

By the time he left the circus hours later, he'd found enough infractions to impound key animals and equipment until those fines were paid. The Cincinnati Zoological Gardens even agreed to house the elephants. Given how much work he'd seen the elephants do in setting up tents and performing during the show, losing those two would be a crushing blow.

After a few more hours wiring other towns, he had a handful of warrants for circus members who'd jumped bail. Most were for petty crimes, but Mr. Beadle himself was wanted for questioning in the disappearance of several adolescent boys. The boys had likely run off to join the circus of their own volition, but the parents insisted the man had kidnapped them. It was enough to hold Mr. Beadle and delay the circus's departure. A delay which would cost the man dearly.

That left Abraham facing his final goal.

Mr. Beadle wasn't likely to drop the charges against Miss Pelton and Miss Plane, especially with the charges and fines lobbed at him. However, paying fines required money, something that keeping that goat would never provide.

Abraham visited the three-legged goat in the stables and did a thorough examination of the animal. He was no veterinarian, but he could tell Tipsy wasn't long for this world. If he had to guess, he'd say the goat had gotten too close to the tiger cage and almost become a meal. The deep gashes festered, and dull eyes barely acknowledged his prodding.

"Hey, Tackett."

The stableman who cared for the horses poked his head out of a stall.

"You used to live on a farm. What's the likelihood of this creature surviving?"

Tackett set his shovel aside and squatted next to the goat. After a cursory examination, he shrugged. "Personally, I'd put her out of her misery, but if someone were determined, it's possible."

"Do you think it would survive traveling?"

"Maybe for a day or two."

"How much do you think it would cost to care for the animal and bring it back to health?"

His incredulous look said it all. "Only a fool would try. It'd cost more than she was worth at her best."

"Thanks, Tackett. That is exactly what I needed to hear."

It would be in Mr. Beadle's best interest to accept Miss Plane's payment for the goat and drop the charges. A much more appealing choice, once slapped with the fines.

Abraham checked his watch. Five thirty. It was time to return to the station and discover if he'd spared Miss Pelton a future as an inmate and himself as a walking target for the Deer Creek Gang.

CHAPTER 5

IF LYDIA EVER NEEDED TO describe the sensation of being smothered by a pillow, she could do so now. The stupid thing was plastered to her face thanks to the stinky goop Papa had slathered on her hives. She peeled the material from her face and gaped at the slant of evening light through the bedroom window. The tonic Papa gave her must have sedated her for a good eight hours. Maybe more. She squinted at the clock on the side table, but her muddled brain couldn't shake the medicine-induced fog.

She swung into a sitting position, and for a moment the world swam.

"It's about time you woke up." Her younger sister, Madelyn, twisted in her desk chair. "Dinner should be ready soon, and I have no intention of taking another meal here. It isn't fair that I be punished just because you stole a goat from the circus."

"I think it's the perfect punishment for always being such a tattler. If you weren't so good at it, maybe Papa wouldn't assign you as my warden."

"Better me than Colonel Plane. You slept through his explosion of temper when he arrived to claim Theresa. I'd say she won't be easily escaping her wardens anytime soon."

"Are you implying that I'll be able to escape you easily?"

Madelyn rolled her eyes and returned to whatever she worked on at her desk.

Not that Lydia planned on escaping through the window like Theresa would. Heights terrified her. No, she would honor Papa and endure her punishment quietly.

Despite the seriousness of her crime, Papa's disappointment in her hadn't been as bad as she'd expected. Yes, he'd called her and Theresa foolish and reprimanded her for not being a leader in the friendship and putting a stop to the escapade. But his fear for her well-being far exceeded his concern for his reputation as a coroner or the repercussions of her crime. Even though he said it was only right that she and Theresa faced them—and Lydia agreed—he planned to hire a good lawyer who could obtain a favorable plea deal without the case going to trial. They would get past this, and he was certain she would learn from her mistake and make better choices in the future.

She hadn't the heart to tell him there were other potential disasters awaiting her. Maybe if she delayed, this whole Dupin-murder-suspect thing would go away without her ever telling him about her pseudonym. The police were too smart to pursue only one suspect who could have nothing more than a tenuous connection to the crime.

The bedroom door opened, and Momma stalked inside. "Good, you're up. I cannot believe what your father told me at breakfast. You are a Pelton, young lady. How could you jeopardize our family's reputation for something so foolish as stealing a goat?" She folded her arms and scowled. "You are going to attend every church service and event from now until the end of the year without one excuse. No writing deadlines. No illness. Nothing. You will prove to our congregation that you are a repentant young woman and model Christian."

She should have known that Momma would react more fiercely to her arrest than Papa. Momma couldn't really enforce Lydia's church attendance, but she well knew how to wield the honor-thy-father-and-mother verse to her advantage. Not that Lydia minded services, and as long as she worked at a steady pace, she'd meet next month's deadline with no trouble.

"Yes, Momma. I promise to do better by you from here on out."

"Maybe when it comes to criminal behavior, but I know you too well, my dear. Your dramatics belong on a stage." Momma's sternness softened, and she flaked off a piece of dried goop from Lydia's face. "You're lucky it was only hives." She shook her head. "Get ready for dinner. Your father should be home shortly."

Madelyn beat her to the bathroom and smirked. "You look like the bride Frankenstein's monster demanded."

"Let me go in. You can use the basin in your room to wash up. I need the bath."

"Fine. I guess you should enjoy your last chance for hot water. I hear they don't have that in prison." She stepped aside, thoroughly pleased with herself. "But don't worry, I'll make sure to box up your things neatly before moving into your room."

"You really don't care, do you?"

"Oh please. It's your first offense and you're a woman. You'll probably just have to pay a fine or something. I'd have better luck getting your room if I played matchmaker and married you off."

Lydia slammed the door on Madelyn's smug face. *Sisters.*

After a quick bath and a change into fresh clothes, Lydia hurried downstairs. She'd grab the newspaper from the porch, then join her family at the table.

But when she unrolled the newspaper, bold letters stretching the width of the page screamed at her.

Four Murders, E. A. Dupin Suspected

Nausea swept over her, and she sagged against the doorframe.

Four murders? And Dupin was the suspect for every one? But how could they possibly suspect someone who didn't exist?

She stepped inside the foyer and devoured every word of the article.

All four victims were from cases that had inspired her Detective Billy Poe novels. More than inspired. She'd researched and studied each victim's case with a fervor that allowed her to create stories that were unmistakably fictionalized versions of their crimes. She'd even dragged Theresa, Nora, and Flossie with her to the various locations of the crimes just so she could get the tiniest details correct.

Now her stories were being brought to life—or rather, death—by someone professing to be her Detective Billy Poe. That someone, the paper claimed, was E. A. Dupin. Who else would be so passionate as to have each man's real-life death mimic their fictional one? But the newspaper missed one very important fact. Never once had the criminals died at the hands of Detective Billy Poe. He was always grieved by their deaths and attributed them to God's hand of justice. Her stomach churned as she reread the full-page article.

> After having quietly staged two of his victim's deaths exactly as they died in the books inspired by their crimes, Detective Billy Poe has laid claim to these and two other murders. By leaving signed messages with quotes from the murder victims' corresponding books on their bodies, Poe warns that no criminal who unjustly walks free is safe from judgment and execution.
>
> But how is it that a fictional man can kill? The answer lies in the very real person who hides behind the pseudonym. Yes, E. A. Dupin's name is as fictional as his characters. Should the name Poe fail to hide his deeds, Dupin can rely upon his carefully constructed alias to protect him. According to an unnamed source, even the police don't know who Dupin is.
>
> The police have attempted to keep this information from you, going so far as to pressure journalists to remain quiet while the police investigate. But with a fourth murder now having been committed without any progress, the *Cincinnati Commercial* believes it is your right to know that Dupin is a menace to society.
>
> In an effort to succeed where the police have failed, the families and the *Cincinnati Commercial* are offering a $100

reward for Dupin's identity and location. Submit any information you have to the *Cincinnati Commercial*, care of Eugene Clemens. If your information leads to the author's identity and arrest, then the reward will be yours.

Beware, E. A. Dupin. The people of Cincinnati are on the hunt.

Drawing her breath was impossible. It didn't make sense. Did no one realize Dupin couldn't be the murderer? Obviously not, because Cincinnati had declared a manhunt. For her.

A knock at the door startled her.

Were they here for her already? Her best friends would never betray her, but had her publisher discovered her identity and turned her over? It was ridiculous to jump to that conclusion, but she couldn't stop the shake in her hand as she opened the door.

Officer Hall stood waiting.

Lydia clutched the doorframe, suddenly weak in the legs.

The law had come for her.

"Are you unwell?" He stepped closer, though he seemed uncertain as to how to assist.

She straightened. "I'm well enough."

"Are you certain?"

"Quite." If this was it, she would go with dignity. "Are you here for me?"

"Yes and no. Is your father home?"

That wasn't the answer she'd expected. Did he wish to notify Papa before taking her in?

She feigned a smile. "Not at present, but he should be soon. Would you like to come inside and wait for him?"

"I suppose I have no choice."

She showed him to the parlor and laid the paper on the table. Though she offered him coffee, he declined. The plush seat, however, he accepted.

For a moment his eyes dipped closed, and the evidence of exhaustion appeared in the dark circles beneath his eyes and slump of his body.

Some of her anxiousness eased in light of his obvious need. The poor man. She should drape a quilt over him. No doubt he'd be out within seconds.

Officer Hall must have had similar thoughts of sleep, because he jumped to his feet and moved to where he had nothing to lean against.

"May I relay a message to my father so you can return to your duties?"

Or bed.

Hopefully he wasn't working the night shift. If so, he might collapse somewhere or be overtaken by crooks.

He massaged the bridge of his nose before conceding. "I suppose Dr. Pelton can verify it with Superintendent Carson if he doesn't believe you."

Verify it? Like she was untrustworthy? How ridic—

Guilt pierced her conscience. Of course Officer Hall wouldn't consider her trustworthy. He only knew her as a criminal.

Officer Hall continued. "All charges have been dropped and the payment for the goat accepted. Another officer is delivering the goat and informing Miss Plane."

So it didn't have anything to do with the Dupin case. The stress of the last few moments sluiced off. "But why? Mr. Beadle was livid. He wouldn't—"

The truth rose like a welt on her face. Papa's political ties. She'd just been a beneficiary of the crooked system she fought against. Her hands fisted against her skirts. "Did my father insist that you persuade Mr. Beadle?"

"No, but his friendship with the mayor worked in your favor."

While the knowledge that Papa remained honorable soothed some of her ire, the fact his friends had no compunction against bending justice to suit their needs did not. "I am sorry to have placed you in such a position. It isn't right for me to escape consequences just because of who my father is."

He regarded her as if measuring the truth of her words. "You didn't seem to mind the deferential treatment last night."

"If you recall, I repeatedly asked to be placed in a cell."

"True." He studied her a moment more, then pulled something from his pocket. "Did you write this?"

The familiar bright orange dime novel cover used by her publisher appeared in his hand.

The blood drained from her face. No, her whole body. She felt behind her for the chair's arm so she didn't miss and crash to the floor as she sat.

How could she have been so foolish to assume herself safe? Someone must have suspected her identity and turned her in. She could lie to him, but that would work against her if he already knew the answer. But if he didn't, there was still a chance to preserve her anonymity.

"I take your response as a yes."

There went lying.

"Does your father know?"

"He does not." Maybe there was a chance she could convince Officer Hall to not tell Papa. After all, he had to realize she couldn't murder anyone. He needn't tell anyone else her identity.

Officer Hall dropped the book on the table and pivoted away.

She focused on the title to see which book had ruined her.

The Gentleman's Ward.

Her romance novel? He wanted to know if a book with her name printed on the bottom was written by her? A relieved laugh bubbled out.

"I guess I shouldn't be too surprised she committed theft." Though he mumbled as if talking to himself, she caught his words.

"And what is that supposed to mean?"

He had the decency to look abashed, but he did not back down. "Dime novels do nothing but glorify evil with their violence, unseemly romances, and bucking of roles for men and women. They are dangerous and pollute the mind."

She arched back, unable to hide her offense. Was he really one of *those* people—the ones petitioning for dime novels to be banned and removed from mail delivery? "Have you even read any?"

"I don't need to. I see the evidence of their corruption on the streets every day."

"A man's heart is corrupted by sin, not by literature."

"That twaddle does not count as literature."

"Twaddle!" She stood, but reminded herself it was a crime to assault an officer of the law. Education was the best way to deal with ignorance, and Officer Hall was in great need of enlightenment. "Very few of those romance novels have unseemly scenes, and almost all of them uphold the sacredness of matrimony and society's roles. And books that do not, use their stories as a warning to the consequences of such behaviors. If you've never read a dime novel, then you are just spouting off the opinions of another without investigating the truth for yourself. You might as well be a parrot."

"I'm knowledgeable enough to form my own opinion. My sister has unhealthy expectations for her future husband due to the romances she's read. No man can live up to those unrealistic ideals."

"Oh, you mean the ones you haven't read? How do you know if they're unrealistic?"

"Men do not have to swim across swollen rivers to save the women they love."

He must have read at least a little of *The Lady's Terrible Secret* to cite that example. "No, they don't. That is just an event to make the story more exciting. I guarantee, what your sister wants is a man who's courageous, true, loving, and willing to do what's necessary for those he loves. Those are not unreachable ideals. I see them every day in my father."

He seemed caught off guard by her argument and did not immediately respond. Dare she hope her words had made an impact?

"I understand your point, and I concede that I should conduct my own investigation of dime novels before proclaiming such a decided opinion." The words indicated victory, but the underlying challenge in his tone declared it a premature assumption. "But how do you explain Dupin?" He pointed to the headline of the poorly folded newspaper. "Is he not proof that dime novels are capable of degrading their readers?"

She should have shoved that paper with its sensationalist bombast in the umbrella stand when she answered the door. "I maintain my position. Just because the killer left behind Billy Poe quotes does not mean Dupin or his stories are responsible. Just read his books. You will see that the only thing they did was reveal the atrocities of the criminals whose stories they were based on."

"And yet four of those men are dead."

"Do you really consider him a suspect, or are you parroting someone else's beliefs again?"

His lips pressed into a thin line.

Antagonizing the man would do her no good—they were on the same side, after all. But she needed him to realize that Dupin was not the suspect the police should be chasing.

"Please, Officer Hall. You are an intelligent man. All I am trying to say is, if you want to catch the real murderer, you would do well to study your suspect—Dupin—in any way available to you. Right now, all you have are his books. One can learn a lot about a person by reading their stories. Read Dupin's. Maybe then you will realize that just because he writes a crime novel doesn't mean he commits murder."

"Why are you so adamant in your defense of him?"

A moment of panic sent her mind scrambling for some logical reason. Thankfully she spotted her romance novel still lying on the table.

"Because we are both dime novelists. We are not guilty of misconduct, merely of exposing truths to the world. Dupin reveals corruption, and I reveal the characteristics in a man that a woman should desire."

"That doesn't mean his stories didn't incite someone else to commit murder."

She shook her head. "A man's heart is corrupted by—"

"Sin and not literature?" He arched a brow.

"Not literature *or* twaddle."

"So you admit it's twaddle." A half smile creased his cheek.

She scrunched her mouth to keep from forming one of her own. Even she had to admit that was a good retort.

"It's good storytelling, Officer Hall. That is all."

"I suppose I will have to judge that for myself. If you'll excuse me, it appears I have some *storytelling* to investigate." He picked up *The Gentleman's Ward*. "If your story is half as challenging as you, then I might be forced to change my opinion—at least on romance."

"You'll have to return when you're finished and inform me if I was successful in such a formidable task."

"With your permission, I'd like to."

Had she just fallen into a romance novel? That was entirely too formal and hinted at more than an interest in discussing the morality of dime novels. Her heart raced in a way that was entirely too suspect.

She lifted her chin in an effort to dispel the sudden effect he had on her. "The invitation was genuinely offered. I won't rescind it just because you accept. I'm not afraid of you."

"I wonder if you're afraid of anything."

"Monkeys. Definitely monkeys."

He lifted a hand covered in scabs and chuckled. "I concur. Good evening, Miss Pelton. This visit was surprisingly enlightening."

He let himself out.

Good gracious! Normally she was the one initiating the flirtation. It was surprising to have any man, let alone her Detective Darcy, take the lead. She'd have to work the conversation into a future story, just so she'd have it to treasure long after he'd moved on like the many other potential suitors before him.

"Who was that, dear?" Momma asked at the parlor door.

"Officer Hall. He says Mr. Beadle dropped the charges. Theresa and I are free." The relief hit her fully then. She need not fear for Papa's reputation.

"Praise the Lord! Your father will be so relieved, but don't think you are free of punishment, young lady. It doesn't change what you did. Now head to the table. I'll grab your father's paper and be there in a moment."

At the mention of the newspaper, Lydia's stomach dropped. They might celebrate her freedom tonight, but Cincinnati was hunting her.

CHAPTER 6

In the five days since the *Cincinnati Commercial* had declared a manhunt, all of Cincinnati's newspapers had frothed with hate and threats toward Dupin. Lydia shouldn't have, but she'd read every word. Many editorials blamed Dupin for the Billy Poe murders and called for Dupin to be dragged into the street and given the same treatment as his victims. The few editorials that had come to Dupin's defense and pointed out anyone could have claimed to be Billy Poe were met with rebuttal. Whether Dupin killed them or not, they said, he was responsible. His books had been the catalyst. The plan for action. He should suffer, and this city would not rest until he'd been pulled from whatever sewage gutter he'd hidden himself in.

Even worse, notices of criminal activity began to include brawls over Dupin accusations and citizens taking out their frustrations on innocent officers. Questions over potential rioting arose. Cincinnati was a city divided.

Something needed to be done.

Lydia could no longer pretend the whole situation would sputter out like a candle's last spark. No, this flame was burning its way down a fuse of unknown length, threatening an explosion that would leave Cincinnati forever marred.

She rubbed her gritty eyes and surveyed Nora Davis's late-afternoon sunlit parlor. Piles of newspapers littered the room. Flossie Gibson sat cross-legged on the floor with her pampered spaniel puppy, a Cavalier named Harold, in her lap, scouring the columns while trying to keep the interested pooch from shredding the pages. Nora sat primly on the settee with her ever-present knitting needles beside her, turning the pages so quietly it was easy to forget she was there. Theresa, who had sneaked out to join them, lay sprawled out on the floor, tossing the papers aside as she finished each one.

These were the Guardians—a secret society turned friendship, born from an oath during their school days to protect their defenseless peers from a lecher and tormentor. Now, years later, they continued in their mission. Only, today, Lydia was the one in need instead of a stranger. Somehow they had to come up with a way to prove Dupin innocent while protecting her identity from the police and Cincinnati.

She returned her attention to the page in front of her—the *Cincinnati Commercial*'s original exposé article. Thanks to it, they had the dates of the murders, but so far, they'd been unable to find one article that provided more details than what the *Cincinnati Commercial* had shared.

With a frustrated huff, she tossed the paper to the table in front of her. "I just don't understand it. How is there so little information on the murders of men whose trials were front-page news for weeks?"

"The *Cincinnati Commercial* did say that the police had encouraged their silence." Nora set aside her newspaper and took up knitting a sock as she spoke. "Besides, Billy Poe didn't lay claim to the murders until Daniel Finn's. The first two deaths looked the same as every other murder in town. Why waste the space?"

Out of the puppy's reach, Flossie held up a front page with the illustration of a burning building on it. "Especially when the toy factory fire overshadowed Mr. Wakefield's death. No one cared about him when the factory fire meant the loss of hundreds of jobs."

Theresa wadded her paper into a ball and tossed it across the room, catching Harold's attention. Smiling at him as he sprang across the room and pounced on it, Theresa added her findings to the mix. "Benjamin Patterson's death was next, but it was overshadowed by the Republican National Convention."

Nora's needles stopped clicking. "I wonder if that's why, when Billy Poe killed next, he claimed their deaths and Daniel Finn's. Do you think he was hoping their deaths would make a bigger impact on the news? He *did* include a warning to those who escaped justice."

That made sense, but it was frustratingly unhelpful in determining a way to prove Dupin's innocence.

"Oh no you don't." Flossie grabbed for her ruby-haired pooch as he pounced on Nora's yarn ball, then held him against her shoulder. "I think it's possible, but his motivation means little. You must prove that Dupin had neither the means nor the opportunity to murder those men."

"I doubt they will take my word that Dupin doesn't have the strength to overpower Mr. Wakefield or the gun mastery to shoot Benjamin Patterson. All I can offer are my alibis for the dates the *Cincinnati Commercial* listed." Lydia frowned at the diary next to her that contained her explanations for each date.

"I still don't see why that is a problem." Nora spoke as if it were as simple as binding off one of her knitted socks.

"Because the number of people present at each alibi could reveal my identity."

"What are your alibis?" Theresa scooped up an armload of newspapers and deposited them in the kindling basket. "Maybe we can discover a way to give them what they need without implicating you."

"I was at a private ball of only a dozen or so couples when Otis Wakefield was murdered. The public lecture given by the Honorable Joseph Kelley during Patterson's death drew a crowd, but I have notes from the lecture to prove I was there. Unfortunately I don't have an alibi for Daniel Finn's death. My next Dupin novel was due the following day, so I was holed up in my room, frantically finishing it. For Joseph Keaton's murder, Theresa and I were either in the process of rescuing Tipsy or sitting in the station, but I can't very well admit that."

Evidently bored with the conversation and being held, Harold lunged at the bow in Flossie's brown hair.

"Not now, Harold." Flossie set him down, then removed and

dangled the ribbon for him to chase. With the dog appeased, Flossie returned her attention to the problem at hand. "I think you're safe. Even if you identify which ball you attended, they'll probably only suspect the men."

Nora nodded. "Then they would have to determine whether any of those men attended the lecture *and* were seen at the station before they would have enough to even consider that man a suspect—which is highly unlikely."

But Lydia hadn't attended those events on her own. Papa had been present at the ball, the lecture, and the jail. Papa also had the intelligence to plan and write those books, was in a position that would require a pseudonym to protect himself, and had in-depth knowledge of the cases—she'd gotten most of her details from his files.

He could easily be mistaken for Dupin.

"Not highly unlikely. Highly *probable*. They'll think Papa is Dupin." Her friends looked at each other, surprised and dismayed, as Lydia offered a brief explanation.

Theresa nodded thoughtfully. "That's a real possibility." Then she grinned and elbowed Lydia. "Especially if that handsome Officer Hall is the one who investigates."

Heat crept up Lydia's neck. By Flossie's and Nora's knowing smirks, they'd noticed. She hadn't told them about Officer Hall or the flirtation she'd indulged in. Of course, the fact he hadn't returned to share his thoughts on her novel probably meant there was no more story to tell. And that was probably for the best. After all, did she really want to continue flirting with a man who thought her novels were immoral twaddle? She'd dismissed nearly a dozen potential suitors for lesser reasons.

"A handsome officer who makes you blush? And you didn't tell us?" Nora thankfully speared Lydia with an arched brow rather than a knitting needle. "I expect the details once we're finished with the problem at hand. The police will never catch the real murderer if we don't turn their suspicion from Dupin."

"The whole city needs to turn their suspicion from Dupin," Lydia muttered.

"And I know just how to do it!" Theresa rubbed her hands together. "Since Billy Poe brought suspicion to Dupin through a letter, Dupin should respond with one of his own. Then we can deliver it to the police, and voilà! They will know Dupin is innocent."

Flossie shook her head. "They're not going to believe a letter claiming to be from Dupin. It could be from anyone."

"But no one's handwriting would match mine." For the first time since they had come together, Lydia had hope they could actually accomplish clearing Dupin's name. "I can insist they compare the letter's handwriting to that of one of the manuscripts turned in to Mr. O'Dell. They can't deny it is me if my handwriting matches a manuscript turned in months ago."

"A letter to the police won't reach the public, but if we give something to the newspapers . . ." Flossie pressed a finger to her lips, and the excitement of a conspiracy lit her face.

"They'll likely print it and share it with the detective in charge." Theresa plopped on the floor and scratched behind Harold's ear. "With all the people who come and go in those places, they won't notice someone dropping a note on a desk."

"Especially if I'm the one to do it." A rare but mischievous smile graced Nora's lips. "No one ever sees me."

Nora wasn't wrong. Even with her red hair, she was as unnoticeable as air wherever she went. People forgot about her with her silent ways. It was the perfect solution.

"And I know whose desk to drop it on." Lydia held up the original article and pointed. "If Eugene Clemens is as ambitious as I think he is, it'll be printed in tomorrow's edition, and this madness can end."

"You write the letter with as vague yet solid of an alibi for each murder as you can while Theresa and I clean up. Nora will deliver it when you're finished. No matter what happens, we'll stand by you. If worse comes to worst, we'll find a patch of poison ivy to line the Billy Poe imposter's clothes with." Flossie winked at the allusion to how they'd ended the unwanted attention of a lecher together during their school days.

Together. That's how they always made it through the challenges, and that was how they would face this one.

Lydia just hoped that they wouldn't need to actually protect her, because poison ivy would do nothing against a raging city or some deranged person who brought fiction to life.

CHAPTER 7

ABRAHAM SQUINTED AS HE ENTERED the basement foyer of Central Station. Moving from the glare of the still-bright evening sun into the dim and dank interior left him blind—and his prisoner too. The man hit his hip on a nearby bench and stumbled, freeing a curse and his arguments. Again.

"You've got the wrong man. I swear it. It was Dupin! And now you're letting that murderer get away."

Abraham ignored the accusation. It didn't matter what he said. The man was convinced, just like the one Abraham arrested yesterday. And the one on the day before that. Three arrests in as many days for brawling over the identity of E. A. Dupin. It was absurd how quickly people lost their heads when a reward hung in the balance. If they used any logic, they'd realize that anyone with access to a Dupin novel could quote the book. Just because Dupin wrote the original words did not make him guilty. It didn't make him innocent either, but Abraham would not draw conclusions until the case came to trial.

He handed the brawler off to be processed and claimed an empty desk to write his report on the incident. Then he'd escape this stuffy building and return to patrolling downtown. He'd take the heat of summer and flaring tempers over the monotony of a clerical job any day. Even on the days when it felt like Cincinnati had gone mad with Dupin fever.

Halfway through his report, someone clapped him on the shoulder.

"Brilliant work on the Beadle case." Talbot Lawson, the most respected detective on the force, stood over him with the gruff appearance of a man who'd missed an appointment or three with his razor. "Both men nabbed and several boys returned to their families. Not every patrolman can claim such success."

Abraham rose and shook the man's hand. "Thank you, sir."

"No *thanks* to it. Good work deserves recognition. When you finish up that report, Superintendent Carson wants you in his office."

"Yes, sir."

Abraham finished his detailed report and turned it in before knocking on Carson's door. When he entered, Eugene Clemens leaned against a wall, and Detective Lawson sat in a chair. The open window behind where Superintendent Carson sat allowed in a wet and sticky breeze from the humid day; however, it did little to cool the sweatbox or dissipate the lingering scent of an extinguished cigar.

"Took you long enough." Carson gestured to the only empty seat in the room—the punishment chair.

"If it's all the same, sir, I prefer to stand."

"Suit yourself. I assume you know Lawson and Clemens?"

Abraham acknowledged each man, and Clemens returned his nod with firmed lips and a cold stare. Their relationship had always been strained at best. While Abraham understood the necessary role the reporter played for the community, Clemens pushed ethical boundaries in order to get his stories. The man was more ambitious than the snake in the garden of Eden, and Abraham was certain he'd learned his trade from that fateful chapter in the Bible. Clemens asked questions that purposely twisted the truth to create stories that couldn't outright be declared false but were far more sensational than they were factual. He was exceptionally skilled at unnerving officers and shaking loose information to include in his articles. Abraham looked forward to the day when he could strike his heel to Clemens's head.

"Let's get right to the point." Carson dropped the pen in his hand and leaned back. "I've removed you from your beat, effective immediately."

Abraham regretted not taking that seat. The blow was almost palpable, but he forced himself to remain standing at attention, awaiting whatever might come next.

"I've reassigned you to assist Lawson in the Dupin case. You'll be working the day shift for now."

Relief washed over him. Officers were often temporarily appointed as assistants. To be delegated partial responsibility for such a public investigation was an honor.

But Carson wasn't finished. "I've been watching your work for several months. You're observant with a keen mind. We need fresh eyes on this case, and I think you'll be an asset. If all goes well, you can expect a permanent detective position."

To become a detective at twenty-six was almost unheard of in the Cincinnati police department. Each detective on the force had well over twenty years of experience. Abraham had a mere three.

Lawson regarded him with fierce appraisal. Abraham must have met his approval, for the man rose and enthusiastically shook Abraham's hand. "Congratulations. I'm eager to begin your training."

"Don't congratulate him yet." As Lawson returned to his seat, Carson gathered papers on his desk and tapped them into alignment. "The negative publicity has drawn Mayor Jacobs's attention. He plans to fire the entire department if we don't bring this case to a swift end. Dupin is our only lead and the driving force behind this madness. Your first priority is to identify the man and bring him in for questioning. Clemens, share what you brought in earlier."

Clemens retrieved a plain envelope from his coat pocket and extended it toward Abraham. "Dupin left this on my desk while I was away."

A quick glance at the signature indicated it was Dupin, but anyone could have signed it. However, it was unlikely anyone else would be so adamant and detailed in the defense of his innocence or go so far as to suggest comparing the handwriting to a Dupin manuscript. Abraham frowned as he read the lengthy letter describing the reasons why Dupin couldn't have committed the murders, including his alibis. Dupin admitted being at home to finish a manuscript was insufficient to persuade anyone of his innocence, but insisted his publisher could verify that he had a deadline the next day. As for the most recent murder, he'd been at the police station when it occurred. A brilliant stroke of luck if they could identify him.

"He was at the station? Which one?"

Lawson shook his head. "He didn't give enough information. Even if we knew, we don't know what capacity his presence entailed. Prisoner, officer, clerk, visitor, lawyer. The possibilities are too wide and undocumented for us to identify a specific suspect."

An unfortunate truth. But it was something to keep in mind. "Did anyone see Dupin when he delivered the letter?"

Clemens shook his head. "I asked around, but no one remembers seeing him. People are always coming and going in our offices."

Lawson scrubbed his chin. "Unless Dupin is familiar with which desk is yours, he would have had to ask for its location. Did you check with the front clerk to see if they could give a description?"

"Of course I did. You're not the only one who can conduct an investigation."

"But why deliver it to you at all?" Abraham asked. "It makes more sense for him to deliver the note to us. We're the only ones who can dismiss him as a suspect."

"He's smart enough to know you'd keep the information to yourselves. He needs me to publish the note and clear him publicly. One hundred dollars is an enticement few men can ignore."

Abraham frowned. "This sounds like a scheme to sell more papers."

Clemens stepped away from the wall toward Abraham. "Then why would I come here before publishing it? We might not always see eye to eye, but I believe in justice as much as you. I just go about it in a different way."

"We have the same aim, gentlemen, and it is in our best interest to work together." Carson rose from his chair, as if preparing to step in should fists start flying.

He needn't have worried. Abraham wasn't given to fighting. Not that he could say the same for Clemens. Rumor had it he was a fierce competitor in the illegal pugilist matches.

"I've done nothing but cooperate. I withheld the story about Poe's connection to Finn's murder just like you asked, but instead of an arrest, another body turned up. I'm printing Dupin's letter."

Carson folded his arms. "At least wait until we have confirmed that this letter is indeed from Dupin. It is too late to go to the publisher today, but we'll pay them a visit and compare documents tomorrow." He extended his hand toward Clemens. "Thank you for the information. I appreciate your support."

Clemens snubbed Carson's proffered hand. "Just be sure Lawson runs every lead down to the ground. Whether Dupin's innocent or guilty is yet to be determined, and Lawson's history doesn't give me confidence that he's the right detective for this case. His negligence has allowed a criminal to walk free before."

He strode from the room without a by-your-leave.

"Don't let him get to you, Lawson." Carson relit a half-smoked cigar. "No one has a perfect career. Some people just can't accept that we're human and make mistakes."

"He has good cause to be upset with me over that particular case, but I've learned not to allow the man's bitterness to affect me."

No specific case stood out in Abraham's recollection of the detective, but Carson's words were true enough. Leave it to Clemens to hold being human against someone.

"Good." Carson sat down. "Familiarize Hall with the details of the case, then put the pressure on O'Dell Publishing to give up Dupin's identity. They know who he is, and we're not going to allow them to keep silent any longer."

Before they examined the files, Lawson provided Abraham a brief tour of the small detectives' office tucked into the back corner of the City Building's basement. Like the rest of the station hidden beneath the city's government offices, small rectangular windows situated at the top edge of the exterior walls provided the only natural light. Of course, that might be for the best. The dimness probably hid the evidence of rodents and grime better, even if it couldn't disguise the musty air.

"That one is yours." Lawson pointed to a dilapidated piece of wood that once upon a time might have been considered a desk. Dark mildew spots streaked the bowed and splintered top while one leg appeared rotted through. With it jammed in the corner as it was, Abraham would have to climb over and risk his neck to reach the chair.

By the amused curve to Lawson's lips, this assignment was part of the usual hazing process.

Lawson relented. "That's heading to the potbelly stove on the first cold day. You'll share with me for now." He pulled the chair free and sat it opposite his. "You're one of us, *Detective* Hall."

"But I've not been promoted yet."

"It won't be long, so you might as well get used to the title. I'll train you so you can run circles around Detective Bradford. You're already capable of running them around Carlisle."

"I heard that, Lawson." A long-faced man with more gray than black to his hair—presumably Carlisle—stuck his head inside the room. "Just remember, if I finish my cases before you finish yours, you're buying drinks for a week."

"No concerns there. I've got an advantage. Meet the boy detective."

Carlisle looked Abraham over and chortled. "Certainly can't be a man. How old are you, boy? Thirteen?"

"Twenty-six, sir."

"Grow some whiskers, or no one will take you seriously. You're nothing but a pup."

Abraham never had a problem earning the respect of those on his beat, whether another officer or a citizen. "Perhaps, but pups have youthful vigor that old dogs do not."

"And brains that don't know when to keep their yaps shut. Watch that one, Lawson. He's calling you old."

"I think we know which of us has the most gray hair, Carlisle. Get on about your business. I've got a week's worth of drinks to earn."

Once Carlisle left, Lawson laid out four stacks of files. "By the time I'm finished teaching you, you'll be the second-best detective in the country. If you have questions, ask. If you notice something, speak up. If you think I'm wrong, think again. If you still believe I'm wrong, speak up. No one here knows Dupin better than me, but you've been brought in for a fresh perspective. We're partners on this, and I expect you to not hold back. Understand?"

"Yes, sir."

"Good, because we have a lot of ground to cover before you take an active role in the investigation. Dupin's written eight novels. So far, four men are dead."

"Have you identified the other four potential victims?"

"Yes, and they have been notified of the danger to their lives. The fools insist they can take care of themselves, unlike those other poor saps." Lawson shook his head. "They don't know the cunning of the man they're up against. It's up to us to ensure they never do."

They spent hours examining and comparing notes from the murders and the victims' original crimes. Lawson hadn't been brought into the investigation until the third murder occurred, and the only original crime he had personal insight on was the Wakefield case a year ago. They had to rely heavily on the reports left behind. Though detailed, nothing pointed to one suspect, outside of Dupin, for all the murders.

As far as Dupin went, the two notes left on the bodies of Billy Poe's latest victims had distinct handwriting. Handwriting that did not match that of the letter supposedly written by Dupin. That either supported Dupin's claim he wasn't Poe or indicated the letter wasn't from him. Until they met with the publisher tomorrow and compared the notes to a Dupin manuscript—assuming Mr. O'Dell cooperated—there was no knowing for sure.

By the time Lawson called it a night, it was well past the end of their scheduled day. Abraham felt strange, leaving only a few hours into his old shift, but Lawson insisted he'd want to get to bed soon, as morning came early. That might be, but Abraham had no intention of being finished for the night. He walked straight home with the Dupin novels Lawson loaned him, grabbed his dinner plate from the warmer, and retreated to his room to eat while he worked. Miss Pelton's assertion that he should study his suspect in any possible manner held merit, and he'd begin with skimming the borrowed books. After all, he'd discovered quite a bit about Miss Pelton by reading two of hers.

Before beginning with Dupin's work, Abraham picked up *The Lady's Terrible Secret*—the cover carefully reattached—and flipped through the pages. That woman had as much flair for the dramatic in her writing as in her real life. Whatever man married her was likely to face a lifetime of adventure and headache. The situations in which she placed her characters weren't scandalous, but they were outlandish. No real man could swim a raging, flooded river to rescue his love from a burning building. If her heroes were any indication of what she desired in a husband, she was doomed to be a spinster. Yes, their qualities reflected the virtues of Christ and a chaste, God-honoring love, but the characters themselves were too perfect. He couldn't possibly live up to her standards—which was part of the reason he hadn't paid another visit.

He also didn't want to admit he'd been wrong in his judgment of her dime novels. They were well written and modeled Christian morals and faith. Actually, not that he would admit it to any of the men on the force, he was finding them more than tolerable and an enjoyable distraction from the grit of his profession. It had nothing to do with the fact that hers was the face of every heroine and his the face of every hero. He just lacked the imagination for anything else.

Suddenly aware of the half grin on his face, he laid the romance novel aside. No time for nonsense now. It was time to see what he could learn about Dupin. He took the top book from the stack and settled in.

Dupin's writing proved easy to read, but the farther he got into the story, the more he was convinced that his earlier opinion of dime novels was correct. The only redeeming points he found were in how descriptions never crossed the line of the obscene and how the hero, Detective Billy Poe, modeled Christian qualities. Abraham also appreciated the close attention Dupin gave to detail. Otherwise, the man's obsession with the dark underpinnings of the criminal world was disturbing. How did anyone find the violence, depravation, and greed appropriate for entertainment?

Whoever Dupin was, he must not keep his eyes on the things above as the Bible instructed. He probably wasn't even a Christian. It was likely, though, that he was an officer or at least connected to the police in some form. The man knew things about investigating crimes that civilians wouldn't.

Including information withheld from the public about the cases that inspired the books.

Abraham frowned as he compared *The Fall of the Philanthropist* to his notes on the latest victim.

Joseph Keaton had been convicted of burglarizing the home of beloved philanthropist Russell Vernon, but not of Vernon's murder. Given Vernon's known medical condition, which made him prone to stumbling, the defense argued that the cause of his fall could not be determined. He could have been pushed down the stairs or simply have become physically unbalanced with nothing to stabilize him. The fact he'd been beaten beyond what a tumble would cause had been completely ignored.

Dupin's description of the novel's murder scene made one wonder if he'd been at Vernon's house during the investigation. Body positioning, mud on the stairs, the portion of the banister ripped from its foundation as if Vernon had caught himself—all of it was too reflective of the actual case. If Dupin had sat in the gallery during the Keaton trial, he might have gleaned some of the specifics, but not all of them. Either Dupin had personal experience, or he had inside information. Tomorrow they'd find out Dupin's identity and how one man had so much access to details he shouldn't.

Far too late for a man who had to be at work by six in the morning, Abraham set Dupin's book beside Lydia Pelton's on his nightstand. Maybe he'd reconsider visiting her after tomorrow's shift. There was much he didn't understand about the novelist turned circus thief turned repentant yet flirtatious angel. Puzzling the riddle of Miss Pelton's character might be the perfect distraction from the darker aspects of his job.

But first Abraham needed to uncover Dupin's identity.

CHAPTER 8

WHEN ABRAHAM AND LAWSON ARRIVED at O'Dell Publishing at ten the next morning, nearly a dozen people were picketing outside the entrance. Signs condemning the publisher for printing immoral books were interspersed with signs demanding Dupin be handed over. The group appeared peaceful, but that could change quickly.

As Abraham and Lawson entered the three-story brick building, one of the picketers who lived on Abraham's beat recognized him as an officer and called him out. The picketer, then the crowd, lobbed insults about the police not doing their job and insisted they arrest Dupin. Lawson appeared unperturbed, but Abraham remained tense until safely inside. Hopefully they'd ascertain Dupin's identity today and subdue Cincinnati's bubbling temper.

Just past the vestibule, locked glass cases displayed copies of O'Dell's printed works with an obvious pride in the material they published. As he approached the secretary's desk, Abraham noted Mr. Dupin and Miss Pelton each had an entire shelf dedicated solely to their works. Only two other authors shared that privilege. They must be the primary moneymakers for the company or perhaps the most prolific of the company's contributors. It would explain Mr. O'Dell's reluctance to expose Dupin. If Dupin were guilty, O'Dell would lose a source of income. His refusal to share Dupin's identity might speak more of his doubt over Dupin's innocence than his presumed desire to protect his author.

A dark-haired man, far too broad for the cramped space provided by the desk, rose to greet them on their approach. "Good morning, gentlemen. I'm Marcus Monroe, managing editor of O'Dell Publishing. How may I help you?"

"I'm Detective Talbot Lawson, and this is Detective Abraham Hall. We're here to speak with Mr. O'Dell."

Monroe's smile faded. "I presume you seek Mr. Dupin's identity."

"It is the only way to clear Mr. Dupin of suspicion." Lawson led the conversation as Abraham watched for any inconsistencies. "As managing editor, you have contact with the authors. Is that correct?"

"Yes, but Dupin is an exception. I've only dealt with him through letters. The man has never set foot in the building."

"Did you know Dupin was a pseudonym?"

"It was agreed upon in his contract, and I've never been told his identity."

It didn't take observing the man's defensive stance or his slight avoidance at meeting their eyes to know Monroe would protect Dupin. Maybe O'Dell would be more cooperative.

"Is Mr. O'Dell available to speak with us?"

"He's in his office." Monroe gestured behind him. "Down that hall, take a right at the end, and it will be the last door on the left. I'd take you myself, but our secretary had a family emergency, and I'm covering for him."

"Thank you, Mr. Monroe. Don't go anywhere; I may have more questions for you afterward."

The dainty chair groaned as Monroe dropped onto it. "As long as you finish with O'Dell before closing, that shouldn't be a problem."

James O'Dell welcomed them into his office with an exuberant handshake and wide smile. Odd, given a crowd protested at his entrance and the police were paying him a personal call. With a magnanimous sweep of his arm, he offered them each a padded seat across from his massive desk. The thinning hair combed over his balding head bounced with each jaunty step to his publishing throne.

"For a man whose author is suspected of murder, you appear quite jovial." Lawson claimed a chair and Abraham followed his lead, though he'd rather stand and keep the advantage.

"What can I say? Murder is good for business." O'Dell rested his hands over his plump belly. "I've sold every copy of his books I had since this whole scandal started. Second-run prints are in process, and I've commissioned special editions to be created with the original news stories at the back."

"I see greed is alive and well." Lawson crossed a leg over his knee and leaned back in his chair. The man was an expert at appearing nonchalant and relaxed, even while delivering an insult.

"*Greed* nothing. It's business. The profit margin of the publishing world is not so great as you might think. Each story we print is a risk, and when I have a moneymaker, I'll run it until there's no more gain to be had."

"Even at the cost of lives?"

O'Dell snorted. "Dupin is no murderer. The man is far too protective of his reputation to stoop to something so risky. Why do you think he uses a pseudonym? No, gentlemen. You're wasting your time. Someone else is responsible for those men's deaths. Not that their passing is any great shame."

Abraham bristled. "Every life is valuable."

O'Dell waved a dismissive hand. "Yes, of course. But you must admit, the world is a safer place having those criminals permanently off the street."

"They were fairly tried and exonerated." The justice system might not be perfect, but it was not the public's place to overturn that decision.

"*Fairly* tried? Had it been anyone else, convictions would have abounded."

"That is a very decided opinion, sir."

"And one shared by the majority of Cincinnatians. The newspapers may be decrying Dupin as a villain, but I guarantee you, there are many more who gather in their parlors and declare him a hero."

Lawson shifted and cleared his throat. "Be that as it may, our investigation requires we examine one of Dupin's manuscripts and for us to speak with Dupin ourselves." He produced his notepad and pencil and slid them across the desk. "If you'll provide his most recent manuscript and his contact information, we'll be on our way."

"I wish I could help, but you'll need a warrant for that manuscript."

So much for Mr. O'Dell's cooperation.

"As far as Dupin's identity, I can tell you honestly, I don't know who Dupin is. Signing him on with that anonymity agreement was the best choice I ever made."

"Then how do you pay him or contact him when there is a problem?"

"All communication and payments are made through another author."

"And that would be?" Lawson nodded toward the notepad.

O'Dell ignored it. "Unless you have a warrant, I'm not at liberty to tell you. I must protect those in my employ."

O'Dell had dozens of authors. Any one of them could be Dupin's contact. No, not any of them. Dupin started writing for O'Dell three years ago. If he insisted on communicating through another author, that person must have already been established here and likely still wrote. Dupin had eight novels, so his contact likely had more. Based on the number of authors with entire shelves to display their work, that fact narrowed things down significantly.

When avoiding answering questions, people often gave themselves away through unintended signals. It wasn't perfect but worth an attempt. Otherwise, Abraham and Lawson would be knocking on the doors of authors all week long.

Abraham stood so that he had a better view of O'Dell's physical responses. "Would Dupin's friend happen to be Rebecca Maney?"

O'Dell remained silent.

"T. G. DiVincenzo."

Again, nothing.

The last author who met Abraham's criteria was one he deeply hoped would result in the same response.

"What about Lydia Pelton?"

O'Dell remained silent, but he visibly tensed while his lips flattened and his Adam's apple bobbed.

Abraham's stomach sank. One response could mean nothing, but all three at once? So much for discerning Miss Pelton's character through her writing. She *knew* the police were searching for Dupin, but instead of revealing her connection to him, she'd suggested Abraham read his books as if that might prove his innocence.

He'd been duped, and he had no one to blame but himself. He should have known a woman who'd steal a goat wasn't to be trusted. At least he'd discovered her character before he'd allowed his heart to become entangled. This would serve as a reminder that, if he wanted a wife, he'd have to make an effort to meet women outside of his professional interactions.

Lawson jumped on O'Dell's physical response. "How is Miss Pelton connected to Dupin?"

O'Dell scowled. "I don't have to answer that."

"I noticed that she has over a dozen books displayed on your shelves. She must be a very popular author. I'm sure you don't want the papers discovering her connection to Dupin. If the papers printed that information, Miss Pelton might feel it unsafe to continue writing for you."

Lawson must be bluffing. He wouldn't really risk Miss Pelton's reputation or safety by sharing her Dupin connection with the papers, would he? Even if he didn't care for Miss Pelton, Lawson must care about his career. Their jobs would not survive to the end of the case if the mayor found out they were responsible for his friend's daughter being exposed to danger.

Thankfully, O'Dell didn't test the bluff. He grimaced and dropped his arms. "I suspect they're romantically involved. Their characters sometimes appear in each other's novels, especially when they have similar deadlines. They must spend a great deal of time brainstorming and writing together. Other than for romance, I can't fathom why they would do so."

"Dupin could be a family member," Lawson reasoned.

"Miss Pelton has no brothers. Her father is the coroner and, while a decent man, does not have the knack for writing. He once submitted a story that was best used for the lining of my wife's birdcage. If Dupin's a family member, then it must be a distant one." The publisher picked up a pen and examined it thoughtfully. When he spoke again, it was in a firm tone. "I'm telling you, her relationship with the man is a romantic one. I pressed her to reveal his identity when his books began to outsell hers, but she refused. Said it would ruin his reputation. Even after promises of secrecy and a threat to fire her, she refused to betray him. She's confident enough in his affections that she declared if I fired her, Dupin would go to a competitor."

Usually, Abraham viewed loyalty with respect, but all he could muster now was dismay. He'd intentionally flirted with her to test for potential interest. She'd flirted back for nothing more than entertainment. Rejection always stung, but at least he'd not given her the opportunity to declare a coward like Dupin a better choice of partner than him. Call him spiteful, but it pleased him that he and Lawson were about to reveal the character of her beau as lacking.

CHAPTER 9

LYDIA KNEW THERE WOULD BE consequences in delivering her almost-late manuscript in person, but she hadn't anticipated facing a crowd of picketers. They looked peaceable enough, but they were angry with the publisher. Would they take out their frustration on her, one of O'Dell's authors? If they knew she was Dupin, they'd likely drag her by the collar to the nearest station—after a good beating.

If her romance novel weren't in danger of being late, she'd go to the post office and mail it. But if it didn't arrive by the end of the business day, she'd be in breach of contract, and O'Dell would love nothing better than to penalize her pay. The man was as greedy as a bank thief and as cunning as a squirrel after birdseed.

All this Dupin nonsense had stolen her focus. But she'd never missed a deadline, and she wasn't about to do so now. Even if it meant turning in the most awful romantic ending she'd ever penned. Marcus Monroe would make her rewrite it, but hopefully this Dupin mess would be behind her by then. It had better be. A dead rat had more life than her creativity, and her new Billy Poe novel was due next month.

She glanced from her manuscript to the picketers and clenched her jaw. There was nothing for it. She'd just have to keep her head down and cut straight through the group. Once she turned in the manuscript, she'd visit the newsstand for the latest on the Dupin investigation.

Mind made up, she exited the hack and braced for insults.

"Well, if it isn't the clown from the police station."

That hadn't been the insult she'd expected. That reporter—Mr. Clemens, wasn't it?—approached her from the edge of the crowd.

"I almost didn't recognize you without welts on your face. What brings you to O'Dell Publishing?" His sharp-minded gaze dipped to the manuscript pages in her hands, and he grinned. "Ah, so you're one of my uncle's authors."

"Your uncle?" That wasn't good. What if Mr. Clemens told Mr. O'Dell of her arrest? Even though the charges were dropped, he could still use it as grounds to dismiss her or, more likely, decrease what he offered her per submission.

"Don't look so disconcerted. I find it as unfortunate a connection as you, but what can you do about family? I assure you, I have no desire to expose your goat thieving to him. It will be our little secret." He winked as if they were the closest of chums. "What's your name? Perhaps he's forced me to read your books."

"I'm surprised that an astute reporter such as yourself doesn't know it already." If he truly didn't know, she certainly wasn't going to provide it to him.

Oddly, he seemed to approve of her. "You are as smart as your characters, Miss Pelton. If you were on the case, Dupin's identity would no longer be a mystery. Please, allow me to escort you safely inside."

He looped his arm around hers, guided her through the throng of protesters, and then physically shielded her identity from those hurling insults at them. She expected him to release her once inside, but he remained firmly attached.

"So do you have any suspicions, Miss Pelton?"

"Suspicions of you? What sane woman wouldn't?" She forced a flirtatious lilt to her voice in hopes of throwing the man off his line of questioning.

His chuckle fell flat. "I was referring to Dupin."

"Mr. Clemens, I was not expecting you so soon." Marcus strode toward them. "I'm afraid your uncle is with the police just now, but if you go upstairs, Simon's wife dropped off a large plate of cookies for the printers."

Lydia didn't miss Mr. Clemens's calculating squint before his face smoothed.

He released her arm and offered a duplicitous smile that many probably fell for. "Marcus knows my weakness for sweets and my dislike of idle waiting. If you'll excuse me."

That man was not after a cookie. He was probably sneaking off to eavesdrop on Mr. O'Dell and the officers. That's what she would do, given the opportunity.

She and Marcus watched until he disappeared around the corner. Then her editor took the manuscript pages from her hands, gripped her elbow, and propelled her toward the exit.

"What on earth, Marcus?" The man had never once treated her so forcefully. Normally he was gentle and kind, even bordering on flirtatious.

"You have to leave. Now. Detectives are questioning Mr. O'Dell, and I'm certain it won't be long before they discover you're who they're seeking."

Lydia stumbled as her stomach vaulted. He couldn't know her secret. "But I'm not—"

He stopped pulling her and stared her down. "I've edited your and Dupin's manuscripts since the beginning. Did you think I wouldn't recognize your writing style or, at the very least, your handwriting? I've known Dupin's identity all along."

Bile burned in her throat, and she covered her mouth. She was going to throw up. Right here in the middle of the foyer and probably on Marcus's shoes.

Marcus's fierce stance eased, and unexpected tenderness further softened his manner. "I've done everything I can to protect you. Mr. O'Dell might be too arrogant to believe a woman capable of writing the Billy Poe stories, but he can obviously connect you to Dupin. We cannot allow the police to discover Dupin's identity. Once they know, so will the papers. Do you understand the danger that will place you in?"

He didn't wait for her answer. "Clemens has no soul. He'll feed you to the masses and watch the carnage, all the while writing articles that will ruin your family. Those protesters are just the beginning. There are others who are more menacing, who would love nothing more than to do the same violence to you as has been done to those murdered men. Perhaps worse when they discover Dupin is a woman."

Definitely worse. She well knew the special dangers that lurked for women. She'd used them as plot points in almost every novel.

Still, a tremor ran through her. Everything she'd feared speaking, he'd given voice to. She wasn't overreacting.

"Go home. Figure out a story to explain your connection to Dupin. I'll stall them for as long as I can, but they will come. I want you to be ready to say whatever is necessary to protect yourself."

She'd never thought to write Marcus as a hero, but here he was, acting the part. Maybe she shouldn't have turned down his invitations to dinner.

Would kissing the man on the cheek be too presumptuous? Probably. And she absolutely didn't need any romantic intrigues at a time like this.

"Thank you, Marcus." She lightly pressed his arm and turned away.

He reached around her to the doorknob. "Go straight—"

"Miss Pelton. What a coincidence. We were just coming to see you."

While Lydia did not recognize the smooth voice, she did recognize the air of authority and underlying warning not to leave that accompanied it. The police had caught up to her. Too bad she was an author of the written word instead of oral tradition. Her drafts were always a mess before she edited them. Telling the first story that came to mind wasn't likely to work in her favor, and there would be no changing the words after they escaped. A dreadful reality.

She forced a smile and faced the man who had addressed her.

If his plainclothes suit was any indication, he was a detective. Though his newsboy cap hid his hair, the white and gray of his close-cut beard indicated he was not a young man. That would make convincing him even more difficult. Papa often equated the age of an officer with his expertise in handling liars and crooks.

Her stomach twisted again. Was she really comparing herself to liars and crooks? What was wrong with her? She hadn't stolen anything.

Except a goat.

And she wasn't lying.

Yet.

Maybe it wasn't too late to vomit on the floor.

"I'm Detective Lawson. Would you be so kind as to join me and Detective Hall in an empty office? We have some things we'd like to discuss with you."

Detective Hall? He couldn't mean the same man as *Officer* Hall. The surname was fairly common, so it stood to reason that they were different people. At least she prayed so. It was bad enough he'd arrested her. She didn't need him investigating her.

However, when Detective Lawson gestured toward the back offices, Officer Abraham Hall stood in the way.

Could this situation get any worse?

Not that Officer Hall didn't deserve a promotion to detective. From what she could tell, he'd be great at it. But not right now. Not on this case. And definitely not with her as a suspect.

Already disappointment cast a pall over his deportment, as if he knew her secret without her ever saying a word. With a disgusted shake of his head, he pivoted and strode toward the offices.

So much for convincing him that she was a woman of upstanding character. She forced herself forward and prayed her terror at what lay ahead remained hidden.

"You too, Mr. Monroe. As you've already seen fit to abandon your post, we have a few questions we'd like you to answer as well."

"I did not abandon my post. I was still in the lobby. However, if you'll allow me to lock up, I will take us to the conference room. It has a table that will more comfortably accommodate us."

Suspicion dipped Detective Lawson's brow, but he said nothing.

After securing the front door, Marcus placed a protective hand on Lydia's back and walked alongside her.

Once they passed the detective, Marcus kept his face forward and whispered, "Keep your secret, no matter what they say. I'll do the same."

CHAPTER 10

DID ALL INTERROGATIONS TURN A room into an icebox? Lydia shivered despite the open window allowing in the summer heat. She accepted the curved-back seat Detective Lawson offered, but she refused to rest her elbows atop the chair's arms. Neither he nor Officer—no, Detective—Hall would be such tyrants as to tie her into place, but they might if they discerned how much she desired to flee. Is this what her characters felt? If so, she'd not done their torment justice.

Detective Lawson motioned for Marcus to claim the seat next to her, then he made himself comfortable in the one across the table from her. Leaning back in his chair with one ankle crossed over his knee, he appeared relaxed and nonchalant. Detective Hall, on the other hand, stood in the corner behind his colleague and cast a thundering cloud over the room. She tried not to squirm under the intensity of his scrutiny, but it was hard not to with how it felt he could see straight past the lies she'd yet to form.

Lies she debated whether or not to follow through with.

Marcus had insisted once the police knew Dupin's identity, so would the newspapers. Her and her family's safety would be at risk, but was deception really the best course of action?

All it took was one peek at Detective Hall to know what his answer would be.

But he wasn't a woman. He had no idea what the ramifications of admitting she was Dupin would be. She had a pseudonym for a reason. Being a romance writer had its own societal risks, but nothing worse than a turned-up nose or denial of entry to some pretentious ladies' club she hadn't really wanted admittance to anyway. Murder mysteries, on the other hand, especially when surrounded by scandal and accompanied by a manhunt—that posed a very real danger. Marcus's description of Mr. Clemens's soulless delight in the carnage only added to the certainty that it would be a fatal mistake to reveal herself.

"Mr. O'Dell tells us that you and Dupin have a close relationship." Detective Lawson folded his hands over his stomach, looking for all the world that this was merely a casual conversation. "Is that true?"

In the chair next to her, Marcus disguised his head shake with a chin rub.

It would be so easy to go along with him—to deny any connection and allow him to step in as her hero. But lies worked like a deck of cards. You might be able to build a house out of them for a little while, but at some point, the whole construction would collapse.

But if she were careful, she needn't fabricate anything. All she had to do was convince them Dupin was incapable of committing those crimes without divulging the full truth of her identity.

"That is true, and I can personally assure you he is innocent of murder."

There. She'd been honest.

Detective Lawson tilted his head, an underlying skepticism revealed in the action. "May I ask how you can be so certain? These murders were committed at night. A time you should have been abed."

The ball might account for late-night knowledge, but not the lecture. And Detective Hall would question her if she revealed she'd been with Dupin at the station. How could she truthfully account for Dupin's whereabouts without revealing herself? She tapped a finger against her leg until a moment of brilliance struck her.

"As I rarely sleep before three in the morning, I would know if Dupin was not in bed when he should be."

There. Let them refute that.

She smiled until she noticed Detective Hall stiffen in the corner, his eyes wide.

Marcus sank back in his chair and covered his face. "I can't believe you just said that."

His mumbled words reached her but didn't make sense. What was wrong with what she'd said? If she was awake and able to verify Dupin's whereabouts, that should clear him of suspicion.

Detective Lawson leaned forward. "Are you insinuating that you share a room with the man and that is how you can account for his whereabouts?"

Heat blazed into her face. *That's* what they thought she meant?

But of course they did.

She should have known better than to say the first thing that came to mind. Her first ideas always needed tossed and completely rewritten.

How could she explain that she knew exactly where Dupin was at every moment of every day without revealing herself or impugning her reputation? Yes, she shared a bed with Dupin, but it wasn't as scandalous as it sounded.

"I assure you as an unwed woman living in her father's home that I have never shared a room with a man."

"Then the question stands, how can you know for certain that he wasn't involved?"

"You'll just have to trust me that I can."

Detective Hall's shrewd and calculating stare warned that he wouldn't allow her answer to stand. "Are you protecting your father? He's the only other man I can imagine whose whereabouts you could track at night."

Oh dear. Implicating Papa was the last thing she wanted to do. "No. My father would never, ever break the law."

"He knows specific details of the crimes. Details that made it into Dupin's books but not into public record."

Her stomach churned. Papa *had* helped with her research, albeit without his knowledge. "Anyone with access to the justice system might be able to obtain those particulars. I'll vow on a Bible that my father is not Dupin."

"Are you saying that Dupin has access to the justice system? What kind of access?"

Evasive answers were more difficult to devise than she'd assumed they'd be. She picked at one of the many splinters on the table's edge. "He knows people and is an impeccable researcher."

Detective Lawson redirected his poorly veiled interrogation. "Are you romantically involved with Dupin?"

Lydia couldn't help the laugh that escaped at the absurdity of the question. Romantically involved with herself? Oh yes, she could see that now. Walking through Burnet Woods at sunset, holding her own hand as she admired her reflection in the water's edge. Hugging herself was possible, but kissing might prove interesting. Although she did buy herself chocolates and flowers on occasion to help spur romantic ideas for her stories. So maybe that counted.

"I don't see what's so funny about that question." Detective Hall straightened and leveled a glare at her that must make the worst of criminals shake in their boots. She certainly was.

"My sincere apologies for appearing to not take the question seriously. However, how I feel about Dupin is irrelevant to the truth of his innocence."

He stepped to the table. "Then give us his name and address. If he is innocent, he has nothing to fear."

"Nothing to fear?" Was he really so naive? Even now, the panic clawed at her throat. "What about those picketers outside? Or the downfall of his and his family's reputation when the newspapers discover who he is? Or the manhunt underway? I assure you, there is plenty to fear."

His demeanor suddenly softened. "Do you fear what Dupin might do to you if you reveal him?"

His sudden consideration and compassion took her aback. It was sweet and heroic but completely unnecessary. "I do not fear Dupin. I only fear *for* him and his family. I'll do anything to protect them."

"Then tell us who his family is, and we'll guard them."

"My father is a coroner. I see the limitations of your resources. You do not have the necessary manpower to do that. Besides, the only way to protect them from scandal is for no one to know who they are in the first place. Dupin is innocent, I tell you. Turn your investigation elsewhere."

"It doesn't work that way, Miss Pelton." Detective Lawson sighed. "He's our best lead, and we must pursue it to the end. Now, you can either choose to reveal his identity, or we can inform Mr. Clemens of the *Cincinnati Commercial* that you are connected to Dupin and allow the public to extract the information from you. Who do you think Dupin would want you to protect more? Him or yourself?"

The cad!

Marcus shot to his feet. "That is an unfair and manipulative choice to require of her. No gentleman would place such a burden upon a woman."

Detective Hall scrutinized Marcus, and the harder his stare grew, the tighter Lydia's throat squeezed. If he'd noticed Marcus's signals or the intimate conversation they'd held in the foyer, it was more than likely Marcus had just made himself the primary suspect.

"Marcus is not Dupin." That was one truth she wouldn't shy away from. He didn't deserve the consequences of a false accusation.

"No one said he was." Detective Lawson tented his fingers. "But your defense of him is intriguing." The corner of his mouth twitched in suppressed satisfaction, probably because he thought they'd out-witted her.

Well, they both were wrong. "I can see the accusation in Detective Hall's face just because Marcus came to my defense."

"Other clues suggest his defense is more than gentlemanly con-cern." Detective Hall crossed his arms.

"It's true that I care a great deal about Lydia." Marcus regarded her with eyes that confirmed he desired more than an editor-author relationship. "And if it will protect her, I will gladly claim Dupin's identity."

"No, Marcus." She stood and gripped his arm. "You are not Dupin. You cannot lie to protect me."

"A hero is always willing to make sacrifices for the woman he admires."

The stolen quote from her last romance novel and his affectionate smile should have made her swoon into his arms and reward him with a kiss. At least that was how her heroine had responded. But not her. Not when it meant the loss of so much. Marcus needed a good shake by the collar and to be told he was being an idiot. Not only would the declaration ruin his reputation and career, but it would continue to waste the police's time.

Or worse, he'd be convicted of something he hadn't done.

She had to make him see reason. "This is a worthless sacrifice. Think of your job. Your reputation. Your family."

"I think I get to determine what is worth the sacrifice and what is not, and you are worth every sacrifice."

"I am sure Miss Pelton will enjoy adding your overtures to her next novel, Mr. Monroe, but we are not searching for heroes." Detective Lawson rose from his chair. "However, you do fit the build of a man capable of committing murder. If you are claiming to be Dupin, then I'd like to see proof. Samples of your writing alongside the drafts that Dupin submitted for editing would suffice. We need to examine one of his manuscripts for another purpose anyway. I assume you have those filed somewhere on the premises?"

Marcus peeked at her, doing a poor job of hiding his distress.

They both knew the bluff would soon be found out and Detectives Hall and Lawson would return to pressuring her.

"It may take me some time." Marcus gave her a meaningful stare that indicated she should use his absence to come up with a better story for Dupin's identity. "The last book released three months ago, and edits were even farther back."

"We have as long as you need. Hall, wait with Miss Pelton while I accompany Mr. Monroe." The subtle glance at her and then back to Detective Hall clearly communicated his assignment—get her to talk.

"Yes, sir."

The door clicked behind their exit, and Detective Hall took the seat Lawson had abandoned.

Resigned, she sat back down, expecting him to dive directly into questioning her, threatening her, or trying to trick her into revealing information she didn't want to disclose.

He said nothing.

The silence lingered.

And lingered.

And lingered.

Lydia tried to think of a plausible story, but she couldn't while sitting under his unnervingly silent observation. Had this silence occurred even two weeks ago, it wouldn't have bothered her, for her mind was never quiet anyway. The voices of characters, story ideas, or snippets of research she'd uncovered would have filled the spaces quite comfortably. But since the newspapers had declared the manhunt for her, the only work her imagination did was on how the world would react if they discovered Dupin's identity.

Maybe if she led Detective Hall to discuss other things, she might be able to relax enough to create a believable story. "Congratulations on the promotion to detective."

"It isn't official yet."

"Still, I'm sure it is well deserved. From what I've seen, you have a sharp mind. An admirable and necessary quality in a detective."

"I'm not sure my mind is as sharp as I thought. I cannot make you out, Miss Pelton. I want to believe that you are the woman of good character you claim to be, but all I see before me is a goat thief protecting a man who may very well be responsible for the death of four men. And you want me to believe that dime novels do not corrupt a person?"

The question may have been rhetorical, but she needed to answer. "I've made many mistakes in my life, but you cannot presume to know me just because you've only seen me at my worst. Just like you cannot presume to know Dupin only by his novels."

"Dupin's continual hiding behind a pseudonym, even when it comes at the cost of lives, declares him to be a selfish brute and a coward."

She clenched her fists beneath the table and hoped the rest of her body would not betray her personal offense. She might be a coward, but she wasn't selfish. She *had* tried to come forward with proof of her innocence. It just wasn't good enough for the stubborn men who didn't have the good sense to start hunting someone else. "Dupin is not selfish. He values justice and truth. Those stories give the victims the justice denied them. He might be a coward for not coming forward, but there is more to his reasoning behind it than you know."

"I'd know if you told me."

"I've already told you. If he comes forward, his life and the lives of those around him will be ruined."

"And what about the lives of those dead men? Their lives and the lives of those around them have been forever altered in ways that cannot be repaired. Why should Dupin be exempt? Would not his own version of justice demand that he suffer for the injustices he's committed?"

"Their deaths were not his fault! He just wrote the stories. He didn't kill them."

"Those men were exonerated of their crimes. Even if they shouldn't have been, it isn't up to Dupin to decide their futures. He could have written any fictional story he wanted. Instead, he chose to rewrite the narratives of real cases, using details so distinct that no one would question who Billy Poe pursued. Their fictional deaths served as an exact guide for the very real deaths of those men. The *exact guide*, Miss Pelton."

The endings of her Billy Poe novels flashed through her mind, and she shuddered. The villains' deaths had always mirrored those of the crimes they'd committed. She'd never been graphic, only alluding to the deaths they received, but had it really been enough for someone to use? The nausea from earlier returned.

"Dupin is not a hero, nor is he a man worth protecting. Even if he didn't physically commit murder, he corrupted a reader to do the deed he wasn't willing to do himself. Dupin is as responsible for their murders as he'd be if he'd slain them himself."

With each statement, the bile built in her throat.

No. Murder happened because of sinful choices, not literature. She was not responsible for their deaths. She hadn't killed them.

Except in fiction.

Did that make her complicit, at least in part?

Lydia wrapped her arms around her stomach as she rocked to abate the nauseating cramp.

But Detective Hall didn't stop talking. "Tell me. Are you still willing to risk your reputation for that man? Is protecting his identity worth what it will cost you?"

Acid burned in her throat, making her voice croak. "It doesn't matter what I say. The end will be the same for me."

Detective Hall rose from his seat and rounded the table to crouch beside her. His voice gentled. "We can keep your name out of the newspapers if you tell us Dupin's identity. You will not suffer the same as he. I promise you. We can protect you."

She shook her head and did the only thing she could do. "You don't understand. *I am* E. A. Dupin."

He didn't believe her. She could see it in the frustrated tension in his face. Feel it in the puff of his breath as he determined his next tactic.

Finally, he stood and shook his head. "I do not understand why you would sacrifice your family for this man. You cannot be Dupin."

The door clicked shut behind her.

Detective Lawson dropped two stacks of manuscripts on the table. "I am afraid she is. Apparently Miss Pelton has a murderous streak."

CHAPTER 11

ABRAHAM GAWKED AT THE MANUSCRIPTS before lifting his gaze to a suddenly green Miss Pelton.

"I'm going to be sick." She lunged from her chair toward the waste bin in the corner.

Though she did not retch, she clung to it like a beloved doll.

Monroe strode to her side and placed a hand on her shoulder, proclaiming apologies for his inability to protect her.

But it couldn't be true. The deaths Dupin outlined in his novels were as vile and sinister as the crimes committed by his villains. Only a soul as dark as the evil lurking in the world could contrive such endings. Miss Pelton's romance novels had been far-fetched, yes, but full of light and laughter. They'd been beyond reproach. But Dupin's novels . . .

They couldn't be written by the same person.

"Come now, Miss Pelton," Lawson spoke in soothing tones. "Calm yourself. You're not in trouble, but I have quite a few questions that need answered."

She moaned, and heaving followed.

A gag choked the back of Abraham's throat, and Lawson fled the room under the excuse of obtaining water for her. Even Monroe patted her shoulder while facing away.

By her physical response, the revelation was true. Somehow both dark and light lived inside that woman, and yet God had declared that an impossibility. Good trees could not yield bad fruit, and bad trees could not yield good. Just who was this woman who'd managed to yield both in her writing?

Abraham ran a hand through his hair and momentarily tugged.

This could not be real. Miss Pelton's character revelation aside, Dupin was their only lead.

Was.

Miss Pelton couldn't possibly be physically capable of murder. She was by no means a small woman, but she lacked the height and strength necessary to kill those men. Joseph Keaton had been dragged a considerable distance through back alleys before being staged to match his original crime. But even if she'd had help, she couldn't be in two places at once. Stealing that goat had given her an alibi that no one could question.

The heaves in the corner subsided, and Monroe aided Miss Pelton to her seat.

With Lawson gone, it was up to Abraham to continue the line of questioning—and he had plenty he wanted to ask. Not all relevant to the case. But he was a professional. Now was not the time to succumb to the personal shock of having fallen prey to the idea of a woman rather than the reality.

He withdrew his notebook and pencil from his coat and focused.

This must be like any other interview. Collect the facts, identify new suspects, and determine how she had gained access to details she shouldn't have had.

Monroe sat close to Miss Pelton, his arm stretched across the back of her chair like she was his. For all Abraham knew, she could be. The woman had proven herself a criminal through and through. Con women flirted and used their wiles, beau or not. Still, it irked him that he'd assumed her unattached and allowed even the beginnings of attraction to set in. He should have known better.

Abraham cleared his throat. "Given the details included in your Billy Poe stories, you are far more acquainted with the crimes of these men than what the papers shared. How did you come by your information? Did your father provide it?"

She jerked upright. "No! He would never share such things. He doesn't know that I'm Dupin."

"Then how did you gain access to details you shouldn't have?"

The large splinter sticking up from the edge of the table suddenly had her full attention. "I . . . sneaked peeks into his files whenever I visited him at the morgue. If I couldn't get the information I needed there, I flirted with a couple of the officers who'd worked the cases and used their bragging to fill in the missing pieces."

Only further proof that she was a good confidence woman. She must have chosen her targets well. Not many officers fell for the wiles of a woman who frequented a police station, even if she were the daughter of their coroner. Once the news reached Superintendent Carson's desk, reprimands would echo through the hallway for hours.

Miss Pelton continued. "For writing the settings of each book, I visited the crime scene locations to collect details that I couldn't determine from the photos."

Of course she'd examined the photos. Scenes that he'd rather never see again were forever carved into his memory because of his job. But for her to seek them out and revel in them? What hardness of heart did it take for a person to find enjoyment in such a thing? Had she pursued something honorable with such persistence, cunning, and resourcefulness, he'd admire her. But this only served to turn his admiration to ashes.

He'd been right. Dime novels were a source of depravation, and Miss Pelton was a prime example of it.

Lawson returned with a glass of water that he offered Miss Pelton, then reclaimed his chair and indicated Abraham should continue.

Abraham obliged, though he wished the man would take the lead and leave him to process the ramifications of this whole fiasco. "Why do you write under Dupin if you already have a successful career as a romance novelist?"

"I actually wrote crime novels first." She glanced at him and shrugged at whatever response she saw on his face. "I know. It doesn't fit what a proper woman should read or write. But I've always loved Edgar Allan Poe, and with Papa a coroner, my fascination with crime and the human mind only grew." She wrapped her hands around the glass and stared into its contents. "Papa runs his practice out of our home when not at the morgue, and officers often come in to seek medical attention for themselves or victims of a crime. When I was a child, I'd hide in the office connected to the examination room and eavesdrop on their conversations. The stories of injustice I heard broke my heart, and I wanted to write stories where the hero always won and those who'd been hurt would get the justice denied them. That's why I write my Billy Poe novels."

The concept was admirable, but the execution lacked the same nobility. "And you write romances for Mr. O'Dell, because . . . ?"

"Because it was the only option I had at first. When I mailed my first detective novel to Mr. O'Dell, he accepted it eagerly—until he discovered L. R. Pelton was a woman. He accused me of passing off a man's work as my own. In his opinion, the only thing women are capable of writing is romance. So I took my novel home and wrote a romance instead. They're fun, but my heart lies with Billy Poe. Eventually, I decided to try again with my crime novels, but this time, I submitted under the pseudonym E. A. Dupin. Mr. O'Dell liked them so well, he agreed to the terms I set for protecting E. A. Dupin's real identity."

"So you lied to get what you wanted."

She frowned at his response. "No. E. A. Dupin is my pseudonym. I made that clear upon the submission. Mr. O'Dell made his own assumptions. I just worked around his prejudice and didn't reveal that Lydia Pelton and E. A. Dupin are the same person. There are plenty of authors who write under pseudonyms. It's part of the business."

Abraham firmed his mouth to keep from pointing out that there was a difference between using a pseudonym and hiding behind one for deceptive purposes.

"It's true." Monroe came to her defense. "Even the famous Mark

Twain is only a pseudonym. They help protect the identities of writers from unwanted attention, and, in this case, consequences. Dime novels are not well received in many circles. Many of our authors circulate among those who despise them and advocate banning their stories. Having a pseudonym is not a crime. It's a safety precaution."

"Perhaps, but Miss Pelton's reluctance to come forward has cost the department a week or more of investigation." Abraham turned his attention back to her. "Do you realize the injustice you've participated in by keeping silent?"

Her face fell, and her voice turned pleading. "I understand your position, but can you not see mine? I've been stuck between providing the justice I desire and ensuring that those who are dearest to me are not hurt. My letter was the best I could offer."

"No, it wasn't. You could have told me when I came to the house to inform you the charges were dropped. Instead, you chose to save yourself. Now that we know who Dupin really is, we can act accordingly."

"You're not going to reveal who I am to the papers, are you?"

The end of her question tremored with fear, and Abraham felt a prick of compassion.

"We assure you, your secret is safe with us." Lawson leaned forward and patted her hand in fatherly comfort. "You have nothing to fear. The city will turn its attention elsewhere soon enough. Just hold out until they print their next story."

"How long will that be?"

He leaned back. "I can't say for certain, but soon. We need a new lead that will satisfy the city. I don't suppose you have any theories as to who is claiming to be Detective Billy Poe?"

"No. None."

Another lie, or does she speak truth on occasion? The harshness of the thought made Abraham shake his head. He would not allow his merciless streak to direct his investigation. Maybe she just didn't know she likely had an idea of who reenacted her stories.

"Do you have any letters from fans of your Dupin novels?"

"A few, but they're at home."

"I'll need every one of them."

She shrank in her chair, her voice matching the action of her body. "Could I bring them to you tomorrow while my father is away?"

"You still want to hide that you're Dupin from him?"

"It's for the best."

"The best for whom?" Abraham felt for the man. It would be a hard blow to discover his daughter wrote such dark stories. "Tell him before he finds out through other means."

"I don't suppose telling him can be avoided at this point." She slouched so much it was a wonder she remained in her chair.

Had the woman learned nothing about keeping secrets? "No, it cannot, and you owe it to him to tell him yourself."

She nodded but said nothing further.

Monroe rose from his seat. "I assume Miss Pelton is free to go?"

Lawson rose as well. "We'll have more questions later, I'm sure, but for now I think Detective Hall and I will return to the station."

Monroe offered his arm to Miss Pelton. "I'll take you home and tell your father that it was at my insistence you used the pseudonym and kept it secret."

Another snake. Abraham's world was filled with them, but at least he could step on this one. "I'd be wary of the man who encourages you to lie, Miss Pelton. He's no hero."

Monroe's face darkened. "A true hero does what is necessary to protect those he loves."

"And he does so without breaking God's law. I'd bear that in mind, Mr. Monroe." Those two deserved each other, one liar to another. "You may leave now. I'll be by this evening to collect the notes."

Monroe huffed in response, but Miss Pelton's chin dipped toward her chest.

When Monroe opened the door, Clemens leaned against the frame with a smug serpent's smile.

"Well, I'll say, Miss Pelton. You are one talented woman. A romance author *and* a crime novelist? Won't that just shock my readers.

I can see it now." He swiped his hand across the air like reading the headline. "'The Queen of Romance Is a Killer at Heart.' Can I have a quote for tomorrow's edition?"

"You can quote this." Monroe drew back a fist and landed it against Clemens's mouth.

Abraham tried not to grin. How often had he desired to punch Clemens? Too bad he would need to arrest Monroe for assault now.

Lawson beat him to it. "It appears I'll be taking you down to booking, Monroe. Clemens, you're with me. I'll have to write up a report for this, and I'll need your statement."

"I don't want to press charges." Clemens spoke through a bloody lip.

"That's fine, but I'll still have to fill out a report. Hall, escort Miss Pelton home. I'll take Clemens's statement here and then meet you at the station."

That was one way to keep Monroe and Clemens away from Miss Pelton. Not that she didn't deserve the consequences of her deception, but Lawson and Abraham had promised to protect her, and Abraham was a man of his word—even if she wasn't a woman of hers.

CHAPTER 12

THE RIDE HOME WAS UNCOMFORTABLY silent as they bounced along in a hack that smelled of stale sweat and unwashed bodies. Lydia had no idea what to say to the man who'd obviously lost all regard for her. No more smiles or banter graced his lips, just stern scowls and silence. Given his opinion of Dupin before he knew it to be her, he must now view *her* as a vile, selfish coward.

And she was beginning to agree with him. At least in part.

If she had come forward the moment she'd heard about the Dupin murders, Cincinnati might not have reached the boiling point it was at now. Tomorrow, instead of settling into a simmer with the revelation, Cincinnati's chaos would likely spill over to burn her and those she loved. What would Papa think when she told him she'd not only written stories capable of being used to plan murders but hidden it from him for three years? Her stomach twisted again, but thankfully there was nothing in it left to heave. She was indeed a coward.

And maybe a *little* selfish.

She'd wanted it all. The ability to write, the satisfaction of making a difference, and the anonymity needed to do so without facing any consequences. But she wasn't completely selfish. Those stories had been written for others. The victims deserved justice, and they weren't going to get it any other way.

But she was not vile. Yes, her stories were dark, but they weren't immoral. And her pseudonym was nothing more than protection.

It wasn't a form of deception. Detective Hall could think what he wanted. His opinion didn't matter to her.

Except that it did. A perplexing nuisance. She'd not cared one whit about the other good men she'd encountered in her life, but for some reason Detective Hall's disdain felt as crushing as a lost dream. Maybe because he'd become Detective Darcy to her, and now she didn't think she'd be able to write that story without seeing the contempt on his face. How could she not mourn the loss of a man who, though he was repulsed by her, spoke up to warn her about heroes not encouraging those around them to lie like Marcus had?

The hack stopped before the combined row house and physician's office she called home. Inside, her unsuspecting father waited, about to learn of her secrets. Secrets that would affect his position as coroner if Cincinnati ever discovered he was the unwitting source of much of her research.

"I'll need those letters now, please."

The use of *please* softened his cold tone. He was upset with her, but he still treated her with respect. Why did that make her feel like a chastised child?

"I'll return with them immediately."

She slipped inside and noted that Papa was taking inventory of his supplies in the converted examination room. Good. She wouldn't have to explain herself just yet. Sneaking past, she went upstairs to her room and retrieved the locked box where she kept her paperwork related to Dupin. The stack of letters was small, but she smiled at them nonetheless. These were confirmation that writing those stories had been part of her calling. Granted, none of the letters were from the families of actual victims, but the readers had thanked her for holding the justice system accountable. She hated to relinquish them, but if they helped the police find the real murderer, then she would do her part.

When she returned outside, Detective Hall was pacing the sidewalk in front of the hack.

This was her last chance to say something to him, for he'd no doubt avoid her after this. There would be no mending his good opinion now, but she could at least offer an apology. "Before we part ways, I'm sorry for having delayed your investigation of the right suspect."

He tucked the letters inside his coat as he regarded her. "A person's character—*your* character—is defined by what you do or don't do, say or don't say, and write or don't write. Choose wiser in the future."

The words pinched, but she appreciated his intent behind them.

"Goodbye, Detective Hall. You are a good man, and I wish you the best." She held his gaze for a moment longer than necessary, then returned inside.

Papa stood in the door with brows furrowed. "Are you in trouble again?"

When she bit her lip to determine the best answer, he sighed and gestured toward his office down the hall. "How bad is it? Should I be sitting or standing?"

She entered the small room with a bookshelf at the back, a locked file cabinet to the side, a spindle-legged desk with its leather chair in the middle, and a single wooden chair for guests. Telling him in here might suffocate them both, but it was the only room in the house with guaranteed privacy.

"You'll probably alternate between them, but I'd start with sitting."

"That bad?" He shut the door and peered at her over his glasses before shaking his head and clearing space in the room.

No matter how much he prepared himself to be shocked or disappointed, it wouldn't be enough. She twisted the necklace at her throat as his leather chair bumped against the tall bookcase of medical journals and reference books. With the desk almost in the center of the room, he'd have plenty of space to pace once he heard the truth.

Papa lowered himself into the seat and planted his elbows on the chair arms. "All right, I'm ready."

He might be, but she wasn't. She gripped the back of the wooden chair to still her jittering fingers and blurted, "I'm E. A. Dupin. The one wanted for those murders."

Not that there was another E. A. Dupin.

He didn't move or speak.

The silence stretched.

"Did you hear me? I, your daughter, am E. A. Dupin, the crime novelist."

He drew a slow breath. "I heard you. I am just struggling to believe that you wrote the novels that fictionally murdered exonerated men."

"They weren't murdered by Detective Poe in the stories, but yes, they did die." There was a difference: Her hero never murdered anyone. Other shadowy characters had done the deed and served as her clear sign of God's justness.

"I've read those books, Lydia. They did not just die." His head shook, increasing with such vigor that he launched to his feet to continue the movement from one side of the room to the next. "What were you thinking, writing such stories? They're not proper for anyone, let alone a young woman like yourself."

"I'm not ashamed of what I write." Maybe ashamed to tell him, but not enough to stop writing. "Our government is unscrupulous and allows criminals to go unpunished. I bring justice to those who have been denied it."

He halted his pacing. "God has ordained governments and judges to carry out justice, and we are subject to those authorities. If those authorities are committing injustices, it is a citizen's duty to vote or petition to have them removed from office."

A lot of good that did her. She was a woman. She couldn't vote. Not to mention, everyone knew the crooked politicians physically controlled the voting polls.

"And if the government is too corrupt for a citizen to have any impact?"

"Then God will judge those He assigned to authority. It is not our place to enact vigilante justice when we feel those officials have failed. To do so is to take on the role of God."

Why couldn't he see reason? "But I write fiction. It's not the same as being a vigilante. I didn't kill those men."

"No, you didn't, but the stories you write reveal your heart and make a statement to the world. You believe you have the right to determine whether those men live or die."

What she wrote was a reflection of God's justice, not personal opinion. "The Old Testament says that the crimes those men committed are worthy of the death penalty."

"We are called to mercy, Lydia. Only God and those He appoints can cast judgment."

"We're going to have to agree to disagree on whether or not my rewriting their stories was wrong or right."

Dismay lined his face. "Perhaps, but this is still very serious, Lydia. How did you even get permission to write those stories? Your publisher came to me when you sought to publish your romance novels."

Only because she'd not reached her majority. "He didn't know I was E. A. Dupin. I submitted it as a pseudonym and requested that my identity be preserved even from him. Otherwise, I knew he would never publish my stories. Not as a woman."

"So you lied to get what you wanted?"

What was it with everyone accusing her of lying? "Using a pseudonym is not a lie."

"No, it's not, but your use of one for deceptive purposes is." He ran a hand over the balding spot on his head. "Has your heart been so hardened that you really cannot discern the truth?"

How was she supposed to respond to that? "I don't have a hardened heart, and I did not lie. He would never have published my stories if he'd known it was me."

"Perhaps that was meant as God's protection from writing stories you ought not to have written." An unpleasant thought must have crossed his mind, for the corners of his mouth curved downward. "Where did you get the details for your stories? I know there were more there than what was available to the public. It's been a discussion among my peers for weeks."

She gulped. He would ask that question. She traced her thumb against the engraved surface of the chair. How could she form a palliative answer without misleading him?

"Out with it, Lydia. I already suspect your answer."

She closed her eyes. "I stole peeks when I visited your office . . . and I convinced a few officers to show me the files when we visited the station."

A thud from Papa's direction indicated he'd dropped into his seat. When she looked, she saw that he leaned against one chair arm with his hand supporting his head. The evident pain and discouragement caused by her answer aged his appearance by years. A new gulf yawned between them, destroying the once solid bond they'd had, and she felt the loss keenly.

Slowly he sat up. "Sneaking around. Lying. Manipulating people. My heart grieves for you. You have deceived yourself. Even if the writing of your stories were acceptable, the means by which you created them are not. How often have you rationalized your actions against your conscience? Do you even hear it anymore?"

The ache behind his words crumbled her defenses. He was right. She had done a great deal of rationalizing her choices to get published and then to acquire the information she'd needed. She still didn't believe the stories themselves were wrong or even responsible for the murders committed, but in the face of Papa's crushing disapproval, she could no longer deny that she had selfishly pursued her desires without consideration of the consequences.

A pit formed in her stomach. "There's more. A reporter has discovered my identity. It will be in the papers soon."

His head angled back against the bookcase as he seemed to beseech the heavens for direction.

"I'm sorry, Papa."

He shook his head. "Please leave. I need time alone to think and pray."

The heaviness of the defeat in his voice tied a millstone around her neck. All that remained was for him to throw her in the river to drown. It took great effort to walk out. Thankfully no one else was about as she trudged up the stairs and shut the door to her bedroom.

What had she done?

The partially finished Billy Poe manuscript sat in a neat stack at the center of her desk, awaiting her to finish its tale.

Her reasons for a pseudonym and for writing her Billy Poe novels were valid. James O'Dell would not publish anything but a romance from a woman. And these stories needed to be shared. The evil of this world might be on full display between the pages, but right always won. Evil always died. Didn't that reflect the ultimate end? Or was she rationalizing a falsehood only she believed?

She laid a hand on the stack of pages.

God, isn't this what You wanted me to write? Why should a man be the only one allowed to reveal the darkness of this world and point people back to light?

But where is the light in these tales? The question arose as if God Himself had asked it.

It was there. Justice won. That was light enough, wasn't it?

Her stomach twisted with unease. This was too much unanswerable thinking. She shoved the pages into her manuscript box, locked it in her desk, and threw herself onto the bed. The right thing to do would be to grab her Bible or pray. But she couldn't. Her spirit was battered and weary enough. She didn't want to read the words that might indicate that Papa and Detective Hall were right about her. She didn't want to feel the suffocating disappointment of not only her earthly father but her heavenly one too. Instead, she lay face down, clutched her pillow, and wished all this would simply go away.

She wrote books. Works of fiction. Certainly she'd done nothing wrong. It was the rest of the world that was wrong. It couldn't really be her, could it?

CHAPTER 13

ABRAHAM TOOK HIS TIME RETURNING to Central despite the imperative task of finding a new lead. How had he missed that Miss Pelton and Dupin were one and the same? He should have suspected her the moment she came so fiercely to Dupin's defense. Or at the very least, he should have noticed the similarities of style between her and Dupin's writing and questioned the possibility then.

But no, he'd allowed attraction to affect his judgment. What a fool he'd been to believe her a misguided, onetime criminal and an exception to the immorality of dime novels. His work had taught him better than to think she was different from every other criminal he'd arrested.

Except that she *was* different. He could feel it in a way that he couldn't explain.

Which was ridiculous.

She was a charlatan, a criminal, and not the sort of woman who should captivate his attention.

Maybe Lucian was right. Abraham didn't get out enough. If he wasn't careful, he'd be doomed to bachelorhood or marriage to an arrestee. Once this case was over, he'd be more intentional about attending events that would introduce him to eligible and desirable women. That should rid him of any lingering detriment Miss Lydia Pelton had inflicted on his judgment.

The hack rolled to a stop outside Central Station. Ordinary citizens flowed in and out of the main entrance, intent on their business attending police court or visiting another government office. Just as plentiful were the dark blues and domed hats of officers as they either returned from their beats with prisoners in hand or headed out to patrol the city.

Abraham grimaced. He did not envy them. Until yesterday, he'd been sweating it out in a uniform that absorbed the heat of summer and baked him like a loaf of bread. The thinner gray material of the everyday suit he wore now was a welcome relief as temperatures continued to climb.

He stepped out of the hack just as Lawson jogged down the stairs.

Lawson pivoted to walk alongside him. "Glad you made it. Did you gain any more information from Miss Pelton during the ride?"

Abraham pulled the notes from his pocket. "I haven't read them, but this is what she gave me."

Lawson didn't even look at them before tucking them away. "What about what you learned from her during your ride? Did she give any indication of who she's working with?"

"Who she's working with? As in, as a suspect?"

"Absolutely. She couldn't have physically murdered those men, but she is most assuredly a potential participant. Haven't you read those books I gave you?" He waved the question aside. "Never mind. You haven't had time."

Abraham might not have read them word for word, but he'd skimmed them well enough to know nothing in them indicated Miss Pelton would be intentionally complicit in murder. But what did he know? He already felt a fool where she was concerned.

Lawson opened the basement entrance to the station, and they passed into the dim interior. He continued speaking without any indication that the stifling, musty air choked the breath from him like it did Abraham every time he entered.

"Miss Pelton's mind is especially keen, and her sense of justice is as strong as any man's I've met. I don't know whether to be dismayed or impressed." Lawson's voice dropped as they passed the rows of desks humming with conversation. "All this time I spent searching for Dupin, I never once considered that Dupin might be a woman."

Lawson's admission soothed some of Abraham's frustration with himself. If a seasoned detective hadn't considered it, why had he expected himself to?

"It boggles the mind to know a woman can lay out such a clear plan of action for serving justice. Did you notice that she didn't appear upset those men had been murdered? Only that Dupin was a suspect? For all we know, she could be pleased that her plan worked."

It was an unsettling image; however, Abraham couldn't attribute the vile mind needed for such pleasure to Miss Pelton.

The elder detective continued thinking aloud as they entered the closet they called an office. "Perhaps she does have a partner. Her stories would be the perfect avenue for communicating without detection. All he'd have to do is pick up her book to know his target and what to do."

"She has the mind for it, but do you really believe she would partner with someone for murder?"

Lawson shrugged. "Everything is possible until proven otherwise. It's best to remember that whenever you are conducting an investigation."

A suspicious mind might have spared Abraham the brief attraction to such a reprehensible woman. He still had a lot to learn about being a detective, and he wouldn't waste this opportunity to tutor under the best. As far-fetched as the theory of communicating through books was, the possibility of a partner held merit. It wasn't plausible for her to have committed those crimes on her own.

"Marcus Monroe seems a likely candidate for a partner," Lawson mused. "He has the size required and no compunction against lying to a detective. His romantic interest in her would serve as motivation for carrying out her plans. His handwriting didn't match that of Billy Poe's notes, but that doesn't necessarily rule him out."

"We should consider James O'Dell as well. He's benefited greatly from these murders." Abraham's suggestion was met with agreement.

"We'll examine those notes for other potential leads, but I'd also like to become more acquainted with Miss Pelton. Maybe she'll reveal something that will lead us to her partner."

Hopefully Lawson would assign himself to the task and have Abraham investigate Monroe and O'Dell. The last thing Abraham wanted was to spend more time with the woman who made him feel like a fool every time he looked at her.

Reading through the two dozen Billy Poe letters proved fruitless. None of the readers seemed overzealous in their admiration of Dupin or Billy Poe, nor did anyone's handwriting match the distinct style of the notes left on the bodies. Only a handful of readers had written to Miss Pelton more than once. Those and the two who'd offered suggestions as to which crimes to write next went to the top of his and Lawson's list of people to question. It would take a few days, but they intended to meet with everyone who'd mailed a letter.

They spent the rest of the shift reevaluating each case's file and searching for others to add to their suspect list. Unfortunately the only clear link between the murders was Dupin's novels. Not one officer, prosecutor, or judge was involved in the process of reporting or investigating all four original crimes. Even the suspected political connections weren't the same between cases.

That meant any of the 250,000 residents of Cincinnati with access to a Dupin novel, a city directory, and the strength, means, motive, and opportunity necessary could have committed those crimes. And that was if only one person were involved. Like Lawson suggested, they could be dealing with multiple perpetrators and a possible leader—albeit Abraham still doubted Miss Pelton qualified as a suspect for any of those positions.

Abraham massaged his tired eyes. Switching to a day shift schedule wasn't easy, but he undoubtedly would sleep like the dead that night.

"Time to call it quits, Hall. Cases like these aren't solved in a single day." Lawson closed his notebook and stretched. "We'll meet here in the morning, then visit Miss Pelton at her home."

"Would it be better if we divided tasks, and I began questioning those who wrote Miss Pelton?" That would keep him far away from the possibility of unwanted attraction distracting him.

"Nonsense. I can't teach you how to be the second-best detective if you're off scampering around on your own. We'll discover what kind of woman Miss Pelton is together. A criminal mastermind or just a talented author."

As long as he kept in mind she was a schemer, Abraham would be fine. At least he prayed so.

CHAPTER 14

THE POUNDING AT THE FRONT door wouldn't stop, no matter how many times Papa yelled for the protesters to go away. Not that they could hear his voice over their chanting.

"Murderer!"

"Strumpet!"

"Bring her out!"

And a few others that were far too descriptive of what they would do if that last demand were obeyed.

Lydia wrapped her arms around her waist as she watched the veiled outlines of the angry group through sheer curtains. They'd wasted no time in coming. The newsboy had only delivered the paper an hour ago. How long would it be before the number of protesters exceeded those who'd picketed the publisher?

Two more people crossed the street, their voices raised above the rest and shouting things that would make the citizens of Sodom proud.

She rubbed her arms, though no movement she made warmed the cold that iced her veins. Why was this happening? Her Billy Poe novels weren't evil, and they never crossed into the obscene as these people suggested. Her detective was valiant, good, and just. Billy Poe was a lauded hero.

But no. It wasn't him they were here to throw stones at. They wanted *her*. She was the villain in everyone's eyes.

Yes, she had misrepresented herself to get published and had persuaded officers to provide information, but she wasn't a criminal. She hadn't killed anyone.

If you hadn't written those books . . .

She forced the thought away. The pen might be mightier than the sword, but *her* pen certainly hadn't the power to end someone's life.

"Come away from the window, dear. What if they should see you?" Momma's pinched face belied the calm, steady click of her knitting needles.

The task was one that always calmed Momma's nerves and allowed her to donate copious amounts of socks, gloves, hats, and scarves to those in need at the church. By the number of socks she'd finished since Papa told her of Lydia's second identity last night, she'd been a perpetual ball of nerves.

At least Momma had the good sense to sit on the far side of the room. Lydia couldn't drag herself away from the window. Perhaps if she stared at the scene long enough, she'd discover this was a nightmare. She would wake up to the world that existed before Billy Poe became a murderer and Dupin his accomplice.

Furniture scraped in the hall, and a moment later Papa rounded the corner with a sheen of sweat across his brow, his breath labored. "That should prevent any attempts at breaking in."

"Do you think they'd try?" Lydia asked. The crowd was angry, but surely they wouldn't stoop to vandalism or breaking and entering.

"The bigger the crowd, the less they think and the more they act on impulse." He wiped the sweat from his brow with a handkerchief. "Henrietta, send Miranda home. Then I want you, Madelyn, and Lydia to pack your bags. We'll go out the back and stay with the Planes until it's safe to return."

Lydia would never argue against staying with Theresa, but the idea that Lydia's stories were cause for her family to flee from their home? It was absurd.

"Can't we send for the police and have them disperse the crowd?"

"I've already made the call, but their presence will only be temporary. It is not safe to remain here." He jammed the handkerchief back into his pocket and paced as he plotted his next move.

Lydia clutched her necklace, trying to soothe her anxiety, and returned her attention outside. More people had arrived within the span of their short conversation. Who knew how long they had until the crowd became bold enough to break in. Thank goodness Papa had the foresight to have a telephone installed as soon as they became available. Too bad Detective Hall was unlikely to be the officer to respond. Although, if they specifically asked for his assistance, he'd probably come, even if he hated her. That was just the kind of man he was.

She sighed. What she wouldn't give to have a second chance with him—or maybe it was a third? Regardless of how many chances she was offered, he wasn't likely to give her another.

Still, a part of her desired . . . What? Friendship with the man? Something more?

She shook her head. That was the foolishness of being an author—the imagination dragged the heart into its dreams.

Another person joined the crowd. What were they up to now, two dozen?

"Detectives Lawson and Hall, sir."

What? Lydia spun on her heel toward the parlor entrance, where the two men stood behind the maid. *Very funny, God. I know my thoughts did not just conjure him any more than my words killed those men.*

Detective Hall's gaze briefly met hers before skipping to Papa's. By the scowl that deepened at the corners of his mouth, he did not wish to be here.

Papa shook each man's hand. "You couldn't have arrived at a better time. I don't suppose you brought any other officers with you?"

"When we saw the crowd, we called for assistance. The station house informed us men were already on their way. The crowd should be dispersed shortly. Your maid let us in through the back." Detective

Lawson directed his attention at Lydia. "I would not stand so near the window if I were you."

"So I've been told."

"Multiple times." Momma's curt tone chastised Lydia. "But Lydia does what Lydia wants."

"So I've learned." Detective Hall's words wounded, but no more than she deserved.

Lydia forced a smile. "Gentlemen, please have a seat. We are glad you've come. Miranda, would you please make some coffee and bring some molasses cookies?" The ones that matched Detective Hall's eyes. She was a glutton for punishment.

The maid bobbed her head before exiting the room. Momma set aside her knitting needles and followed, claiming to offer assistance. More likely, she desired to escape the growing tension. Detective Hall took the vacated seat while Detective Lawson joined Lydia.

"I thought you said you wouldn't stand so near the window." She gestured toward the growing crowd with her head.

A wry smile curled one side of his mouth. "I said, 'if I were *you.*' I'm not the target of hate from those outside. I thought it best that I be close enough to render aid should they decide to do more than shout at your door."

Some of the tightness in her chest eased. This was why she wrote detective stories. She admired their tenacity, their intelligence to solve crimes, and the protectiveness they all seemed to possess. She felt safer with one by her side—even if she did wish it were Detective Hall instead of his partner standing next to her.

"Thank you, Detective Lawson. I appreciate your consideration. What brings you today? More questions for me?"

"Yes. I'm hoping that if I can better understand you, I can better understand the mindset of our killer."

Was he implying that he thought her the murderer? How ridiculous. He had to be too smart for that foolishness if he'd made it to detective.

"Don't look so disconcerted, Miss Pelton. I know you couldn't have committed any of those murders, but the simple fact is you are our only lead in this case. Let's start with why you chose to kill your criminals at the end of your books rather than jail them."

Papa angled away, obviously not wanting to hear. His disappointment in her seemed only to have grown in the time since she confessed. Her answer to Detective Lawson's question wasn't likely to improve matters, but she had no other explanation to give.

Not wanting to see his reaction, she watched the veiled street, where two officers encouraged the group to move along. "Those men already had their chance in court and escaped the justice they deserved. I suppose I could have written it where they were convicted after a trial, but my reasons were twofold. My readers expect evil to be defeated, and evil would live on in a jail cell if I didn't ensure their demise. The other reason is it felt right for these men to die in similar ways to how they'd killed others. It was justice served in the best way possible."

"Do you really believe murder is the best form of justice?"

The question came from Detective Hall, and it pinched. Honestly, saying her motivation aloud left her feeling dirty instead of proud. Was it really an injustice to allow the criminals of her stories to languish in jail instead of face death? If she had the chance to write the stories again, would she do it differently? "Writing a character's demise in a book is not the same as killing a real person. I'm not responsible for these men's deaths."

"But you do think the real criminals should have died for their crimes?" Detective Lawson asked.

Papa looked her direction with a hopeful expression.

How she wanted his approval, but she wouldn't lie just to appease him. "I'm not sure. All I want is for the corruption in our justice system to end. Citizens should feel safe in their city, and that means criminals need to face the consequences of their crimes."

Disappointment once again claimed Papa's demeanor, and it hurt. All night long, she'd wrestled with what he'd said. She couldn't agree that writing her stories had been wrong, but perhaps she needn't have killed the characters to get her point across. After all, it wasn't as if killing them had changed the city's morality. Every week, a potential story walked free from their crimes. As far as the real men's fates? She didn't claim to know how they should be sentenced, but they did deserve to face some sort of punishment. It just shouldn't have been murder.

"Miss Pelton?" Detective Lawson touched her elbow.

"I'm sorry. My mind drifted. Did you have another question?"

He leaned closer, and his eyes narrowed.

Unnerved by his nearness, she leaned back, but his focus was beyond her.

Before she could ascertain what troubled him, his arms wrapped around her.

Glass shattered.

He jerked her around and shielded her with his body. A dull thud and Detective Lawson's pained grunt indicated something had hit him.

Police whistles blew on the street. Calls of "run" and "stop" added to the sense of chaos out of view.

Lawson released her, spun on his heel, and hopped over the shattered window's ledge to the grassy area on the other side. "Hall, stay with the Peltons." Command given, he joined in chasing the protesters.

Still trying to understand what exactly happened, Lydia studied the floor. Glass lay in glinting shards around her. A brick edger from their front garden lay at her feet. Crudely scraped white letters stood out against the red clay.

Murderer.

A lump formed in her throat. Had someone thrown that at her?

Don't be stupid. Of course they did. Bricks don't tattoo themselves, grow wings, and attack.

Someone had deliberately tried to hurt her.

A tremor traveled down her spine. Name-calling she could handle, but she was under no illusion that she could withstand a physical attack. If they were trying to harm her while in her home, what would they do if they caught her on the street?

"Are you hurt, Miss Pelton?" Detective Hall's concerned voice came from just behind her.

Lydia glanced at the glass, the broken window frame, then back at the brick. If it hadn't been for the quick reflexes of Detective Lawson, that brick would have hit her.

"I'm fine, but someone threw that at me!" Lydia jabbed a finger in the brick's direction. "I don't understand. This isn't my fault. I'm not the murderer. Whoever is pretending to be Billy Poe is."

Again, her eyes sought the accusation literally thrown at her. That was poetic justice. A written word with the power to actually kill had it hit her just right. She hugged herself tightly.

Detective Hall guided her gently away from the glass field.

When he transferred her to Papa's care in the foyer, she couldn't hide the tremor in her hands.

Papa wrapped his arm around her shoulders, and though his disapproval hadn't abated, compassion softened his features. "Our words have power, Lydia, no matter if they are meant to be fictional or not. We must always be careful in what we say or write and be sure that it is God-glorifying and edifying to those around us."

He didn't say that her Billy Poe novels didn't measure up to that standard, but it wasn't necessary.

"What happened?" Madelyn was halfway down the stairs before Papa could stop her.

"Go pack a bag. We'll be staying"—he glanced at the gaping hole in their wall where a window should have been—"elsewhere."

He probably feared someone still lingered nearby and might overhear their new location.

Madelyn opened her mouth to argue, but when she saw the mess in the parlor, she glared at Lydia. "This is your fault. I was supposed to have friends over this afternoon."

"Madelyn."

At Papa's stern rebuke, Madelyn stomped back upstairs and slammed her bedroom door.

"George?" Momma called from the kitchen with an edge of panic.

Papa ran a hand over his balding spot before addressing Detective Hall. "If you'll please stay with Lydia and ensure no one enters the house through the parlor, I must calm my wife."

Papa left them in the foyer. They had a clear view to the kitchen, where Momma stood twisting a towel in her hands. Behind her was Marcus Monroe.

What was he doing here?

Marcus glanced Lydia's direction, worry etched deeply in his face. He didn't approach her or even call for her but extended a piece of paper to Papa. He shook his head at her before guiding Momma and Papa farther into the kitchen.

If he thought to exclude her from a conversation with her parents, he was sorely mistaken.

She marched toward the kitchen.

"How did you determine which men should live or die?"

Detective Hall's question brought her to an abrupt halt.

"Excuse me?" She turned to face him.

"How did you determine which men should live or die?"

She stared at him for a moment before the words made sense. "I did not choose for these men to die." At his arched brow, she amended, "Not in real life. I'm not a murderer."

"No, but the only connection between each of the murders is your Billy Poe novels. It seems to me that if you had not written their stories and defiled some poor soul's mind, those men would still be alive."

She'd come to realize that being called a liar or manipulator was accurate enough, but to be called the one responsible for someone else's wickedness? That was not to be borne. "I stand by my belief that sin corrupts a man's soul, not literature."

"Yet the murderer chose to become *your* character and kill the men *you* selected."

A new and terrifying thought struck her speechless. If she'd written about different crimes, would those men have been the ones to die? Her stomach twisted, but she forced a calming breath. The answer didn't matter. She still wasn't responsible for another's choice.

"I need to know how you chose your stories. It could impact the investigation."

Whatever it took to end this madness. "I chose cases where men were undoubtedly guilty but walked free because of dishonest dealings."

"I can name half a dozen more that fit your parameters but haven't made it into your stories."

"Because I can only write so fast. Out of necessity, I wrote about the ones occurring at the time I was writing. Otherwise, needed documents would've been harder to access without garnering unwanted attention."

At his glower, she rolled her eyes. They'd been over this already.

"Perhaps it was wrong of me to obtain information that I shouldn't have had, but—"

"Only *perhaps* it was wrong? Have you learned nothing?"

"Fine. It was wrong of me to obtain the answers I did in the manner that I did it, but I am *not* guilty of murder."

"Did you write those stories to communicate your plan to a partner?"

"Have you been drinking?" It was the only explanation for such a ludicrous question. "There are more efficient ways to communicate with a partner than through writing a book that takes months to draft and as many months more to edit, then publish." She crossed her arms despite her determination to keep her temper under control. "My stories are a means of serving justice, not communicating dastardly plans for murder. I may be a broken and sinful woman, but I do not delight in death."

"Your books would indicate otherwise."

He really did believe her vile. How disappointing. Her Detective Darcy would never be so blinded by prejudice.

Detective Lawson appeared at the window. One glance at the standoff between her and Detective Hall, and his countenance wrinkled like a prune. He clambered over the windowsill and strode toward them.

Before Detective Lawson reached them, Detective Hall speared her with another question. "Are you upset that those men are dead or only that your pseudonym is exposed?"

"That is enough, Hall." Detective Lawson's words came out hard and reprimanding.

"I'll ask no more, *after* I hear your answer, Miss Pelton."

Lydia looked Detective Hall directly in his stubborn eyes. Forget comparing them to delectable molasses cookies. They were mud brown, just like the words he slung. "I do not revel in their deaths, and I am sorry that they were murdered, but I cannot say I feel any remorse for rewriting their stories. They were criminals who escaped the punishment they deserved."

The harshness of her own words boxed her ears. She still believed the sentiment behind them, but Papa's rebuke of last night pricked her conscience. Was she taking God's place by insisting her execution of justice was better than His?

Detective Lawson touched her back. "I think it best you go pack. It won't be safe for you to stay here until that window is fixed. Hall, I'll meet you outside."

Detective Hall didn't even acknowledge her as he strode toward the kitchen to leave. Papa met him and handed him a piece of paper. After a quick perusal of the sheet, he glared at Marcus, who stood behind Papa, then pivoted back toward Lydia and Detective Lawson.

"It appears you have a letter from Billy Poe."

CHAPTER 15

LONG AFTER DETECTIVE HALL LEFT with the letter, Lydia sat at the table, numb. No, *numb* wasn't an adequate description. A maelstrom of emotions—fury, guilt, grief, fear, and more she couldn't put names to—twisted and knotted her insides so tightly that she doubted she'd ever eat again.

Marcus scooted the cup of tea she'd shoved aside back in front of her. "At least drink this. Your father said it would help."

More like send her into oblivion. But she didn't deserve that. No, she deserved this misery. For all her life, she would remember Billy Poe's words. They were seared onto her memory like a cattle brand.

> *My dearest Lydia,*
>
> *When I first read "Shadow in the Night," I knew we had something special. With your pen and my sword, we can right the wrongs of Cincinnati. Do not fear for your safety. I am near and diligently protecting you. When the time is right, I will retrieve you, and the future we've longed for will be ours to create. Together.*
>
> *Ever yours,*
> *Billy Poe*

Acid burned in Lydia's throat.

This man truly believed himself to be a purveyor of justice—and the sword to *her* pen.

Detective Hall was right.

She was responsible. Her words had corrupted a soul.

And now some madman believed they belonged together like some bizarre pairing of wine and rat poison.

Marcus lifted the cup nearer her face.

The sweet aroma of Papa's concoction filled her nose. She gagged and pushed it away, sloshing the green-tinged liquid onto the table.

Marcus set the cup aside. "Please, Lydia. I know you're worried for your safety, but I won't let anything happen to you. None of us will. Even Detective Lawson has vowed to ensure you are safely transported elsewhere. No one is going to harm you."

For a man who edited fiction for a living, Marcus had a severe lack of understanding of this situation. Of course someone was going to try to harm her. The only question was who would get to her first—Cincinnati or Billy Poe?

Billy Poe might have delusions of love now, but once she condemned his actions, would he turn on the creator of his vigilante world and write *her* ending? Would he stab her to death with a pen? Or perhaps he'd slice her with a million paper cuts and then douse her with vinegar so her agony would be drawn out. That might be extreme, but if her mind came up with it, would his? What if he didn't believe her denouncement of his actions? Would he enact the plot of her romance books and kidnap her to make her his bride? Would he even recognize he fulfilled the villain's role instead of the hero's? There were so many ways she could write this, and none of them were experiences she desired.

And what would he do while he waited to kill or kidnap her? Four books still remained for him to choose from to enact her version of justice. Four men whose lives were at risk because she had deemed they should die. She was going to vomit again.

She swallowed the bile and rose from the chair. "Thank you for coming, but you should go."

Marcus clasped her hand. "You know I couldn't stay away, not once I saw what Clemens published. I knew those people would come for you."

Those people.

She shivered. It felt like a lifetime ago that she'd watched their veiled figures picket her stoop. Had it really been only a few hours? She no longer heard the chants echoing down the hall, largely thanks to Detective Lawson. Detective Hall had skedaddled from the house as quickly as his feet would carry him, under the guise of taking the letter back to the station as evidence. But not before he'd interrogated Marcus like he was Billy Poe.

Lydia studied Marcus for herself. With brows furrowed deep enough to plant corn in, hazel eyes pinched with anxiety, and lips downturned, he didn't strike her as a murderer. His large hand encompassed hers with a firm, protective grip—so much like the heroes she'd created. He couldn't possibly be guilty. He was too kind and far too worried about her *because* of the threats Cincinnati and Billy Poe posed. Delivering the letter did not make him a villain.

Neither did it make him a hero.

She slipped her hand from his. "Thank you for your concern, but my family will be safe. We're staying with—" She bit down on the information. He might not be Billy Poe, but she didn't want anyone to know their new location. She'd put her family in enough danger.

Marcus frowned. "With whom? I can be sure to check on you there."

"I'll contact you when I can. You understand that I cannot take any unnecessary risks for the sake of my family."

"It's only me. I won't divulge the information to anyone else." When she continued to hold back, hurt edged the earnestness in his face. "I kept your secret about Dupin for three years. Do you not trust me?"

"Please forgive me, but I cannot even trust myself. I'm sure we won't be away for more than a few days. I'll contact you when we return."

He nodded, though a puppy with its bone taken away couldn't have looked more crestfallen.

He left through the back, and Papa appeared in the kitchen doorway. "It's time to leave. Detective Lawson will escort you, Madelyn, and your mother to the Planes' while I sort out this mess with the window."

"My bag—"

"Is already packed and loaded into the carriage. Go out the front and straight to your seat."

Lydia hesitated. "Papa?"

His unusually impatient glare demanded she obey immediately.

"I just want to say, you were right. I wrongfully justified my actions so that I could achieve what I wanted, and others have paid the consequence for those decisions." A tear slipped out as the fullness of it weighed upon her. "I could have written anything, anything at all, but I chose to rewrite their stories and kill them, because I thought my plan for justice was better than God's."

"Oh, my dear girl." He pulled her into a hug and sighed. "Acknowledging that we have done wrong is the first step toward forgiveness and restoration. Confess it to Christ and then allow Him to begin the work of changing you. It won't be easy and it will hurt, but discipline is meant to restore us to each other and to Him. Don't mistake that discipline for not loving you. Because we do. God and I love you so very much." His voice grew thick, and he released her from their embrace. "Now get outside. Each moment you delay is a risk to your sister and mother."

Lydia nodded, her throat too tight for words.

When she reached the door, onlookers gathered across the street, where officers held them at bay. Mr. Clemens stood among them. She stopped walking and fisted her skirts. Billy Poe might exist because of her, but this mob existed because of him. He'd been the one to turn the fury of Cincinnati toward her family, and she'd love nothing more than to retrieve the brick from her parlor and show him her fury. Her conscience twinged. Cincinnati's unrest was a consequence of her actions. She would not shift the blame to someone else. Even him.

Detective Lawson grasped her arm and created a protective barrier as he ushered her into the closed carriage. "Keep the shade drawn and your head away from the window."

Once she claimed her seat next to Madelyn, he shut the door, and the carriage dipped as if he'd swung up top with the driver.

So much secrecy and protection needed for her family, all because one reporter couldn't keep his mouth shut. Of course, if she'd just come forward at the beginning, this situation might have been avoided. She cringed. She'd already apologized to Detective Hall yesterday, but she owed Detective Lawson an apology as well.

All through the ride, Lydia's mind turned over Billy Poe's words. Did she share in the responsibility for those men's deaths? Would Billy have acted without her words? If she'd never written them—if she'd only written her romance stories—would the men still be alive?

The ride to Theresa's took twice as long as normal and varied in speeds from heart-racing to plodding as they wended a path she'd never taken.

Detective Lawson handed her down onto the drive of the castle-like home. "I'm sorry for the unusual ride, ladies, but there were several people attempting to tail us. We've lost them, but I suggest staying away from windows and refraining from venturing out of doors."

"Thank you, Detective Lawson," Momma said before she bustled past, ushering Madelyn inside.

Lydia held back.

"Please, Miss Pelton. I need you to adhere to my advice."

"I will. I just wanted to apologize for what I have cost this investigation by my silence. It was wrong of me, and I ask for your forgiveness."

"There is nothing to forgive. I understand that you did what you thought was best to protect yourself and your family. I am only sorry that we could not preserve your secret."

"You are too kind, but being exposed is only what I deserve."

He offered a compassionate smile. "Don't be so hard on yourself. We all have our secrets. Now go inside and stay away from the windows. Detective Hall and I will see to it that this case ends quickly so you can go back to writing your stories."

Lydia thanked him again, but it sounded as hollow as she felt.

Papa had said acknowledging her wrongdoing was the first step toward forgiveness and restoration, but was it too late? Four men were dead. Her silence had delayed the police from searching in the right direction. If another man died . . . Christ might forgive her, but could she forgive herself? And what about justice? What did that look like now? She had a lot to consider over the next few days of hiding, and she suspected that this period of self-reflection was going to be exceedingly miserable.

CHAPTER 16

TWO DAYS LATER, ABRAHAM CROSSED the street from Central Station and glanced at the horsecar. Sweaty bodies elbowed one another for a chance at the breeze stirred by the horse-drawn conveyance. He could pay the fare and be home in half the time, but his shirt and vest already stuck to him like fresh plaster. Riding with that crowd would turn his entire suit into a rancid rag. Besides, a walk would provide the solitude and silence he needed to think that working with Lawson denied. Who knew the man would be such a squawking hen? Not that Abraham didn't appreciate the instruction on becoming a detective, but the constant chatter left him little room to make his own observations.

He bypassed the horsecar and unbuttoned his coat to allow in what little air he could. Although he and Lawson had interrogated all the picketers, they were no closer to identifying Billy Poe. The man remained a faceless menace with an uncanny ability for delivering notes unnoticed. Oh, Abraham and Lawson had their suspicions, but nothing beyond speculation.

Monroe's story about how he'd found Billy Poe's letter sounded as true as an out-of-tune piano. Why would Poe pretend to be a picketer, drop the note at the corner of the house—half-hidden in the bushes, no less—and leave the discovery of it to chance? The obvious answer? He wouldn't. Poe *wanted* Miss Pelton to read that letter, and dropping it outside the house was a senseless gamble. The wind could have whisked it away, someone could have picked it up and taken it, or it could have gone unnoticed altogether. No, that story made no sense for a man as meticulous and prepared as Poe. More likely, Monroe had crumpled and stepped on the note himself to make it appear trampled before bringing it into the Pelton home. The man plainly had a romantic interest in Miss Pelton, and Poe was quite clear in his admiration of her.

Not that Abraham or Lawson could prove that Marcus had made up the story. True to the nature of a mob, no one had seen anything. Not Marcus. Not the letter. Not even the man who'd hefted the brick through the window, despite the cheers that had accompanied the sound of shattering glass.

Abraham's jaw tightened until his teeth ached.

Praise God for Lawson's quick reflexes. Miss Pelton was no wilting miss, but being hit by a brick might have sent her into hysterics. Worse, she might have been injured. Lawson had a bully of a bruise that he tried to hide the discomfort of, but Abraham saw the older detective wince each time he leaned his back against a chair. If a man with enough grit to smooth wood felt the pain of it, what would a delicate woman have suffered?

Although, in truth, the word *delicate* did not describe Miss Lydia Pelton. Foolish? Yes. Dramatic? The queen of it. A liar and a thief? Facts no jury could ignore. But not delicate. No woman who wrote what she did and refused to feel remorse for it or accept responsibility for the murders penned by her hand could be called delicate. Callous, more like it. And selfish. All that time wasted on finding Dupin because she refused to speak one word.

If he never saw Miss Pelton again, it would be too soon.

Tightness between his brows indicated he'd started to scowl. A passing lady glanced at him, then gave him a wide berth, meaning it must be a fierce one. He massaged his forehead to erase the tension. His family did not need him bringing home the stress and anger this case and Miss Pelton created in him. They didn't expect him to pretend all was well, but they certainly didn't deserve a quick temper.

He blew out a breath. Miss Pelton was of no use to his case. They'd interviewed a few admirers who'd corresponded with her. So far that had proven fruitless. Only one had the physical potential for murder, and his alibi had been confirmed by three reliable witnesses. The remaining people on their list were unlikely candidates but would still need to be contacted.

The best evidence they had for determining Poe's true identity were the notes he'd left behind. The unique handwriting would make matching it to its owner simple. Unfortunately, at least for now, it effectively disproved Monroe as the author. Still, something about it didn't feel natural. It was both controlled and uncoordinated at the same time. The letter formations were shaky and slanted at an odd angle, as if created by a child just learning penmanship. However, there was a sense of skill in that each character was compact both in width and height—something a new writer rarely achieved. But how could an author be both proficient and amateur with the use of a pen? Given that the readability improved with each message, Abraham would bet Lucian a dinner at the Hotel Emery that Poe was disguising his handwriting. But how to prove it?

Abraham turned the corner to his street, and the hairs on his neck rose. A closed carriage stood in front of his house. Who in their right mind would travel with the curtains drawn tighter than a hangman's noose on a day like today? With the temperatures above eighty and the humidity thick enough to bathe in, anyone inside would simmer in their sweat. Too long in that oven box, and the meat would fall right off their bones.

Even rumbles announced the driver asleep before Abraham reached him. Leaning at a dangerous angle, the man slouched in his seat with crossed arms and a tugged-down hat. The tall pile of dung and ammonia-rich puddle beneath the horses indicated they'd been here for some time.

Sunday sometimes meant guests, but usually Mother warned him beforehand, and rarely did anyone have a carriage wait for them. He glanced at the front door for a clue to who had come. He was in no mood for Mother's matchmaking schemes, and even a visit from the minister would be unwelcome today.

Jake shot through the door. "Don't go inside!"

The driver startled but resettled into sleep at a safer angle, so Abraham faced his brother, who spoke in wide-eyed horror.

"Girls are inside, and it's all squeals and prattle. I'm going to Michael's." He glanced over his shoulder like he feared the women chased him. "Don't send for me until they're gone."

Abraham collared Jake before he could run. "What girls?"

It wasn't unusual for Jake to make himself scarce when Clara's friends visited, but unease wended through Abraham and coiled with warning.

"Dunno. Some author lady and her family."

God wouldn't be so cruel, would He? "Do you mean Miss Pelton?"

"Sounds right." The scamp wriggled free and called back, "Good luck with *her*." Then he darted down the street at jailbreak speed.

A wise man would follow suit. And Abraham was no fool.

"There you are." Mother's voice came from behind.

Curse his hesitation. He turned, and she stood on the stoop with far too bright a smile.

"Hurry inside and freshen up." Mother held the door open for him. "We have guests."

"I'm in no mood for guests. Especially not Miss Pelton."

"Nonsense. She risked her safety just to have a private audience with you."

"You should have sent her away the moment she arrived."

"Abraham!" The shock mixed with reprimand declared she'd raised him better than that, but Mother had no idea of the viper she'd let in.

"She's a fraud and a schemer. What's more, she feels no remorse for writing the stories that have cost the lives of four men. Do you really want her to influence Clara?"

As if to emphasize his point, Clara's breathless voice carried outside. "I've found it! Would you sign this one too?"

Mother tugged the door closed. "Miss Pelton arrived on our doorstep as the picture of repentance and remorse. She's done nothing but encourage Clara to be a better woman than she. I'd say that humility is a beneficial example to your sister."

Humility? Bah! "Don't believe anything that comes from Miss Pelton's mouth. She only says what she needs to get what she wants."

"And what, pray tell, do you think she wants by apologizing?"

"To prove she's not responsible for those men's deaths."

Mother frowned. After a quick glance around, she lowered her voice. "You believe Miss Pelton murdered those men? I confess, I don't see it."

"Not physically, but her words influenced someone else to do it for her."

"Oh, my boy." A mixture of pity and compassion colored her tone as she cupped his cheek. "You are too smart to believe that. She's no more responsible for their deaths than Mother Goose was for your sticking a thumb into a hot pie to find a plum. Your decision was yours alone, just as this was Billy Poe's."

His thumb ached at the memory of that long-ago burn, but Mother's words didn't change how he felt about Miss Pelton's responsibility. Those men might be alive if it weren't for her. "She is culpable for her words and her actions, whether the results were intentional or not. Do you know the things she did to get those stories published?"

"I am not saying she is innocent of all things, but she is not guilty of murder. She has come to you today as a broken and repentant woman to make her apologies."

"I don't have time for apologies from a hypocrite." It was safer that way. The less he respected her, the easier it was to squash any potential attraction. He'd built up his wall, and he intended to keep it intact.

"God is making her new. Allow her to say her piece, then go from there."

"She deserves condemnation, not alleviation from guilt."

Mother rested a hand on his arm and held his gaze. "Mercy, Abraham. It's the gift of *not* giving someone what they deserve. It is what Miss Pelton needs and what God requires of you. She is not escaping consequences by you listening to her or forgiving her. I am certain this experience has left an indelible scar on her soul, one she will never forget the pains of. Go speak to her."

All right. He'd listen to her, but that was the only concession he'd make.

At his nod, Mother led him into the parlor, where Miss Pelton leaned over a stack of orange-leafed dime novels. Joy beamed from her countenance as she made large swoops and swirls with the pen in her hand before finishing off with a flourish.

So much for a remorseful Miss Pelton.

Once the last book was signed, Clara scooped up the pile and clutched it to her chest. "Thank you so much! I'll treasure them forever. In fact, I'm going to hide them somewhere safe right now." Clara turned to leave with her precious loot and spotted Abraham. "You'll have to find your own copies to read now. I'll not lend these out to anyone. Even you."

"You needn't worry about that, Pages. I have no interest in ever reading a Lydia Pelton book again."

At his voice, Miss Pelton's happy glow of a moment ago was snuffed out. Panic flickered across her face before she dipped her head and folded her hands like a somber funeral attendee. If she meant to convey shame and earn his pity, she failed. It was just as he told Mother. This visit was a ruse.

"Mrs. Pelton, Miss Madelyn, would you do me the honor of joining me in the kitchen for some cake?" Mother gestured toward the back of the house.

"Thank you, that would be delightful." Mrs. Pelton gently pushed an obviously reluctant Miss Madelyn to exit the room.

Silence fell.

The remaining woman knew well how to play her game. Her solid dark-blue gown could pass as puritanical. Add how her shoulders sagged and her chin nearly touched her chest, and someone less knowledgeable of the underworld would be convinced that she felt remorse on a soul-deep level. She'd even tried to tame those wild curls into a tight bun, but they—like their owner—were rebellious and unruly. He almost wanted to go and pluck out however many dozens of pins she'd used, just to show her she could not hide her true self from him.

How was he supposed to show her mercy? And what did that require of him? If he gave Miss Pelton a thread of compassion, she'd unravel his whole neatly woven world.

CHAPTER 17

UNWILLING TO REMAIN IN THE same room with Miss Pelton any longer than necessary, Abraham stationed himself at the threshold, arms crossed and stance wide enough to brace himself against any manipulations or deceptions she lobbed at him.

"Say what you came to say. Then leave."

Miss Pelton fisted a handful of her dress and drew a long breath before releasing them both. Though she stood to face him, her eyes remained fixed on the floor. "A few days ago, you told me a person's character is defined by the things they do, say, and write. You also exhorted me to make wiser decisions, like I'm not someone to be trusted."

Abraham opened his mouth to reply that she wasn't but clamped down on the response. He'd not engage with her more than absolutely necessary. With the words sounding so practiced, this had to be artifice.

"It appears you were right about the nature of my character, and I was too blind to see it. While I may not have personally killed these men, my stories and my need for self-preservation have played a part in their deaths. Thank you for your persistence in finding Dupin. I'm sorry that I did not have the courage to admit my pseudonym. I have wasted valuable time and resources and can do nothing to repair the damage I have caused." Her voice shook like she held back tears.

"I do not ask for forgiveness, for I do not deserve it, but I felt you should know that I have been convicted by the High Judge and am working on reforming. I am not the same woman you first met, and I'll forever be grateful for your being a tool in God's hand. If there is any way that I can help your investigation, please know that I am at your utter disposal."

How convenient. "And allow you to use this case for your next story? I think not."

She recoiled a touch at his response but nodded. "I understand. While my word means nothing, I assure you, this experience will not become fodder for any future novel."

"You're going to continue to write?" If that didn't prove she hadn't changed, he didn't know what would.

"I am under contract for one more mystery and one more romance. As Mr. O'Dell has demanded that both contracts be fulfilled regardless of the current situation, I have no choice."

"You could choose to break them."

"I could, but there are significant financial implications, and more importantly, it would mean going back on my word."

"Some promises should be broken. Even David went back on his rash vow to kill every male belonging to Nabal. Your next story may very well condemn another man to death. Should not that promise be broken in light of saving another's life?"

Her gaze drifted away. After a long, quiet moment, she sighed. "I will pray over what you have said and give it honest thought."

When her attention returned to him, it was a struggle to maintain his defenses against the brokenness he saw there.

"I really do want to be the woman God desires me to be—even if it comes at a cost. Thus, my coming to apologize. You don't know me well enough to understand, but apologies are not something I easily hand out. And I *am* sorry. More than you can ever know."

Her regret felt genuine, but she was a good storyteller. And her machinations had been proficient enough to go unnoticed for several years. He couldn't allow her to chip a breach into his wall. At the first sign of his stance softening, he stiffened. She would not win him over with her pitiful eyes or earnest tone. She was the enemy. The criminal. He was an officer of the law, and it was his job not to be swayed by her.

After an extended silence, her chin dipped. "Thank you for listening, and I wish you well on your case. Good evening, Detective Hall." She didn't lift her head as she scooted past him into the foyer to collect her hat and shawl from the hatstand.

Good. He'd survived her attack with his wall intact. She could leave, and he'd be safe from her influence.

Except some traitorous part of him demanded he believe her. Worse, it demanded him to recant and grant her mercy and grace.

He pinched the bridge of his nose.

God, she doesn't deserve it. A niggle of Mother's reprimand chastised him. *But I suppose none of us do.*

He sighed, trying to focus on Mother's wisdom. It wasn't his place to judge the genuineness of Miss Pelton's contrition. Only God could see the heart, and was not this moment revealing that he had a heart as judgmental as hers? His mouth twisted. What a pair they made.

He dropped his hand and discreetly observed her.

She angled away from him, but the mirror to her left revealed the slip of her confident veneer. Momentary, wretched grief crumpled her face as she stared at the white shawl too long. She clenched her eyes shut, took a deep breath, and adopted a mask of composure as she swung the shawl around her shoulders. With hat in hand, she stepped toward the kitchen—presumably to announce their departure.

Hang it all. "Come back and have a seat, Miss Pelton."

Apprehension and confusion played across her face, but she returned, claiming the edge of a chair.

Abraham forced himself to sit across from her and prayed for guidance, because he had no idea what he was going to say or do now. "An apology, while appreciated, does not make you trustworthy."

"No, it doesn't, especially when I've spent a great deal of time fooling everyone—perhaps myself most of all."

The slouch to her body and the heaviness in her tone exposed the burden she felt far better than her earlier speech had. These were the words he could trust. Unrehearsed. Raw. Guileless.

Her hands knotted together, her fingers working themselves into odd positions. "God has been quite merciless with His sword of the Spirit over the last few days. Or maybe I should say *faithful*. He's revealed my shortcomings and outright defiance in painfully clear ways." Her voice turned thick, and she stared out the window rather than at him. A stray tear slid down her cheek, and she scrubbed it away with the heel of her hand. "I meant it, Detective Hall. I am truly sorry for the abominable person I've been."

"I've known worse."

She snapped toward him. "Really? I think it would be pretty hard to top a dime novelist who sentences men to death with her pen."

"And as a dime novelist who writes about police, you should know you don't even come close to the wickedness I've seen in this world." Oddly enough, his voicing that made her seem less of a reprobate.

She'd never set out to hurt anyone. Her intentions had been flawed and misguided, but at their core, they were admirable. Who didn't desire justice for the defenseless? Wasn't that why he did his job?

Miss Pelton sniffed and flicked away a few more tears that had escaped down her cheeks. "Thank you for not hating me."

"I try never to hate anyone. Although, I admit, you sorely tempted me."

"What can I say? People either love me or hate me these days." Her light tone indicated she jested, but the evident weariness of her countenance and posture proved the truth of her statement had been keeping her up at night.

"Do you feel unsafe at Miss Plane's?"

She gave a half chuckle, half snort. "More like a barely tolerated guest. Theresa is thrilled to have us, but her grandfather isn't exactly a pleasant man. If it weren't for the fact my father saved Colonel Plane's life in the war, he probably would have turned us away. He runs his house like a military camp and treats us as his personal soldiers. But I do feel safe. If anyone tried to throw a brick through his window, Colonel Plane would have them captured and court-martialed before they could think to turn around. And if they tried to come inside, they'd have to get past the impervious Mrs. Hawking first. That woman could have scared Stonewall Jackson into surrendering if someone had given her the chance."

"Even so, obey the rules and stay out of sight. I don't want my key suspect ending up like her victims."

She gaped at him, her horror at his statement clear.

What kind of fool was he to make such a jest? "Forgive me. That was in poor taste."

She blinked and then a slow smile curved her lips. "I suppose a hero can't be expected to say the right things all the time."

"Oh no you don't. You are not to make me a character, especially not a hero."

"Well, I did consider making you a villain for a short time. But truly, you make a much better hero. Any woman would swoon over you." She slapped a hand over her mouth as if doing so might stop the words that had already escaped.

Did she carry a torch for him? He almost laughed outright. Not with his abominable treatment of her. However, she might be discerning that he no longer considered her a wolf in sheep's clothing. He still couldn't quite call her an innocent lamb, but she'd found his thread of compassion and was wrapping it around her finger. It was dangerous, this discovery of how much they had in common and the easy banter that passed between them. It would be too easy to forget she was a criminal, not a potential wife. He'd best snap the thread loose before she unraveled the whole of him.

"Please refrain from swooning in my presence. I'm a dreadful catch and would likely drop you instead of sweep you off your feet."

Her laughter was far from the sweet chimes described in her novels and more like a squeaky mouse. It was rather endearing in its own odd way. "You don't have to worry about that. There isn't a man on this planet who could physically sweep me off my feet and carry me away. But I suppose that makes me kidnap-proof."

Abraham frowned at her self-deprecating humor. "That was by no means a reference to your size, Miss Pelton. You are a very beautiful woman and very much in danger of being kidnapped." Whether by Billy Poe or the many other men who surely found Miss Pelton desirable.

"You don't have to be so kind. I wasn't fishing for a compliment. However, I do wonder . . . Do you think . . . Would it be possible for us to start over? I mean, I know we can't start over literally, but I have a desperate desire to prove to you that I'm not the horrible creature you've met. Or, at least, I'm not going to *stay* this horrible creature."

Abraham thudded back in his chair. Was she proposing friendship or courtship? Neither was safe. She might desire to change now, but that was no guarantee. Allowing Miss Pelton any more space in his life than necessary was risky.

He'd already given her too much.

That ember of admiration he'd thought doused had reignited unnervingly fast in these last few minutes. Had she sensed that and decided to exploit it for her purposes? Her hopeful and earnest face suggested not, but friendship with her posed too many risks.

"It's not wise to befriend a suspect."

Instead of being put off by the reminder of her status, she grinned and leaned in. "But befriending the enemy allows you to know what they're up to. Wouldn't it be wiser for you to keep your enemy close? Perhaps even closer than you would a friend?"

It was difficult not to chuckle at her determination, which only proved how dangerous it was to let his guard down around her. "We're not enemies, Miss Pelton."

"Oh good; that means we're friends." Before he could deny it, she clasped his hands. "I know there is nothing I can say to dissuade you from believing I played a willing part in Billy Poe's actions, but this Billy Poe is not *my* Billy Poe."

The desperation for him to understand played in the depths of her eyes and the creases that formed around her mouth. She was sincere in what she said. Either that or he was a fool. The former was possible but the latter definite. He should pull free of her grasp, but there was a sweetness to her touch that he couldn't help but indulge in.

She continued on, passionate and pleading. "All I've ever wanted to do was to improve the world around me. To display God's justice and love through a man who had the power to do right where I could not. This man who pretends to be Billy Poe is a monster. And like Frankenstein's, the monster is one I regret creating and whose actions I do not condone. I want Billy Poe caught just as much as everyone else in Cincinnati. More so, even, because he has taken what was meant for good and used it for evil."

This woman. Why did she have to be so convincing? However, if there were any truth to her words, he would only know through a closer acquaintance. He regarded her from the escaping curls to her contrite expression. A flutter of anticipation filled his midsection. It had to be gas. Men did not get butterflies in their stomachs—and certainly not over a potential friendship with a woman who had already proven to be trouble.

"All right, Miss Pelton. I'll agree to a tentative friendship, but that doesn't mean I trust you."

"I'd expect nothing less. Thank you for giving me the chance to prove I am changing and that I do not belong on your suspect list."

"That remains to be seen, but I look forward to finding out." The edge of a smile sneaked out, heedless of his effort to keep it hidden.

She grinned. "Thank you. I have a feeling we'll make much better friends than enemies, and as our first order of friendship, I insist on you calling me Lydia."

"That is a bit much, considering I'm still investigating you." He pulled his hands free.

"I concede that would make your position awkward, so I'll refrain from calling you Abraham during your official duties. But if you don't call me Lydia when we're in private, I'll have to create a character after you in my next book, and I'll make him a dreadful bore."

"Is that supposed to be a threat?"

"I could make you the hero of my next romance novel if that's not threat enough. Oh! And I'll make the heroine a criminal of the worst sort."

Abraham folded his arms. "I thought you weren't going to use this case as story fodder."

"If you're insinuating that I'm casting myself as the heroine, you are mistaken. I'd make a better villain with what I put my characters through. That being said, I think it best if I take my leave, Abraham." Her eyes sparkled in a way that made him nervous. "I've just had the most brilliant idea for an actual story."

"I'm afraid to ask."

"You should be." As she rose from her seat, her demeanor sobered. "Thank you. You've given me hope that I'm not beyond redemption."

"All I've agreed to do is be your friend."

"'Faithful are the wounds of a friend; but the kisses of an enemy are deceitful.' You have already proven a greater friend than many by speaking truth even when it was not welcomed."

She nodded to take her leave, and all Abraham could do was watch her walk out the parlor door to the kitchen. He wasn't sure what had just happened, but he was certain this case had just taken an interesting turn.

CHAPTER 18

ONE WOULD HAVE THOUGHT MOMMA had the sense to miss evening service considering their situation. But no. She had deemed the timing of their departure from Abraham's house providential. Lydia called it the curse of her life turned into a dime novel. They shouldn't be here at all, but no one defied Momma about church attendance. Except maybe Papa, who wasn't with them. Normally Sunday nights only had a handful of attendees, as Pastor Evans repeated the morning's message for those unable to attend earlier.

But nothing since stealing Tipsy from the circus had gone according to plan.

The thrum of more than a hundred voices bounced off the stone walls. People crowded the sanctuary entrance, searching for seats. Or rather, searching for her. Dozens of copies of that morning's *Cincinnati Commercial* crinkled in eager hands with the headline "Meet the Face Behind the Killer Queen." Somehow that snake Eugene Clemens had discovered where she attended church and paired that delicious fact with her face and fed it to the ravenous mobs. He was probably around here somewhere, waiting to watch the carnage the moment she was identified.

By God's grace and mercy, Flossie spotted their arrival before anyone else. Momma didn't even argue when Flossie demanded they leave. Madelyn led the retreat but abruptly stopped just outside the door. A group of men stood guard around the hack, ignoring the driver's commands that they disperse. So much for escaping the way they came.

Lydia pulled Madelyn back inside and faced Momma and Flossie. "Flossie, take them upstairs to the choir loft and keep them safe. I'll hide in the robe closet." It was the safest place she could think of.

Flossie scowled but didn't argue. Using her flowing red-and-white choir robe to obstruct anyone's view of Lydia, she rushed Lydia across the foyer and into the alcove where the closet was tucked.

Lydia stepped inside and tried to close the door.

Flossie stuck her foot into the narrowed opening. "I don't like it. Guardians do not leave each other to fight alone."

Hopefully there would be no fighting to it. All Lydia needed to do was hide until service was over so Flossie could sneak her out without being spotted. "Just keep Momma and Madelyn safe."

"I still can't believe your mother insisted you attend." Flossie's face bunched. "Actually, I can, but still! Your father is going to have a fit of apoplexy."

"I know. Now go. The longer you stand here, the more likely you are to draw attention."

She nodded, then shut Lydia into the dark box.

The closet might be the safest place Lydia could think of, but that didn't mean she was safe.

If she were writing this as a story, she'd have the heroine frantically search for a way to escape and find none. Then, when the villain exposed the heroine's hiding place, the hero would swoop in and save the day. That's how romances worked. But she wasn't living one of those. She was caught in a Billy Poe mystery. Worse, Billy was the villain and the outcome yet unknown.

She needed a plan, and not one where she twiddled her thumbs and waited for some imaginary hero to rescue her. This damsel in distress needed to become the hero. Since Billy could never again fulfill that role, she would have to consider the situation through the eyes of her new hero, Detective Darcy. He was smart and resourceful. He would scrutinize what the closet held and devise some way to use whatever he found to his benefit. Unfortunately there was little to work with. It was an empty box with a rod going across and cramping her headspace. The door had no lock, and the crystal knob was uncomfortable to hold when she applied any strength to the grip. If someone wanted in, there would be no stopping them.

She could rip the rod down and wield it as a weapon. But Pastor Evans would be livid if she damaged church property because of her overactive imagination. Best to wait until—

Someone knocked on the door.

If Flossie knocked, she'd use their secret code. Madelyn would just yank the door open, and Momma would whisper through the door. Which meant, more than likely, a foe awaited her on the other side.

Lydia wrapped her hands around the smooth wooden rod.

The door opened wide on silent hinges. A boulder of a man blocked most of the foyer light, casting him into an ominous shadow. Maybe she'd been too quick to tell Abraham no man could carry her away. This one appeared capable of tossing her over his shoulder as though she were nothing more than a potato sack.

"Looks like Miss Pelton attends service like she writes her books. In secret." His bass voice belonged in the choir loft with how much it boomed in the small space and shook her courage.

Be Detective Darcy. Firm. Confident. And for heaven's sake, Lydia, don't let your sweaty hands lose their grip on the bar.

She lifted her chin and tried to meet the man's shadowed gaze. "I believe you've mistaken me for someone else."

"You telling me you're a monkey come to swing in a closet? If you want to swing, I've got a rope to help you along."

From behind him, a woman's voice squawked. "It's too dark in there. Are you sure it's her?"

He grabbed Lydia's chin and forced her forward into the light as he shifted aside. A squat female, about the same age as the man, lifted the *Cincinnati Commercial* to Lydia's face and nodded sharply.

Cruel excitement lit the man's exposed face.

She would not cower. She was Detective Darcy, and Detective

Darcy would yank this rod free and vanquish the villain without even disturbing the service.

She jumped and used the full weight of her body to pull the bar free.

Only the stupid thing remained firmly anchored.

Arms thick as Roman columns wrapped around her waist and tugged. Unlike the rod, her sweaty hands gave way without resistance.

The organ and a multitude of singing voices covered the sounds of their scuffling.

Her angle was all wrong to knee the man. She'd never get enough momentum for him to drop her. That left her with only a damsel-in-distress tactic.

The woman shoved material into Lydia's mouth before she could so much as squeak. "We'll have none of that. You'll come with us nice and quiet, and I won't have to do to you what Billy Poe did to my boy, Joseph."

Joseph Keaton. The half dozen limestone steps might not kill her if they tossed her, but that didn't mean a serious injury couldn't occur.

Lydia nodded her acquiescence and walked down a few steps between the two abductors.

"Miss Pelton, is that you?"

The familiar voice came from behind, and she peered over her shoulder to find Mr. Clemens beaming at her.

There was no way he could miss the giant wad of material in her mouth, and yet he smiled? Was he part of this outlandish plot?

He jogged down to stand in front of them with his notebook and pencil in hand.

By all that was holy, if that man was slowing them just to get a story, she'd lay him out flat and then kiss him for the delay. If it resulted in someone else coming to her aid.

Confusion squished her kidnappers' faces, indicating he wasn't a part of their scheme.

"Ah, Mrs. Keaton, Phillip, you're both looking well. If you'll recall, I'm Eugene Clemens with the *Cincinnati Commercial*. We met last week to discuss seeking justice for Joseph's death."

"You should mind your own business and move along. We've got our justice." Phillip yanked Lydia down another step.

Mr. Clemens moved to block his path. "Cincinnati will hail you as heroes. Tell me." He scooted closer and whispered eagerly. "Since your son's death matched his crime, will you be breaking Miss Pelton's fingers to match her own?"

Heavens above! Was he really giving these two suggestions?

Phillip's bottom lip protruded in consideration. "That's not a bad idea."

No! It was a terrible idea.

"It's not," Clemens agreed. "But I think we could do better. Where were you planning to do the deed?"

Was she really just standing here, listening to them debate how to best torture and kill her? She lifted her leg and slammed her boot down on Mrs. Keaton's bread loaf of a foot. The woman yipped, and Phillip yanked Lydia around so she stood with her back pinned against his chest.

The man didn't even break conversation with Mr. Clemens. "I don't trust you."

"Nonsense. I love a good story of poetic justice. Anything I write will, of course, protect your anonymity. I wouldn't want the heroes of Cincinnati to be carted off when they were only doing what the police would not."

Mrs. Keaton leaned over to rub her foot and glared at Lydia. "The alley's close."

"Not poetic enough." Mr. Clemens tapped his pencil against his lips. "A library might work. No! Her house, where she writes the books. It's been empty the last few days, so you wouldn't run into anyone there."

"That so?"

Lydia couldn't see Phillip's face, but his whole body leaned forward, eager for the information.

"It is. And there would be no witnesses to interfere."

These people were insane. If she didn't escape now, she was going to end up dead at her desk with fingers broken and a pen jabbed through her heart. Or, more likely, her neck. At least, if she were staging it, that was how she would do it.

And that was an unsettling thought in its own right—planning her own murder.

A murder that would occur if she didn't stop letting her mind run ahead of her situation.

She jerked from side to side and threw in a few kicks for good measure. Phillip was not amused and tightened his hold until her chest hurt. Mr. Clemens completely ignored her plight while the men who guarded the hack watched with delighted curiosity.

It was one thing for this scenario to happen in a book—she'd written it often enough—but shouldn't there be at least one decent man in the world willing to rescue her? Where was Abraham when she needed him?

Phillip attempted to force her farther down the steps, but Mr. Clemens slid in his way. Phillip growled. "Move aside. You want to write your story, write your story. But stop delaying me."

"One more minute. I want to make sure I understand your plans correctly. You're taking Miss Pelton against her will to her home, where you will proceed to break each of her fingers in poetic justice before killing her yourself?"

"It's only what she deserves," Mrs. Keaton asserted. "Joseph was getting his life turned around, and that wench had him killed."

"Getting his life turned around, really? I find that hard to believe given the current situation. But please, don't allow me to stop you. I have what I need." Mr. Clemens stepped to the side as he drew something from his pocket to his lips.

The shrill of a police whistle rent the air. Lydia winced, and her ears rang at its being so near.

God bless Mr. Clemens, even if he was as addlepated as a Longview resident.

Phillip's head swung back and forth, his chin bumping against her head.

The whistle stopped, but no officer rushed to her aid.

The momentary hope she'd felt deflated. Addlepated indeed. One would think Mr. Clemens would ensure the police were nearby before giving himself away.

Phillip gave a mirthless chuckle before he passed Mr. Clemens and hauled her toward the alley. It appeared they weren't going to stage a poetic death at her home after all.

A second shrill whistle blew behind them.

Another joined it as an officer rounded the church corner, gun drawn and leveled at Phillip.

The only problem with that plan was Lydia stood trapped between. Of all the times she'd written something similar, she'd never imagined how her legs would turn to water or that her ears would drum so loud it was all she could hear. Her vision tunneled to that narrow metal cylinder, steady in the officer's hand but still as capable of firing at her as Phillip. Would she see the bullet fly from the end before it struck her? Or would a searing pain in her chest be the only announcement of the death she received? At least she could go to her grave knowing she didn't scream like a ninny in the face of a gun.

The arm around her waist disappeared.

Without Phillip's support, her legs gave way, and she thudded to the ground. Her hip and elbow caught the edges of the steps and zinged with pain.

Sweet, blessed pain—the sign of life no one wanted but she was glad to have.

Around her, chaos ensued. Two officers wrestled Phillip to the ground. He flailed and kicked, sputtering curses and condemnation down on their heads. Mrs. Keaton was halfway to the corner with an officer giving chase. The men by the carriage had scattered. Only Mr. Clemens stood unoccupied by a task.

With his hands in his pockets, he watched Phillip being shackled. "I always seem to get my timing off." He shook his head, then offered a hand to help her stand. "I hope you'll forgive me, Miss Pelton. I had to stall for time until the officers stationed inside could reach us."

Lydia stared at his hand and considered biting it, but first, she needed to deal with the dratted gag. Pulling out the wadded material as it stuck to her tongue and the roof of her mouth sent a shudder through her body. Never again would she shove something into her characters' mouths. A neat and tidy strip of material tied at the back of the head would be much more palatable.

Ignoring his hand, she pushed from the ground. "I don't know whether to thank you or to slap you. It's your fault that they're hunting me."

Some of his swagger disappeared. "I thought a stint at Longview Insane Asylum would be the worst they'd do once they discovered you were a woman. I never expected this."

"The worst they'd do?" *Slap him. Definitely slap him.*

She drew back her arm, but he deftly caught it and tucked her arm around his. "Allow me to escort you back to Miss Plane's. I have a hack waiting around the corner."

She stiffened and dug a boot heel into the space between cobblestones. "How do you know where I'm staying?"

"I'm a reporter. I have eyes everywhere, especially on you. You're the story of the century."

The notion he'd been watching her more than unsettled her; it downright sickened her. "I want an officer to escort me and my family home. Not a reporter."

"Especially not this reporter?" He quirked a brow and offered a knowing smile. "While I understand your hesitancy, I promise you, I'm not the fiend Detective Hall paints me to be."

"It's your own actions that declare you one, sir!"

"You must admit that, at the moment, I'm more hero than fiend. If it had not been for me, Phillip and Mrs. Keaton would have you in the back alley, breaking those beautiful fingers of yours. Or worse, killing you."

"All the same, I'd rather someone else take us home."

Mr. Clemens nodded, though his displeasure was clear. "Then allow me to deliver you into Officer Lucian Atwood's capable hands. You might not trust me, but I won't chance someone else whisking you away."

Lydia refused to respond to that. She *didn't* trust him, and one act of heroism wasn't going to change that. However, she couldn't help but be thankful for his consideration once she met Officer Atwood. He was the perfect officer to soothe her fears. He assured her of his protection and never moved more than a few feet away.

It took longer than expected to give her statement, see Phillip and Mrs. Keaton taken away, and to have Madelyn and Momma retrieved. But eventually, Officer Atwood escorted them to Plane Manor in an open-air hack. With the cool breeze and his smooth words, he managed to calm Madelyn's hysterics, stop Momma's berating herself, and fill the drive with easygoing chatter. Despite his jovial personality, however, Lydia couldn't relax. A trembling anxiousness held her in its grip, muddling her brain and icing her veins, though it eluded her how, on such a baking day, she could feel so cold.

The hack pulled directly in front of the portico, and Theresa opened the door to greet them with a half-eaten bouquet of flowers.

By the grim set to her mouth, these flowers weren't a simple casualty from Tipsy.

"Billy Poe sent you these and another note."

Lydia pressed a hand to her throat, trying to quell her rising fear. "He sent them *here*? To your house for me?"

Theresa nodded. "They were left on the steps not ten minutes ago. Tipsy found them first when . . ."

Whatever else Theresa said was lost to Lydia.

Ten minutes. He'd been here, at this spot, ten minutes ago.

Oh, Lord above! What am I supposed to do?

There was no doubt in her mind that he watched her. Wherever he stood, his eyes bored straight into her. How long would it be until looking wasn't enough?

CHAPTER 19

"Abducted? Where? How?" Abraham rammed a hand through his hair. Lydia had been here not two hours ago.

Lucian stood in uniform at Abraham's door even though this section of town wasn't his beat. "Her mother insisted on attending church service, and Keaton's father and mother were waiting for her."

Were all the Pelton women without sense? "Tell me all."

After a brief report, Lucian shook his head. "We always talked about becoming detectives, but I'm not so sure I'm interested anymore."

"The grass is always greener on the other side, but that usually means manure was involved in the making of it. Are you saying you're afraid of a little muck?"

"Nope, I just like being home with my wife. If you're ever free again, stop by the house for a visit. Verity says she misses you."

"Only because she wants me to marry her sister."

Lucian shrugged. "You're not getting any younger."

Too bad the only woman who interested him was the one he shouldn't consider.

Abraham thanked Lucian for the information and walked to the nearest horsecar stop. Lydia must be a hysterical mess by now. Any woman would be. In all likelihood, Dr. Pelton had given her a sedative, and she wouldn't be awake to question. Still, Abraham would go. A new Billy Poe note might hold a crucial, time-sensitive development. It didn't matter that his shift had ended only a few hours ago. As Lawson had warned, the case's needs dictated his schedule. Breaks would come when there were lulls.

He took a seat on the half-empty horsecar and scrubbed his face. Climbing over the detective fence had indeed landed him in manure. An unpredictable schedule, a partner who abhorred silence, and a murderer as elusive as a snipe. Throw in this attraction to Lydia, and he was up to his neck in muck. Maybe if he was lucky, this trip would only take a few hours, and he'd be home and in bed with enough time for a full night's sleep. Lord knew he needed it. Never before had his job stretched him so close to his limits, and this was only the beginning of the case. If his gut was right, they still had a long way to go before they apprehended Billy Poe.

Twilight shrouded Plane Manor in a haunting gray by the time he arrived. Not that the Gothic stone building needed any help in appearing menacing. Wings and bays towered three stories tall, with parapets and pinnacles giving the illusion of guards keeping vigilant watch from above. The only warmth emanating from the building came from the glow of the front window.

He sighed as he caught a glimpse of Lydia pacing behind the window in plain view. So much for her being sedated. That was probably best for his case, even if he'd have to reprimand her for not staying out of sight.

Mrs. Hawking, the Planes' housekeeper, refused to open the door until he identified himself, then swung it open to reveal a rifle in hand. Rail-thin, dressed in black, and hair twisted into a fierce bun, the woman made the house's outside feel welcoming in comparison. With a no-nonsense comportment and tone, she led him into the packed parlor.

Except for Lydia, the Pelton family was seated together near the door. Dr. Pelton sat next to his wife, holding her close while he scowled at some distant thought. Lydia's younger sister lounged on the sofa and paged through a lady's magazine.

"Maa."

Was that a goat bleat? Abraham glanced at the floor near Lydia. Next to Miss Plane, the three-legged animal lay on a blanket and chomped on what appeared to be the remainder of a bouquet of flowers. Wasn't that creature supposed to be dead by now? Miss Plane must have a healer's touch, because the goat appeared well on her way to recovery.

"I didn't expect to see you until tomorrow."

Abraham turned at Lawson's voice.

"Officer Atwood informed me of the situation." Abraham's eyes strayed to where Lydia continued her back-and-forth path in front of the window.

Instead of a face puffy from tears, a tempest raged. Her hands alternated between fists and flexes as she muttered to herself. He should have known better than to expect to find her a swooning mess. To write the stories she did, she must have a constitution stronger than steel.

Movement from the corner snagged his attention, and Marcus Monroe stepped away from the wall where he leaned.

What was he doing here? No one was supposed to know Lydia's location.

Monroe gripped her elbow before she stepped out of reach. "Stop fretting. I'll see to it that all will be well."

Lydia shrugged out of his hold, and the thud of her footfalls intensified. "I'm not *fretting*. I'm angry."

Lawson leaned over and whispered, "She's been like this since I got here twenty minutes ago. I've tried my hand at calming her, but I think she's just a woman who has to pace through her emotions until she collapses."

"How long has Monroe been here?" Abraham watched Monroe continue to convince Lydia to be still.

"Longer than me. Says he followed Atwood and the Peltons from the church."

"But I thought he's Catholic. Why would he be at her church?"

"That is the question, is it not?" Lawson arched his brow meaningfully.

"One of many."

When Monroe grabbed Lydia's arm again, Abraham strode toward them. "Hello, Miss Pelton. Mr. Monroe."

Lydia yanked away and shifted so that Abraham stood between her and Monroe. The scowl on her face eased into a small smile as she addressed Abraham. "I didn't think I'd see you so soon."

"It appears that if I want to know what my enemy is up to, I need to stick closer to you."

Her smile broadened. "'There's a friend who sticks closer than a brother.'"

The reference to Proverbs made him shake his head. "As admirable as that sounds, I hope I do not need to lay down my life in order to ensure your safety. After all, this is not a romance novel."

Monroe grunted. "It sure sounds like you're trying to make it one."

"Not in the least. I am only here to do my job."

Jealous skepticism flashed across his face.

Great. Just what he needed—another reason for Marcus Monroe to make his job more difficult.

"My life is neither a romance novel nor a Billy Poe novel." Lydia shook her head, and worry lines creased around her eyes. "Except perhaps it is. I *was* almost abducted and murdered in a way befitting my crime."

Instead of dissolving into a fit of uncontrollable sobbing and meekness, her lips thinned, her hands flexed, and she reclaimed her angry pacing. If Billy Poe happened to appear before her, the man would likely end up as the recipient of a floorer. The reaction shouldn't have surprised Abraham. Most of the women in his life—Clara included—generally faced problems head-on, even if tears eventually became involved.

Lydia continued ranting. "Between Cincinnati out to kill me and Billy Poe out to woo me, I might very well be in the midst of both a romance and a mystery." She pivoted and marched back in Abraham's direction. "Do you know that he's been watching me closely?" She stopped at the window and searched the streets before shaking her head and continuing on her warpath. "He knows what I'm reading. He's seen Theresa and me caring for Tipsy. He even talked about how delicious my pork roast looked and smelled. I'd say he was in the house, but it's only been my family, the Planes, and Mrs. Hawking here."

Those were unsettling details indeed, but those activities could be seen from the ground-floor windows. Not that it made the situation any better.

"Even worse, he intends to prove his love through a gift only he can give."

Now *that* was disturbing news. "May I see the note?"

She gestured to Lawson, who retrieved it from his pocket.

Abraham unfolded the parchment to reveal the familiar writing. Though filled with words of admiration, it was barbed with phrases like "ordinary heroes give chocolate and flowers; I give you justice." His hints at a special gift waiting just for her meant there would be no going home once Abraham left here. He and Lawson would be chasing down the remaining potential victims to inform them of the heightened risk to their safety. Poe planned to murder again soon, and all in the name of love.

Abraham refolded the letter and slipped it into his coat's inner pocket.

Lydia's tirade resumed. "What kind of man believes love equates to flowers and dead bodies?"

"You do have similar views of justice." Lawson shrugged. "And you did kill those men in your books. Isn't the greatest form of flattery imitation?"

Lydia stumbled to a stop, her face pale. If Lawson was trying to determine if she were part of a conspiracy, her responses were evidence enough that she was not.

"Perhaps Billy Poe should read your romance novels. Then he

could start re-creating the right scenarios of love." Miss Plane's teasing tone was decidedly out of place. Upon seeing Lydia's horrified expression, Miss Plane's shoulders sagged. "I'm sorry. I was only trying to help lighten the mood. What do you call it in your stories? Comedy relief?"

Lydia shook her head. "Comedy relief only works when it's well-timed. Your attempt was not."

Monroe touched Lydia's shoulder. "She's not wrong to lighten the mood. You need to calm yourself and leave Billy Poe to us."

She jerked out of his grip and stumbled backward into Abraham.

He caught her against his chest. Her citrus-scented curls bunched around his nose, and the warmth of her back against him branded him in a way it shouldn't have. She was just a woman.

Yet even as he thought it, that *just a woman* came back to slap him. Lydia Pelton was far from common, and holding her was as dangerous to his sensibilities as holding an adder.

He righted her and stepped away to create space.

Lydia stepped with him, keeping them unsettlingly close.

Monroe glowered at Abraham like he'd identified his newest adversary.

"Go home, Marcus," Lydia said. "I appreciate your coming, but I don't need your coddling. I'll deliver the next Billy Poe novel on time, but I ask that you leave me alone until then."

"I'm not here about your novel. I'm here for *you*. I've made clear my regard for you. Please don't push me away because you're scared."

"I'm not scared. I just need to sort this out in the same way I do everything."

Miss Madelyn piped up from the couch without lowering her magazine. "You might as well leave, Mr. Monroe. Lydia will stomp and talk aloud until she reaches a satisfactory conclusion, just like she does with every story she writes. It's downright annoying, and at this rate, she'll be all night. Save yourself the aggravation and go home."

That was a surprising defense, even if it did come in the back-handed fashion of sibling derision.

Lawson glanced disapprovingly at Abraham's closeness to Lydia, but placed himself between her and Monroe. "Come, Monroe. The lady told you to leave, and I have a few questions to ask you about the church incident. Miss Plane, may I beg the use of another room?"

Miss Plane scratched the goat's ear before rising. "My grandfather is out doing target practice in the carriage house, so you can use his office. Just don't touch anything."

As they passed him, Abraham bumped Lawson's shoe and whispered, "Tail him when he leaves."

After a frown that communicated Lawson did not appreciate being told what to do, the trio disappeared down the hall.

Lydia sighed before facing Abraham. Had they been a romantic couple, their faces were close enough to steal a kiss without giving away his intent. Not that he'd ever take something that wasn't his or freely given, but the thought was enough to have him put a proper distance between them.

"I know I can't ask you to leave, Papa, but Momma, Madelyn, would you please allow me some privacy to speak to Detective Hall?"

Mrs. Pelton hesitated, but after a glance at her younger daughter, who plainly tried to hide her interest behind the magazine, she acquiesced. Miss Madelyn grumbled about leaving just when things were getting good, but accompanied her mother.

Finally alone, Lydia gestured for Abraham and Dr. Pelton to sit. "There is no reason for you to stand just because I can't be still."

Dr. Pelton claimed the seat Mrs. Pelton had vacated, but Abraham refused. Not that he expected Lydia to swoon, but should something happen, he wanted to be close. In fact, it would be in their best interest to close the curtains. Before doing so, he surveyed the yard and street. Lit rooms from the neighboring mansions cast rectangles of light, but no streetlamps existed to push back the dark. If Poe were out there, he had plenty of shadows to hide in. Abraham tugged the curtains closed and turned toward Lydia.

All pretense of anger had vanished, leaving behind the distraught woman he'd expected to find when he arrived. The shimmering tears, quivering chin, and almost shrinking into herself were so common to his job, he could ignore them. But her eyes, the haunted brokenness that pleaded with him to make everything right, left him aching and wishing he could hold her until her torment subsided and she felt safe once more.

"I confess, I lied to Marcus." Her voice cracked. "I'm scared. Terrified, really. What if Billy Poe is watching me right now?"

Before Abraham's restraint broke, Dr. Pelton filled the role of comforter. He rose and encased his daughter in an embrace and silently pleaded over the top of her head for Abraham to find a quick end to this case.

If only Abraham could promise to do so. "With the curtains closed, Poe cannot see you." He closed the door. "And now he cannot hear you."

She gave a watery nod and allowed Dr. Pelton to lead her to the sofa. Like a frightened child, she tucked her legs beside her and leaned into her father's hold as if Dr. Pelton alone could protect her.

Unfounded jealousy pricked Abraham. She might not view him as her protector, but it was his duty as an officer, and now her friend, to share that responsibility. She could depend upon him. He would be that companion that stuck closer than a brother.

He pulled up a chair and rested his arms on his knees as he leaned in. "Do you have any idea how Billy Poe found you?"

"No, but I have at least two suspects in mind." Her temper sparked.

It amused him more than it should, but he was glad to see the spunk alive and well despite her tears.

"I never told Marcus where I was staying, but he arrived here only minutes after we did."

As much as he'd like to hold Monroe responsible for Billy Poe's actions, they had no proof that he had prior knowledge of Lydia's location. Not that a lack of proof meant he was innocent. "Lawson said Monroe followed you, but the flowers and note preceded you. How could Monroe be responsible for them?"

Lydia's forehead bunched, and her mind stalked off to hunt down an explanation.

Abraham worked to suppress his delight at watching her. The woman was fascinating in her approach to everything. She swung from cowering child to rampaging detective all within a few breaths. No wonder she was an author. One had to be half mad to think and behave the way she did and then commit it to paper for the world to read.

In her hunt for an answer, her finger tapped against her arm. Soon her teeth played with her bottom lip, and she nodded. A grin crept up one side of her mouth before she unleashed it fully.

"I know how he did it." The excitement of solving a puzzle lit her whole countenance.

He couldn't help but answer her smile with his own, even if it might give her the wrong idea about his interest in her, which was strictly professional, of course. The fact he'd just discovered a shared interest—solving puzzles—meant nothing more than their friendship might actually work.

Lydia scooted to the edge of the sofa. "The flowers and note did arrive before him, but if Marcus overheard Mr. Clemens's offer to escort me to Theresa's, he would have known who that was. There was a season where my edits had to be directed here while I cared for Theresa during her recovery from a near drowning. Considering how long we were at the church, he had time to act."

That was doubtful. Abraham wasn't in the habit of sending flowers, but on the rare occasion he had, the ordeal had been time-consuming. "Do you really believe it long enough for him to have written the note, ordered flowers, and had them delivered?"

"It's a Sunday. The flowers weren't from a market. They were mostly weeds found in the empty lots between here and the church. Theresa said they only discovered the note and flowers a few minutes before we arrived. Marcus could have placed them, then waited nearby until he saw the hack deliver us."

Her explanation could fit, and if Monroe was close enough to overhear Clemens—

"Did you say Clemens was there?"

"Yes, and I suspect him as much as I do Marcus. He's the one who stepped in when Mr. and Mrs. Keaton tried to abduct me, which means he had to be following me." She huffed. "He even had the gall to suggest more 'poetic' ways to kill me. According to him, it was to buy time for the police to arrive, but there is nothing like hearing someone plan your death while you're forced toward an alley."

Her shudder and subsequent curling against her father had Abraham fisting his hands. Lydia might be a dime novelist with an unsettling interest in the macabre, but no one should be subjected to such conversation. Whether Poe or not, when Abraham next saw Clemens, he was going to have a few words to share about inappropriate stall tactics.

Dr. Pelton frowned. "How did he know you're staying here?"

Even though her head remained against Dr. Pelton's shoulder, her eyes rolled in annoyed melodrama. "He's a reporter. He has eyes everywhere. I'd like to poke his eyes out, especially since he made a point to say he was keeping them on me in particular. I don't care if he thinks I'm the story of the century; it's unnerving."

Clemens's interest in Lydia was definitely more than the story called for, but pitiful if that was all it truly was. "Given we still have twenty years to go, he must be anticipating a pretty uneventful career."

She chuckled at that, and the accompanying smile eased some of the fear that had taken hold of her countenance.

Dr. Pelton was far less amused. "In the morning, I'm demanding a restraining order."

Even Dr. Pelton wouldn't be successful at getting one of those. "You don't have enough to prove he's a threat and worthy of such an order, but I'll speak to Clemens and make it clear he is to keep his distance."

"A lot of good that will do if he's Billy Poe." Lydia's whole body deflated.

Abraham grasped her hand. "You are not alone in this. Between your family, me, and Detective Lawson, you will be safe. Finding Poe is my top priority, and I won't rest until he's arrested and convicted."

Lydia's face took on a shine that mirrored Clara's after reading a heroic rescue. That it was directed at him should have made him run from the room. Instead, it made him wish she would write him as the hero not just of her story but of her life.

Dr. Pelton coughed before sending a meaningful look toward Abraham's and Lydia's clasped hands.

Abraham pulled away quickly. Speaking with Lydia was a maze of obstacles and traps. If Abraham wasn't careful, he might find himself facing a future with a former criminal as his wife.

The fact that the thought brought a smile and not a frown unsettled him all the more.

CHAPTER 20

AFTER TWO HOURS OF TRACKING down two of the four potential victims, Abraham was so weary he could feel the ache in his bones. He leaned his head back against the hack's frame and closed his eyes. With the breeze cooling his face and the semi-comfortable position, he could sleep until next week. Unfortunately he couldn't spare even a hack ride's worth. He still had to meet with Lawson to confirm all four potential victims were accounted for, safe, and warned. Abraham forced himself upright and angled so the door handle regularly jabbed his side. At least another hour, maybe two, lay ahead before he could collapse into his bed.

With any luck, Lawson's two potential victims had been more co-operative than Abraham's. Kimball Sullivan had mistaken Abraham for a moneymonger he owed, and had taken off. Abraham could have let him go, but he'd pursued the man instead. Better to be winded and tired than to have a man die because Abraham hadn't done his job to the fullest of his ability. After a lengthy chase, he'd finally collared Sullivan. The ungrateful brute had landed a decent punch before Abraham got him pinned to a wall and managed to convince the man that he was an officer. With a shrug, Sullivan had said he had bigger problems than a crazy vigilante who *might* be after him, and then disappeared down an alley. Considering Sullivan owed Weidel the Short a considerable amount of money, it probably was in his best interest to leave town and take care of two threats with one move.

Wesley Xavier had been only slightly better. He'd been deep in a bar brawl when Abraham found him. After breaking up the fight and enduring a few more well-aimed fists, Abraham had hauled him to the nearest station. At least the man would spend the night protected by a jail cell. Once arraigned in the morning for disorderly conduct, it would be up to Xavier to take Abraham's advice and lie low or continue visiting his favorite haunts for Poe to find him.

All too soon, the hack stopped in front of the McManus Boardinghouse, where Lawson lived. Abraham hated knocking after midnight, but with the door locked, he had no choice. It took several rounds of pounding, but eventually, grumbles came from the other side.

The door opened to a spindly man in a housecoat that swallowed all his features but the fierce scowl. "What do you want?"

"I'm here for Lawson."

"He has his own entrance so I don't have to deal with this." He gruffly directed Abraham down the side alley to access the back entrance to the apartment at the top of the three-story building.

A door with three different locks met Abraham at the top of the stairs. Lawson certainly took preventing break-ins more seriously than any other officer Abraham knew. Then again, Lawson had been on the force longer than most and had probably had lots of experiences that reinforced his vigilance. Lawson answered the door with wet hair, clean clothes, and a grin that turned into a grimace when Abraham mentioned waking Mr. McManus.

"Sorry about that. I should have warned you that I have a separate entrance." Lawson methodically secured the locks. "After too many middle-of-the-night interruptions from officers needing to speak to me, McManus cleared out the attic and refitted it for my use—at a higher rent, of course."

Abraham glanced around the open space.

The kitchen was a decent size compared to most apartments Abraham had visited, even if it did share the floor with a large round table with the remnants of an abandoned card game. The place could benefit from a good cleanup. A faint rotten odor tainted the air, probably from the overfull waste bin. When Abraham left, he'd do the man a favor and toss it onto the pile in the alley waiting for sanitation. On the opposite side of the room, two plush chairs framed a large bookshelf filled with the bright orange covers of dime novels intermixed with more reputable titles. The only indication the man might have a family was a photo of Lawson with a teen girl hanging on the wall.

"Not bad for a bachelor, eh? Since I never had a missus, I turned the extra bedroom into an office so I can continue working after my shift."

"If you've never married, who's the young woman with you in the photo?"

"My goddaughter." His tender smile revealed a fatherly love, but it dipped into grief a moment later. "She passed just under a year ago."

"I'm sorry."

He waved away the condolence. "I keep that picture there to remind me why I do this job. It's a hard one, Hall. It's best you find your reason for choosing this career, so when the days get long and you get discouraged, you can keep moving forward."

It was good advice, and something Abraham would have to think on. Up till now, his reasons for becoming an officer had to do with protecting the innocent and upholding justice. They weren't bad reasons, but they were rather generic. He studied the picture of the young woman. Who would serve as his reminder of why he did this job? Lydia's distraught face came to mind, and he shifted uncomfortably. Shouldn't someone closer to him, like Clara or Mother, cross his mind first? This attraction to Lydia was growing unwieldy.

He purposely redirected the conversation and his thoughts. "Is it necessary to have an office in your home? Shouldn't you leave your work at the station?"

Not that Abraham could throw stones. Since starting this case, he'd gone home every night and continued working the puzzle on his own time. But that wasn't sustainable. Was this to be his life as a detective?

"Not much else to keep me busy in the evenings, but I do a lot of reading and have weekly card nights. You just missed the last one, but you ought to come next week." Lawson collected the empty glasses and dumped ashes into the trash on his way to the sink. "Have a seat. I've got some ham in the icebox and a bottle of bourbon calling our names."

Abraham declined and chose a hard wooden table chair rather than a plush one, where the risk of falling asleep was too great. A half-read copy of *Shadow in the Night* sat splayed open.

Abraham picked it up and frowned. "I thought you lent me this."

Lawson rattled around in the icebox, stacking thick ham, a hard-boiled egg, and an apple onto a plate. "I have several sets of the books. I've been studying Dupin since before these murders. Even tried my hand at writing my own dime novel once, but it was flatly refused."

"You wrote a dime novel?"

"O'Dell should have burned the awful thing instead of sending it back." He settled at the table with the odd assortment of food and a double portion of bourbon. "It's locked away in my desk drawer until I finally get up the nerve to do the job myself. Any luck tracking down your two potential targets?"

"Sullivan's been warned, and I arrested Xavier for disorderly conduct. You?"

"Noah Grant was diagnosed with consumption last week and has traveled to Colorado for treatment. He's out of Poe's reach for now. Samuel Ross hasn't been home for over a week, but his neighbor says he frequently disappears without warning. She wouldn't know or care except that he leaves his dog in the house. She's been tossing scraps through a broken window just to stop his howling."

Scraps weren't likely enough with as long as Ross had been gone. Still, Abraham could do nothing about it tonight. "Did she know where Ross went?"

"No. We'll just have to wait for him to come home or for his body to show up."

"Which book was he from? We should watch the area where he died in the story."

"Not a bad idea, Boy Detective. You'll have me beating out Carlisle yet." Lawson abandoned his plate, examined a row of dime novels, and pulled one out to flip through. "Ross's character was beaten, bound, and gagged, then shoved into an attic with a plate of food and glass of water out of reach. It fits Ross's crime. Officers found his children locked in the attic, living in their own feces, starved, and half clothed in the middle of winter. One was barely three and almost died. Ross was convicted and sentenced to Longview Insane Asylum, but his government friends bought him a pardon from the governor. The children were returned to him until family found them locked in the attic again. They won custody, but he didn't get charged again."

"Ross is a special breed of scourge."

"Makes you want to drag your feet in rescuing him from Poe's hands, doesn't it?"

Abraham refrained from responding. It wasn't his place to execute vengeance, but it made him sick to think of how the children had suffered under Ross's hands and how the justice system had failed them. They deserved better. The heinousness of both acts were enough to make a man jaded.

No matter how hard Abraham worked to rid the streets of evil, evil won more often than not. Dime novels couldn't even begin to touch the horrors. Newspapers provided glimpses that were quickly lost to claims of sensationalism. The public walked in blissful ignorance of the fathomless darkness and corruption that surrounded them. The sort of corruption that allowed a man like Ross to not only go free but to have another opportunity to slowly kill his children.

As much as Abraham wanted to deny it, he understood why Lydia wrote her stories and even why Poe chose to take matters into his own hands. Abraham was tempted to take matters into his own hands too, if only by delaying his inquiry into Ross's whereabouts.

Lawson broke the lingering silence. "I've been thinking about Clemens being the one to rescue Miss Pelton at the church. I hadn't considered that he has a connection to each of the cases, *and* he has a very personal association with the first murder victim. Otis Wakefield was the man exonerated for violating Clemens's fiancée. She eventually took her own life."

Abraham sat up in his chair. "What? How did we miss that?"

"It's easy to miss when reporting on the murders is part of his job. His personal association didn't cross my mind, because he had no connection to any of the other murders at that time."

That shed new light on Clemens's interest in Lydia and the Billy Poe case as a whole. Clemens was the reason behind Cincinnati's push to expose Dupin's pseudonym. If that article hadn't been published, much of Cincinnati would still be oblivious to the murders. Had he seen Dupin as his partner but was now no longer satisfied by the distance Dupin's pseudonym created? Stooping to incite citywide upheaval was just the type of unethical strategy Clemens would employ to uncover Dupin's identity.

Now that Clemens knew Dupin was a woman, he'd convinced himself that they were a perfect match for serving justice. A love match. The thought disgusted Abraham almost as much as Ross's treatment of the children. Clemens's attachment to Lydia would explain why he had been nearby at the church, especially given what his fiancée had suffered at the hands of a man. If the love of Abraham's life were violated, he was pretty sure murder would cross his own mind.

"We need to question Clemens."

Lawson waved the statement away. "Not yet. Everything we have is circumstantial. At this moment, he doesn't know we suspect him. If we try to question him, he'll walk free and with the advantage of knowing we're on the hunt. He's not our only suspect either. Monroe has just as much potential to be Poe. Both men need our attention, and Miss Pelton needs our protection. The department won't cover the cost of an officer's staying with her or the family, but we can take turns with our off shifts. I'll take tonight. You resemble a busted punching bag. Get some ice on your face and then some sleep. I'll see you in the morning."

"What about checking Ross's attic?"

"We can do that tomorrow. One more night won't kill him."

Abraham wasn't so sure about that, but there wasn't much he could do to argue. He was dead on his feet, and what were they going to do tonight? Bang on the door until the dog's howls woke the neighborhood? He didn't like it, but tomorrow would come.

Hopefully with answers.

Sleep should have come the moment Abraham's head hit the pillow. Instead, he tossed and turned, the horsehair mattress stiff and unyielding. Just like his conscience.

One more night won't kill him.

But what if it did? They knew Poe actively sought his next target in an attempt to impress Lydia with his affections. If Poe were re-creating the victim's crimes, Ross wasn't likely to starve over the course of one night. Still, lying in bed, knowing there was a man whose life was potentially in danger didn't sit well with Abraham, no matter how exhausted he felt. He had a duty to serve and protect. They had reasonable cause to enter Ross's house and check on his well-being. A warrant wasn't needed. On the other hand, if Ross were waist-deep in criminal dealings, they wouldn't be able to use the evidence against him in a case, and a jail cell might be the safest place for him.

After struggling to sleep for over an hour, Abraham rose from his bed, redressed, grabbed a hand lantern, and slipped out of the house.

Three a.m. meant Lucian still patrolled his beat. It covered a section from Smith to Pearl to Broadway to Water Streets, an impossibly large area to find one man on the move. Still, after how the other two victims had received Abraham this evening, having a second person with him when he knocked on Ross's door seemed prudent. Abraham found the nearest police box and used his key to access the phone Cincinnati had installed the year before. The dispatcher at the station house informed him where Lucian had last checked in, and Abraham headed in that direction.

It took another half hour to locate Lucian, but his friend didn't hesitate to change course and join him. All was quiet on the dark street. The drinking establishments had closed their doors hours ago, and their patrons had either stumbled home or into a gutter somewhere. Even the gas streetlamps seemed too tired to do anything more than cast a faint glow over the cool mist hanging above the rutted street.

Abraham raised a fist to knock on the door but paused. "You have that baton ready to keep the dog away, right?"

"Got better than that. If it's as hungry as you say, I've got a meat pie in my pocket." Lucian pulled out a grease-blotched paper wrapped around an odd-shaped lump.

A treat for any dog, hungry or not.

Abraham hammered with a force that echoed down the street and made the door shudder. "Mr. Ross, this is the police. We need to speak with you."

No sounds came from within. Not even the dog. Abraham frowned. Was the poor creature too weak with hunger to respond?

Abraham pounded and yelled louder. A dog inside the neighbor's house barked, and a stooped salt-and-pepper-haired woman yanked open the door of her home.

"Land sakes, man. I told that other officer that Sam has been gone for over a week. No need to go on trying to wake a man who ain't there."

The dog nosed its face between the thin material of her wrapper and the doorframe. He snarled, and the woman pinned its head between her leg and the frame. "Hush, Butcher, or I'll put you back where I found ya."

"That wouldn't happen to be Ross's dog, would it?" Lucian asked as he pulled out the meat pie and tossed it at the woman's feet.

The dog pushed through and pounced on the morsel of food. A waft of urine and rotted meat slammed into Abraham at the animal's nearness. Matted fur couldn't hide the ribs that protruded enough to be counted. Ross's utter neglect of the living astounded him.

"Butcher's not Ross's anymore. He got out this evening, and I'm not givin' him back."

"How did he get out? We have reason to believe Ross may be in danger."

"Oh, he's in danger all right. If I ever see his face again, he'll wish he were back in Longview." After a glare that indicated Poe had competition, she waved to the narrow alley between their buildings. "The door out back has been rotting for years. Butcher probably finally busted it open."

Without a further word, she pulled Butcher inside and slammed the door.

The farther down the alley they proceeded, the worse it smelled. An animal's carcass must be nearby. No wonder Butcher broke out. He probably wanted to eat it.

Though the door remained closed, the bottom corner had been chewed through. Abraham knelt to take a better look, and the miasma of death assailed him.

God, let that be a dead animal.

He wrenched the door open with ease and, with the hand lantern, moved through the kitchen where the dog had scrounged for food. Empty sacks lay strewn and shredded on the floor. Cans punctured by teeth marks provided an obstacle course. The kitchen led into a main room that wasn't much better. Having given up on food, Butcher had gnawed on cushions, furniture legs, and any exposed wood. There was no sign of Ross, but as Abraham and Lucian climbed the stairs to the second floor, the air turned from pungent to putrid.

Lucian tugged his coat over his nose and nodded to the closed door at the top.

When Abraham reached it, furious buzzing hummed on the other side.

Flies.

How many did it take for the noise to be that loud?

Please let a family of raccoons have gotten in and died.

There was little hope for it, but he prayed it all the same. After a bracing breath through the material of his coat, Abraham opened the door.

The potent stench exploded from the room with the force of dynamite.

Lucian took the stairs two at a time but didn't make it to the bottom before casting up his accounts.

Bile rose in Abraham's throat and threatened to make him follow Lucian's example, but he battled against the response. He needed to see, to know for certain.

A quick glance was all it took.

A black cloud of startled flies hovered over a bloated body stretched across the floor. Gagged, bound, and chained to the wall, the body was clearly Ross's. A plate of dried-out food sat next to a tipped-over water glass, inches from where Ross must have fought to his last to reach.

In contrast to the death and decay, next to the plate stood a fresh bouquet of roses with a note addressed to Lydia in Poe's handwriting.

He'd beaten them again.

CHAPTER 21

THE BORROWED PLANE MANOR CARRIAGE dipped as it hit a rut on the darkened streets of morning's twilight. Lydia's shoulder brushed against Detective Lawson's, stirring the unease in her stomach. She shouldn't have come. But how could she stay home and sleep? If indeed that fitful twisting and turning of her mind could be called sleep. The moment Detective Lawson knocked on her parents' door to summon Papa as coroner, she'd known.

Her words had killed another person.

In her foolish need to see what horrors her pen had wrought, she'd pressed to join until Papa and Detective Lawson acquiesced. Neither man would share which of the remaining four victims had met their end, but as the carriage turned onto Main Street, she knew.

The derelict row house of Samuel Ross sagged beneath the weight of the horror that stood within.

God, forgive me. That man's fictional demise had been her most disturbing one to write, but she'd done it nevertheless. The vile, evil monster that was her soul had deemed torture and a lingering execution the only sorts of justice Mr. Ross deserved. Where had been her mercy—or her conscience, for that matter? It should have rebelled at such a callous, hideous thought. Had she really learned to strangle it so much that it had gasped its last? Were her heart and mind so degraded that, even now, the Lord had given her over to depravity and washed His hands of her?

No. That was a lie straight from the devil. She'd repented, and God had promised to help her change. But *could* she change when the stench of her own wickedness spilled out into the streets from the attic above?

The carriage stopped on the opposite side of the street from where the windows and doors stood flung open. Death mingled with the mist to haunt the air with a foreboding that warned all to turn back. Even with a handkerchief pressed over her nose, the rot seeped into every fiber and breath.

How many days, hours, and minutes had Mr. Ross suffered in the sweltering heat of a summer attic, dying of hunger and thirst while relief lay in sight but forever out of reach?

This wasn't justice for those poor, abused, and neglected children. This was revenge.

No wonder a vigilante as deranged as Billy Poe had thought her a perfect match for him. It was only natural that one monster should be attracted to another.

"Do not get out of this carriage." Papa did not wait for her agreement, but grabbed his bag and hopped to the ground.

For once, she had not the slightest objection. She'd lost her courage to face her sins almost as soon as she'd entered the carriage.

"I'll station an officer to stand with you once I get inside," Detective Lawson said. "You won't be alone."

Gooseflesh pricked her skin.

Though he'd meant his words for comfort, they reminded her that Billy Poe likely watched her. A glance around revealed neither Marcus nor Mr. Clemens, but a small group of curious gawkers with cloths over faces gathered nearby. Any of them could be Billy, should she be wrong about his identity.

She wrapped a hand around the horseshoe she'd nabbed from Theresa's carriage house. It wasn't a great weapon, but it would give her punch more potency if she needed to slug Billy.

An officer staggered outside, yanked his face covering down, and heaved near Papa's feet.

Lydia dipped her chin and took slow breaths to abate the queasiness of her own stomach. How bad must the smell be inside for that to be his reaction?

After a few moments, the sounds stopped, and she sought Papa's reaction. Ever the kind soul, he patted the man's back and offered him a handkerchief. Once assured the officer would be fine, Papa retrieved the perfume-scented strip of fabric Momma kept in his bag and secured it over his nose. He glanced at Lydia one more time before going in to see the depths of depravation his daughter's words had instigated.

Never again would their relationship be restored. Not after he saw what awaited him in that attic. What a fool she'd been. Published mysteries were not worth all that she'd lost. All the *lives* lost.

The officer, who'd since composed himself, approached the carriage. "Detective Lawson assigned me to watch over you."

"Lucky you."

"You have no idea."

"Is it that bad inside?" By God's grace and mercy, may her mind have conjured images worse than reality.

Still pale with a tinge of green, the stout man shook his head and shuddered. "You don't want to even imagine it. It'll give you nightmares."

She sat back, nauseated. Five men now had died via her nightmares, with three more anticipating their turn. Her current villain still awaited his fate, but her deadline loomed. Soon the pages that sat on her desk would soak up her ink and sentence a real man to a brutal end.

What was wrong with her? Was she still such an ogre that she'd condemn *another* man?

Yes, breaking her contract came with consequences, but what were those in comparison to a man's life?

But maybe she didn't have to break her contract. What if she changed the victim? After these events, no one would consider Billy Poe a hero. Perhaps it was time for him to experience his own demise and allow for a better detective to rise and take his place.

"Good almost-morning, Richards. I heard we have another Billy Poe body."

Lydia startled out of her thoughts as Mr. Clemens appeared next to the carriage.

Upon noticing her, he faced her fully. "I didn't expect to find you here. Come to inspect your handiwork, have you?"

She worked to infuse confidence into her posture. Fear was no option in the face of such evil. "Do not jest with me, Mr. Clemens. I do not approve of this."

"Tell me." He leaned against the door of the carriage. "What do you think of Ross getting what was coming to him?"

Did he seek affirmation from her for what he'd done? She'd only suspected he was Billy Poe, but did this serve as proof that he really was the sword behind her pen? Her grip on the horseshoe turned white-knuckled. She would not, under any circumstances, encourage the man further.

"I think his murder excruciatingly vile. I'm horrified to ever have written such a thing. If Billy Poe thinks he is showing me his love through these acts, he is mistaken on what overtures of love should look like."

"'Overtures of love,' is it? Hmmm. What sort of 'overtures of love' would the Killer Queen of Romance desire if not these? I doubt she is a woman swayed by flowers, sweets, and poetry."

She glared at him, determined to stop this madness. "There is nothing Billy Poe could ever do to convince me to love him, but if he should stop his vigilante ways, then I might not kill him off in the next book."

"Still seeking justice through fictional murder, are you?"

The blood drained from her face—no, her whole body. He was right. Killing Billy Poe in her next book wasn't any different from what she'd done before. Had she really changed so little? She might have sought forgiveness and repentance within the last few days, but was she so far gone that even God couldn't make her a new creation? Her stomach churned.

"Clemens!" Abraham's voice cracked like lightning striking a tree.

Lydia recoiled from the shock of it, and Mr. Clemens jolted upright.

Abraham strode from the house with the force and fury of tornadic winds. Whether coming to her defense or to arrest the man purely for the sake of his job, Lydia didn't care. She'd never been so grateful to have a man with fists clenched and eyes narrowed storming her direction.

Mr. Clemens recovered quickly from his shock and adjusted his coat before pulling out his notebook. "Ah, Hall. Glad to see you. How about you help a fellow investigator out and allow me a peek into the attic?"

"You're a reporter, not an investigator. Go home. You're not welcome here."

"Can't. I have a job to do. If you won't allow me into the attic, what about sharing some details? Anonymously, of course."

"Go. Home."

Undeterred by Abraham's crossed arms and wide stance, Mr. Clemens pressed on. "How would you describe the scene inside? A body chained to the wall? Food and water just out of reach? Just exactly how closely does the scene resemble Miss Pelton's story?"

Given the speed at which he rattled off the questions, he couldn't truly expect verbal answers. What was Mr. Clemens's strategy?

"Was Billy Poe as meticulous as always? Or now that he knows who Dupin is, has he taken to adding his own panache? Perhaps placing chocolates or roses with the dead body as a show of affection?"

When Abraham stiffened, Mr. Clemens's smile grew.

So that was it. Mr. Clemens was reading Abraham's unconscious responses. The body had a language all its own, and apparently Mr. Clemens was fluent—just like the Billy Poe she'd penned when she believed him valiant and superior. The flesh-driven part of her wanted to reach out and strangle Mr. Clemens for ruining Billy Poe. However, Spirit-filled conviction demanded she get hold of that murderous thought and discard it. Murder was not justice.

Maybe she was changing. Nevertheless, at the moment, it would be nice to shove aside conviction and give in to her fleshly desire to slug the man.

"Richards, escort him to the station. I will stay with Miss Pelton." Abraham glared at Mr. Clemens. "Let's see how you like cooling your heels in a jail cell."

"Are you charging me with something? Because if not, I'm free to go as I please. You cannot hold me."

"Detain him as a suspect in Mr. Ross's murder."

Clemens shook off Richards's reach for him. "What? That is an outlandish and falsified reason."

"Is it? Your description of the crime scene is reason enough."

"Anyone who's read her books could describe the scene up there. I haven't even seen it, and evidently I did a good job of it."

"Take him in. I'll be in to question him later."

Richards gripped Mr. Clemens's arm. "Come on, Eugene. I'm sure it will get straightened out at the station."

Mr. Clemens held his ground. "What did I say that makes you think you can blame me?" After a moment of silence from Abraham, his eyes widened and lit with delight. "It was the comment about chocolates and roses, wasn't it? It's the only thing not described in the story. So which was it? Flowers or chocolates?"

Abraham pointed toward the end of the street. "Get him out of here *now*!"

Mr. Clemens rubbed his hands together. "How's that for romantic overtures, Miss Pelton? It appears the Killer Queen of Romance has found her king."

No doubt he'd make that tomorrow's headline. At the rate he fanned the flames of Cincinnati's fury, she'd be burned alive at the stake before sunset.

Abraham stepped closer, fists clenched and ready to finish the job Marcus had started. That would never do.

Lydia jumped from the carriage and placed herself between the two men. Foolishness, she knew, but she wouldn't have Abraham getting in trouble for starting fisticuffs with Mr. Clemens, even if Mr. Clemens *was* Billy Poe.

Lifting her horseshoe-clutching hand, she jabbed a finger of her other hand toward Officer Richards. "Do what you've been told, Mr. Clemens. I'd hate to see you hurt."

Mr. Clemens eyed the piece of iron and laughed. "Are you trying to threaten me or wish me luck? Because I have to say, that is the oddest weapon I've ever seen."

Abraham reached around her and plucked the horseshoe from her hand. "Go with Richards, Clemens. The more uncooperative you are, the guiltier you seem."

Clemens glanced toward the row house, and his face lit with excitement. "Ah, so he left roses for her. A far cry from the earlier wildflowers."

Lydia stepped back, colliding with Abraham. There was no way he could have known about the wildflowers. Tipsy had most of them eaten before even she arrived.

Mr. Clemens really was Billy Poe.

Detective Lawson joined them, carrying a vase of pristine roses, their beauty defiled by the stench of decomposition. "You're not welcome here, Clemens. This is an active investigation. You can get your details at the station once we're done."

"I've already instructed Officer Richards to escort Clemens to Central for questioning." At Detective Lawson's responding scowl, he added, "He knew about the flowers."

"I only suggested there might be flowers or chocolates in response to Miss Pelton's enlightening comment." Mr. Clemens snagged a rose and sniffed it before making a face and extending it toward her. "You wanted overtures. It appears Mr. Poe is quite ready to give them. A man doesn't like to be rebuffed, so I'd be careful of your next move. Billy Poe has already proven himself unstable."

When she didn't accept the flower, he dropped it to the ground.

"What a shame. It appears I will have to spin this as a tale of unrequited love." He tsked and strode off with Officer Richards.

Lydia remained rooted against Abraham, afraid that if she pulled away from the strength he provided, she'd collapse. Would it not add to the scandal of the morning, she'd steal a page from her romance novels. She'd turn around, bury her face into his coat, smell his masculinity—perhaps a sandalwood or bergamot cologne—and allow his arms to wrap around her in a protective barrier from the horror that surrounded them.

"For a man as smart as Billy Poe seems to be, Clemens sure is painting himself guilty." Detective Lawson shook his head. "Unfortunately we only have circumstantial evidence, and he's smart enough to cast reasonable doubt if this were to go to court. We can't do anything. Yet." He shifted the vase to his other arm and retrieved a note from his pocket. "Mark my words, he's starting to slip up. It won't be long and we'll have him, and this is the first nail to his coffin."

Lydia accepted the note with trembling fingers and unfolded it.

Abraham snagged it from her hands. "It serves no purpose for you to read it."

While she appreciated his attempt to shield her, not knowing would make it worse. She turned and faced him. "I have an overactive imagination. It is best that I know the words rather than guess them."

His lips firmed into a hard line, but he flipped it open and read it aloud to her. "'To my Killer Queen. A gift to you as proof that I've long held you in regard, even before I knew who you were.'"

Her gaze flitted to the building. Did his words mean that Mr. Ross had suffered for more than a week? With the August heat, the need for a drop of water must have been of the utmost torture as he eyed the whole glass—perhaps watching in desperation as condensation rolled down the side and soaked into the wood.

Curse her imagination. It conjured the scene, the whole experience, with morbid clarity.

Though she shouldn't, she leaned her head against Abraham's chest. Instead of the soothing and romantic scent of sandalwood or bergamot, all she smelled was rotting flesh.

His arm came around her, and he squeezed her shoulder in a familiar yet brotherly way. Given that he couldn't stand to be in the same room as her less than twenty-four hours ago, she'd take the kind gesture and try not to allow her mind to spin it into something more. "Do you want me to stop reading?" he asked.

She shook her head and croaked out a no just in case he couldn't determine her answer.

He continued. "'Ross suffered less than he deserved, but thanks to you and me, at least his children will endure it no more. Dead bodies don't make for the greatest declarations of love, but I hope the justice I have served and these flowers will assure you of my unwavering ardor. Until we meet again, stay home—even from church. Stepping in to rescue you was an honor, but an unnecessary risk. It's easier to keep you safe at Plane Manor. Ever yours, Billy.'"

"What a horrid note." Tears stung her eyes and clogged her throat.

Glass clinked against wood, and she lifted her head.

Detective Lawson straightened from setting the flowers inside the carriage. "The only person who has ever called her the Killer Queen of Romance is Eugene Clemens, and he's the one to have stepped in to rescue her from the Keatons. It's not enough to arrest him, but it's a start."

"I don't think it's safe for Lydia to remain here." Abraham's voice rumbled against her ear. "I'll escort her back to Plane Manor and finish out the night there."

"Lydia, is it?" Surprise and incredulity lilted Detective Lawson's voice.

The bob of Abraham's throat pressed against Lydia's head. Obviously that had been a slip of the tongue.

She pushed away from him and swiped at her eyes. After a sniff to stop an embarrassing stream from her nose, she faced Detective Lawson. "Yes. I insisted that he call me by my Christian name. You should as well." She extended the offer more as a cover to the faux pas than out of genuine desire, but it couldn't be helped.

Detective Lawson glanced between them. Disbelief and suspicion crinkled the corners of his eyes. "If that is to be the case, then you must refer to me as Talbot."

"Thank you, Talbot. I'm sorry to have insisted I come, only to return so quickly."

He waved away her apology. "I will take her, Hall. You should head back home and rest."

"You just arrived at the scene. You should give it your experienced eye. I've already been here long enough for putrefaction to seep into my skin." Abraham pressed a hand to her back and directed her toward the carriage. "We'll compare notes when we meet later."

Detective Lawson frowned but did not argue further. And was she ever glad for that. He was nice enough, but Abraham was the man she wanted by her side right now.

The death flowers blocked her entrance to the carriage. What a diabolical display of romance. She picked up the vase with her fingertips to minimize contact. Those foul blooms were an appropriate display of Billy Poe's love. He'd taken something beautiful and meant for good and transformed it into something that she would forevermore revile. She transferred the vase to the ground, then settled herself on the bench. Let the rats find and devour them.

Abraham joined her on the same bench, leaving the opposite one empty. He adjusted his truncheon so it didn't smack against her as he shifted. A flush of warmth crept through her body.

This is not a scene from your romance novels. Stop. Don't let your mind go to hand-holding and secret kisses.

Drat. It was a mistake to even scold herself. She sat on her hands and clamped her mouth shut. She would behave. No lacing fingers through his and definitely no daydreaming about Detective Darcy finding a bride.

"Take care, Hall." Detective Lawson picked up the abandoned vase. "There is no guarantee Clemens didn't give Richards the slip, and I fear what he might do if he discovers there is any familiarity between you two. Jealousy is a dangerous emotion."

Abraham didn't deny the familiarity but nodded. "I'll see you in a few hours."

It was a valid concern. How many times had she employed jealousy as a villain's motive? She sidled closer, hoping neither man noticed, and retrieved the horseshoe from where it sat between them. It wasn't much, but if necessary, she'd protect Abraham and deliver some bad luck right to Billy Poe's face.

CHAPTER 22

IF MRS. HAWKING HADN'T AWAKENED Abraham before dinner and demanded he go home to bathe because he smelled like a decomposing carcass, he'd still be asleep on that sofa, despite the day being well past noon. Two baths later, the only thing about him that had changed was now he felt like a resurrected carcass instead of a rotting one. With the way his feet dragged and how heavy his limbs hung, he'd probably soon be mistaken for Frankenstein's monster and chased through the streets by a mob with pitchforks. His siblings had shown him no mercy. Why should strangers?

Clara had insisted he use her secret stash of face paint so that no one would mistake him for a raccoon, thanks to the punches from Sullivan and Xavier.

More bothered by Abraham's stench, Jake had stood as far down the hall as he could and pinched his nose. "What'd you do? Die in a barrel of perfume?"

Maybe Abraham shouldn't have doused himself so thoroughly with Cristiani's Florida Water Cologne.

He raked a hand through damp hair as he slogged up the Plane Manor drive to resume his duties. The spicy aroma of dandified corpse still clung to his skin, though he'd gone back to the tub and scrubbed until bright red. If Mrs. Hawking turned him away, he'd resort to a tomato bath. If it worked on skunk spray, it'd work on him.

Mrs. Hawking opened the door before he reached it, and gave him a wide berth as he passed.

"Detective Lawson wasn't pleased that you left Miss Pelton unprotected, but I convinced him you had no choice."

At the slight grin to her sharp-featured face, Abraham knew Lawson had discovered what a reckoning the housekeeper could inflict. Abraham had no doubt that the reason not a crack of outside light made it into the foyer when she closed the door was because even the curtains didn't dare neglect their duty under her command.

Mrs. Hawking continued. "Detective Lawson said he'll return after his interview with Mr. Clemens."

"Thank you. Where is everyone else?"

"Miss Lydia's in the parlor, Miss Theresa is caring for Tipsy in the carriage house, Colonel Plane is at the printshop, and the rest of the family is resting."

Abraham bristled. "They left her alone?"

After the attack through the window and the near abduction, shouldn't Dr. Pelton have at least confined Lydia to the second floor?

Mrs. Hawking sniffed as if personally offended by the accusation in his voice. "She's safe enough. Besides, you won't want to stay in there either, I wager. The girl's pacing and muttering up a storm. She must be arguing with her characters again."

Keen disappointment weighed upon him. So she still planned to fulfill her contract?

The woman was as persistent as a bad case of lice. How could she even consider continuing writing after last night? The putrid odor still coated his throat and tainted everything he ate or drank. She might not have witnessed the scene, but her experience from the street should have been enough to make her see reason.

He massaged his forehead. *God, give me the patience needed with this woman. You've called me to be her friend, but I don't know that I can silently accept her choice.*

"Thank you, Mrs. Hawking. I could use a full, bracing pot of coffee, if you have it."

"You'll need more than that with her. I'll put some cotton on the tray for your ears." She pivoted with a crisp about-face and marched down the hall.

God bless that woman, but it would take more than cotton to escape Lydia's antics.

On a well-rested day, he didn't know what to do with her. In his current state? She'd truss him up while spouting off some romantic delusion all before he could react.

But if Paul could live with a thorn in his side, then Abraham supposed he could live with Lydia as his.

At the parlor door, he rested his forehead against the cool wood. He just needed a moment to gather his wits before facing the chaos that was Lydia Pelton.

Agitated footsteps approached from the inside. He drew a fortifying breath. He wasn't ready, but clearly God thought he was.

"I just don't know what to do." Lydia's voice grew and faded as she passed the door and continued on. "I mean I know what to do, but I don't want to do it, God."

God? Was she using Him as a character in a book, or was she praying? If the latter, it would be indecent of him to continue listening, but if the former, he could linger outside a few minutes more.

"Writing has been everything to me. It's not just what I do; it's who I am. How am I to process this world, let alone impact it, without a pen in my hand?"

Her frustration and desperation kicked him in the gut. It was so easy to believe the worst of people, but Lydia was evidently wrestling with her desire to change. He'd intruded on a raw and unguarded conversation that she expected only God to witness. Abraham should walk away and allow her the solitude and space needed for such a deliberation. Lord knew how often he'd gone on solitary walks to achieve the same purpose.

He lifted his head to turn away but felt a staying hand on his shoulder. He peered around, but no one else stood in the hall.

Are You telling me to eavesdrop, Lord?

He scoured his memory for some verse that implied it was wrong, but nothing came to mind. *Lord, forgive me if I'm interpreting this moment incorrectly.*

It still didn't feel right, but he turned his ear to the crack between the door and wall.

Lydia's voice sounded from the other side of the room. The speed at which it grew closer meant she must be eating up the perimeter. "I don't even know what justice is supposed to look like anymore. If I quit writing, how am I to figure that out? Yes, I know I'm supposed to lean into You and Your Word, but even You spoke through stories. Of course, Yours brought people back to You, and all mine have done is lead to murder and riots."

The fast click of heels against wood indicated her steps continued, though her silence lingered for several long moments.

"What am I if not a writer? Are You sure there isn't another way for me to change into the woman You want me to be?"

Quiet and stillness settled like she waited for God to audibly speak.

An uncomfortable sense of responsibility sprouted within Abraham. Surely God did not expect him to be His spokesman. Just because Abraham believed Lydia should walk away from writing didn't mean God agreed. Perhaps Abraham should join Mrs. Hawking in the kitchen and leave Lydia to grapple alone.

The floor shook, and glass rattled against tabletops.

Had Lydia taken to stomping like a toddler?

A muffled scream of frustration stretched out before she yelled a clear, "Fine! I'll quit. No more mystery or romance novels."

Perhaps Lydia should write children's books instead. The temperamental tots and she had much in common.

"But You have to help. I'm not as courageous as my characters. I can't just march into Mr. O'Dell's office, slap a stack of advance money on his desk, and stride out the door. I just can't. Not alone. He'd eat me alive."

Please don't be asking me to do what I think You are, Lord.

Abraham almost laughed when struck with how similar his and

Lydia's prayers were. If he didn't think it absurd to declare so soon, he'd say they belonged together. That possibility created a spark of excitement that he wasn't exactly sure what to do about. He might complain even to himself about being thrust into a friendship with the woman, but in truth, he was eager to discover what it was about her that captivated him so.

Perhaps it was testing God, but Abraham gently pressed against the door. It creaked open.

All right then. He'd take that as a sign God wanted him to do this. He fully opened the door. "You wouldn't be going alone."

Lydia screeched and whirled around, lifting that ridiculous horseshoe in the air.

He approached with raised hands to assure her he meant no harm. "If you need the support of a friend, I will accompany you."

Her arm lowered, and she gaped like a widemouth bass.

A chuckle escaped at the bizarre comparison. He really must be tired beyond reason to compare the curly-haired beauty in front of him to a slimy, cold-blooded lake dweller.

He stopped outside of swinging range. A horseshoe thrown by her may not pose any real danger, but he'd rather not end up with a headache. "Do you really believe a horseshoe can protect you?"

"Well, no, but I can't imagine it would feel too good hitting your face."

"True, but there's no need to lob it at me. I'm not here to hurt you." He slowly reached for it, arching a brow in question. He wouldn't put it past her to test how hard she could swing.

Her head tilted, and she peered at him with a calculating squint. "Are you afraid of me?"

Not in the sense she meant, but he'd never admit that his glimmer of attraction for her frightened him senseless. "You are unpredictable, but I'm confident that I can handle anything you attempt."

"Is that so?" Mischievousness illuminated her face and curved her lips. "Tell me, Abraham, are you confident enough to make a wager?"

"It wouldn't be right to take your money."

"I propose a wager that entails nothing more than bragging rights. I bet I can knock you right off your feet. If I'm wrong, you get to brag that you can read me better than a novel. If I win, I get to brag that I outwitted a real detective."

Abraham studied Lydia from head to toe. She wasn't too much shorter than him, and she was solid enough to make him *oomph* when thrown into him, but there was no way she'd take him down. "I will not wrestle with a woman."

Her squeaky mouse laughter bubbled out. "I don't need to wrestle you to win. Trust me, brains win over brawn every time."

Perhaps not every time, but he had both to work with in this particular instance. "Fine. I'll allow you one shot, but no weapons allowed." He nodded at the horseshoe.

"Agreed, and just to show you I can play fair, you may take my sole weapon." She extended the horseshoe toward him.

There was something not quite right with this offering. Did she expect to yank him off balance? That would be the most likely tactic, and one easily avoided. He spread his stance before wrapping his larger hand around the iron. Their knuckles brushed, but he ignored the tingling sensation as he prepared to thwart her plan.

The grin that spread across her face screamed a premature victory.

Just as he anticipated, she jerked her arm backward.

He remained firmly planted, but Lydia flew forward. She crashed into him, and he dropped the horseshoe to catch her around her waist before she fell. Once she was secure against his chest, he looked down to declare his victory.

Her brown eyes danced with humor, and before he could react, she popped to her toes with lips puckered.

CHAPTER 23

JUST BEFORE LYDIA'S LIPS CRASHED into Abraham's, her brain caught up to her impulse. What was she doing? The touch of his chapped lips lasted less than a second, but the feel of them branded her a hoyden.

They thrust apart at the same time. He stepped back to keep his balance, but caught the corner of the low table. Lydia flung out an arm to catch him. Instead, she whacked him across the nose as he fell.

The thud of his landing shook the floor, and for a moment she feared he'd cracked his head against the edge of the sofa. One leg draped across the table, foot dangling in the air, while the rest of his body sprawled across the rug. Watery eyes peered at her like she was a lunatic, and his hands shot to cover his nose.

Oh heavens. Had she broken it, and blood gushed already?

She dropped to her knees beside him, determined to assist like Papa might. But what should she do? Abraham didn't need his pulse checked. By the glare he leveled at her, his heart was furiously beating. Should she check for broken bones? Perhaps a busted rib or fractured arm? No, the only thing likely to be broken on him was his nose. She reached to pry his hands away, but he averted his face so quickly he banged against the floor. A muffled word she likely didn't want to hear escaped.

She winced with sympathetic pain. The poor man had been

nothing but kind, and here she'd done with great success just as she'd promised. Blast her competitive nature. Abraham was sure to regret his offer now and condemn her to facing Mr. O'Dell alone. Perhaps it was best to make light of the situation.

"It seems I've knocked you off your feet." The chuckle she meant to give came out as a choked whimper.

He sat up and released his nose with a flinch. "I'm the one who gets kissed, trips, then receives a blackened nose, and somehow you're the one crying?"

She sob-laughed but couldn't get any words out. It really was absurd. If anyone should be crying, it should be him. Although that felt equally laughable. Men cried, she knew, but over a kiss and being hit by a girl? Maybe if she were in pinafores and Abraham in short pants. Which actually made quite an adorable and distracting picture. He must have been devilishly cute, and probably a holy terror, if what she heard about raising boys was to be believed. Abraham, the rascal child, now an upstanding officer. What a contrast.

A smile sneaked through, and she sniffled into her handkerchief to hide it. If the man could read her mind, he'd abandon this tenuous friendship for the safety of Cincinnati's riotous streets.

Abraham shook his head as he rose to his feet, and then offered her a hand up.

She accepted, unsure if the warmth that shot through her at the feel of his firm grip was embarrassment or pleasure. Either way, her face was sure to be the color of Marcus's editing ink.

Once she was standing, he put more distance between them and folded his arms. "I underestimated you. A kiss and a shove, all to win a wager? How often have you pulled that stunt?"

The heat in her face blazed into an inferno. Her lips had never touched a man's until now—not that Abraham would ever believe that after such a flippant display. Twenty-two years of saving her first kiss for a romantic encounter with the man she loved, and she'd tossed it aside to win a bet. What was wrong with her? It didn't matter that it was Abraham, her own personal Detective Darcy. She'd conducted herself as carelessly with that gift, that blessed treasure of a first kiss, as she had with her words.

Words that must come to an end.

Thankfully, the unpleasant duty of meeting with Mr. O'Dell would serve as a distraction from that lackluster kiss.

She cleared her throat and focused on the table's askew doily. As she slid it back into place, she asked, "Will you still go with me to break my contracts?"

"Avoiding the question does not reflect well on you. Am I to take it you've employed that tactic often?"

Her head jerked up. "No! You're the first and only. I'm sorry. That did not go how I intended. It's my stupid competitiveness. I don't know what I was thinking. I should have never—"

"Lydia. Stop. I can see your mortification. I believe you." His voice held a nasal quality that hadn't been there earlier.

Oh dear. His nose must be swelling. Now every time he spoke, she'd be reminded of her scandalous behavior. Even worse, she'd feel the momentary brush of their lips. How could she ever look at him again? He'd see the red and know what she was thinking.

If she did write another book, she'd turn this whole scene into a comedy. Or maybe she'd write it as a tragedy and let the heroine die of embarrassment right on the spot. She certainly wished she had.

"We'll move forward as if nothing happened." His eyes dropped to her lips, then immediately darted to the door. "I am still your friend, and I will go with you."

"Thank you. We had better leave before I lose my courage." Or did something else to jeopardize their friendship.

"I'll be right by your side." He pressed a guiding hand to the small of her back, then seemed to think better of it. His hand dropped like a boulder off a cliff. By the speed of his stride to enter the foyer ahead of her, his shoes had caught fire.

She shook her head. He'd be right by her side, eh? More like scurrying out of reach so she couldn't pounce on him again. Moving forward like nothing happened must have a different meaning for him than her.

He was almost outside when she caught up to him.

Placing the half-closed door as a barrier between them, he directed her to stay inside until the carriage pulled up. "I'm going to search the grounds for any sign that Poe is watching."

His exit felt like a retreat as the door shut nearly on her nose.

She parted the curtains wide enough to peer out with one eye.

Abraham stared skyward as if praying or, more likely, complaining to God about her. After a moment, he slapped his hat against his leg, repositioned it on his head, and strode out of view.

This was going to be a long and awkward ride to O'Dell's.

Twenty minutes later, Lydia burst from the coffin-like carriage into the glorious fresh air in front of the bank. Who would have ever thought she'd consider the repugnant summer smells of horse droppings, urine, and factory smoke pleasant? She waited until Abraham turned to give the driver instructions before gasping, then drawing in slow, deep, clearing breaths.

She'd been right about the ride being long and awkward, but she had no idea it would be because of Abraham's . . . unique scent. When he'd sat diagonally from her, she'd believed he wanted to put distance between him and her potential leap across the seat to kiss him.

Then the minutes passed.

Hot, stagnant air captured the truth and made it more potent with each passing street. She'd discreetly coughed and then shifted to sipping breaths. When her eyes began to water, she'd dabbed at them with her scented handkerchief and prayed he assumed she was still upset over the knocking-him-off-his-feet stunt. He didn't ask, and she didn't offer an explanation. They'd spent the entire ride staring silently in opposite directions at the closed curtains.

Never in her life had she been so glad to exit a carriage—and she'd pulled off many escapades where that had been welcomed. The unpleasantness of the city air returned, abandoning its brief victory of being considered fresh. Still, it was a relief to breathe normally. Never again would she smell Florida Water Cologne without gagging. If ever she reached the point of giving Abraham gifts, the first one would be a new cologne.

After one final cleansing breath, she focused on the imposing stone monstrosity in front of her. She'd chosen the bank because of its proximity to O'Dell Publishing—a blessing for more than one reason should she be able to convince Abraham to walk rather than ride the remaining distance.

She smelled Abraham before she felt his touch on her arm.

"Stay close. The closed carriage is drawing too much attention," he mumbled. "We should have taken an open-air hack."

On that note she could agree, but most likely not for the same reason as his.

He offered his arm and nodded toward the entrance. "Shall we?"

Her eyes slid to the decorative wood doors, and her chest constricted. The one benefit to Abraham's odor was she'd been too focused on not smelling it to think about her dilemma. But here it was. The beginning of the end. The climax of her story. Except she was the villain, and hers would not be a happy ending.

Together they walked through the busy foyer and selected the shortest line. Abraham stood rigidly next to her, inspecting the room as if searching for danger. Which, likely, he was, and he should. Only yesterday had the Keatons tried to abduct her. She shivered against the memory but immediately suppressed the shiver, and the memory, when Abraham's attention snapped to her.

He arched a brow in silent question.

"I'm fine."

His doubtful gaze lingered on hers for several beats, then returned to its vigilant watch. "I'm right here. No one is going to hurt you or take you from me."

His words, accompanied by a reassuring tightening of his linked arm, were worth a swoon. Detective Darcy needed a story and a girl of his own—a heroine just like her to keep him on his toes and provide many opportunities for danger and adventure.

Her heart pinched, and her soaring thoughts crashed. She would not be the one to write those stories. She meant what she'd promised God. She'd do what He wanted, even if that meant she never wrote again.

"Next."

Lydia stepped to the window and cast a sidelong glance at Abraham. Papa had signed for her to open the bank account, but not even he knew how much she'd tucked away between her thirteen romance and nine mystery novels' payments. "I'd like to withdraw three hundred and forty dollars in large bills, please."

She couldn't miss the surprise on Abraham's face when the cashier slid the money and a receipt with her remaining balance through the opening in the wire wickerwork grate. Even after such a large withdrawal, she had over two thousand dollars to her name. With no real expenses, she'd been able to save most of what she earned. She'd dreamed of surprising her future husband with it, so they could buy a house somewhere between her parents' and Theresa's. Her account wouldn't grow after today, but it would still suffice for at least a modest home.

Lydia stepped aside, separated the money into two folded stacks, and tucked them into her reticule. She delayed facing Abraham's unspoken response to her wealth by playing with the purse strings. "It's the advance for two books as well as interest. I know Mr. O'Dell well enough to be prepared for his demands."

"Come along. That sum alone is enough to make someone target you." He guided her toward the side exit.

Not two steps later, a familiar voice spoke from behind them. "I see the killing business pays well."

Lydia swung around to face Mr. Clemens and a companion, who eagerly pulled out a notebook and pencil.

"Put that away, Egleston. This story's mine." Mr. Clemens appraised her like one might a roast at the butcher's.

Her mouth dried at the hunger she saw there. Whether Billy Poe or not, the man's ambition scared her more than the tiger at Adam Beadle's circus. Abraham pulled her closer to himself, and she scooted until his strong frame supported her whole side. Maybe his scent would transfer to her and force Mr. Clemens outside.

"Not this time. I need the story more than you do." His companion cut in front of him.

"You steal this one, and I'll ensure Josephine knows that you borrowed money from me to pay your gambling debts."

"Committing blackmail in front of an officer, Clemens? I thought you were smarter than that." Abraham reached into his coat as if fishing for his handcuffs.

Mr. Clemens raised his hands in surrender. "Egleston, the story's yours."

The man smiled and immediately scratched out a few lines on his notepad. "So, Miss Pelton, have you discarded Billy Poe's affections for another?" He eyed Abraham's proximity to her.

Mr. Clemens scowled. "Must have, if she's insisting on standing that close to a man who smells like he belongs in a morgue."

Lydia lifted her chin. If she was going to be in the newspapers, she would provide information for her benefit. "Detective Hall is escorting me for the sake of protection. I am on my way to break my contract with Mr. O'Dell. There will be no more Billy Poe novels."

"What?" Mr. Clemens's voice echoed off the stone walls.

"This is marvelous! I'm finally going to undercut you with a story and win a spot on the front page." Mr. Egleston scribbled furiously. "Why the change of heart?"

"The Billy Poe I created is not the brute who claims his persona. I can no longer, in good conscience, write stories that twist justice into vengeance."

"Some of those men deserved their deaths." Mr. Clemens stepped forward.

Abraham shifted her behind himself, but she peeked her head around to continue talking.

"It is not our place to serve as judge, jury, and executioner. We must abide by the decision of those God has placed in authority, even if we don't agree. He has His reasons."

"I'd like to see if you still hold that opinion when a crime has been committed against you." Hostile intent burned from Clemens's eyes, and the hair on the back of Lydia's neck lifted.

Lydia ducked back behind Abraham and grasped his jacket. Best to leave the situation to an officer of the law.

"That is enough. Egleston, you've got your story. Clemens, remove yourself from the premises or be charged with disorderly conduct." This time, Abraham really did remove his cuffs from his coat—their clinking sounded as threatening as his words.

"I haven't done anything to warrant that, and you know it."

The way Abraham leaned forward, Mr. Clemens must have done the same. She peered around the room, and patrons observed with open curiosity. Whispers and fingers pointed at her indicated she was no longer a nameless customer. She and Abraham needed to leave before someone other than the reporters decided to approach them.

Egleston gushed over the display. "Won't this be a juicy piece to add to my story. You squaring off with her new lover. Excellent."

"I am not her lover." Abraham's words were sharp and unyielding. "And I'll not have you slander her or my reputations."

"Then I'll use the term *beau*. People can make of it what they want. All that matters is, Poe's lady love has dropped him and his books." Egleston snapped his notebook closed and darted out the door.

This was turning into a disaster.

"You're going to regret this outing, Hall. And Miss Pelton?" Mr. Clemens stepped closer, and Abraham immediately thrust a distancing hand to his chest. "Don't think you're safe from Poe just because he declared his ardor. He's a dangerous man, and regardless of your choices, I don't want anything to happen to you."

Mr. Clemens stormed out of the bank, leaving a wake of whispers and gawking.

Abraham spun toward the exit and hastened them out the door. Though her legs trembled, she followed him into the carriage. After what had happened inside, she didn't want to walk anywhere. Being trapped with a man who smelled like a perfumed corpse was better than becoming one.

CHAPTER 24

ABRAHAM WATCHED LYDIA THROUGH A side-glance. The ride between the bank and O'Dell Publishing was hardly sufficient for her to regain her composure. Even with the carriage's curtains pulled back, she looked wan and frightened. The fact his name was about to appear in the papers as Poe's competition for Lydia's hand didn't sit well with him either. Not that the idea of being Lydia's beau wasn't enticing, but the announcement could escalate Poe to violence toward him—or worse, toward Lydia. Though the desire to hold and comfort her ate at him, Abraham remained anchored in place. Friendship was all he could offer. That, and his protection and determination to find and arrest Billy Poe.

When he and Lydia arrived, picketers maintained their demands for accountability. Abraham instructed the driver to find an entrance at the back of the building. The alley was free of obstructions, and nothing that indicated a threat hid in the slanted afternoon shadows. Still, tension pulled at Abraham's shoulders as he assisted Lydia from the carriage and ushered her to the door. Not surprisingly, it was locked.

"I'll bang on Marcus's office window and have him let us in." Lydia took a few steps deeper into the alley but paused when he followed. "Wait here. I'm not sure how he'll respond if he sees you with me."

The placating smile she offered did little to comfort him, but it was only a dozen feet. He would still be close enough if trouble occurred.

Lydia peered through Monroe's window, then rapped.

It opened in a rush. "What are you doing here? It isn't safe."

Even from this distance, Abraham could see the distress pinching her face. He took a few steps toward her, but she waved a hand below the view of the window to stop him.

"I must speak with Mr. O'Dell."

"Climb in. I'll take you to him." The window lifted the full height, and Monroe's arms stretched out.

Lydia stepped out of reach, and the reprimanding tone that accompanied her words would make any mother proud. "I am a lady, Marcus. I absolutely will not climb through that window. Come open the door like a gentleman."

There was some mild grumbling before he closed the window.

She rejoined Abraham and folded her arms. "I swear, the man thinks I'm just like the characters in my books."

"Not to defend him, but you did steal a goat from the circus while dressed as a clown."

A mischievous smile softened her frustration. "And I've walked George Street in the dead of night, pretended to be a server at a gambling den, and shot a rifle, all for research. But have no fear; a target could be three feet in front of me, and I'd probably miss."

"That's more worrisome than knowing you could hit a man at twenty yards. If you're going to shoot, you should do it right." In fact, all of it was worrisome. George Street? She was lucky she hadn't walked away ruined or ended up dead.

"Are you volunteering to teach me?" She fluttered her lashes and clasped her hands to her chest in dramatic fashion. "You are my beau, after all."

The door flew open.

"He's your *what*?" Surprise and outright anger burst from Monroe.

Of all Egleston's words for her to have chosen to proclaim at that moment.

"She was jesting," Abraham said.

"Don't be silly. He'll read about it in the papers soon enough." Lydia looped her arm around Abraham's and smiled sweetly at Marcus. "Thank you for letting us in."

She and Abraham passed Monroe, who struggled to subdue his temper into a mask of composure. Abraham stiffened. Giving his back to Monroe opened the chance for the man to stab him with a pen. Thankfully Monroe must have left it behind.

"Is Mr. O'Dell in his office?" Lydia's voice feigned lightness, but underneath, Abraham discerned fear.

"You had better let me announce you. He was in a foul mood this morning." Monroe cut between them with such force, Lydia was forced apart from Abraham.

After catching her balance on the wall, she glared at Monroe. "I know you're upset, Marcus, but really? Was that necessary?"

"It couldn't be helped. The hall's not wide enough for the three of us." He stalked ahead of them and banged on O'Dell's door before disappearing inside.

Abraham lowered his voice. "You shouldn't antagonize him. Now we are both targets, which makes protecting you even harder."

"Nonsense. You're a police officer. You'll be fine. You deal with danger all the time."

How could a woman who wrote the stories she did and had a coroner as a father be so naive? "This isn't a romance novel, Lydia. Officers don't have immunity from death. Every day is a day I might not come home. Just last week, Officer Chumley was murdered *inside* the Ninth Street station house with three officers standing right next to him."

Wide-eyed horror mirrored his own reaction when he'd first heard the news. He should regret his bluntness, but she needed to know this was serious.

Her head shook in violent denial. "That won't happen to you."

Would that her proclamation could make it true. He clasped her shoulders and tilted his chin down so that she couldn't escape his gaze. "It could, especially with a jealous madman on the loose."

"Oh, Abraham. I'm so sorry. I . . ." Her eyes' shimmering depths declared she really did care for him.

She kissed you to win a bet.

The reminder was supposed to be a warning, but it just made his attention flick lower. What she'd done couldn't be called a kiss, and her absolute mortification had proven it done without thought. Still, the soft whisper of her lips against his had shot through him with shocking force and left a lingering desire to see what something longer might feel like.

O'Dell's door opened, and Monroe stepped out. "You may come in." The frost in his words matched the stabbing icicles of his glare.

Lydia stepped out of Abraham's hold and offered Monroe a weak smile as she entered the office. Abraham followed, and Monroe shoved a shoulder against his back under the guise of standing too close while shutting them all, himself included, into the room.

O'Dell didn't bother to rise. "You had better have that manuscript with you, Miss Pelton. Someone broke in last night and destroyed our largest press. We're rushing the edits for both your latest romance and your newest Poe novel. I need them out while your popularity still allows for twenty-five-cent sales instead of the normal fifteen."

The greed of that man astounded Abraham.

Lydia looked to him, and the earlier fear and insecurities she'd confessed to God showed on her face. Abraham had promised he'd stay by her side, and that was what he'd do. He stepped forward and laid an encouraging hand to her back. No words passed between them, but he felt the deep breath she took for courage. She lifted her chin and reached into her reticule.

"Actually, I've come to return the advance given to me for the next Billy Poe novel." She laid the folded money on the desk and stiffened her posture. "I won't be writing it or any future novels."

"What?" That brought the man and his large girth out of his chair. "You cannot break your contract."

"On the contrary, according to the penalty clause, my contract can be broken provided the advance is returned with forty percent interest."

Forty percent? Abraham knew moneymongers who required less.

O'Dell sputtered for a moment, then regained his slimy, self-assured composure. "Without a Poe novel, I won't publish your next contracted romance. You'll owe me the advance plus forty percent for that one too."

"I expected as much." She retrieved more money and laid it on the table. "This is the full sum plus interest for breaking both contracts. There will be no future submissions from me. I will not be picking up a pen again."

Monroe rushed forward and turned her toward him. "You can't let them win. You must keep writing."

Abraham forced himself to remain rooted in place. Lydia made no attempt to remove herself from Monroe's grip, nor did she appear more uneasy than before. Unless she or Monroe gave him a legitimate reason, Abraham would not intervene, no matter how much he desired to pull her to safety.

Lydia shook her head. "I can't."

"What you do is more than write words. You give hope and justice to those who cannot find it any other way. Think of the letters you've received. This is your purpose in life. You can't give it up."

Her face softened with compassion and strength. "No, Marcus. I'm finished pretending I know better than God. Those men were exonerated, and whether I agreed with that decision or not, I didn't have the right to condemn them to death. I will not be responsible for one more lost life."

"You aren't responsible for their deaths. They are just words. Meaningless words."

Monroe stood as a pillar of contradictions. First, what she did was more than words, but now those words were meaningless? It was the sort of twisted logic a man like Billy Poe might believe.

Lydia folded her arms and cocked her head. "If they are so meaningless, why are five men dead, three fearing for their lives, and Cincinnati crying out for my own indictment? All words have meaning and power, Marcus. And I have wielded that power in the worst possible way. I cannot do it any longer. Please don't ask me to."

He stepped back from her, his face twisted in betrayal and disgust.

O'Dell rounded his desk. "You're making a mistake. With your popularity, you could become a very rich woman." He waved the money from his desk in the air. "This is only the start of what you will be losing."

"Saving a man's life is worth the cost. Good day, gentlemen. Our association is now over." Lydia pivoted toward the door, and Abraham rejoined her side. For a brief moment, her hand clasped his, as if she were garnering the courage to walk out, then she grasped the brass knob.

Mr. O'Dell cleared his throat. "Not quite so fast, Miss Pelton. Given that your manuscript was due soon, I assume that you have a good portion of it already written. Is that true?"

Lydia remained facing the door. "It is."

"And do you still have that unfinished manuscript?"

"I do."

"I will purchase your unfinished manuscript for the price of your Billy Poe advance, minus the interest. Marcus is familiar enough with your writing. He can finish it."

She glanced at Abraham, then slowly turned around.

No. She couldn't be considering that offer. Her savings might have suffered from her choice, but if her bank statement were any indication, she could well leave that money behind and still have plenty to buy whatever baubles she desired.

Abraham whispered, "Don't be tempted. Remember what's at stake."

She took a step closer to O'Dell. "You do know if you were to publish it, a man might die?"

"The police will catch him long before that. This book has the potential to give him a second chance at life. Just think. He'll have

205

escaped a jury and a vigilante. It might very well be the thing that turns him into a model citizen."

The slithering snake. Given the man was Clemens's uncle, it must run in the family.

A glimmer of hope sparked in Lydia's eyes before a frown dug its furrows in her forehead. The war of uncertainty showed her as susceptible as Eve to Lucifer's tongue. O'Dell knew the lengths Lydia had gone to be published, had heard her arguments for quitting, and now, instead of releasing her, he sought to entrap her by her desires.

That might have worked if she were alone, but Abraham would not stand idly by. Ultimately the decision was hers, but he would fight for her even when she battled against herself.

He slipped his arm around Lydia's and leaned in. "Why are you debating? You know what you came here to do and why. Nothing has changed."

Her head snapped toward his, and their noses brushed. The painful reminder of her victorious bet shot straight through and made him flinch.

Lydia angled away and offered an apologetic smile. "Sorry, and thank you." The next response she directed at O'Dell. "As tempting as your offer is, I cannot accept. Good day."

"Both advances, then."

She shook her head and turned her back, Abraham gladly following her lead.

"Both advances *with* the interest returned."

She stilled, and Abraham could feel the battle resuming.

O'Dell sensed it as well and jumped on her indecision. "Three hundred and forty dollars is more than I've ever paid for a manuscript, and you don't even have to finish it. You'll get the money and potentially save a man's soul."

Abraham closed his eyes and waited for the battle to be lost. Change was too hard. The temptation too great. Greed always won out, leaving someone to be hurt in the end.

"No." The single, confident word left no room for more argument. Lydia released Abraham's arm and exited without a backward glance.

In that moment, Abraham could honestly say he'd never been prouder of another person. He grinned as he trailed her into the hall and closed the door on O'Dell's attempts to offer a more enticing bribe.

O'Dell's muffled voice rose, but Lydia kept marching.

By the time she reached the corner, Abraham had caught up. "I'm proud of you."

"Thank you. I don't know that I could have walked away without you there." Her steps slowed, and a heaviness seeped into her tone. "The money didn't tempt me so much as the thought that maybe there was still a purpose for my writing. What if he was right and this last story didn't bring judgment but restoration?" As they reached the door, her eyes found Abraham's. "What if my stories actually made a positive difference?"

The desperate, broken wistfulness pleaded with him to understand, and made his chest ache with compassion for her. "God may not be calling you away from writing forever. He may choose to restore that part of your life some day in the future."

"Not after what my stories have done. There is no hope of restoration for my writing."

He cupped her cheek and prayed she heard his next words down to her very soul. "With Christ, there is always hope. After all, He's the Author of life."

"And I have been the author of death." She pulled away and walked into the alley.

"You give yourself too much power, Lydia. Remember, it's sin, not literature, that corrupts a man's heart."

Her eyes shimmered with sadness as she stopped at the hack's step. "You can't use my words against me when you don't even believe them yourself."

"Maybe I didn't at first, but I do now." He grasped her hand under the guise of aiding her, but he didn't let go as he joined her inside. The need to be physically connected to her as he spoke was too strong. "You and this case have challenged my thinking. I still disagree with the existence of your Billy Poe novels, but the deaths of these men are not your responsibility. Stop writing for now, but be open to the possibility that, after a time, God may call you back to it." He reluctantly released her hand to sit across from her.

The tender way she regarded him made him reconsider his declaration that they forget about her kiss.

Monroe burst out of the building's rear exit. "Lydia, don't leave!"

Curse that man. Abraham closed the carriage door before Monroe could reach them, but Lydia leaned out the window.

"I'm sorry, Marcus, but it's over. I can't do this anymore."

"You don't have to. Just give me the manuscript, and I'll write something you'll be proud of."

"There is no ending to a Billy Poe novel that I could be proud of. He's ruined it for me. Goodbye." She pulled back from the opening.

"I'll pay you whatever you want. Double, even triple, what he offered inside."

She heaved a sigh and leaned back out. "It's not about the money."

"Maybe not for you. He *needs* that story, Lydia. He's already spent the money from advance orders on those special edition reprints."

"That was his poor decision, not mine."

"Then do it for me. O'Dell will fire me if I don't get this story from you."

Abraham frowned. Desperation made a man dangerous. It was time for them to leave. He tapped on the roof and silently indicated for Lydia to take her seat.

"I'm sorry, Marcus. My answer's still no."

The carriage jerked into motion, and Abraham steadied her with a hand until she sat across from him.

Monroe ran alongside them, his shouts filling the carriage's small space. "After all I have done for you, you would treat me like this?"

Abraham tugged the curtain closed. There was no reason for her to witness such a demonstration.

"You're making a mistake! People will forget you, but they'll never forget Billy Poe." Monroe's words became breathless, but they held no less sting as they echoed down the alley. "You're abandoning your legacy, your purpose! *What are you if you're not a writer?*"

Lydia flinched as if Monroe had physically landed a punch.

Abraham slipped to her side and wrapped an arm around her shoulders. "You did the right thing."

Tears slid down her cheeks as she clenched wads of her skirt together. "Just keep telling me that until I believe it. In my head, I know it's true, but my heart is breaking. He's right. What am I, if not a writer? How will I accomplish anything good in this world now?"

She turned into him, and her silent tears turned into soft cries. Abraham brought his other arm around her and held her like he might Clara . . . only this was different. Far different. Lydia nestled in and fit like she belonged there. There was no brotherly desire to pat her on the back, make a joke, and let her go when they were done.

"We'll get through this, Lydia. Whether you're a writer or not, God has a purpose for you. After this is over, we'll figure out together what that purpose is. In the meantime, let's focus on keeping you safe and tracking down Poe."

After today's fiascoes, Poe had more than enough reason to seek Lydia out. And Abraham doubted very much it would be to deliver flowers and a love note.

CHAPTER 25

BY THE TIME THE CARRIAGE rolled onto Theresa's drive, Lydia had composed herself. The knowledge she'd never write again still made the idea of curling up under her bedcover for the rest of her life appealing, but Abraham's presence and silent support made facing the world bearable. Barely, but enough. If only she could hold his hand or lean into him whenever the brokenness of her situation overwhelmed her and threatened to drown her. Yes, knowing God was with her at all moments was a consolation, but there was no denying the relief Abraham's physical presence brought.

How was it that a man she'd met twelve days ago and agreed to friendship with only yesterday had become her anchor? She'd written plenty of romance novels with fast friendships and whirlwind romances, but she hadn't actually believed them realistic. Was it possible she was living a dream? Considering the fantastical turn everything had taken with her Billy Poe novels coming to life in the most horrific manner possible, she shouldn't be surprised that her romance novels decided to vie for a position in her reality. But was this reality? Or would Abraham, like a fictional detective, disappear once the book was closed on the Billy Poe case?

He ducked out of the carriage to the graveled drive and turned to assist her. His tender and compassionate smile promised her that he wasn't going anywhere, but her imagination was an atrocity that shouldn't be trusted. She was simply reading too much into his expression. It didn't matter that crying in his arms made her feel loved, cherished, and safe. He was her friend—whether temporary or a forever sort—and that was all.

His warm hand wrapped around hers, and a zing traveled up her arm.

No. No. *No!* Zings and locked, longing gazes were only supposed to happen in romances. They didn't happen in real life.

Yet here she stood, half ducked at the door, completely unable to remove her attention from the molasses-colored eyes that made her heart thud harder. Friends didn't stare into each other's eyes for no other reason than to enjoy the sight of them. That was what lovers did. She flicked her gaze away, but instead of going somewhere safe, it found his lips.

You have to stop this, Lydia. He is not the hero of your novel, nor are you the heroine.

Her foot overshot the narrow metal step, and she tumbled forward. Abraham moved quicker than her fall, and she found herself tucked safely within his arms.

Or rather, hanging from them.

The tips of her toes dug into the gravel, and her knees hovered inches above the ground, thanks to his strong hold.

Abraham's voice rumbled against her cheek where it pressed against his chest. "If you were trying to knock me off my feet again, you missed your target. My lips are higher up."

Good gracious. Had he noticed her attention on his mouth? Her face flamed even though she could hear the jesting in his tone. If he jested, that was a good sign, right? Inside jokes between friends were special—especially those that referenced a kiss. Friends kissed on occasion, right? Not that she'd ever kissed Theresa, Nora, or Flossie, but the French did, didn't they? Surely the Hall and Pelton surnames had some French history somewhere . . .

He hefted her higher, and she gained her feet—although they weren't much in helping her to stand when her legs were as firm as jam under this man's amused smile and supportive grip. He didn't even smell like a perfumed corpse to her anymore.

This is not a romance novel. Stop it. Now.

Lydia let loose a nervous giggle and stepped away, not at all sure that she'd be able to stay upright. "I thought we were moving forward as if that never happened."

"Some embarrassing moments are too good to let go. Especially when I'm presented with an opportunity to bring them up again."

"I'll keep my lips to myself from now on, thank you very much. And that's a promise."

A suppressed grin peeked out. "Don't make promises you can't keep."

"Oh, and you think we're bound to kiss again?"

"I'm saying, if the possibility exists, you shouldn't make promises against it. I am your beau, after all."

At his wink, a true swoon threatened to overtake her. Another inside joke? Or did he not consider it humorous at all? Was there truly a possibility for them?

"You can't court her. It's unprofessional." Detective Lawson's reprimand, harsh and unyielding, came from behind Abraham.

The teasing dropped from Abraham's expression, and he stepped aside, creating distance between them and a clear view to his partner. "We're not courting. It was a jest in reference to a reporter's interpretation of my escorting Lydia to break her contract."

"Reporter? What—" Detective Lawson's scowl swung toward her. "Wait. You've broken your contract? The one for more Billy Poe novels?"

"I have. There will be no more Billy Poe or romance novels from me."

He stared at her as if not comprehending.

"There can't be more bodies if I don't write any more books. I should've never written them in the first place."

He blinked at Abraham. "And you allowed her to do this?"

"Of course. I encouraged it, even."

Detective Lawson massaged his forehead for a moment, then gestured for them to walk toward Plane Manor. "You are young and shortsighted. If we don't catch Poe before he fulfills the other novels, we will have no way to predict his next victim."

Lydia stumbled at the implication. "Are you saying you fear the other three men will die before you catch him and that you need more potential victims for him to claim?" The thought was horrifying. "I cannot condone or be a part of such a plan."

"We'll catch him. Have no fear." Abraham's confidence reassured her like a soft touch. "We won't need future novels to lure him out."

Mrs. Hawking opened the door, and Lydia led the men into the parlor.

Theresa popped to her feet from the sofa and rushed to her. After a brief inspection of Lydia's face, Theresa pulled her into an embrace. "You did it, didn't you? Oh, Lydia, I'm so sorry."

She pulled back, and the friendship from their youth that bound them in sisterhood meant nothing else needed to be said. Theresa knew the depths of Lydia's pain in walking away from writing, and Lydia knew by the ferocity of Theresa's expression that the woman was ready to go to war for her. If Billy Poe wasn't arrested soon, Theresa would blow the battle horn and call their clan of Guardians together for a trap-plotting session.

"I'll be okay." Lydia put up a courageous front. "But I wouldn't be opposed to your sitting with me for a while." A much safer alternative to the possibility of Abraham claiming a position next to her on the sofa.

Obviously she was too emotional to think clearly. Her imagination was reveling in the freedom to take every kind gesture from him as the potential for something more.

Detective Lawson claimed the seat directly in front of Lydia. Abraham chose to stand farther away, but there was a protectiveness in the way he watched her—like he was prepared to step in and rescue her should Lawson's questioning become too much.

Theresa pressed Lydia's hands and drew her attention—and, thankfully, her imagination—away from Abraham. "How did O'Dell take the news? Was it as terrible as you thought it would be?"

"I think he took it better than Marcus, but Mr. O'Dell did practically beg to buy the unfinished manuscript from me."

Detective Lawson scooted to the edge of his seat. "You have an unfinished manuscript?"

"I was almost finished when I discovered the Billy Poe murders were occurring. I haven't been able to add a word since."

"That could be the piece we need to lure Poe out of hiding. May I see it?"

He couldn't be serious. Yes, it could work for bait, but she would not be so foolish as to believe there wouldn't be consequences to such a scheme. "No, you cannot. Not one person, aside from me, has seen it, and I intend to keep it that way. I'll not risk giving Billy another target."

"But don't you see? That manuscript gives us control. Your best choice is to hand it over to us. You can trust us to keep it safe and use the information only when necessary."

"*When* necessary?" It wasn't even a matter of *if*. She tried her best to hold the disdain from her voice, but it slipped out thick as syrup. "If you can't catch Billy Poe before he murders three more men, then I'm not going to give you the means to provide him with another."

"There won't be three more deaths. Two have fled the city after the report of Ross's murder, and the third might as well be dead. He's in a consumption sanatorium in Colorado." Detective Lawson leaned his elbows onto his knees, imploring her with his nearness. "Your manuscript is the only way to direct his next move."

"No. Absolutely not. There are other ways to trap him than to put another man's neck in the guillotine and dangle the drop rope for Billy to grasp."

"Lydia's right." Theresa's countenance brightened, a sure sign of the suggestion about to fly from her mouth. "If you allow her, Nora, Flossie, and me to put a plan together, we'll have Billy Poe trapped and begging to be arrested rather than deal with us within a few days."

A choked laugh came from Abraham. The curve of his lips betrayed his thoughts—probably along the lines of her and Theresa being enough trouble even without the aid of Nora and Flossie to force Billy to beg for mercy.

At Lawson's scowl, Abraham schooled his countenance. "I have to agree with Lydia, Lawson. It's an unnecessary risk, and we can't force her. It's bad enough that having the manuscript makes her more of a target. Marcus knows she has it, and is desperate to retrieve it."

"All the more reason for her to give it to us."

Lydia jumped to her feet. She hadn't walked into Mr. O'Dell's office and broken her contract just to turn around and use the manuscript anyway. "I'm not going to do it. I'd rather burn the thing."

Detective Lawson leaned back in his chair with a heavy sigh. "I will not force you to give it to us, but I do encourage you not to burn the manuscript. Having written a story myself, I know how much work goes into creating one. Once this is over, you may change your mind and choose to publish it. Don't allow your emotions to drive your decisions."

"Just because I show my emotions doesn't mean I allow them to rule me. I am capable of sound judgment. Don't you dare make that face, Abraham." She didn't even have to look at him to know he either smirked or gave her a dubious frown.

"I'm not making a face," Abraham said. "You absolutely are capable of sound judgment. Whether you *use* that judgment is another story."

Lydia snapped her attention to him, ready to knock him off his feet by a completely different method, but his stupid smile disarmed her. Teasing her was entirely unfair. The familiarity of it drew her in like a novel's promise of a happily-ever-after.

"You're lucky you're so charming, or I might have to show you sound judgment isn't the only thing I can deliver."

His eyes sparked. "Are you implying that you want to knock me off my feet? Because I don't think that would be wise. I just might turn around and teach you how to do it properly."

His answer completely discombobulated her. She didn't know whether to blush, melt into a puddle, slug him, or run away and try to figure out what on earth was going on between them. Friends. They were *friends*.

Theresa cleared her throat. "Whatever Lydia decides about her manuscript, she needs time to think it through"—she pulled Lydia toward the door—"without your influence. She'll present you with her decision tomorrow. Until then, I suggest you two review the case while Lydia and I discuss her options. Oh, and since Detective Hall helped Lydia so much today, I think it best if he goes home tonight."

Oh no. Lydia inwardly groaned. Theresa must have picked up on the unspoken conversation. Had Detective Lawson?

His scowl hadn't changed much since she'd declared she'd not give him the manuscript. Maybe she and Abraham were safe.

Well, at least they were safe from Detective Lawson. If Theresa's giddy and mischievous expression were any indication, Lydia was about to be in serious trouble.

CHAPTER 26

"WHAT IS GOING ON BETWEEN you two?" The question barely waited until Theresa closed her bedroom door. "And don't give me some fish tale about there being nothing."

Lydia forced herself not to chew on her bottom lip as she tried to compose an answer. But how could she when she didn't know the answer herself? What *was* going on between Abraham and her?

"I won't dishonor our friendship by denying there is something between Abraham and me, but I honestly have no idea what that something is." She dropped onto Theresa's pristine bed. "He and I have only been friends for a single day."

"Broderick and I were friends for years before we shared the sort of silent looks you and Abraham just did. I don't think we shared even one like that until *after* we'd kissed for the first time." Theresa's eyes widened. "Did you two kiss?"

"No. Yes. I mean . . ." Lydia drew a deep breath and tried to state the facts simply, except there was nothing simple about them. "I kissed him, but it wasn't a real kiss."

"Nonsense! A kiss is always a kiss. When did this happen?"

"Does it really count as a kiss if our lips barely brushed before we pushed away and I literally knocked him off his feet?"

"Is that what all the knocking-you-off-your-feet talk meant? Good gracious, Lydia! The man just practically threatened you with a deep and passionate kiss."

So it wasn't just Lydia's imagination taking his meaning further than she should. With his superior sitting right there, Abraham had threatened to kiss her.

She grabbed the novel sitting on Theresa's bedside and used it as a fan. "Nonsense. We're giving his comment more meaning than he intended."

Theresa sat back and folded her arms with her you're-being-absurd face. "I was nearly married to Broderick, Lydia. I recognize when a man has more than a passing interest, and Abraham was absolutely implying he would kiss you breathless."

"But was it an invitation or a warning not to try?"

"Nora, Flossie, and I can arrange an opportunity to test it out."

"Theresa!"

She shrugged and smiled. "It's only fair that a romance author should experience her own love story."

"I'm not a romance author anymore. And obviously Abraham was right. I have the ability to demonstrate sound judgment, but what I lack is the application. You cannot allow Abraham and me to be alone. I desire his friendship, and I don't want to jeopardize it."

"Is friendship really all you want? Or are you denying the fact that you wouldn't be opposed to something more? *Mrs. Hall* does have a certain ring to it, after all." Theresa waggled her brows.

The idea that Abraham hinted at an invitation set her heart racing and her palms sweating. As a gentleman, Abraham would wait for her permission before pursuing such a scintillating activity, but she'd read and written enough novels to know the danger in that. If a real kiss from him was half as good as she envisioned it to be, they'd best go after a short courtship and engagement.

But she didn't just want passion in her romance; she wanted true love. Something that could endure the hardships of life. Someone who would stand by her side even when she was at her worst. She'd watched Theresa's devastation when Broderick had left her when she needed him most. Lydia wanted better for Theresa and for herself.

Abraham stood next to Lydia as her friend for now, but how long would that last?

"I don't know which one I want it to be, Theresa. All I know is I want a real love and not just some fleeting, passionate kiss."

"And that right there shows you're far wiser than you give yourself credit for." The pain of abandonment played across Theresa's face, fresh as the day she discovered Broderick was gone and never coming back.

Two years, and still Theresa grieved. And why not? Everyone had thought Broderick and Theresa were the embodiment of true love. They were best friends turned more, passionate and faithful. But that hadn't stopped him from leaving. What hope for love did anyone have with an example like that? Lydia and Abraham were barely friends. There hadn't been time for something deep and lasting to form between them. No. If she were going to have a chance at any future with Abraham, kissing had to stay firmly out of the picture.

After a moment, Theresa shoved her melancholy aside and replaced it with a gleam of mischievousness. "If a kissing opportunity should arise, Nora, Flossie, and I promise to turn our backs to afford you some privacy. You never know what a kiss might lead to—matrimony or just a sweet memory to relive in your dreams. My bet is on the first though."

"You're incorrigible. There is no need to turn your backs, and I'd rather you not. I'm certain once this Billy Poe case is over, Abraham will be as good as gone."

"I'm not so sure about that. Abraham might end up as steadfast to you as your father is to your mother."

Now there was true love. Lydia's parents had met and married within a year. Devotion had laced every letter exchanged while Papa served during the War Between the States. Despite miscarriages, financial hardships, and an often-chaotic life, they'd remained faithful in their love. Sweeter still, they were affectionate to the point of embarrassment. Of course, most of the embarrassment came from Lydia watching them when they thought they were alone. That was what she wanted in a husband. A man she could respect, trust, be affectionate with, and lean into during the hard times.

One day of friendship did not make Abraham that man.

But he could be.

That idea needed squelched. Detective Lawson was right. She should not make any hasty decisions while her emotions ran high. Abraham must remain simply a friend, and *if* a future existed for them, she would explore it after this Billy Poe madness was over—something that needed to happen sooner rather than later.

It was time to call together the Guardians.

"I think it's time we bring Flossie and Nora in to create a plan to capture Billy Poe. It's obvious Detective Lawson has no confidence in the police's ability to apprehend him before there is another death."

"I was hoping you'd say that." Theresa rubbed her hands together. "I'll have Mrs. Hawking send them each a note to meet here first thing in the morning."

"What should I do with the manuscript?"

"Is it here?"

"Of course. I was supposed to be working on it."

"Keep it until the girls arrive. You shouldn't be alone when you say goodbye to writing. Flossie, Nora, and I will be by your side as we burn your manuscript in a symbolic ceremony of your tossing out the old and becoming something new."

Lydia cringed. "I'm not sure I want to be compared to changing from paper to ashes."

"But what about the verse about God making beauty from ashes? The first step is to become those ashes."

"That sounds painful."

"It seems to me that you've already endured the pain. You might as well go the full distance and see what reward God holds for you on the other side."

Why did that reward sound so ominous? "As long as that other side isn't an early entrance into heaven. I don't think Billy is going to be happy with me when he discovers in tomorrow's newspaper that not only am I not writing any more books but Detective Abraham Hall is my supposed beau."

"You didn't tell me that bit of news."

"Yes, well—"

A rap at the door saved Lydia from further explanation.

Mrs. Hawking marched in, stiff as a soldier on parade. "Miss Lydia, Mr. Monroe is here to see you. I tried to send him on his way, but Detective Lawson insisted you be notified. He wants you to lure Mr. Monroe into stealing your manuscript by hinting at where it is located."

So much for not using her manuscript for bait.

But that didn't mean it had to be located where she told Marcus it would be. Theresa could be trusted to hide the manuscript without reading it, so long as Lydia didn't *tell* Theresa not to look. That woman's desire to rebel increased whenever presented with a rule. How she'd managed to survive as the ward of a militant grandfather was beyond Lydia. Then again, Theresa was a master at evading Mrs. Hawking and Colonel Plane.

"Theresa, would you grab the manuscript from the desk in my room and hide it in your armoire while I speak with Marcus?"

"Are we not waiting for Flossie and Nora to set the trap?"

"Tonight, we'll execute Detective Lawson's plan. If it doesn't work, then tomorrow, the Guardians will form one that does."

Perhaps it was arrogant to believe four women could do what an entire police department could not, but Lydia was tired of passively waiting for Billy Poe to be arrested. She was an author, after all. She was used to plotting the end of a story, and she was ready for the climax. Too much time had been spent wading through the muddy middle.

Lydia met Marcus in the foyer, where he stood with his coat still on and hat in hand. No hospitality had been offered him, and she wouldn't make him feel welcomed either. It was best to plant the seeds and then leave them to take root as quickly as possible.

Neither Abraham nor Detective Lawson were within clear view, but it was probably Abraham's feet that caused the dark lines in the light beneath the parlor's doors. It was a comfort to know he would be within reach if she were to need him. However, it wouldn't be long before Theresa finished her task and grabbed a vase to heave from the landing should Marcus cause trouble. The plan had been laid out since she and Lydia were children imagining villains in every shadowed corner. If Marcus *were* Billy Poe, he had no hope of abducting or hurting her without immediate consequences.

Still, Lydia stood well outside of Marcus's reach while addressing him. "If you're here to beg for my manuscript again, you can leave."

"Please, Lydia. You have a gift. You can't give it up."

"Gifts are meant to be used to glorify God. All I ever did was glorify evil. Tomorrow I will take that manuscript from Theresa's guest room and burn it. No one else will die by the ink of my pen."

He stepped closer but stopped short when she retreated. Hurt clouded his countenance. "I would never harm you."

"You might. You could be Billy Poe."

Hazel eyes pleaded with her. "You can trust me. I'm your friend, and if you give me your manuscript—"

"No." If she'd had any doubts over his true reason for being here, they were gone now. "I'm sorry, but you are no longer welcome here. Please leave."

"You would end our friendship over this?"

"You don't actually care about our friendship. All you want is that manuscript so that you can save your job. I'd rather risk your job than the life of another man. It's over, Mr. Monroe."

He flinched at the formality.

"Leave and do not return. There is nothing for you here."

The brim of Marcus's hat crumpled within his fists, and his nostrils flared. However, he wasn't red-faced, nor did any of his veins bulge. He might be upset, but he was far from a raging bull.

Lydia held her ground and waited him out.

At last, he jerked a nod, jammed his hat on his head, and strode out the door. It slammed with such force, she jumped at the crash.

Abraham emerged from the parlor with his gun still in hand. Detective Lawson followed close on his heels and slipped outside.

Abraham touched her elbow as he holstered his weapon. "Are you all right?"

"I'm fine." It wasn't completely true, but how was she supposed to explain the ache of shoving a former friend away despite his possibly being a vile vigilante?

"Lawson is tailing Monroe. I'll stay until he returns, then I've been ordered to go home for a good night's sleep."

"But Billy might try to break into the house tonight." Involuntarily, she drew nearer to him.

He didn't move away, instead caressing her arm with gentle encouragement. "You'll be safe. Lawson's bringing back several men to watch the house. Besides, I can't always be around. Sleep with Miss Plane tonight and keep this handy." He withdrew a hidden derringer from near his ankle.

"You did hear me tell you that I can't shoot an object within three feet of me."

"And that's why I'm going to teach you in the carriage house. Colonel Plane has an area he uses for target practice."

Lord, have mercy on her soul. The man was going to teach her to use a gun? How many times had she written such a scenario into her books? It had seemed so romantic when she'd written of masculine arms steadying the woman's aim, the man and woman cheek to cheek as they lined up the sights. Now the only thing she could imagine was accidentally shooting her hero when she missed so badly the bullet hit something metal and ricocheted back at them. Or worse, she'd just put the bullet straight into him.

"I don't think this is a wise idea. You greatly underestimate how poor a shot I am."

"I think you've just had poor instructors. If you're still not comfortable after I teach you, we'll find another weapon for self-defense."

Should she tell him Theresa likely had that covered? Or should

Lydia allow him the opportunity to improve her shot, and herself the chance to enjoy a romantic gun outing with her "beau"?

One glimpse into his imploring eyes and she melted. He could ask her to learn how to dance with a cobra and she'd say yes. She only hoped he wouldn't regret it.

CHAPTER 27

"IS IT LOADED?" LYDIA TURNED the gun to check.

Abraham's heart jumped to his throat. With a quick and controlled movement, he pushed her arm down and pulled the gun from her hand. "Didn't anyone teach you not to look down the barrel of a gun?"

Her face paled. "Well, yes, but I got so nervous, I forgot."

Lord, help them. There were too many safety rules for anyone to forget just because they had a bout of nerves.

He flipped back the barrel, removed the bullets, and shoved them into his pocket, then flipped and locked the barrel back into place. "Rule one: *never* look down the barrel of a gun, even if you think it's empty."

"What if someone is pointing it at me? I don't think I'll have much choice then."

"If someone is aiming a gun at you, either do what they say or run for cover. A moving target is harder to hit than a still one. Of course, the *best* course of action is to never be on the wrong end. Which brings us to rule number two: never point the muzzle at something you don't intend to shoot."

"You mean, like my face."

"Exactly. If the derringer were to accidentally go off, you'd want the bullet to go in a direction where it can't possibly shoot anyone. This means you should always know where you're pointing and what's beyond it. Bullets have the potential to pass through your target, so be aware of what else it might hit. Colonel Plane has those sandbags stacked four deep and ten tall to stop any bullets from passing through to the other side of the carriage house. That's the only place we are going to aim this gun, loaded or not. Do you understand?"

"Yes, sir."

"Good. Now give me your hand."

She stuck it out, and he adjusted her position until the derringer would be directed at the sandbags. Once sure her aim would be correct, he carefully wrapped her thumb and three bottom fingers around the grip. When her pointer finger automatically went to the trigger, he pulled it off.

"Keep your finger off until you have your sights on your target and you've made the decision to shoot. Not one moment before. Otherwise you may shoot before you intend to."

She nodded. "There's a lot to keep in mind."

That wasn't even half of what he intended to teach her about handling a gun. She still needed to support the base of the grip with her other hand, learn how to aim, be able to hold steady while pulling the trigger, and maintain control of the weapon during the recoil. And eventually he'd have to get up the nerve to actually load the gun and let her shoot it.

Maybe this wasn't such a good idea. His earlier visions of teaching her to become the best markswoman in the country in one lesson had been foolish.

"It's a deadly weapon, Lydia. You can't forget any of these rules without jeopardizing your life or someone else's."

"I know. That's why I've only fired a gun once. It was enough to realize I was a danger to myself and others." She lowered the weapon so that it pointed down, but failed to notice the muzzle was directed at her foot instead of the ground.

And her finger was once again resting on the trigger.

Abraham released a prayer of thanksgiving that he'd had the foresight to remove the bullets before allowing her to keep the derringer in her hand. "It appears that is still true. You're about to put a hole in your boot." He retrieved the gun, reloaded it, and knelt to return it to the holster at his ankle.

"What? You're not going to teach me anymore?"

"I think our time would be better spent determining other ways to protect you."

Her shoulders drooped. "You don't think you could teach me if you were behind me and helping me to hold the gun? Maybe use your arms to support and guide mine?"

He looked up at her and rested an elbow over his knee. "You've been reading too many romance novels. If you can't control a gun on your own, you shouldn't be holding one."

"Maybe you could try one more time?"

The pleading in her voice was tempting, but . . .

"Did you fake struggling in hopes that I'd come up behind you like in one of your stories?"

"I wish I could say yes, but, unfortunately, I'm just that bad."

He'd laugh if the situation weren't so serious. He rose to his feet. "We're done using a gun. I'm not risking your life in an attempt to teach you how to protect it."

She sighed. "Truthfully I have no desire to learn anyway."

"You just desire to be in my arms, is that it?"

By the immediate flame to her face, the jest proved as true as her inability to shoot. He focused on adjusting his pant cuff over the weapon to hide his own struggle with that revelation. He didn't mind holding her. He rather enjoyed it—far more than an officer should with the woman he was supposed to be protecting. She no longer served as a suspect in his mind, but that didn't change her standing in Lawson's. Any sort of relationship with her was unprofessional.

But if this trap proved effective, then their relationship wouldn't be restricted to professional etiquette. Friendship would be theirs to explore. Except Lydia wasn't the sort of woman he could confine to friendship. Either something more lay in their future or he would have to walk away at the end of this case. The trouble was determining which course he should take.

He cleared his throat. "So how would you write this scene if it were in your next book?"

"You're trying to trap me. There will be no more novels, romance or otherwise."

"But if there were, if God were to call you to write just romances, how would you write this scene?"

Her head tilted as she contemplated. "After today's experience, it might be fun to play with the expected. I suppose the lesson could go wrong. The hero could be accidentally shot, requiring the heroine to nurse him back to health."

"I'm not a fan of being shot."

"This is a fictional story. I have no intention of shooting you. Besides, you've already put that threat out of reach."

He dared a step closer. "How about if the hero asked the heroine to join him for a stroll instead? What then?"

She blinked. "Ummm . . ."

Was it his imagination, or had the speed of her breathing increased?

"I'd probably have some witty banter or some revelation about the character's past or dreams for their future."

"And what dreams do you have for the future?" He reached out and brushed her knuckles with his fingertips.

Her rapid retreat and darted glance outside warned he'd misread the situation.

He stepped back. "I'm sorry. Forgive my forwardness."

She chuckled but kept her face averted. "No apology needed. Friends share things like dreams for the future."

Awkward silence fell between them. Lydia's attention remained on the view of the animals waiting outside for the shooting lesson to be over. Her finger tapped against her arm, indicating she mulled over thoughts. How he wished he could be privy to them.

Or maybe he didn't. He'd greatly overstepped. She might very well be planning to grab a horseshoe off the wall and chuck it at his head. He deserved it. What sort of cad was he?

He was about to suggest they return to the house when she finally spoke.

"I find the dreams I had for the future are shifting dramatically." Her arms crossed over her chest in a protective stance that declared her insecurity. "Before this, I dreamed of being a lifelong author; one who could support herself if necessary or share her wealth with a husband who didn't mind that she bucked society's expectations of a proper lady. That fantasy has suffered a fatal blow, and I'm floundering to know what else there might be to hope for." Her eyes found his. "In the immediate moment, I desire to be able to protect myself while you're gone. I confess, I feel safer when you're around. Detective Lawson is nice enough, but I don't know. He's not you. I don't trust him the same way I do you."

That was encouraging, but he'd not assume it was because she felt the same draw to him that he felt toward her. "Why not? He's the real detective on the case, with decades of experience. I'm only an assisting officer, not even a real detective yet. If anyone is to outwit Billy Poe, Lawson is the most likely candidate."

"I disagree. How long has he been working on this case? It's only been since you've come on that he's made any real progress."

"I'm not sure that you can count what we've learned as progress."

"You're down to two suspects: Mr. Clemens and Marcus."

"True, but there is still a chance that neither man is Poe."

She shuddered and stepped closer to him, though not near enough for him to touch her again. "I'd rather it be just two suspects. It's terrifying to have no idea who your enemy is. I don't know if I'll ever be able to go out on my own again without fear causing me to look over my shoulder."

"You shouldn't have been going out alone before. You've only had the illusion of safety. No matter where you go, there are broken men who would like nothing more than to make a beautiful woman like you theirs for a short time."

"I know. You are a good friend to worry for me."

Friend.

Was she putting him in his place? His timing left something to be desired, after all. Romantically pursuing a woman in the midst of a crisis was in poor taste. If Abraham wanted to see if they had a future together, he needed to stop flirting. He could wait until after the case. A slow pursuit would be difficult, but he couldn't walk away without at least trying.

"Should we bring the animals back inside, then return to the house?" She offered her arm and waited with expectation.

At least she wasn't afraid to have him by her side. He gladly accepted and guided her toward the door. "I'll escort you inside and then take care of them myself."

"That's probably a wise decision. I imagine Detective Lawson will be returning soon, and I don't think he'd be happy to see us alone together. Not with knowing how you're my beau and all." She bumped his side and offered him a shy smile.

Was she teasing or flirting? Why couldn't the woman be more straightforward in what she wanted?

Well, if she opened the door, he wasn't going to ignore the opportunity.

"Speaking of beaux . . ." *Please don't let me make a muck of this, Lord.* "I've read several of your novels, but I can't seem to figure what it is that you desire in a man."

She shrugged as they passed outside into the glow of a setting sun. "The heroes in my books aren't written for me. They're written for the heroines of the stories. Each couple has their own unique qualities necessary to make the match true and lasting. I've not written a hero who matches exactly what I want."

"Oh. Then what sort of hero would you design for yourself?" Nervous perspiration formed under his arms, and he prayed the lingering stench from Ross's death would cover the potential smell.

A small smile curved her lips like she knew what he was about but wasn't willing to let on. "I suppose I want a man who loves Christ, loves his family, and loves me."

"That's all? You're not waiting for someone who rescues you from a burning building by swimming across a flooded river?"

Her squeaky laugh escaped. "I suppose that would be admirable, but not a requirement. Sometimes it's just fun to write the ridiculous and see how far I can take it before readers denounce my stories as utter rubbish."

The smile in her voice revealed how much her writing was a part of her. She derived absolute joy from it. No wonder she'd sobbed in his arms at the death of her future novels. If only she'd stuck to romances instead of adding mysteries. Then again, they might never have crossed paths had she remained strictly on the acceptable feminine publishing path.

Lydia stopped walking and angled them toward the back hedges, where the sun sank. A painter's palette spilled across the sky in hues of orange, pink, and purple. The view was far from perfect, but it must have been enough. Her voice took on a dreamy lilt as she continued speaking.

"No. What I desire above all things is real love, and real love comes from the ordinary. Only, to those two people, the ordinary becomes something extraordinary. Little touches, walking through the trials of life together, fighting for each other as needed. That's what I want. An ordinary man who becomes extraordinary simply because I love him."

An ordinary man. Right. Because that is what sold romance novels by the thousands. The woman must be lying to herself. She didn't want someone ordinary. She wanted a hero disguised as ordinary.

"And how exactly does one move from the ordinary to extraordinary in your eyes?"

She arched a brow. "You mean, aside from what I've already stated?"

"Little touches and walking through the trials of life together aren't exactly specific."

"Then allow me to be more specific." Impishness edged the corner of her mouth upward as she turned back to the fading sunset. "To move from the ordinary to the extraordinary, my future beau must remove a monkey from my hair, speak difficult truths into my life even when unwanted, sleep on my friend's sofa to guard my family, and read my dime novels even though he thinks them twaddle."

He gaped at her profile. Had she just . . . Did that mean . . . Future beau? Though he tried, not one coherent thought could muddle itself together. When words did form, they jumped out before he could think them through. "Are you saying that you love me?"

His chest constricted in anticipation of the answer, though what answer he wanted, he couldn't be sure. It was too soon for something like love, but the chance at it? That was something to hope for.

"I'm not sure."

Now was not the time to be coy with him. He grasped her shoulders and turned her toward him. "But you are saying you find me extraordinary. Or am I misunderstanding you?"

Her head dipped demurely.

Gently he lifted her chin and held her gaze, imploring an honest answer.

"I do indeed find you extraordinary."

He released the breath he hadn't realized he'd been holding.

"But—"

At her additional word, he sucked in another breath and waited for the rejection to come.

"Despite what my books say, I'm not one to rush into love. We've barely known each other two weeks, and we only agreed to friendship yesterday. I think it would be irresponsible for me to say *I love you* so quickly."

That was an answer he could respect. Like her, he didn't wish to rush into love, but the fact they both agreed the potential existed made him bold. Either they had a future or they didn't, but wavering between the two would drive him mad.

"As you said, love is proved by walking through life together. That requires time. Time we've barely begun to share." He swallowed hard against the nervousness threatening to cut off his next words. "May I have the honor of spending more time with you and seeing if our walk together is a lingering one? Once this case is over, of course."

"Are you saying we should skip straight into a courtship?"

"As long as your answer is yes. If it's no, then that's not what I'm saying."

She laughed, then sobered. "Whirlwind romances only belong in books. What happens if we discover we don't suit each other?"

The very thought of it sent an unexpected pain through his chest. "Then we go our separate ways, wishing each other well. I'll be honest, Lydia. I'm not sure I'm capable of just being friends with you."

"To make such a declaration, you really must have hit your head when you fell after our bet. You make it sound as if we're either destined for a happily-ever-after or a heart-wrenching goodbye."

She did have a way of making things sound more dramatic than they were. But in truth, that is what they faced. "As you've stated, our friendship is very new. We could end it now and finish this case merely as acquaintances, saving us both from an unpleasant goodbye. Or we could explore the possibility that whirlwind romances do exist."

Feigned shock widened her eyes. "Don't you know that possibilities are what make every story exciting?"

By the growing anticipation tingling through him, he did indeed, even if he hadn't been able to put it into words before now.

The playfulness fell away. "Would you mind giving me a minute to pace and pray? I've learned the hard way that I do not turn to God or listen to Him enough."

The fact she wanted to seek God in prayer chastised him for not suggesting that himself. Rushing her into an answer was foolish and unwise. "Take all the time you need. I don't need an answer tonight."

"You might not, but I do. I confess, I'm already smitten, and to walk any farther would make goodbye all the more painful."

The admission gave him hope, and he stepped back a few paces. "I'll be right here, praying myself."

While they prayed, he kept his eyes on Lydia, lest Poe make an attempt to kidnap her while Abraham was unprepared. She paced beneath a tree beside the house, her undecipherable mutterings reaching him. This woman was not a passive participant in life. Whatever she did, she did it wholeheartedly. What would it be like to be wholeheartedly loved by her? And to love her wholeheartedly back? They still had much to learn about each other, but this ability to envision a future with her was new and enticing. No other woman had inspired such an intense desire to pursue a forever life together. And now all he could do was pray that a future with her was God's intention. For if God called them to go their separate ways, it would hurt like no other experience thus far in Abraham's life.

As the darker shades of evening pushed out the remaining light of sunset, stars appeared along with a low-hanging moon. Nearly full, it lit the grounds enough to see Lydia's pinched lips as she approached him. Gas bubbles—not butterflies—formed in his stomach.

She stopped in front of him. "As a lover of stories, I'd like to explore the idea of a happily-ever-after future with you."

Though he wanted to whoop, he found her hand and lifted it to his lips. "I'd like to go on that adventure with you."

Maybe they didn't have to wait until after Billy Poe was arrested. Right now, the idea of kissing her tantalized him.

Her thoughts must have run alongside his. "Do you know that aside from this morning, I've never kissed a man?"

"That does not count as a kiss."

"Whyever not? Our lips touched. Isn't that the basic definition of a kiss?" A hint of sauciness played in her tone, but there was also hope undergirding her words that he would contradict that definition.

"Maybe in the strictest sense, but a real kiss races your heart and steals your breath."

Doubt clouded her face. "I'm sure you have a lot of experience with that. Many women must have counted you extraordinary over the years."

Oh no. He wasn't about to be trapped that way. Jealousy never served to aid a relationship. "I won't lie. You're not the first woman I've kissed, but I have a feeling you will be the last."

"Oh, that sounds lovely." She leaned in, and he took that as an invitation.

He wrapped his arms around her waist and pulled her close.

Their lips met, and he intended to teach her exactly what a knock-you-off-your-feet kiss entailed.

"You two might want to reconsider that!" Miss Plane's voice shattered the moment. "Detective Lawson just returned!"

Lydia and Abraham pulled back from a kiss that barely lasted longer than the first.

Lydia let out a puff of breath that bounced a curl lying on her forehead. "I suppose that is my just deserts for all the times I interrupted her and Broderick."

As much as Abraham wanted to curse Miss Plane for her timing, the truth was, a kiss of the nature he desired to give was best served much later in a courtship. "It's wise we wait. Until Billy Poe is caught, we really shouldn't be courting, much less kissing. And I haven't even asked your father for permission."

She chuckled. "Yes. Well, I'll pray for you on that one. He's quite good at scaring off potential suitors."

"Not this one. You're worth the fright."

Her pleased sigh carried a dreamy quality. "That was the most perfect thing I've ever heard said."

"Don't get used to it. I more often get it wrong than right." The sigh he released wasn't so pleased. "Speaking of getting things wrong . . . for now, we must stick to simply being friends. No flirting, no touching, and especially no kissing."

"I don't like it when you're right." She stepped away. "It's probably best that you're going home. I'm afraid I've lost my senses and need some time to regather them."

"Be safe tonight, Lydia. It doesn't sit well with me that you're un-protected."

The confident grin he was slowly growing to anticipate appeared. "Just because I don't have a gun doesn't mean I'm unprotected. Theresa and I have long had a plan for deterring and protecting against intruders. If Billy Poe tries to enter our room tonight, he'll be unconscious before he can get three steps inside."

"All the same, I'll be praying for your safety."

"And I, yours. You're in as much danger as I. Especially if Billy Poe saw any of the last few minutes."

She wasn't wrong, and he dreaded that almost as much as leaving her.

CHAPTER 28

SHARING A ROOM WITH THERESA on the same night Theresa had witnessed Abraham and Lydia together served as a warning for Lydia to do better at hiding her budding romance. Theresa's endless teasing and incessant desire to know every detail made it difficult to focus on listening for Billy Poe. The guest room shared a wall with them, meaning Billy could sneak into Theresa's room by mistake. Not that he could get in unscathed with the ceramic pitcher strung up and ready to swing into his head if he opened the door. Confident in their trap, Theresa slept soundly—after she'd finally tired of making predictions about Lydia and Abraham's future together. Lydia, however, spent the night wide awake, vacillating between euphoria and questioning her sanity.

How on earth had she gone from insisting she wouldn't risk her friendship with Abraham to agreeing to a courtship with the man in less than an hour? Oh, she knew why—Abraham was the hero she'd never dared to write—but real life rarely lived up to fiction. And now she couldn't decide if she was glad for taking the risk or if she regretted it.

If it worked out and they did develop that steadfast love her parents possessed, she'd be richly blessed indeed.

Already she and Theresa had chosen the perfect house for her and Abraham to live in. It belonged to their former tutor and had a room on the main floor that could host a ball, an office for Abraham to conduct his work, and plenty of space for them to raise their half dozen children. It was even the perfect distance between her parents' and Theresa's homes. They'd spent an hour imagining the quiet evenings she and Abraham would spend together curled up before the fire. She and Abraham would talk, kiss, read together, kiss some more, then enjoy a round of checkers before finishing off with more kissing. The kissing had been Theresa's idea, but Lydia didn't mind dreaming about it—even if she'd yet to experience the knock-her-off-her-feet variety that Abraham insisted existed. Yes, if this sudden jump into a courtship worked out, she'd have a life better than any romance novel.

But if it didn't work, Lydia's loss would be significant.

In all her years of measuring every potential suitor against her high standard of what made a hero, none had come close. Not until Abraham. She didn't want what society defined as a perfect hero. Bulging muscles, fashionable facial hair, and classic Renaissance features—they disgusted her. Who wanted to cuddle a rock, get hair in her mouth, or marry a painting? No, Abraham was perfect. Not just in his looks, but more importantly, his character was everything she admired in a man. Confident but not arrogant. Kind even to criminals with welts on their faces. He cared enough to confront a friend when he saw them straying, but was humble enough to admit when he'd made a mistake.

Admittedly no one was perfect. She suspected a few of his flaws already. After all, he was very decided in his opinions and believed her romance novels twaddle. But courting and marrying her own Detective Darcy was a dream worth chasing, not just because he was Detective Darcy but because Abraham Hall was a man of flesh and bone who loved Christ, loved his family, and hopefully one day would love her too.

When Lydia finally did drift off to sleep, swoonworthy dreams of kissing Abraham and nail-biting nightmares of Billy Poe alternated, then swirled together. One moment she was anticipating a kiss as Abraham's face neared. The next, a deranged combination of Marcus's and Mr. Clemens's faces laughed maniacally as the men wrapped her in arms that turned into rope. She struggled against the rope's hold, kicking and screaming until finally her foot connected with something hard.

Pain in her toes jolted her awake. She yelped before curling on her side to hold the ailing little piggies. Apparently, she'd kicked the bed frame.

Something shattered behind her, and someone grunted.

Lydia shot up in bed and twisted toward the door.

Early morning light filled the room, illuminating the open door and a dazed Mrs. Hawking sprawled on the floor amid shards of ceramic.

Lydia scrambled from the bed. "Mrs. Hawking!"

Theresa followed, and they carefully avoided the ceramic field to reach the poor woman's side. Blood trickled from a cut on her temple. With her eyelids closed, it was impossible to tell if her eyes had turned glassy or not. Was she even breathing?

"Papa! We need a doctor!"

Lydia knelt and pressed her ear to Mrs. Hawking's chest.

Mrs. Hawking gasped.

"Praise God!" Theresa dropped to the floor, heedless of the danger. "I thought we'd killed you."

"You'll wish you had." Mrs. Hawking pressed a hand to her head and groaned.

Theresa cut a glance to Lydia and grimaced. Colonel Plane would put them in front of a firing squad for this. Or, more likely, he'd set them to cleaning the baseboards and floor seams with a toothbrush.

Papa rushed into the room with his shirt half tucked into his pants, barefoot, and his black bag in hand. When his eyes landed on his newest patient, they widened. "Good heavens! What happened?"

"Ummm . . . We might have booby-trapped the room and forgot to tell Mrs. Hawking." Lydia eyed the dangling rope that still held the pitcher's handle within its loop.

"Of course you did. No, don't sit up, Mrs. Hawking. I must

determine if it is safe for you to move first." He pulled Lydia to her feet and waved Theresa to do the same. "Put your wrappers on and collect your clothes for the day. You'll dress across the hall so I have the space necessary to treat her."

They did as bidden and left Papa feeling for breaks in Mrs. Hawking's skull. Detective Lawson and the other officers he'd brought gathered in the hall. Before Lydia could enter the room her parents shared, the detective gripped her arm.

"It wasn't Billy Poe, was it?"

"No. Only Mrs. Hawking taken unawares by our trap."

"I suppose I shouldn't be surprised at your creative means of protection, given your stories." Detective Lawson glanced to where Mrs. Hawking's prone legs and feet could be seen through the open door, and shook his head. He returned his attention to Lydia and eyed the rolled-up dress and underpinnings. "Once you're ready, meet me in the parlor with your manuscript. Poe never showed, but that doesn't mean he won't still try. We'll figure out a safe place to store it until this is over."

"There's no need. My friends should arrive soon, and we'll burn it not long after."

"I still say that's a rash decision."

"You can think what you wish, but it is my story to do with as I please, and it would please me very much to know I've stolen the identity of Billy's last potential victim from him."

Detective Lawson frowned but nodded.

By the time she and Theresa emerged from the room, Papa had assisted a concussed Mrs. Hawking back to her quarters and Nora and Flossie had arrived. Lydia retrieved the manuscript box from the bottom of Theresa's armoire while Theresa retrieved the kindling bin from the kitchen. Then Lydia locked the four of them plus Flossie's puppy in the parlor. Abraham had barged in on her yesterday. She would not allow Detective Lawson to do the same and attempt to steal even a single sheet for his purposes.

Lydia faced her three friends, already forming a line in front of the fireplace. The ceramic Guardian brooches Flossie had designed and fired in her home kiln stood out prominently on their dresses, declaring this was no ordinary meeting among friends. From a distance, someone might assume the design a flower, but upon closer inspection, four swords came together over a shield of blue and purple with some greenery spreading out at the bottom. The colors were specifically chosen to represent the group's ideals of justice, harmony, and loyalty. Whatever would she do without these ladies?

Harold didn't seem impressed by the display of bold friendship and chose instead to chase his fluffy tail.

"Thank you for coming." Lydia clutched the box with the unfinished pages to her chest. "The first order of business is to protect the identity of Billy Poe's next victim by"—emotion she hadn't expected lodged within her throat, and she had to swallow hard to continue—"burning my latest story."

Unrestrained compassion showed on her friends' faces, and some of her burden lifted.

"I'll remove the summer cover and attach the grate." Theresa broke from the line and prepared the coal fireplace.

"And I'll go get coal." Nora started toward the door.

"We won't need it," Lydia said. "I intend to burn my manuscript box as well."

Nora stopped and stared at her. "But that was your first purchase to celebrate becoming a published author."

"And it will be the coffin for the last manuscript I ever write." Though Lydia had tried to sound confident and unaffected, the tears that built pressure behind her eyes also warbled her voice.

Flossie scooped up Harold and exchanged him for the manuscript box. "You need the love of a puppy."

Harold's tongue immediately began exploring Lydia's face. "At least I'm finally getting kissed by someone."

Theresa snorted from her squatted position as she attached the coal grate to the surrounding frame. "I think Detective Hall was quite successful doing that last night."

"Not too successful. You interrupted him," Lydia muttered.

Flossie squealed. "You finally got your first kiss?"

"He insisted it didn't count. Our lips barely touched."

"Oh, what a disappointment. You'll have to try again." Flossie said it so flippantly that, if Lydia didn't know better, she'd think Flossie kissed every man she met. But Flossie would never allow a man who did not first support and encourage her suffragist activities anywhere near her lips. So far, such a man proved as elusive as a unicorn.

"Ignore Flossie." Nora retrieved scraps of wood from the kindling bin and handed them to Theresa. "The only kisses she knows are Harold's."

"And I suppose you have your own superior experience?" Flossie retorted.

"No, and I'm not going to try for one. Especially since there likely isn't a man willing to take me on with my family's trouble."

"You just haven't met the right man." Flossie's momentarily sympathetic tone returned to teasing. "I know there's one out there crazy enough to put up with your family."

Lydia winced at Flossie's choice of the word *crazy*. There was a reason none of them joked about Longview Insane Asylum around Nora. It wasn't some abstract place. It was her mother's residence.

But Nora seemed unbothered by the slip. She shook a piece of frayed wood at Flossie as Harold's head and eyes followed the stick's movement. "That's certainly more likely than one who'd be willing to put up with yours."

Harold leaped from Lydia's arms, snagged the stick, and darted beneath the couch, where he must have thought no one could reach him.

"Let him have it." Flossie waved off his behavior. "He'll stay out of trouble that way. I'll sweep up the mess later."

Theresa sat back on her heels and pulled the box of matchsticks from a nearby drawer. "Do you want to light the fire?"

Lydia shook her head and reclaimed the manuscript box. The only part she wanted in this was laying her career to rest. Building the pyre to cremate it was not something she was ready to take part in.

Flossie wrapped an arm around her shoulders. "If this is what you really want to do, we're with you every step."

"I want to do this. It's the only way to protect this man's life."

"All right then. We all know I love a good fire." Flossie grabbed the matchbox from Theresa, struck a stick, and held it to the kindling.

Slowly, the splinters of wood smoked, curled, and then caught. Flossie fed the fledgling flames some discarded newspaper while Theresa arranged two larger pieces of wood over the top.

"Whenever you're ready, the fire is." Theresa rose and stepped to the side.

Flossie followed suit.

Lydia ran her hand over the varnished wooden box she'd spent a portion of her first advance on. The dark sheen had contrasted perfectly with her name, engraved by Theresa with fanciful swirls, and a feather pen beneath. At some point or another, each of her books had been nestled inside. This box had been filled with love and hate, and even now contained the harsh judgments of a woman who no longer believed them hers to make.

"You're saving a life. Remember that." Nora's soft voice soothed the growing ache in Lydia's chest.

With a deep breath, Lydia stepped forward. It was time to relinquish this part of her life. May God make beauty out of ashes.

She arranged the box so that it stood upright with her name facing forward, then she stepped back.

Her friends gathered alongside her, holding her hands and touching her arms as they watched what had once been a treasured career go up in flames.

The varnish caught quickly, and flames licked across the surface. The crackling of the fire grew louder, indicating the wood itself, and not just the kindling and varnish, had succumbed to the flames. It was a thick box and would take some time to fully disappear, but she'd stay until every last word smoldered.

"Fire!" Detective Lawson's voice cut through the door into the room.

Of course there was a fire. That's how one burned a manuscript.

Pounding shook the door. "The carriage house is on fire! Everyone to the water pump, or there'll be no saving it."

"Tipsy!" Theresa broke from the group and ran for the door.

Flossie and Nora looked at each other, then at Lydia, before rushing after Theresa.

Lydia stayed, watching the flames. Until the manuscript was completely burned, she couldn't leave.

"Come on, Lydia." Detective Lawson remained at the door, waiting for her. "We need everyone's help if we're to keep the fire from reaching the hay. Once it finds that, the carriage house and the animals inside will be lost."

Still Lydia hesitated. Flossie and Nora were probably even now trying to drag Theresa back from rushing inside to save every living creature. Staying here meant abandoning her dearest friend, but neglecting the manuscript left a man's life vulnerable.

The kindling shifted, and the flame-engulfed box dropped deeper. The lid separated from the bottom and leaned toward the grate. A few pages fell with it. The white edges curled and ignited. It wouldn't be long before the fire ate up the pages whether the box burned quickly or not. The manuscript was safe to leave unattended. Unlike the carriage house.

"Come on, Lydia. I can't leave you here unprotected from Poe." Detective Lawson waved her toward the door.

She slipped past him, casting one last glance at her career turning to ashes. He pulled the door closed and followed her as she rushed out the front door to join the fire brigade.

Chapter 29

A dark cloud of smoke billowed behind Plane Manor as Abraham's hack pulled into the drive. Calls for buckets and water mingled with Miss Plane's hysterical screams.

Had the kitchen caught fire? More importantly, had everyone gotten out of the house?

Abraham jumped to the ground and raced around the side of the mansion to find the source of smoke. The carriage house, not the manor, crackled beneath the wrath of the roaring flames climbing the building's back corner. By the looks of it, the fire hadn't been going long, but it was quickly eating up wood.

Mrs. Pelton and Miss Madelyn burst through the kitchen door carrying all manner of pots and bowls. The officers who'd spent the night waiting to pounce on Billy Poe now pounced on the water vessels and sped toward the water pump, where Dr. Pelton primed it with the vigor of a man half his age. A yapping puppy darted in between and around legs. One officer caught himself before falling, but a second skidded forward across a dirt patch. Two women—probably the friends Lydia had spoken of—physically restrained Miss Plane, whose screams clearly stated her intent to barge into the burning building to save her animals.

Colonel Plane raced past Abraham and flung open the carriage house doors. A smattering of barn kittens sprinted out, quickly disappearing into the hedges and the safety beyond.

Miss Plane broke free and sprinted inside. Her two friends hesitated, then rushed after her.

Three friends, but no Lydia.

His heart jolted at the realization, and his eyes once again roved each face. Setting the carriage house on fire would serve as the perfect distraction for Poe to kidnap Lydia.

"Theresa! Nora! Flossie! No!" Lydia's scream came from the front corner of the house.

Abraham whirled in her direction. Lydia darted toward the carriage house's doors, intent on joining her friends in needless danger. While he admired her foolish bravery, he wasn't about to allow her to add to the number of those who might need rescued from a collapsed building. He stepped in her path and caught her around the waist before she made it past.

She shoved against his chest. "Let me go. I've got to help them."

"It's too dangerous."

"Abraham Hall, if you don't let me go, I'm going to knock you off your feet in a way that doesn't involve lips."

"Do what you must, but you can't go in there."

Two horses pounded out of the carriage house, wild-eyed and willing to barrel over anyone in their way.

Abraham jerked Lydia and himself out of their trajectory and held tight as Lydia fought against him. Her heel stomped on his toes. Her elbow slammed into his gut, and she attempted to kick off his legs to lurch forward. She didn't claw at his face like some arrestees had in the past, so maybe she wasn't fighting as hard as she could. He hoped not. If this was the best she could fight, Poe would have no trouble overpowering her.

Miss Plane sped out of the building with a bleating Tipsy in her arms and her two friends right behind. Colonel Plane followed, waving his coat at a brood of hens, directing the squawking and confused birds from danger.

Lydia slumped in his arms, her voice choked. "Thank God they're okay."

He waited until he was certain the three women were far enough away from the carriage house that they wouldn't race back inside, then released Lydia.

She stumbled forward, calling them a thesaurus full of words for their foolish behavior as she went.

Abraham kept close to her heels. Poe was nearby. He had to be. There was no other reason for the carriage house to catch fire. They weren't in a drought. The sky was clear of clouds or the possibility of lightning. Nothing contained within that building would lead to a spontaneous fire.

"Quit your mother-henning and go help the others put out the fire." Miss Plane sidestepped Lydia's wagging finger, and continued her determined march. "I'm taking Tipsy to the kitchen to tend her burns."

The look Lydia shot Miss Plane expressed both the desire to strangle the woman and a sisterly love that felt relief at her safety. "Flossie, Nora, run to the neighbors' and rouse more hands and buckets."

The women hustled off, and Lydia strode toward the fire.

"What do you think you're doing?" Abraham kept close, scanning their surroundings for Poe.

"Joining the fire brigade, just like you."

He had every intention of hauling buckets, but a woman in skirts near an unpredictable flame was as dangerous as leaving her unguarded. "Help your father at the water pump. I don't want you near that blaze." Or alone.

She rolled her eyes but didn't argue. When they reached the pump, she relieved her father, who began exchanging filled containers with empty ones.

As Abraham reached for a full bucket, he leaned close to Dr. Pelton. "Poe's about. Don't allow her out of arm's reach."

Her father's gaze darkened, and he nodded. At least now Abraham could leave her side and know that someone guarded her.

He rushed to the flames, which battled against the barrage of splashing water. Unfortunately the efforts meant little unless the fire department arrived soon with their steam engine and fire hoses.

Trip after trip, he lobbed water at the climbing flames. His muscles burned from the exertion, and his lungs ached from the smoke. Each grateful smile Lydia gave him when he exchanged buckets renewed his determination.

Finally the bells of the fire engine rang in the distance. Soon they'd have help.

Abraham drew back a bucket. Something red and round flew past his face. It crashed against the carriage house's wall and shattered. Flames exploded with invigorated life and leaped from the wall toward him.

On instinct, Abraham dropped the bucket and lifted his arms to protect his face. He twisted away, but the inferno hit him with such force he stumbled backward.

His mind barely acknowledged his screamed name. The urge to escape the painful blaze overpowered every other sense. Heat seared up his sleeves and spread along the side closest to the fire. He ripped off his coat and flung it as far as he could.

Still, it felt as if flames torched his clothes and kissed his skin.

Startling cold water struck him in the face, then from opposite directions. Relief mingled with the sting of burns on his arm and hand, but thankfully his neck and face just felt wet. He swiped away the water and glanced around.

Lydia, Dr. Pelton, and another officer holding empty buckets stood nearby. Beyond them, Lawson knelt on the ground, pounding at the flames on Abraham's still burning jacket with his own.

Lawson's coat burst into flames, and he jerked away with a howl. Too late, another officer doused the material.

Lawson sat on his haunches, cradling a hand already red and blistered.

"Madelyn, grab my bag from my room!" Dr. Pelton glanced over Abraham. "Lydia, I'll need your help. Go with Detective Hall to the kitchen. Detective Lawson and I will be right behind you." He rushed over to assist Lawson, leaving Abraham and Lydia alone.

Abraham doubted Dr. Pelton really needed her help, but the sly way of keeping her from Poe's reach served its purpose.

Distress pinched her face as she slipped her arm around Abraham's waist. "Does this hurt you?"

"No, but I'm perfectly capable of walking without falling over. Do not feel like you have to bear me up."

"What if I'm the one who needs bearing up?" She turned exaggerated wide eyes on him and fluttered her lashes. "I just might faint without your sturdy presence to keep me going."

When she wanted to flirt, Lydia could be as laughable as her books. Even so, he couldn't deny he liked it. It was nice to have a woman concerned for him and to banter with. And that amusement was just what he needed to distract him from the growing discomfort on his hand and forearm.

He returned her flirtation. "I'm happy to be of ser—"

The bells of the fire engine overwhelmed his gallant response as horses led the engine and half a dozen firemen around the building. Soon the fire would be well in hand and its source determined.

The memory of glass shattering just before the flames erupted slammed into him. That small explosion was no natural event.

He pulled free of Lydia's grip and pivoted toward the fire. There, scattered on the blackened ground, lay the undeniable remnants of curved glass. A fire grenade would leave that sort of debris, but those were filled with salt water or carbon tetrachloride. They were meant to extinguish a fire. Whatever had been within that glass vessel was an accelerant, not a suppressant.

And it had been thrown right when he was closest to the flames.

Abraham's attention snapped to the area around them. Two dozen people now swarmed the fire. Several men dragged the cotton-jacketed rubber water hose into place while another connected the engine to a hydrant. Others continued to refill buckets and haul them back. If Poe were someone other than Clemens or Monroe, he could easily blend in, and Abraham would never know it. But more than likely, he had run as soon as he tossed the fire grenade. Poe was too smart to stick around.

Abraham clenched his fists, ignoring the painful protests of his burns. Poe's targeted attack had come much quicker than he'd expected. The newspaper declaring his and Lydia's romantic relationship hadn't yet been delivered when he'd left his house an hour ago. That left Clemens and Monroe fighting each other for top suspect.

"What's wrong?" Lydia pressed a hand to his shirtsleeve, reminding him of the urgency to get them both out of the open.

"We should get inside."

If Poe tried for another attack, Abraham didn't want Lydia caught in the cross fire.

He gestured for the nearest officer to walk with them as he led Lydia toward the house. "Ask around. Determine if anyone saw who threw that fire grenade."

The officer nodded and left to do as ordered.

"What are you thinking?" Anxiety edged Lydia's voice.

With as smart as she was, she likely had more of an idea than she let on, but he refused to answer until they were inside.

When they entered the kitchen, Miss Plane was sitting on the floor, wrapping linens around her goat's legs. She glanced up and frowned when she saw Abraham's coatless and sooty appearance. "I see you got too close to the flames too. That salve on the counter works for people as well as animals."

Lydia directed him to a chair next to the white tin Miss Plane indicated. Once he was seated, she cupped his chin and turned his head so she could better see. Cool fingers of her free hand trailed lightly up the side of his face as she scrutinized the damage. Nothing hurt where she touched, so that was good. However, when she reached the area where his hair should be, her fingers scraped against his scalp and short, stiff hairs. Her hand slid higher into a longer section and attempted to comb it over the singed portion.

"You'll be lopsided until you visit a barber, but thankfully I don't think there is any damage to your face or throat. Now roll up those sleeves so I can inspect your arms for burns." She focused on tending his injuries and lowered her voice so that Miss Plane could not hear. "Tell me why you instructed an officer to question people."

He leaned forward and tried to ignore how her fingers gently traced the edges of the red blotches forming. "That fire was set."

She sighed and reached for the tin. "That was my fear, but what makes *you* think so?"

"There is no logical explanation for why the carriage house would spontaneously catch fire. As fast as it ate up that corner, Poe had to have used an accelerant."

"Like what?" The pungent, spicy scent of Henry's Carbolic Salve wafted up as she opened the tin.

"Kerosene, mineral spirits, turpentine. Any of those are highly flammable and easy to obtain."

Lydia dipped her fingers into the waxy salve and then turned his palm face up. Her gentle ministrations as she slathered the sticky goo soothed him as much as the salve's cooling properties. If the subject weren't so serious, he'd be tempted to lean back and let her nurse him all afternoon.

"But why would he burn the carriage house?"

"As a distraction to steal you away, just like his note said."

Her brows drew together as she stared at his worst burn. By the downturn of her mouth as she wrapped a strip of linen around his hand, she worked his explanation over in her mind.

All at once, she straightened, a ghastly horror contorting her expression. "No. It wasn't a distraction to steal me away. It was a distraction to steal my manuscript!"

She dropped his hand and ran from the kitchen.

CHAPTER 30

ABRAHAM JUMPED TO HIS FEET. "Where's her manuscript?"

"We were burning it in the parlor." Theresa shoved supplies off her lap.

He didn't wait for her to rise from the floor but raced into the hall.

Lydia was feet from reaching her destination.

"Don't go in without me! Poe may be in there."

Why he expected that knowledge to make her wait for him, he didn't know. Instead, Lydia swiped a vase off the foyer table and darted into the room with it held above her head.

Abraham fumbled to draw his revolver and winced at the pain required to fully grip it.

Glass shattered.

He stopped short of rushing through the door, peering around the corner with his weapon pointed to the floor instead. Even if Poe were inside, he'd take no unnecessary risks.

But only Lydia stood there, the vase she'd held in her hands now a mess of shards on the floor.

A haze of smoke tainted the air, growing thicker as dark curls rose from the smoldering hook rug. Blackened wood chips tipped with glowing embers threatened to consume the ready fuel. The last thing they needed was another fire.

He tucked his weapon in its holster, grabbed another vase of flowers from the table behind the sofa, and dumped the water over the charred space. The hissing sound and puff of steam indicated he'd put it out. Just to be sure, he called for Miss Plane to bring more water. With the sole of his boot, he brushed the debris onto the brick hearth and against the ash tray littered with the remains of kindling. Flames still danced along the two thicker sticks lying at odd angles across the fire grate. With the potential fire starters safe within the confines of the fireplace, Abraham turned his attention to Lydia.

"It's gone." Her small, pained voice suggested more than the loss of her writing career was responsible for her distraught response. "He must have rushed in and taken it the moment Lawson and I left."

"Are you sure it didn't just burn to ashes?"

Her countenance called him daft. "I'm positive. There are not enough ashes here for even a small portion of the manuscript to have burned. Maybe if I'd just burned the pages, but I was an idiot. I decided my career needed a symbolic coffin, and burned the story in my wooden manuscript box."

That would slow the burning process considerably. Abraham stared at the empty spot on the grate. "How much of it had burned before you left?"

"The box had just caught, and the lid popped open, giving the fire access to the pages, but that's all. I didn't think the pages would last more than a few minutes."

"So it's possible he just has a box of ashes."

"Possible, but I doubt it." She pointed to the fire poker sticking out from beneath a chair. "It appears he yanked out the box, then smothered the fire."

The poker wasn't the only indication Poe had been in the room. Smudged with sooty fingerprints, an envelope with Lydia's name written in Poe's distinctive handwriting lay flat on the settee.

Lydia must have spied it at the same moment as he. She snatched it from the chair. "Why? Why does he have to exist?"

Abraham reached around her and plucked the envelope from her hand. "I think it's best if I read this first."

She scowled at him. "Absolutely not. I won't be shielded from his monstrosity."

Miss Plane and her two female companions rushed into the room with buckets of water, Lawson and Dr. Pelton just behind.

"What's happened?" The redheaded friend's eyes swept the room, stopping on the smoldering rug. She charged over and dumped her bucket onto the spot, then indicated the other two should douse the smoking trail to the fireplace.

"He got it, and he had the audacity to leave another letter." Lydia snagged the envelope back from Abraham's hand and dropped onto the chair.

She ripped it open and started reading silently.

Her friends crowded behind her so tightly, he'd never be able to read over her shoulder.

Lawson joined him, his own hands bandaged from fighting the destruction that was Billy Poe. "What does she mean, 'he got it'?"

"The manuscript. Apparently, she was burning it in a box. When everyone was distracted by the fire, he nabbed it."

"So he has his next target?"

"It appears so."

Paper crumpling drew his attention, and Lydia launched her note toward the dying fire. Thanks to her brown-haired friend's quick reflexes and swatting the ball a different direction, the paper landed in the middle of the soggy, soot-stained rug.

"Good job, Flossie," Dr. Pelton said before admonishing Lydia to think through her actions even when upset.

Lawson gingerly collected the paper and smoothed it out on his leg.

Lydia pushed from the chair and paced. "He insists I am wrong about him, that I should trust him."

Abraham tensed. Just last night, Monroe had said she needed to trust him. Was this another attempt from him? He took the note from Lawson, intending to read it, but Lydia's agitation made it hard to focus.

"He wants me to be ready to run away with him so he can prove it! Is he mad?"

Flossie scoffed. "I think we know the answer to that one. The brute will probably get off on a declaration of insanity and be allowed to live out the rest of his days in the asylum."

"*Allowed* to live out the rest of his days?" A quiet but fierce tone of disbelief sharpened the redhead's soft voice. "There is no *allowed* about it. Life in an asylum is a fate worse than death. I'm not sure I'd wish it even on him."

"We can worry about what happens to him after we trap him." Lydia stopped her pacing and faced the group with a determined lift to her chin. "This can't go any further. He has the means to determine his next victim."

"The means, yes, but not the name." Sly delight colored Flossie's response. "You always change the villains' names. He'll have to read enough of the story to determine which crime it matches before he can do anything."

"Even if some of the pages burned, I fear he still has enough of the story to figure it out."

"Then we need to beat him to his next victim." Lawson positioned himself directly in front of Lydia. "The time for you to keep your secrets has passed. Who were you writing about?"

Lydia glanced at Abraham, silently begging with her eyes for him to disagree.

But he couldn't. "'To every thing there is a season . . . a time to keep silence, and a time to speak.'"

She closed her eyes on his last word and dipped her head. "Uriah Ingram. He was released for good behavior a few months ago, having only served eleven years of his twenty-year sentence for brutally murdering his employer."

The same man who'd escaped the noose while his partner had swung, all because Ingram had connections the other did not. It made sense why Lydia had chosen him, given the criteria for her stories.

Giving up on reading the note for now, Abraham slid it into his pocket.

"Ingram will take some time to track down." Lawson frowned as he stared off in the distance. "Bringing Clemens and Monroe into the station will slow their hunt while we get Ingram to safety."

"Agreed." Abraham faced Lydia, who stood with defeat etched on her face. "You must stay inside. Don't leave this house for any reason."

"She's not staying here." Flossie stepped forward and linked arms with her. Immediately the other two linked with them, forming a line of solidarity.

"Poe already tried to burn down my carriage house." The blaze in Miss Plane's eyes warned she'd not obey any plan but whatever she and her friends had concocted. "What else might he try if he discovers he can't get to Mr. Ingram?"

"She needs to go somewhere neither Mr. Clemens nor Mr. Monroe knows about." Flossie smiled at the redhead. "Nora?"

The quiet woman nodded. "Father is away for the next day or so. The four of us can booby-trap the house. There is nowhere safer for her to be."

"I am not leaving you girls alone." Dr. Pelton scowled. "That is asking for trouble."

"Only the best kind, Papa." Lydia clapped as best she could with linked arms, a plan clearly forming in her head. "Have any of you read my romance novel *The Switching of Ladies*?"

He hadn't, but he could already tell he wasn't going to like whatever she had to say.

CHAPTER 31

"I DON'T LIKE IT. DISGUISING someone else as yourself is a common enough ploy that Poe will expect it." Abraham looked just as displeased as Papa with the plan.

"Exactly. We will use his expectations to our advantage." How could Lydia explain it where they would finally understand how brilliant this plan was? "I did it as an author. The trick is to twist those expectations in unexpected directions."

"Three decoys before actually removing you from the house is going to take more time than we have." Detective Lawson argued from his position on a nearby chair, where he elevated his burned hands. "Hall and I need to apprehend Monroe and Clemens before going after Ingram. Poe knows where you are, so he's not likely to come after you first. We're wasting time by staying here any longer."

"Then we can do this without you. Papa will go with Madelyn, Theresa with Momma, and then Flossie, Nora, and I will slip out afterward. It's not four rounds, but three should suffice to outwit him."

"It isn't safe for any of you women to travel alone." Papa's vexation seeped into his tone.

"We will be fine. Flossie, Theresa, Nora, and I have been traipsing all over Cincinnati without an escort for years. Any time we've encountered trouble, we've managed to escape with nary a scrape." Usually.

He shook his head. "Your plan is too convoluted. It might work in a piece of fiction, but I will not allow you to risk the safety of your mother and friends just so you can test the viability of a plot."

"There is safety in numbers. Poe can't successfully try anything if you are together." Abraham flexed his hand and winced.

No doubt he was thinking about how quickly he would have gone up in flames had he been alone instead of there being so many people around to toss water on him. The horror of watching the flames spread over his clothes would probably live in her nightmares for years.

"We'll not argue further about this, Lydia." Papa unrolled his shirtsleeves in preparation to leave. "We will travel as a group. An officer has already secured the house, so there is no need for these dramatics."

What was wrong with everyone? Didn't they see the danger of a location Billy Poe knew?

"I concede that traveling as a group is best," Lydia said, "but our home has been unattended for days. Billy has probably explored it and made plans for my return. We can't assume it safe just because an officer is there. Billy would have planned for that."

Papa's jaw ticked, and Abraham and Detective Lawson appeared to be considering the problem as well. She needed to give them a little push. Then maybe they'd at least agree that her going to Nora's was best.

"Perhaps if we were only concerned about Billy, we could be prepared. But what of Cincinnati? We've had picketers, a brick thrown through our window, and numerous mailed threats."

Papa's brows shot downward. "How do you know about those?"

"It doesn't take an author to imagine that they've been pouring in. But you have to admit, those threats give us more than just Billy to worry about. Nora's house is the most reasonable place for me to go. There is nothing that would point either Cincinnati or Billy to her address. Marcus and Mr. Clemens have no knowledge of Nora."

Detective Lawson stood. "She has a point, but a group traveling from here to Miss Davis's will draw attention."

She wanted to whoop at her victory but forced herself to stand as somber and staid as a spinster. By the slight curve to Abraham's mouth as he regarded her, she wasn't performing her act very well.

"Miss Plane will remain here to assist her grandfather," Detective Lawson continued, "and Miss Gibson is to return home. Dr. Pelton, you'll escort Lydia and Miss Davis to the Davis house. Once an officer arrives, I suggest you join your wife and other daughter at your residence. You'll want to be available to protect them should the need arise."

"And leave two women unchaperoned with an officer?" Papa objected. "Not only is it unseemly, it's also not safe enough."

"Our reputations will be just fine, Papa," Lydia said. "Besides, Nora's a crack shot, and we'll have that house so booby-trapped that tomb robbers wouldn't dare set foot inside. Just look at what happened to poor Mrs. Hawking."

Lydia wasn't sure what Papa's stern mouth with bright eyes meant. Was he proud of their booby trap but upset that Mrs. Hawking had fallen prey to it? If that impressed him, he should see what else she and the Guardians had concocted over the years. Most were set as experiments for her stories, but they'd tested and refined each one. Truly, she and Nora would be safer than Queen Victoria's crown jewels.

Abraham stepped forward. "I'll have my friend, Officer Lucian Atwood, bring his wife along with him to guard the women tonight. They'll be completely safe and have a chaperone to protect their reputations."

If they didn't have an audience, Lydia would throw her arms around Abraham's neck and kiss him. Papa trusted Abraham, and Abraham's bringing in a friend meant Papa might agree. It was brilliant. With the addition of Theresa and Flossie—for they undoubtedly would ignore Detective Lawson's instructions to stay home—the house would be so full, Billy wouldn't have a chance of sneaking up on them.

But even with Abraham's assurances, Papa refused. "We must stay together. It's the only way to keep everyone safe."

Lydia touched his sleeve. "I know you want to protect Momma,

Madelyn, and me, but my presence at home is more of a danger to them than my hiding separately at Nora's. I know I've lost your trust, but you can depend upon Abr—Detective Hall."

At her near slip, Papa arched a brow. There was no way he'd let that mistake pass without an interrogation. Poor Abraham wasn't even going to have a fair chance at asking Papa for permission to court her before she'd have to admit their interest in one another.

"Even if you don't trust this young pup"—Detective Lawson elbowed Abraham's side—"you can trust me and my word. Your daughter is right. For the sake of the rest of your family's safety, you should return home once Officer Atwood arrives. I promise we'll keep her safe."

Finally, Papa acquiesced.

"Good." Detective Lawson turned to Lydia. "Would you please write down Miss Davis's address?"

"Yes, sir." She did a terrible salute before scurrying out of the parlor and down the hall to Colonel Plane's office.

Blank paper sat on his desk, but no pen. She rummaged through a drawer, and something sharp pricked her finger.

"Ouch!"

A red bubble immediately formed at the tip and began to grow. Of course she would find the sole splinter in the whole thing. She stuck the offending pointer in her mouth and carefully finished her search for a fountain pen. With as meticulous as Colonel Plane was, she could at least count on his having the reservoir filled. After dropping into his desk chair, Lydia used her elbow to hold the paper still while she continued to suck her finger. Just like in the days when she became bored with schoolwork, she gripped the pen with her left hand and scrawled the information Detective Lawson needed across the page.

"I thought you were right-handed." Abraham stood at the door.

She pulled her finger free, checked that it had stopped bleeding, and then covertly wiped it dry on her skirt. "I am, but I can write just as well with my left if the situation calls for it." She scribbled the same information below the original with her right hand, then showed it to him.

He scrutinized the writing, and then his attention shot to her. "It doesn't even look like the same person wrote it." Instead of showing surprise or pride, his eyes crinkled like he was puzzling out a problem.

Abraham retrieved the note from Billy out of his pocket and set the two sheets side by side. Leaning over them, he traced the lines of each and ended with a tap.

"Look. Your left-handed writing has similarities to Poe's."

He pointed out how both had letters that slanted to the left and were smudged from their hands passing over still-wet ink. Her handwriting was clearly the most practiced, as her letters varied little in formation, while Poe still seemed to be determining the best way to form some of his. The *e*'s and *a*'s especially varied from use to use— much like her early days of learning to write left-handed.

Billy was brilliant. She'd give him that. "He's disguising his writing."

Abraham frowned. "Which means the writing samples we took earlier aren't going to match Poe's. They were written with Clemens's and Monroe's dominant hands."

Excitement thrummed through her. This was just the evidence they needed. With a little work, they'd be able to determine whether Mr. Clemens or Marcus was the real Billy Poe. "Get new writing samples, but dictate a sentence that has the same words, in a different order, as the Billy Poe letters. They won't have time to think about how to disguise their handwriting that way."

He straightened and gently clasped her arms. "We're going to catch him, Lydia. He doesn't stand a chance now. All we have to do is get Clemens and Monroe to the station."

That victorious smile looked ridiculous with his half-singed head of hair and double black eyes, but it was adorable in a way that she would always treasure. She couldn't help but grin in return. Not just because this nightmare would *finally* be over but because it signaled a new beginning. For her. For them. Maybe a beginning that would grow into a lifetime.

"Then I think it's time we put our plans into action so that you can defeat the villain and rescue the damsel in distress."

The bandage-wrapped hand scratched against her cheek as he cupped it. "I've never wanted to be someone's hero so much. Tell me. Does this hero get to knock the heroine off her feet once this is over?"

Lydia giggled. "Maybe, but the suspense is in not knowing. You'll just have to wait to find out once we reach the end."

"Then we had better get going." He dropped his hand and led her toward the door.

CHAPTER 32

BY THE TIME ABRAHAM ARRIVED at his friend's, Lucian and his wife were finishing up their midday meal. Abraham declined the offer to join them but accepted Verity's generosity in making him a sandwich to take with him. While she put the small repast together, he explained the situation and his request to Lucian. Thankfully, Lucian readily agreed to help.

"I owe you, friend." Abraham passed Miss Davis's address to Lucian.

The wide grin on Lucian's face told Abraham he would pay dearly for this favor. "A whole night with the woman who's managed to catch your fancy? And a criminal clown turned deadly author, at that? I can't imagine my wife and me spending my night off in any better way." Lucian rubbed his hands together. "What stories should I share about you? Maybe the time we dressed as streetwalkers to lure out that violent cad? She might appreciate the details of how horrible you look in a dress."

"I looked a far sight better than you."

Given the first time he'd met Lydia she'd been wearing trousers, he didn't find the threat too frightening. She was well accustomed to doing what was necessary to accomplish a task. Still, knowing Lucian had unrestrained access to share stories with Lydia didn't sit well with him. It wasn't that he feared Lucian would scare off Lydia. No, it was far worse. If Lydia ever picked up her pen to write again,

Abraham had no doubt those stories kept between friends would make their way into fictional stories for the world to read.

Lucian shoved the address into his pocket, his face turning serious. "Be careful going after Poe. I don't like that he's already got one up on you." He pointed at Abraham's wrapped shooting hand. "I can go with you as backup to bring in Clemens."

"As much as I'd like you by my side, I need you protecting Lydia more. Logically, Poe should be going after Ingram and not worrying about Lydia, but *logic* and *Poe* don't belong in the same sentence."

"Maybe not, but watch your back. If he catches you alone, I wouldn't count on him playing fair."

Abraham gingerly flexed his burned hand. The burns weren't as bad as Lawson's had been, but they were enough to put Abraham at a disadvantage.

"I'll be careful. Just make sure Lydia and her friends stay inside. I wouldn't put it past them to become vigilantes themselves and try to catch Poe."

"I'd say you're overly worried, but they did try to steal a goat from the circus." Lucian slapped him on the shoulder. "May the morning dawn with news that this is over, and you can begin courting and taming that wild woman."

Abraham shook his head, then Lucian's hand, and headed toward the station. He wasn't foolish enough to confront Clemens on his own. He'd enlist at least one officer to go with him to bring in Clemens. Once Lawson had Monroe, the detectives would hopefully know who their man was, and Mr. Ingram could live out the rest of his life without knowing how close he'd come to facing death again.

Tracking down Clemens proved harder than Abraham imagined. The first logical place to visit had been the *Cincinnati Commercial* office, but Clemens's boss said he'd sent in a note claiming to be sick. The timing was suspicious, but Abraham tried to withhold judgment.

Everything they had was circumstantial and didn't prove that Clemens was Billy Poe. The man really could be sick with a summer cold.

Only, when they went to the boardinghouse where Clemens resided, the landlord said he'd been gone since early that morning.

Abraham rubbed his thumb over the linen bandages and scowled. The timing fit for Clemens starting the fire, stealing the manuscript, and throwing the fire grenade. As much as Abraham disliked the man, a part of him hadn't wanted to believe Clemens capable of the deeds Poe performed. Yes, the reporter was a snake, but they'd worked begrudgingly alongside each other for three years now. But knowing someone didn't make them innocent. Clemens was like a dog with a bone—he fiercely went after what he wanted. And Poe was exactly the same kind of man. Abraham hated to think that Poe had been under his nose this whole time, gleaning information without much question from the very men who wanted to protect Cincinnati.

"If Clemens should return," Abraham said, "please inform an officer as quickly as you can without alerting Clemens to your doing so."

After agreeing, the landlord closed the boardinghouse door.

Officer Richards, Abraham's assistant for the task, scratched at his beard. "What now?"

They should petition a judge for a warrant to search Clemens's room. With the trouble this case had caused for the city, he might accept Abraham's reasoning as good enough. However, that would take more time and likely yield little direction in where to find Clemens. The day was already edging its way into late afternoon. No, Abraham wouldn't waste precious time in that futile effort. Clemens was a smart man, familiar with sensational stories. He would quickly recognize Ingram as Lydia's story's inspiration. If Abraham were Clemens, he'd secure his next victim, possibly kill him first, and then retrieve Lydia before dashing off into the concealing fog of obscurity. Ingram was his biggest lead, so that was where they should go next.

Abraham retrieved his notebook from his pocket and referenced the address. Of course the man would live in the Deer Creek Gang's area. Assaults were less frequent in the daylight, but it was best not to take any chances.

"I hope you're well-armed. We're heading to Hunt Street."

Officer Richards grimaced but double-checked that his revolver was loaded and ready.

When Abraham called in to Central to report his plans, the switchboard operator delivered surprising but welcomed news. "Clemens is cooling his heels in cell two. He was brought in not long after you left for slugging James O'Dell."

"He punched his own uncle?"

"Yep, and he's got a mean right hook. He's waiting for you to question him."

Thank You, God. It was a bigger break than Abraham could have ever dreamed.

At the station, Abraham found Clemens as the lone occupant of a cell, stretched out on the wooden bench with his coat as a pillow. The man looked entirely too comfortable for being in danger of losing his job. The *Cincinnati Commercial* wasn't likely to keep him on once they discovered their reporter had been arrested for brawling. Then again, maybe they wouldn't care. After all, it wasn't like the newspapers cared much about anything except selling the next edition.

Abraham banged his handcuffs against the iron bars. "Wake up, Clemens. I have questions for you."

The man startled but didn't sit up. Instead, he readjusted his coat and crossed his arms over his chest. "By all means, ask."

If the man didn't mind his business being bandied about where the other cells' tenants could hear, Abraham wouldn't argue. They could move into a private interrogation room once the Poe allegations arose. "Mind telling me why you thought your uncle deserved a black eye and a broken nose?"

"He deserves more than that, and he'll get it soon too."

Was Clemens plotting murder as he lay in a jail cell? Granted, the dank accommodations didn't inspire warm feelings, but that seemed a bit much even for him. Unless he was truly Poe. "Are you planning on giving O'Dell a Billy Poe ending?"

"Me? No. Miss Lydia Pelton has done it for me. Breaking her contracts is going to destroy O'Dell Publishing."

"Losing one or two author contracts won't kill a business."

Clemens snorted. "Maybe if the owner wasn't a greedy lowlife. Good ol' Uncle James sank his profits into printing and selling new editions of the Poe stories at double the normal price. He has no funds to purchase new manuscripts or to fix the machines that angry protesters destroyed. He'll be out of business by the end of the year." The smile in his tone declared his pleasure at the thought.

"If Miss Pelton has already ruined him, then why did you punch him?"

Clemens sat up, and a photo slid off his chest and fluttered to the floor. He quickly retrieved it. Whoever was in the image must be someone Clemens revered, given the way his thumb gently stroked it.

His demeanor hardened, and a dangerous fury replaced the reverence. "Because the cold-blooded leech had the audacity to promote the special edition of my fiancée's ruination on the anniversary of her suicide. I don't care if it is also the date Wakefield's case was dismissed. There were six Poe novels published before that book, but he had to go and grind his heel into the pain of all those who loved her."

He spat on the floor as if it were his uncle.

Abraham couldn't blame Clemens. He might have done the same thing had it been his loved one. He referenced the notes from the arresting officer. There could have been time after the fire for Clemens to fight his uncle, but the timeline was tight. As much as Abraham hated to admit it, Clemens as Billy Poe looked improbable.

"Where were you between eight and ten this morning?"

Clemens's head jerked up eagerly. "Has there been another body?"

"Your location and any witnesses."

"I'm not Poe, and my fiancée's parents, Thelma and Patrick Napier, can attest to it. We met around nine for breakfast at Maggie's favorite restaurant, took the half-hour trip to Spring Grove Cemetery, and visited her grave. On our way home, I saw *Shadow in the Night* displayed in the window with a sign saying, 'Celebrate justice for Maggie with this special edition.' I went straight to O'Dell Publishing and showed Uncle James exactly what I thought of him. I've been here ever since."

Abraham bit the inside of his cheek. That meant Clemens was clear, at least as far as the carriage house fire and manuscript theft went. His alibis for the murders were weak at best, but good enough to cast doubt over his being Poe.

"So who did he kill? I heard Sullivan and Xavier skipped town, and Grant is awaiting his death from consumption in Colorado. Who's left?"

Keys jangled at the barred entrance to the cells.

"We've got our Poe." Lawson held a handcuffed Monroe in place behind the jailer.

The gate swung open, and Monroe stumbled through after a shove to his shoulder. His eyes were glazed over, and a euphoric smile played across his lips. His movements were sluggish, and he seemed oblivious to his surroundings. Was the man under the influence of opiates? Is that how he was able to fulfill his delusions and vile murders?

Abraham stepped aside and frowned at Monroe's hands as the jailer opened Clemens's cell. One hand was crudely wrapped, but ugly white blisters surrounded by unnaturally brown skin peeked out from the edges. The man was severely burned—like he'd pulled a manuscript box from the fire. Unfortunately it was his left hand. There would be no getting a writing sample from him now. Were the burns enough to claim him Billy Poe? After all, both Abraham and Lawson bore similar burns from this morning's events.

Monroe's head listed to one side, and he muttered almost incoherently, "She's safe now. I did it for her."

His words certainly sounded like those of a madman.

"He's been speaking deliriously since I found him at his home with the burned manuscript box in his possession, along with Miss

Davis's address." Lawson released Monroe from his iron bracelets and shoved the man inside.

"Her address? But how?"

"He's been watching her long enough that he probably discerned who her friends were and then used the directory to find them." Lawson clapped Abraham on the shoulder. "We were just in time, Hall. Ingram and Lydia are safe."

Praise God for that. "What about the manuscript pages?"

"Mostly ashes. I doubt Monroe could discern that Ingram was his next victim."

Good. Not that it mattered now. "We'll need a warrant to thoroughly search his home and office for more evidence."

"I'm taking care of that next. You'll interrogate him while I'm gone. See if you can get a confession. It might take you a while to though. Those opiates need to leave his system first."

Abraham cast a doubtful glance Monroe's way. He'd lain down in the middle of the floor, curled around his burned hand, and continued to mutter incoherently. It would be hours before he could be interrogated if this demonstration were any indication.

Lawson continued. "I found him trying to treat the pain with an opium pipe and lamp."

Not surprising with the severity of his injuries, but putting together an opium setup one-handed didn't fit. He gestured for Lawson to step away from the cell and lowered his voice. "Was there evidence someone else set it up for him? Maybe a partner?"

Lawson's brows drew together as he seemed to go back to the scene and mentally walk it. After a moment, he shook his head. "I didn't see any, but I was more focused on hauling him in while he was easy to control. But you're right. He couldn't have done it on his own. You get that search warrant paperwork written up while Monroe recovers. I'll transfer Lydia to a new location and stay with her. Officer Atwood will remain with Miss Davis to protect her and be prepared to capture Monroe's partner."

"I'll transfer Lydia and see to her safety."

"After your kiss with her last night? I think not."

So Lawson had seen them. The collar around Abraham's neck seemed to tighten, and he tugged it loose.

Clemens gave a low whistle. Apparently they hadn't been speaking low enough. "Maybe you're not as straight a die as I thought. Trying to pass off a night with your saucy miss as duty? I don't think there's a person in town who'd believe her innocence intact. Not with your relationship in the papers and all."

The insult to Abraham and Lydia's integrities couldn't be ignored. "We would never allow anything of the sort to happen. Her safety is my priority."

Lawson folded his arms. "Even the most upstanding men can fall to temptation, son."

"By that logic, her going with you, an unmarried man, would be just as much a temptation."

"Do you see how much gray is in my hair and beard? I'm not a young, hot-blooded man anymore. She'll be safer with me than you. I'm pulling rank on this one. You don't get the choice."

Abraham chafed, but there was little he could do. With Clemens watching, Lydia's reputation was at stake if he insisted. "Where will you take her?"

"I'll leave directions on your desk. I wouldn't want curious ears to hear."

He had a point. As soon as Clemens's bail was set, he'd be out. And it was possible that Clemens and Monroe had worked together. The more he thought about it, the more that made sense. "God be with you both, sir."

Lawson left the cellblock, but Abraham lingered. Maybe with a few well-pointed questions, he could determine if Clemens was Monroe's partner.

"What time did you and the Napiers leave the cemetery?"

Clemens's wits weren't clouded by opium, and it showed in the calculating glint to his eyes. "I'm not Poe's partner. I departed Spring Grove with the Napiers around eleven thirty this morning and did not leave them until I lost my temper at seeing the book around noon. I went straight to O'Dell Publishing, where I was placed under arrest by one. I've been in this cell ever since."

That was disappointing. Abraham would have to verify Clemens's story with the Napiers, but if it checked out, Clemens couldn't be the one who helped Monroe set up the opium lantern. Perhaps O'Dell?

"Did O'Dell go to a hospital after your fight?"

"Uncle James doesn't have the wit nor the stomach to partner with Poe in anything but the written word. I am certain he went to the hospital. The man has less tolerance for discomfort than a newborn babe."

In truth, Abraham agreed. He couldn't envision O'Dell physically committing the murders, nor being the one to plan them. But someone had to have helped Monroe with the opium equipment. Abraham needed to petition for that search warrant and determine the possible partner's identity. He pivoted on his heel and strode toward the detectives' office.

"Hall! Where are you going? Let me out." Clemens's voice rang out behind Abraham.

"You'll have to wait until bail is set. I've got more important work to do than chew the fat with you."

CHAPTER 33

LYDIA RUBBED HER STOMACH TO soothe the aching muscles. She hadn't laughed this hard since she couldn't remember when. Abraham would no doubt kill his friend Lucian once he discovered how many embarrassing stories Lucian had shared with her and her friends.

"You should have seen the look on that cad's face when he realized he wasn't propositioning a woman but a hairy-limbed man." Lucian's exaggerated face brought another round of laughter from Lydia, Nora, Theresa, and Flossie.

"Lucian! That is not an appropriate story for young ladies!" his wife, Verity, admonished as she came in bearing a tray of midnight snacks.

He waved her words away before he snagged a wedge of cheese from the top. "Miss Pelton's the daughter of a coroner. I'm sure she's heard worse."

That was true, although Papa would be horrified to know she had overheard the stories he shared with friends.

"The man took off at such a pace that Abraham had to hike his skirts up to his thighs in order to catch up and tackle him."

The image of ankle-high boots and bare, hairy legs both incited embarrassment and laughter. The next time she saw Abraham, she'd have to work exceedingly hard not to peek at his legs and recall the picture her imagination had conjured.

"But I tell you, Abraham saved the day for the women of George

Street. That scoundrel had a bad habit of beating his women near to death and leaving them in the gutters to suffer their fate."

The levity died instantly. Those poor women. How many times had she observed them from afar or read about them with disgust? They had chosen that life, hadn't they? Greed over virtue? At the sick twist of her stomach, she knew herself to have been judgmental. Some of the women might have willingly chosen that career, but what sort of life had they lived to believe that was their only or best option? She could not know the heart of a person, and condemning them only served to show her own lack of mercy.

Lord, forgive me. Keep teaching me to see people through Your eyes, to allow You alone to be Judge.

She released a sigh and stroked Harold's soft fur. "Abraham is a true hero to stoop to wearing a dress in order to save those whom society would rather pretend didn't exist."

"If that is your view, then I have been a good friend to Abe." He winked. "Can't have his future bride thinking of him as anything less than a hero."

The heat climbed up her neck to the roots of her hair. The idea of being Abraham's future bride was incredibly enticing, even if a bit too soon. And to have his best friend declare such a thing? Oh heavens.

Flossie, bless her, shifted the conversation. "Once Poe has been caught, do you think Cincinnati will leave Lydia alone?"

Lucian shrugged. "It may take a week or two, but I'd imagine their anger will shift to the actual murderer rather than the inspiration for the murder."

Lydia winced, but there was no denying her part. What a twisted dream—to want to be an inspiration to others, only to have it lead to the destruction of so many lives.

"Well, girls. It's nearing midnight. What do you say to going to bed?" Verity couldn't be more than a year or two older than them, but apparently becoming a married woman meant every unmarried woman her age was to be considered a girl in need of mothering.

By the exaggerated roll of Flossie's eyes behind Verity's back, Lydia wasn't the only one to be annoyed by Verity's behavior.

Nora rose from the settee and offered a gracious smile. "Thank you, Officer Atwood and Mrs. Atwood, for your kindness in staying tonight. If you need us, we'll be sharing my room."

Lydia knew what her friend really meant was *We're happy to leave you two alone so we can go upstairs and begin our real plotting to capture Billy Poe should Detectives Lawson and Hall fail.*

Before they made it to the stairs, someone beat on the front door.

Lucian's demeanor immediately shifted from relaxed and jovial to tense and serious. He retrieved his gun and gestured for his wife to move behind a wall, then for Lydia and her friends to go to the top of the stairs. Once he was sure they were out of immediate danger, he slid to the side of the door and raised his voice. "State your business."

"Lawson here. Let me in."

Lucian's body visibly relaxed. Still, he didn't put his gun away until the detective entered the house and the door was closed and locked.

Though she'd much rather Abraham be the one to bring news, Lydia rushed down the stairs. "Does this visit mean you've caught Billy Poe?"

The look Lawson gave Lucian did not inspire confidence. "We've caught one Billy Poe, but unfortunately we believe he has a partner."

"A partner? But who was Billy Poe? And who do you think his partner is?"

"Marcus Monroe has a burned hand and your manuscript."

Though she'd suspected Marcus, the news still came as a wallop to the gut. They'd been friends of a sort and, for a brief moment, potentially more than friends. She'd often written of betrayal, but she'd never really tasted it until now. What a poor job she'd done of depicting it. Yes, it tasted of bitter disappointment, but there was something more. A loss so deep it made her chest ache and her limbs heavy. If she felt this for a man she would only claim as a close acquaintance, how much worse must it have felt for her characters when a loved one had driven the dagger into their backs?

"We believe his partner could be James O'Dell, Eugene Clemens, or even someone unknown." Detective Lawson hesitated a moment before adding with gravity, "There was also a note with Miss Davis's address on Monroe's desk. There is a chance his partner knows where you are and is even now coming to collect you."

"Then let him come." Theresa's voice carried with challenge. "We'll be ready for him."

Lydia smiled at her friend's confidence. With all the booby traps they had planned, Marcus's partner didn't have a chance. It would take some time to rig them, but soon the house would be as impenetrable as a fortress. Yes, the betrayal hurt, but eagerness to prepare a defense had her rubbing her hands together. Which plan should they implement first: the swinging pots over the doors or boards with nails beneath the windows?

"Out of an abundance of caution, I'm taking Lydia to a hidden location that has no connection to her." Detective Lawson selected the wrong shawl from the hall tree and handed it to her. "Officer Atwood will stay with you ladies in case Monroe's partner decides to make an appearance."

Nora stepped forward and switched the shawl with the correct one. "But where are you taking Lydia?"

"I am afraid I cannot disclose that. Detective Hall and I believe it is safer for her if only the two of us know."

Lydia regarded her three friends, each held a troubled countenance. "If Abraham thinks this is best then we'll go along with it. Booby-trap the house for your safety, and then I'll see you tomorrow. Just consider this your chance to catch the villain. It'll make a great story to tell our children and grandchildren one day. I'm jealous that you get to have all the excitement."

One by one, they hugged her tight.

Nora was last and held on a little longer, keeping her voice to a low whisper. "Remember, knee to the groin, fingers to the eyes, then run like hell's hounds are on your heels."

Leave it to Nora to give fighting advice. "Thank you, friend. Soon, we'll celebrate the end of Poe's reign."

CHAPTER 34

IT TOOK A COUPLE HOURS to get a judge to sign off on the search warrant and another to conduct it. The search revealed little evidence but enough to incriminate Marcus. A few matching handwritten notes lay on his desk. The most recent Poe novel, the margins of which were filled with personal annotations, sat next to his reading chair. A list of the names and addresses of each exonerated criminal with a line through the ones who'd been murdered served as a bookmark. It was a little too easy to find, and it unsettled Abraham.

Shouldn't the man who brought Billy Poe to life be smarter than that? And shouldn't there have been more than just those three items?

It was well past the end of his shift, but Abraham couldn't go home and sleep. He considered visiting the address Lawson had left him, but he didn't want to risk leading Monroe's partner to Lydia. Abraham returned to the office and pored over their notes on the case. Monroe wasn't a clear fit for most of the murders. The only connection he had to them was being the editor of the books. He didn't have any tangible relationships with the exonerated criminals or their victims. That alone didn't make him innocent, but everything felt a little too . . . staged? But surely not.

Still, that niggle of skepticism bothered Abraham.

Logically Monroe made sense as Billy Poe. His regard for Lydia. His knowledge and access to the stories. His insistence that Lydia's purpose lived in those stories. That what they published was right and good. He had even suggested the men got what they deserved.

Abraham examined the burned manuscript box again. This was the first condemning piece of evidence brought in by Lawson. Proof that Monroe was Poe. Cinders covered the majority of the bottom half of the box, and the charred corners testified to the burning process having begun. Enough of it remained solid that the interior appeared mostly unharmed—except for the smattering of soot at the top and the white powder of pages turned to ash at the bottom. Wouldn't the entire interior have become blackened if dozens of pages had burned?

He sifted through the ash and rubbed the contents between his fingers. There might be enough for a few pages, but not for an entire novel. Not even when combined with what he remembered from Plane Manor. They hadn't found any of the manuscript pages in Monroe's home, and his hearth and kitchen stove were as cold and empty as anyone would expect during summer temperatures. Abraham tossed the box back onto the desk, sending a puff of ash into the air.

Maybe he should go home to bed. He could revisit the case tomorrow with a clear head, and by morning Monroe would be able to answer their questions without the confusion of an opium haze. Tonight, Lydia would be protected by Lawson, and if Monroe's partner *did* show up at Miss Davis's, Lucian would be able to capture him.

"I don't think Monroe is Poe."

Abraham looked up from his desk to find Clemens, a grim line to his mouth, standing in the doorway.

Abraham leaned back in his chair, his muscles complaining about the hours of hunched searching. "I take it bail was finally set."

"Uncle James decided to drop charges." Clemens shifted uncomfortably. "Probably in large part due to my mother's influence."

So the reporter was a mama's boy. That was a surprising revelation. What did the woman think of her son's dealing in sensationalism?

Clemens cleared his throat and straightened. "Come listen to Monroe. I believe Lawson's framed him."

"Framed?" Abraham blinked, then outright laughed. He was too tired for that nonsense. "By Lawson, no less? That's more implausible than a Lydia Pelton romance novel."

"Not implausible. Do your job. Question the man."

Abraham bristled at the command but rose from his seat. As much as it galled him, Clemens was right. Abraham had a confession—or at least an explanation—to wrangle out of Monroe. What evidence did Clemens think Monroe had to be able to accuse Lawson of framing him? The watch attached to the chain hanging from Abraham's vest indicated the time was past midnight, meaning Monroe had been sleeping off the opium for hours. There might be enough lucidity to him by now to get a decently straight answer.

Though Clemens nearly begged to be allowed in the interrogation room, Abraham required he wait in the hall with an officer to ensure he didn't try to barge in.

Abraham closed the door and stood until the jailer brought in a clear-eyed Monroe. Pain twisted his features, but by all appearances the man had returned to his right mind.

As soon as Monroe laid eyes on Abraham, he took long, urgent strides. "You have to go to Lydia now."

The jailer restrained him, then shoved him down into a chair.

Monroe's hand slammed against the table. The accompanying yelp left him curling around his injury in agony.

Was he still in the same crude bandaging as when he arrived? The thought that they would leave a man—even one deemed Billy Poe—in such obvious need sickened Abraham. He addressed the jailer. "Has a doctor tended to his burn yet?"

"No, sir."

"I've got him. Go fetch whatever physician you can. We are not monsters. He obviously needs medical attention."

The jailer left Abraham alone with Monroe, and he waited until the man no longer writhed in pain and gasped for breath.

Though sweat beaded across his forehead and his pallor indicated he should be lying down, Monroe leaned forward as if he meant to beg. "You have to go to Lydia now. Lawson's going to take off with her and kill Ingram."

"That's a serious accusation to hurl at a long-revered detective, especially considering the proof we have that *you* are Billy Poe."

"Any evidence you found was planted!" He hissed at the accidental movement of his hand but continued his rant. "Lawson burst into my home with Lydia's scorched manuscript box under his arm and threatened to shoot me if I didn't cooperate. He said someone needed to take the fall for Poe, and I was the easiest one to frame. He even forced me to burn my hand in order to *prove* I'd stolen the manuscript from her house."

That was some story. "You're too large a man to be forced to do anything. As severe as that burn is, your hand would have had to been held inside the flame. I can't see you willingly subjecting yourself to that torture."

"If you had a gun to your head, you'd hold it until your hand burned off. Lawson drugged me so that I couldn't reveal what he'd done until he was gone. Tell me, how many hours have passed since you last saw him?"

"Your words don't count as evidence."

"What about the fact *he* has burned hands?" Monroe sat back and leveled a challenging glare.

"I saw him receive those burns myself when we were fighting the fire at the Planes'."

"Are you sure that's when he got them? Or was he only using that display as a way to cover up the fact he'd burned them when retrieving the manuscript himself?"

Abraham's stomach soured. It would be a brilliant and very Poe-like ploy. But this was Lawson they were talking about. He had twenty years of experience serving as an officer in various places and positions and was admired for his ability to solve even the murkiest cases.

Monroe must have sensed the uncertainty he'd evoked. "Go to Lawson's apartment. Search it. He might have planted things at my home, but I guarantee you'll find more evidence in his."

The door opened behind Abraham, but he wouldn't allow the doctor to take Monroe away until he had his questions answered.

"What possible reason would Lawson have to kill those men?"

At this, Monroe deflated. "I don't know. Maybe he was as angry as the rest of us that any criminal with the right connections or enough money could get away with their crimes."

"I know why." Clemens's voice came from behind. "At least the first murder."

Abraham was going to throttle that officer for failing his duties to keep Clemens out.

Clemens closed the door and strode to the table's end. "The first murdered criminal was Otis Wakefield, the man who violated my Maggie and got away with it."

Abraham stood, refusing to allow Clemens to tower over him. "Why would that matter to Lawson? It seems to me that would give you more of a reason to be Poe than it would him."

"He never told you? Lawson was Maggie's godfather."

The photo on Lawson's wall and his words that she was the reason he kept going slammed into Abraham. No picture of Maggie had been included in the Wakefield file, and Lawson had always talked about the case in such a detached manner that Abraham never entertained the potential for a personal connection. But was that really enough to make Lawson a suspect?

Abraham studied Clemens. He was wily enough to use that information to cast doubt over the character of a good man, but Abraham's gut warned that everything he thought he knew about Lawson was about to be turned on its head in the worst possible way.

After allowing the full impact of the information to clobber Abraham, Clemens continued. "Lawson doted on her as one would a daughter. When I failed to walk Maggie home from work the day she was attacked, Lawson blamed me and swore that he would take care of Wakefield. Lawson went after him with such a focus and force that Wakefield's connections were able to make allegations of falsified evidence and coerced witnesses to successfully get the case dismissed.

Wakefield walked away a free man while my Maggie became a prisoner to the horrors his actions wrought."

Abraham remembered reading the headlines that blamed Lawson for Wakefield's release, but he'd dismissed them as another sensationalist story meant to cast a pall over the integrity of the police. Lawson was too highly respected and good at his job to consider anything else. Now Abraham wished he'd read the articles. Had he allowed his own prejudices to interfere with his being a good officer? Was Lawson a credible suspect? It might explain the man's incessant prattle. The constant redirecting of Abraham's thoughts had prevented Abraham from remembering Lawson's connection to the Wakefield case. That detail alone was troubling.

Clemens's nostrils flared, and a vein popped out along his temple. He took several deep, slow breaths before he spoke again. "I'd been reading Dupin's novels for a few months when *Shadow in the Night* released. Within pages, I knew that story was Maggie's. I showed it to Lawson. Instead of being disgusted by the exploitation of her pain for profit, Lawson was elated. Claimed it was exactly the justice Wakefield deserved. Lawson disappeared for a week about a month later. I'm pretty sure it was the same week Wakefield was murdered. Use your brain and then try to tell me that Lawson's not involved."

It was circumstantial. Conjectures of a hurting man.

But the possibility could not be ignored. Abraham would have to verify Clemens's story. Perhaps this was an elaborate ruse to deflect suspicion or get revenge on Lawson for allowing Wakefield to walk away. "Why didn't you tell me any of this sooner?"

"Because I didn't connect the details until Monroe accused him in the cell. I started thinking, and once I started . . ." Clemens shrugged. "I despise Miss Pelton for profiting from Maggie's torment, but I wouldn't wish her dead. I'm too vindictive for that. I'd rather she live with a ruined reputation from her Dupin stories. She wasn't a hero for writing them. She was and is a villain."

The hatred spewing from Clemens exposed a new and festering depth to the man. Justice was meant to bring restoration, but this?

This was judgment without mercy. Condemnation that darkened the soul and made one incapable of seeing the light, hope, and forgiveness of Christ. Abraham pitied him.

"Careful there, Clemens. The words you're speaking reveal your heart to be as vengeful and judgmental as Poe's. You might not like it, but you and Lydia both make a living off the misfortune of others."

"I report truth. I don't take it and twist it into a story for entertainment."

Abraham could debate that rebuttal, but it wasn't worth it. God would have to do the work of changing Clemens's heart. Right now, the only thing Abraham wanted to do was determine if Lawson indeed was the threat Monroe and Clemens painted him to be.

CHAPTER 35

THE CARRIAGE RUMBLED ALONG SIXTH Street, and Lydia shifted uncomfortably on the bench next to Detective Lawson. He'd assured her where they were going was safe and secluded, but wasn't this area of town known for Deer Creek Gang attacks? Very few places struck fear in the hearts of the men Papa worked with, but she'd heard them whisper about this place as if it were a living nightmare that might eat them.

Thick humidity made the night sticky and hot, but Lydia tugged her shawl tighter around her shoulders. She'd lived enough of a nightmare over the last two weeks. Adding an interaction with the Deer Creek Gang was not something she wanted.

What few gas lamps that existed along the street were either unlit or flickering in fear behind broken glass panels. The two people they'd passed since entering this part of town had scurried along with furtive glances over their shoulders and hands clutched around objects as if prepared to wield them for defense. At one point, Lydia swore she heard gunshots fired in the distance.

Detective Lawson seemed unconcerned as he relaxed into the corner with his arm stretched out along the length of the padded seat back. Perhaps the gang only attacked easy targets who traveled on foot. Being trampled by horse hooves and carriage wheels might be a grim enough prospect that they avoided it. The driver did seem to urge the horses faster through the street now than he had when they'd been in the well-lit part of town.

The carriage slowed to a stop. Detective Lawson opened the door and hopped down before reaching back inside to assist her.

Lydia withdrew. "This is where Abraham agreed for me to hide?"

"He trusted my judgment. Monroe's partner would never suspect to find you under the protection of the police here."

It made sense, even if it unnerved her. She accepted his hand and stepped onto the dark street. Detective Lawson paid the driver and waited for him to drive away before guiding her farther down the square and into an alley. Another precaution to hide her location, he assured her. As they cut between several buildings, Lydia's heart raced. It didn't help that Detective Lawson walked with his gun out, ready to fire. Didn't the man know she was an author and dreaming up all sorts of horrible scenarios? He was an officer, for heaven's sake. The Deer Creek Gang would gut him alive and do unspeakable horrors to her if they caught up to them.

Before a single scenario came to life, Detective Lawson trotted up the steps of a porch at the back of a two-story brick building. Iron bars protected the lone window. Black lettering on the door indicated they were at Napier's Dry Goods. Napier. Wasn't that a victim's name from one of the original cases? Before she could sort through her mental files of research, Lawson gestured for her to precede him up the outdoor stairs to the next level—likely the living quarters for the merchant owner.

"Are we staying with friends of yours?" That would protect her reputation—not that she had much of one since the Dupin debacle.

"No. The living quarters are being renovated before they move in, but he's allowing me to stay here for a few days."

She noticed his lack of the word *us*. "Does he know I'm going to be with you?"

He put his gun away and retrieved keys from inside his coat, ostensibly ignoring her question.

She supposed his friend's ignorance couldn't be helped. He had said the fewer people who knew her location, the safer she'd be.

The keys jangled for a moment, and then he ushered her into a dark vestibule before locking the outer door behind them. A faint light glowed under the door leading to the living quarters.

That was odd, considering the urgency with which Detective Lawson had removed her from Nora's home. Had he come here ahead of time to prepare for her arrival? Or was someone already here? Maybe Abraham?

Detective Lawson guided her into an unfinished kitchen. A single lantern stood on a table with a shotgun propped up so that it aimed at a door on the other side of the room.

What on earth was a booby trap doing facing toward a room?

Her eyes traced the thin cord looped around the trigger backward and up to the ceiling, where it connected to a pulley behind the gun. After passing through the pulley, the line drooped to the door handle and was secured in place. Should anyone from the other room pull the door open, the tension would pull the trigger and fire the gun at them.

But that didn't make sense.

A booby trap like this should be set up on the inside of the room if the goal was to protect from intruders.

Her stomach dropped. This wasn't for protection. It was created to imprison.

She glanced at Detective Lawson.

Pride quirked his mouth as he joined her. "Quite ingenious, isn't it?"

Surely they couldn't have been *that* wrong about Billy Poe's identity.

When she didn't answer, he slid an arm around her and led her to the door, where he carefully removed the cord from the knob. "This setup made it where I could leave Ingram here alone safely. Not that I expect he's escaped his restraints."

Restraints? Ingram?

Good gracious. Detective Talbot Lawson *was* Billy Poe. How had she not suspected him? She was an author, for heaven's sake! Twists and unexpected villains were supposed to be her forte.

Detective Lawson turned the handle to reveal her would-be prison.

Enough was enough. She was tired of being the victim of her own stories. This heroine was going to fight, not calmly submit and pray her hero would rescue her.

In a move that would make Nora proud, Lydia twisted to face Detective Lawson, jammed her thumbs into his eyes, and rammed her knee into his groin.

As he yelled and then doubled over, Lydia raced to the vestibule and unlocked the outer door. Lawson's feet pounded behind her as she flung the door open and ran.

Halfway down the stairs, the man grabbed a fistful of her hair and yanked.

Her hands flew to where his fingers sank into her curls, and, not for the first time, she cursed the unruly locks. No matter how she tried, she couldn't pry his fingers away. When she continued to fight against him, he heaved her backward. Her back slammed into the sharp edge of a step, and she looked up at the reddening face of a man she'd thought one of Cincinnati's finest.

"That is no way to treat your hero, Lydia."

For some unfathomable reason, he released her hair.

She scrambled to her feet and pivoted just as a metallic click sounded behind her.

She froze. A person didn't have to hear that sound more than once to know exactly what it meant. The step above her creaked, then the cool circle of a barrel touched her temple.

"Turn around."

Would he really shoot her? Supposedly he was in love with her.

Rule number two: never point the muzzle at something you don't intend to shoot.

Her stomach flipped at the memory of Abraham's words. Detective Lawson would not make the same mistakes she had. If he had the muzzle directed at her, he intended to shoot.

Slowly she turned. The barrel shifted so that she faced it head-on. So much for the best course of action to never be on the wrong end of a gun. She'd never be able to run for cover, which left only one option. Do whatever he wanted.

"Good. Now take us to our room."

The use of *our* stole her breath, but she forced one foot in front of the other as Detective Lawson backed his way up the stairs, maintaining the barrel at eye level. He kept his free, bandaged hand tucked against him and elevated above his heart, a sure sign that it pained him. If she could gouge it with her fingers, his agony might last long enough for her to escape.

If he didn't pull the trigger and blow her down the stairs first.

That plan wasn't going to work, at least not right now, but she'd keep it tucked away for the perfect opportunity.

At the entryway, Detective Lawson shifted to walking behind her. She studied the dangling cord. If she yanked it at just the right moment, the shotgun would go off.

Once again, Abraham's rules stayed her hand.

Always know where you're pointing and beyond it.

Well, the gun was pointing at Detective Lawson's back, but she was just beyond him. If the shot passed through him, she might end up shooting herself too. Why couldn't gun rules be more helpful to her in a situation like this instead of keeping her prisoner to the man's delusions? It was too much to hope for, but maybe Detective Lawson would forget one and accidentally shoot himself.

They passed through the door into a small room. A man about the size of Marcus Monroe—presumably Mr. Ingram—sat in the corner with shackles around his ankles, hands secured behind his back, and a gag over his mouth. He wriggled and made noises, but nothing discernible. He would be no help in forming an escape plan. And honestly, should she trust a man who had beaten his employer to death? Although "the enemy of my enemy is my friend" had merit.

If writing had taught her anything, it was to keep her mind open to all the possibilities. When she had a better idea of where she stood with Detective Lawson, she could sort through for the most plausible and unexpected option.

There wasn't much to the room. A narrow bed with a carpetbag at the end took up one wall while a desk with a stack of pages on top sat opposite.

Her manuscript.

She didn't need to get close enough to read the words to know. The brown-singed edges and soot-smudged top were enough to give it away. What she didn't recognize was the second stack of written pages next to it. She stepped closer. The red-inked scrawl of Marcus's editorial marks covered the top sheet. Curiosity was too much. She read the first page and then the second. The words weren't hers but the amateur work of someone trying to write a crime novel.

"You haven't reached that part, but Ingram was my choice of victim too." Detective Lawson spoke at her elbow.

She jammed her hip against the desk in her instinctive attempt to put distance between them, but there was nowhere to go.

His satisfied smirk sent chills coursing down her spine. He toyed with her sleeve, alternating between rubbing the material between his fingertips and drawing flirtatious curved paths up and down the length of her arm. "I wrote this years ago, right after Ingram's poor excuse for a sentencing. It proves that even before I knew you, we were of the same mind. You and I recognized the need for justice and carried it out when no one else was brave enough to do so. Don't you see—I've waited my whole life for a woman who understood me. We belong together." He clasped her shoulders with a light touch communicating the possession he claimed over her.

If only she could sink her nails into his burns—but it would only make him angry, and she had nowhere to go. Lydia forced herself to meet his eyes, expecting the deranged gloss of a madman's. Instead, penetrating clarity stared back at her. He wouldn't be easily fooled, but maybe if she could balance playing to his delusions and questioning them, she could manipulate him into thinking she supported him. After all, Momma often declared Lydia's theatrics fit for the stage.

"What about Abraham?"

A muscle along his jaw twitched. "What about him? He'll never support you or your vision for justice. He's just a young pup who doesn't understand the injustice in the world he serves. It'll be years before he realizes that what *we* do is the only way to protect and avenge the innocent."

"He's a good detective. It won't be long until he realizes that you are Billy Poe. *My* Billy Poe." One word had the power to change the meaning of a sentence and its reception.

As she hoped, claiming him as hers eased his stance. It was disgusting, really, but now more than ever she needed to use the right words from the very first moment she said them. There would be no editing.

"I know. I'd hoped youth would prove his folly, and he'd take my observations and conclusions as his own, but he's too independent for that. It won't be long before he realizes Marcus is nothing more than a decoy. We'll need Ingram's death staged and us out of the city by morning's light. Otherwise I might have to kill Hall, and I am loath to do that. But I will."

Morning light came early in the summer. She checked the watch pinned to her shawl and drew a steadying breath. One o'clock. Roughly five hours until sunrise. She needed to stall Detective Lawson much longer than that. The only tool she had available was writing.

Lord, let it be enough.

"I never finished my manuscript. Ingram doesn't have an ending."

The racket from Ingram grew louder as the man fought against his restraints and yelled muffled words at them. Her stomach twisted. It had been alarming enough to be abducted by Mr. Keaton's family, knowing they wanted to hurt her, but listening to Mr. Clemens talk about the most poetic way for her to die had been a horror she wouldn't wish on anyone. Not even Mr. Ingram. Nevertheless, if she had to stall for time, she would do it, and hopefully save his life.

She hated to admit it, but Mr. Clemens wasn't quite the cad she'd thought him to be.

"He does in mine." Lawson tapped the pages. "I submitted this story to O'Dell last year. Only, Monroe called it 'lackluster drivel that would better serve as kindling' and sent it back."

No wonder he'd had no qualms framing Marcus—he'd experienced at least a partial edit from the man. She well knew how direct and cutting Marcus could be when critiquing a manuscript. But this would provide her the perfect way to stall for time. Editing. The good Lord knew how much she dragged that process out with every manuscript. They could spend days just figuring out the best way to rewrite one scene.

"I'm sure we can work through it together."

Pleasure at her suggestion eased a bit more of the tension in his stance.

"I'll need to read your whole manuscript first though. And time to think through the possibilities. The perfect ending is never the first one I write."

He pulled out the chair and indicated she should sit.

"I'm quite tired. Could you make me a pot of coffee or tea?" If he left, she could rummage through the room and see what was at her disposal for escaping.

Suspicion crinkled his eyes for a moment before a smile re-formed. "Of course. Be warned, if you try to open the door, the shotgun will fire, and a blast of buckshot will go through the wood and plaster. There isn't a safe place for you."

It felt as if the blood had drained from her face, but she hoped it didn't show. She offered a fake smile and picked up Lawson's manuscript. "Why would I do that? I have reading to do."

She studied the first page, only half paying attention to the words, and waited until he'd left.

Soon she'd have hot liquid for a weapon. The trick would be coming up with a plan that would save not only herself but Mr. Ingram as well.

CHAPTER 36

ABRAHAM SPREAD OUT THE EVIDENCE he'd collected from Lawson's apartment on Superintendent Carson's dining room table. Pages and pages of practice notes with his left hand. Files of information used for plotting the timing, location, and methods for murder, along with details on the victims' daily patterns. He'd been methodical and careful. All of it had been locked in a safe hidden behind a bookshelf in his private office. If Abraham hadn't noticed the faint grooves in the wooden floor from the constant moving of the shelf, he might have missed it.

"Sir, we need every available officer searching for Lawson. Miss Pelton and Uriah Ingram are both missing."

The knowledge that he'd encouraged Lydia to trust the very man they sought made him ill. Why hadn't he seen the signs? Lawson himself had told him everything was possible until proven otherwise.

Carson bent over the table and sorted through the evidence, shaking his head. "I can't believe it. He's been our best detective for years."

"I'm afraid we're on limited time. I need your permission to pull together all available officers."

"You have it. Any idea where he might be holed up?"

Everyone on the force knew Lawson's face. He'd want to avoid any chance of running into someone who would recognize him and report him once they learned he was a wanted man. If he'd already killed Ingram, Lawson was probably on a train out of town. But not with Lydia. He'd never get her on a train without her creating a scene. That was Abraham's sole hope the man remained in town.

If Lawson had stayed in the city, he'd have chosen a place officers would eschew.

There was only one place that immediately came to mind. "It's nothing more than a hunch, but if I were him, I'd hide in the Deer Creek Gang's area."

"Pull every Deer Creek Gang file we have and see if there are any connections to Lawson. Maybe he befriended one of them and is hiding in their home."

Abraham gritted his teeth. Somewhere, Lydia was being held against her will, and all he could do was dig through files? Lawson knew their methods for investigation, and he would avoid every potential connection they might find. More than likely the only result in searching for a paper trail would be wasting time. All the while who knew what Lawson was forcing Lydia to do? Participate in Ingram's murder? Watch it?

There had to be a better way.

Carson pulled a photo from the evidence pile. "What's this? Who's with Lawson and Clemens here?"

Abraham peered at the photograph of Maggie Napier. He'd brought it as proof of Lawson's personal connection to the Wakefield case. Was he still close with Maggie's parents? If so, they might have a better idea of where Lawson might be hiding.

"Lawson was close to the family of one of the original victims. I'll talk to them. Carlisle can begin searching the files while I do."

"Whatever you think is best. I'll be in the office shortly. Get everyone searching now."

After obtaining the address for the Napier family, Abraham used the nearest call box to reach dispatch. They would alert the patrolmen to be on the lookout for Lawson and get officers to each train station, just in case. Someone would rouse Carlisle from his bed and get him working through the Deer Creek Gang files. With that settled Abraham headed to the tenement where the Napiers lived.

Lights from their bottom-floor home indicated they were up, and Clemens answered when Abraham rapped.

Abraham frowned. "What are you doing here?"

"Probably the same thing as you. Come inside. I think I know where Lawson's hiding."

Clemens allowed him to pass into the main room, where Mr. and Mrs. Napier sat, in obvious distress, on the settee.

"It's true then." Mr. Napier hugged his wife closer. "The police believe Talbot is Billy Poe."

Abraham hated to be the bearer of such news to a family who'd already suffered so much. "I am afraid so, and we believe he's holding a young woman and his next potential victim hostage somewhere."

The man ran a hand down his face before rising to his feet and heading to a hook on the wall, where a set of keys hung. "I've expanded my business to a second location, one with living quarters above the store. I'm having some renovations done before we move in, but Talbot came by yesterday to ask if he could stay there for a few nights. He said his roof had a leak and the landlord needed him gone while it was repaired."

"And as his friend, you didn't give it a second thought."

"None. He's been like a brother to me since we were schoolmates. I just can't believe this of him." He handed Abraham the keys. "But I'd rather you check the premises and be wrong than for me to deny you access and be the mistaken one."

"Thank you, sir. If you will give me the address, I will return these to you as soon as we're finished searching."

Clemens grabbed his coat and hat from the table. "I know the address. I'll take you there myself."

"You'll get your story later, Clemens. I won't risk your nosiness costing a life."

"This is more than just getting a story." His voice lowered. "I failed Maggie in not protecting her. I may not like Miss Pelton, but she is a woman and doesn't deserve the likes of whatever Lawson has planned." Clemens pulled on his coat and plopped his hat in place. "Besides, you need me. I've connections in the Deer Creek Gang. If you run into them without me, you're a dead man before you even reach the store."

"I'm not going in there alone. I'm taking a group of officers with me."

"Then you'll have a bloody war in the street. It's safer to go in as two men than to drag a bunch of officers to their potential deaths."

He was right about a large group being more trouble than a pair of men, but going in with no backup was foolish and reckless. This wasn't a novel. Lawson might be one man, but he was cagey and would have no compunction against using a hostage to negotiate his way out. And with him suspecting how Abraham felt about Lydia, Lawson would use her against Abraham.

"I'll call for pairs of officers to join us at the store's location." Abraham stood his ground. "We're not looking for trouble with the gang, but I'm not risking facing Lawson alone while he has two hostages."

After making the necessary arrangements, Abraham checked that both his guns were loaded and that he had ample ammunition. God willing, not a single shot would be fired.

Clemens didn't carry a gun, but he swore he wouldn't need one. Words were his weapon of choice, and when those failed he'd rely on his champion pugilist skills. Abraham ignored that information. Pugilism was illegal in Cincinnati, though prizefights happened regularly in the remoter or more abandoned sections of town.

He and Clemens entered the Deer Creek Gang's area on foot so as not to draw attention from any gang members who might be lurking in the streets, searching for early morning factory workers to rob. Dawn would soon be lighting the sky, meaning nearly an entire night had been spent in discovering evidence and Lawson's whereabouts. Hours that Lawson had time to do whatever he'd planned and escape.

Lord, please have delayed him from any action, and keep Lydia and Ingram safe.

Ingram might have been a murderer and a scoundrel, but death at a vigilante's hand was not how Abraham wished for anyone to go.

Twilight dusted the sky but gave no light to the streets. The few working gaslights only served to make shadows harder to discern. The normal noises of night animals sifting through refuse or getting into fights broke up the silence. Abraham and Clemens had yet to see anyone, but occasional lit windows in tenement buildings indicated workers were beginning their morning routines. Soon it would be difficult to predict if the sound of footsteps meant a dangerous gang member or a harmless citizen.

Abraham kept his head down and his hands in his pockets, though his eyes constantly surveyed his surroundings. The burns ached and complained at the cramped space, but it would appear odd to have only one hand in his pocket, and he needed to have quick access to his gun without it being obvious he carried one. In contrast, Clemens walked like he owned the night: head up, slight swagger to his step, and a whistle on his lips.

"Keep it quiet. You don't want to alert anyone that we're here."

Clemens just whistled louder. When he reached the end of "Yankee Doodle," he started over.

Midway through the second time, Abraham was ready to collar Clemens and shove a gag in his mouth. Before he could give in to the temptation, a group of seven men stepped out from the alley and blocked their way.

This was exactly what he was afraid of.

"Well, if it ain't ol' Bloody Knuckles himself." The tallest and leanest man of the group pushed forward.

His cronies took up positions around Clemens and Abraham in a near full circle.

Abraham clenched his jaw so hard his teeth ached up to his temples. He should have forced Clemens to stop whistling the moment he'd started.

But Clemens stood there with a grin on his face. "Just the man I was looking for. I told you I'd be able to find the Bonecrusher." He elbowed Abraham and nodded at Bonecrusher. "The old man can't resist my rendition of 'Yankee Doodle.'"

"It's so awful, ya should be tried for treason."

Clemens barked a laugh. "The only crime I'm interested in is a good rough-and-tumble. What do you say to a rematch? I'm short on rent and could use an influx of coin."

"Might wanna reconsider that fight, seein's how losin' is what took your rent money the first time."

"What can I say? I'm itching to punch someone. Might as well be your ugly mug."

"Ya cocky . . . Ya ain't even gonna draw blood before I have ya spillin' yours on the pavers."

"Care to put your money where your mouth is? Round up a crowd and meet me in front of Napier's Dry Goods in fifteen minutes. London Prize Ring rules. None of that Queensberry rules nonsense. I want to feel the crunch of your nose beneath my fist."

Bonecrusher cracked his neck. "You're gonna have more than bloody knuckles when I'm finished with ya. See ya in fifteen. If ya turn chicken, I'll be comin' to find ya."

The group split, each man knowing where to go to draw the crowd that Clemens wanted.

This time, Abraham really did collar him. "What sort of imbecile are you?"

"You ought to be thanking me. If you don't want Lawson using Miss Pelton as leverage for escape, we need to draw him away."

"And you think he'll abandon his plans for Lydia and Ingram just so he can watch a fight?"

"I think he'll investigate what's going on and allow you to intercept him or get Miss Pelton and Ingram out of harm's way."

"And you didn't think to communicate that before initiating this foolish plan? Lawson is bound to recognize you and realize what you're doing. Not to mention, I have officers sneaking into that building you just planned a fight in front of. We're trying to avoid a war with the Deer Creek Gang, not start one."

Clemens yanked Abraham's hand off his coat. "Lawson's familiar with my choice of entertainment and won't suspect a thing. As for the gang, they'll be too engrossed in the fight. More than likely, half of them will join in on it themselves anyway. You just make sure you're in that building before someone shoots the gun to announce the start of the fight."

Except Abraham couldn't control when the rest of the officers would show up, and he couldn't notify them of this plan. Clemens had single-handedly taken this situation from bad to worse. Men might die, and if they did, Abraham would hold Clemens responsible.

CHAPTER 37

TIME WAS GROWING SHORT. LYDIA could tell by Lawson's agitated pacing behind her.

She'd stalled for four hours reading and commenting on his manuscript and another thirty minutes in brainstorming a list of poetic methods of justice to inflict upon Mr. Ingram. If she managed to stay Lawson's hand for another half hour, she'd consider it a miracle.

Nothing was going according to plan. The coffee idea had been futile. He kept the pot and only put enough in her cup for one or two sips at a time. And all that time he'd spent away preparing it, she'd not managed to find one suitable piece of anything that could be used to free Mr. Ingram or stop Lawson from overpowering an escape attempt.

Not that she wanted to free Mr. Ingram anymore. She'd removed the gag so they could form a plan, and less than a minute later, she'd stuffed it back in his mouth. Nothing but profanities and threats toward Detective Lawson and her had spewed from his mouth. She was the villain, and he intended to get revenge. Given the man had been convicted of murder, she was willing to take him at his word on that particular threat. Especially now that he'd heard her help Lawson cultivate ideas that made her nauseated to even think about.

"You have thirty ideas written on that sheet." Lawson jabbed a finger toward the page in front of her. "One of them has to be grand enough to prove to the world that justice should be upheld and not twisted for personal gain."

"I'm so tired, I can't even tell anymore." It was an excuse but not a pretend one. Her head still ached from his yanking her hair, and her eyes felt like they were crossed. "Maybe we should sleep on it for a few hours and then pick one."

"The sun will be up soon. Patrick is an early riser. He'll show up not long after that to stock the shelves."

All the better, in her opinion. Then she could scream for help.

Somewhere outside, a gunshot cracked.

Had the police arrived? Or was the Deer Creek Gang creating mischief outside the building?

Muffled shouting arose, like a riot had broken out in the street.

Lydia jumped from her chair and skirted around Mr. Ingram to yank open the only window. The shouting grew louder, but she couldn't tell what was transpiring. Another building blocked the view of whatever was happening on the main road. What little she could see of the alley below was empty. With a deep breath to overcome her fear of heights and falling, she leaned out and peered to her left. A crowd of men pressed forward, jumping, yelling, and waving money in the air.

It didn't look like a riot. But it didn't look like the police either.

Lawson yanked her back and took her place.

The thought to grab his legs and shove him out the window flitted through her mind, but he straightened and slammed it shut before she could act.

"I'll find out what's going on." He pulled a set of handcuffs from his waist. "You stay put. I can't risk your trying to get their attention." He locked one bracelet around her wrist, then forced her to the foot of the brass bed, where he locked the other around a pole. "If you manage to get free, don't forget that gun will fire at you if you open the door."

He strode from the room. The handle jostled, proving his warning wasn't an idle threat. The cord waited to thwart any escape attempt.

Well, if she couldn't escape, she could at least block the man's return.

She adjusted the bracelet lower on the pole and gripped the bottom of the bed. With much grunting, huffing, and sweating, she managed to shift the bed so that it stretched the width of the room and blocked the door. The only problem was that left her wedged between the bed and the wall. It was a precarious position to be in should the gun go off, but Lord willing, Abraham would come along and dismantle the thing before that ever happened.

Only Officer Yount made it to the building before spectators gathered for the fight. Eager to prove himself, Yount volunteered to stand guard at the front entrance stairs despite being surrounded by Deer Creek Gang members. He tucked his coat and hat behind some crates and ruffled his hair to blend in with the other spectators. Nothing could be done to conceal his uniform pants, but hopefully the fight's patrons would be too engrossed in the boxing match to notice.

That left Abraham to enter through the back and face Lawson alone—at least until other officers arrived.

He should wait, but Clemens was already working the growing crowd into a lather. The man was more worried about garnering bets than tempering the crowd until Abraham could reach the access stairs undetected.

As groups of men arrived and formed a human fighting ring, Abraham crept as close to the wall as possible down the alley. Just as he reached the cover of the porch, a gunshot rang out from the front.

The fight had begun, and time was against him.

Abraham slipped up the stairs. Keeping his weapon ready, he gritted his teeth against the pain as he used his burned hand to unlock the door and gently push it open. The darkened vestibule led to another door, where light shone beneath.

Confirmation that someone, hopefully Lawson, was here.

He lifted a prayer, then gently pushed on the second door. It swung partially open without squeaking. Footsteps moved at a quick pace, growing fainter as they neared the building's front. Everything else was quiet.

He slid through the half-open door into an unfinished room coated in sawdust and stacked with construction supplies.

If he'd had any doubts as to Lawson's purpose in hiding here, they were gone the moment he spotted the propped-up, single-barrel shotgun, ready to fire. At least he knew where Lydia and Ingram were.

Now the question was, did he take Lawson by surprise or free Lydia and Ingram so they could escape the building before Lawson returned?

Scraping sounds came from the room, like someone was dragging a piece of furniture across the floor.

With the noise going on inside there, Lawson was bound to hurry back.

Abraham pressed himself against the wall next to the door leading to the front.

By the time the scraping stopped, Lawson's footfalls announced his return.

Abraham held perfectly still, his weapon ready to press against Lawson's head the moment he stepped into the room.

The footsteps slowed, then stopped.

A moment too late, Abraham realized the lantern cast his shadow across the open doorway.

Lawson came through the door low and jammed the muzzle of his gun into Abraham's gut.

Abraham dropped the muzzle of his own gun to Lawson's temple, careful to keep his finger away from the trigger. He wanted Lawson alive. "You fire, and you're a dead man."

"So are you, only my death will be quick, and yours will be a lingering, suffering one." Lawson slowly stood his full height, keeping his muzzle pressed into Abraham's belly. "I always knew you'd make a great detective. You just weren't supposed to become one so quickly."

Abraham supposed he should take that as a compliment, but at the moment it felt like an insult. The man he'd admired and hoped to learn from had betrayed all who knew him—betrayed the oath they took. "How could you turn your back on everything you've stood for?"

"I didn't turn my back. The courts did that disgrace. We risk our lives every day to bring in these swine, but when we catch them and turn them in with an undeniable bounty of evidence, they walk free. What's the point of our jobs if we can't fulfill our oaths to serve and protect? The only honorable thing left is to mete out justice ourselves."

"And what is the honorable thing here? You've committed at least five counts of murder—six, if Mr. Ingram's dead."

"Not yet, but Lydia and I have settled on a plan."

The inclusion of Lydia relieved Abraham more than the knowledge that Ingram lived. "Even so, by all rights, you deserve to face the noose as much as your victims did."

"An executioner is not guilty of murder."

"You are no court-appointed executioner."

Lawson's mouth twisted. "No. I'm God's, and I'll not be condemned for it. It's an honor to serve Him as His right hand of justice."

Only Jesus could rightfully claim that honor, but there would be no reasoning with Lawson. That insanity ruling might genuinely be needed. Abraham's partner was even more delusional than he had thought. If he didn't choose his words carefully, they'd both die.

"I've committed no crimes, Lawson, and we're friends. Would God count it as justice if you kill me?"

Indecision flickered over the man's countenance. "I don't want to kill you, but if you force my hand, God will allow it."

"Then I guess we'll stand here in a stalemate until one of us passes out from exhaustion. The only way you're leaving here is in iron bracelets or a casket."

Lawson's gaze slid to the gun pressed against his head.

Victory sparked in his eyes as he pulled his gun back and then rammed it back into Abraham's midsection. His free arm swept up and bashed Abraham's arms against the doorframe.

The calculated risk worked. Abraham tried to keep hold of his gun, but with his burns making gripping difficult, the weapon flew from his hands and skidded somewhere into the dark room beyond. Abraham might have lost his gun, but Lawson's momentum allowed Abraham to twist away from the muzzle at his gut and shove Lawson to the floor.

As soon as Lawson hit the ground, Abraham stomped on his wrist and dropped a knee to his chest. He pounded on the man's hand until he released the gun. When Abraham reached for it, however, Lawson rolled, bringing with him a punch that landed solidly against Abraham's jaw. Light shot across his vision, and ringing shrilled in his ears.

Using his advantage, Lawson maneuvered to the upper position. His hands wrapped around Abraham's throat and squeezed.

The rough material of bandaged hands told Abraham exactly where to retaliate. He pried his fingers beneath the man's grip and curved them into a claw as he pulled Lawson's hands away.

Lawson roared and reared back in pain.

Abraham shoved him off and scrambled to his feet. He wasn't interested in a fight to the death, but he would fight for his life.

Lawson was standing before Abraham could pin and handcuff him. Head down and arms out like bull horns, he charged forward and tackled Abraham's midsection.

They flew across the room and crashed into the table.

It cracked along the middle and collapsed to the floor with Abraham caught in the V of the two halves and Lawson on top of him. At the same time, the shotgun fired, someone screamed, and glass shattered.

The room plunged into darkness, only to reignite as flaming kerosene spread across the floor from the broken lantern.

Lawson's eyes illuminated wild and crazed as he raised his arm for a lights-out punch.

Still pinned in by the broken table and Lawson's body, Abraham could only move his head and arms, but the shotgun had landed near his head in the fall. He wrapped his hand around the barrel and swung it with all the force he could muster. The cord attached to it jerked with resistance about halfway through the swing, but then released with a cracking sound. The stock of the gun connected with Lawson's head and was followed by something heavy from above.

Lawson's deadweight tumbled backward off Abraham and landed on the floor. Abraham scrambled to his feet. In the light from the flames, he identified the pulley that had probably saved his life lying next to Lawson's head. Unwilling to chance the older man's coming around, Abraham slapped handcuffs on him, then tossed his coat over the flames and stomped them out.

With the fire out and Lawson either unconscious or dead—Abraham really didn't want to know which for sure—Abraham took stock of himself and his surroundings.

Early morning light was just beginning to brighten the room. His burned hand stung like it was on fire again, and his entire body hurt but probably not as bad as it would later. He was alive, and that was a miracle considering the gun he'd had jammed in his gut less than five minutes ago. A glance at Lawson confirmed that he'd be no trouble, even if he roused. It was safe to go in and retrieve Lydia and Ingram.

He approached the door, then froze. A dozen holes tightly peppered the lower half corner of the door and wall. Soft whimpers came from the other side. Had Lydia been shot?

He turned the knob and pushed, but something solid blocked the door from opening.

"Lydia!" He rammed against the door, and whatever was on the other side scraped against the floor.

She yelped. "Stop. That hurt."

Her voice came from the side where the buckshot had hit the wall.

His chest constricted, and his attempt at a calm voice failed. "Have you been shot?"

"Yes." Her whimpers tore at him.

"Where and how badly?"

"Arm. Don't know."

Depending on which arm and where, it could be a fatal wound. His heart raced as fast as his mind. He needed to get her out and now.

"I can't open the door. What's in the way? Can you move it?"

"The bed. I can't."

Great. She could be bleeding to death, and he couldn't even get to her. That store had to have something of use in it, and Yount could run for the doctor.

"Don't move. I'm going to find something to break down the door."

CHAPTER 38

DON'T MOVE? THERE WAS NO chance of that if she could help it. Novels made gunshot wounds sound like nothing worse than paper cuts. Men always gritted their teeth and ignored the pain as they fought valiantly to rescue their loves. Then they'd shrug them off as nothing more than flesh wounds and sweep their women off their feet before kissing them senseless.

What a load of poppycock.

Lydia had endured a plethora of paper cuts in her life. This torment was no paper cut. Not even one dipped in lemon juice. And forget sweeping anyone off their feet. She didn't even want to lift her arm—not that she could have anyway, considering it was the one still handcuffed to the bed.

Praise God she'd flattened her body against the wall and slid her legs beneath the bed in order to have the least amount of exposure to a potential shot. If she'd been resting her head on her arm?

Bile rose to her throat. She wasn't ready to die. Oh, she knew where she was going. Jesus was her Savior and all, but Abraham hadn't even properly kissed her. What a tragedy dying without that would be.

But she wasn't dead. At least not yet.

She lifted her hand away from the two bullet holes and yelped at the fresh wave of pain.

Bad idea.

With only a glance at the oozing blood, she returned to applying pressure. What good was it to have a doctor for a father if she didn't adhere to the medical advice he gave others?

Thwamp! Crack!

Lydia jumped at the sounds and let out a cry at the sudden movement.

"Lydia!" Abraham's panicked voice came from the other side. "Did I hurt you?"

She looked up to where the sharp blade of an axe had cut through the door.

Which would hurt more, a blade or a bullet? She laughed at the ridiculousness of her thoughts even as she whimpered from shifting.

"Lydia?"

She blinked to clear her head . . . better that than shaking it and jarring her arm again. "No. I startled, and it hurt."

He muttered something and then spoke louder. "I'm sorry. I should have warned you. I'm going to create an opening so I can get through. Are you far enough away to stay safe?"

She'd probably get covered in wood chips, but there wasn't much to be done about that. "Go ahead. I'm fine."

The next axe swing was his only reply. She dipped her head to curtain her face with her hair as chunks and splinters of wood clinked against the brass frame and fell around her. By the time Abraham finished, her arm and lap were littered with debris.

"Stay as you are. I'm going to climb through onto the bed and come around to you." Abraham grunted, the bed squeaked, and then his boots thudded against the floor.

From the other side of the room, Mr. Ingram fussed and struggled.

"You don't look hurt, Ingram, but the lady is. I'll release you after I tend to her."

Lydia carefully tipped her head back, wishing she could shake the hair from her face but too afraid of the stabbing sensation it would cause.

Abraham reached the narrow opening at the end of the bed. "Where is the worst pain?"

"My arm. The one attached to the bed."

"Attached to the . . ." A growl rumbled in his throat. "I have a key to unlock it, but I don't think there is any way around jostling your arm to do it."

She forced a shaky breath. What was a little more suffering if it meant freedom? "Do whatever it takes."

"I'll be as gentle as I can."

He climbed onto the bed and leaned over the end. Anxiety furrowed his brow and flattened his lips as he assessed her, then the bloodied area of her arm. By the anger that sparked in his eyes, Lawson would have a reckoning once this was over. If only she could cup Abraham's cheek and assure him she'd be okay. Although, releasing the pressure and allowing the blood to flow freely just so she could touch him probably wouldn't alleviate his fear.

After evaluating the situation, Abraham spoke. "I'm going to unlock the one attached to the bed first. Then, once we get you out of that hole, I'll remove the other one."

He slipped his arms between the bars and twisted the key in the keyhole. The cuff released, and Lydia stiffened her arm to slow its drop. The resulting pangs brought tears to her eyes, and a whimper she'd tried to hold back escaped.

Abraham's thumb brushed at an escaped tear. "I'm sorry. Just a bit more, and then you can be still until a doctor arrives."

As long as being still meant he was holding her in his arms, she'd endure whatever movements necessary to get there.

"Can you turn and get your legs out from beneath the bed? I need to move it away from you and the door."

With a whole lot of scrunching her face as if that might ease the throbbing, she twisted until her feet no longer stretched beneath the bed. Her arm screamed, and each breath came with a gasp that threatened to turn into a sob. She tried to focus on Abraham's comical half-singed hair and handsome—albeit bruised—face, but they weren't enough of a diversion. "Talk to me. Please. Distract me."

He climbed off the bed and repositioned himself to pull it away. "What do you want me to say?"

She leaned her head against the wall and closed her eyes against the radiating pain. "Anything. Nursery rhymes. Stupid jokes. Math problems, for all I care." A moan slipped out as her arm jostled with the bed's movement.

Metal scraping against the wooden floor interspersed his words. "Two plus two is four. Four plus four is eight. Eight plus eight is—"

She laughed even as her arm chastised her. She hadn't meant him to take her so literally.

His shadow fell over her, and she sensed him lowering himself next to her. "What? Would you prefer something more along the lines of 'I think you are the bravest and smartest woman I know'? Or that I'm going to thoroughly knock you off your feet the first chance I get?"

"Better."

His chuckle was strained as he held her hand still while he removed the other handcuff.

The force applied by his twisting of the key made her jolt upright and cry out.

"I'm sorry, but it's off now." He released her hand. "Don't try to stand or move. The last thing we want is for your heart to pump blood faster."

What happened to his talk of thoroughly knocking her off her feet? Surely that was better than reminding her of her injury.

Pounding feet entered the kitchen, and the announcement of the police's arrival prevented any more talk. Abraham directed one officer to send for Papa, another to contend with Detective Lawson, and a third to find something in the store below to dress the wounds. A fourth officer confirmed that the Deer Creek Gang had dispersed after Mr. Clemens delivered a prize-winning blow. The only blood in the streets would be pugilist blood. Relief relaxed Abraham's stance even as he warned the dispersing officers to stay vigilant against attack. If her head weren't swirling with dizziness and nausea, she might have been tempted to pull a fictional swoon.

Abraham knelt next to her again and put his hand over hers, increasing the pressure on the wound. It was probably wise and more successful at slowing the bleeding, but the resulting sting made her breathe rapidly. Maybe she would swoon after all.

"Lydia, look at me. In." He inhaled slowly. "Out."

With great difficulty, she focused on his delectable gaze, which comforted better than the cookies she now associated with him. Good heavens he was handsome. God better plan for them to be together, or she was in trouble. From now to evermore, Abraham Hall would be the only man for her. By the way his eyes caressed her face, he felt the same.

When her breathing matched his, Abraham said, "I never thought I'd care so much for a woman so quickly. I don't want to wait any longer to—"

From the other side of the room, Mr. Ingram yelled curses at the officer who'd released him. Abraham jumped to his feet, pivoted, and reached for his holstered gun in one fluid motion.

No. No. No! She was shot. He was doctoring her and showering her with words that promised sweet romance. She hadn't just lived through both a mystery and a romance novel just to have the happily-ever-after ripped away from her. If it didn't hurt to move so much, she'd reach out and draw Abraham back to her. He didn't want to wait any longer for what? To kiss her? That definitely would suffice as a pleasant distraction. And wasn't that how every good story was supposed to end?

If Mr. Ingram stole this from her, she might . . . might . . . Well, she'd do *something* mean and awful. She just needed her arm to stop hurting enough to think of what.

Mr. Ingram strode toward them, jabbing a finger in her direction. "This is your fault. I ought to—"

"Careful, Ingram. Threatening the woman could get you in trouble." The deadly calm tone of Abraham's words would give anyone pause.

"She's the one who needs to be arrested. She helped him plan my death."

"To stall for time!" Her shrillness hurt her own ears, but she couldn't let that accusation go. "Should I have allowed him to act on his first thought and kill you right then and there? You would have been dead hours ago."

Anger flushed his face, but he had the wherewithal to keep the rest of the thoughts rolling through his head to himself. But it didn't stop him from taking another intimidating step forward.

"You've escaped death twice now, Ingram." Abraham angled so he better shielded her. "Don't waste your gift of life. God obviously has something in mind for you, and I don't think it is to earn yourself another trial."

Maybe she could appease Mr. Ingram with an apology. She owed him that much and probably a lot more. In a way, this *was* partially her fault. "I'm sorry, Mr. Ingram. I should never have written any of the Billy Poe stories. If God has deigned to give you a second chance at life, it is not my place to execute judgment. May we both take this undeserved opportunity and learn to use our lives for God's glory instead of our own."

Mr. Ingram snorted. "I should have known you'd be a religious loon. Just don't ever cross my path again." Then he stalked out the door.

She sagged against the wall as Abraham directed the officer to obtain Mr. Ingram's statement.

The man who'd been instructed to procure supplies passed Abraham what appeared to be a cheesecloth. "It was the best I could find."

"Thank you, Nichols. I'll take care of Miss Pelton. See if Yount needs any assistance with Lawson."

The man exited, leaving the room blessedly empty and quiet.

"How are you feeling?" Abraham lowered himself to the floor and gingerly began wrapping her arm.

He would ask that right now. She clenched her jaw and waited until the stabbing pain eased to throbbing.

"Like I've been shot. Does it always hurt this bad?"

"I can't say. You've beaten me to the experience." His half grin did little to ease the strained lines of concern on his face.

"I don't recommend it."

He finished securing the makeshift bandage. "Is there anything I can do until your father arrives?"

"You can either tell me what you don't want to wait any longer for . . . or distract me with a kiss."

He chuckled and cupped her cheek. "How about both?"

"Both is good."

He leaned in, careful not to bump against her body, then stopped a hair's breadth away. "I don't want to wait any longer to court you, which means I can also do this."

His lips pressed against hers and lingered there, inviting her to keep it sweet or dive deeper. She leaned in, determined to fully experience the moment despite the pain trying to intrude. Twenty-two years of saving this kiss, her first real kiss, for the man she intended to wed was worth it. Because, God willing, she would marry Abraham.

Tender. Passionate. Full of promises, hopes, and dreams of a long future lived together. If a person's character could be discerned through a kiss, this moment revealed Abraham's as steadfast, though perhaps impatient at times, certain of what he wanted, gentle, considerate of her needs, and blessedly forgiving of her inadequacies. But she didn't mind his guiding instruction in this. He could teach her all day long.

Until a particularly sharp pain sliced through her consciousness, interrupting the absolute euphoria. She whimpered.

Abraham leaned back abruptly. "I'm hurting you."

"No, the holes in my arm are hurting me, and even that knock-me-off-my-feet kiss cannot distract me from the pain."

He brushed her cheek with his thumb. "Since you aren't on your feet, I'm going to say that doesn't count as knocking you off them, so we'll just have to try again later. And if that one doesn't suffice, we'll try again."

"I fear you'll never actually succeed."

"You never know. Once we get you through this, I have a whole future to prove you wrong."

Now there was a line that belonged in a romance novel.

CHAPTER 39

WHIRLWIND ROMANCES WERE NOT JUST things of fiction. Four months into courting Abraham, Lydia had already planned their wedding details with the Guardians, chosen her wedding dress's design, and hired someone to begin making it. Now all she needed was for the man to actually propose. Given the not-so-sneaky behavior of Theresa, Nora, and Flossie, Lydia suspected Abraham had a plan for that, either for Christmas or the new year.

She bounced her knees in excitement as she finished wrapping Abraham's Christmas present—a bottle of French eau de cologne. It was a perfect blend of lemon, bergamot, and rosemary, with no association of rotting corpse. She'd rather not have the moment of his proposal tainted by flickering memories of the murders guided by her pen.

It was a bit early to exchange gifts, but they'd decided to do so today in an attempt to brighten what was sure to be a difficult afternoon. The trial for Talbot Lawson had concluded, and a swift guilty ruling was expected. Of course, with Lawson's connections to people in high places and his past as a respected detective, there was no telling what would actually occur. Whatever the jury's decision, Abraham would take it hard.

In the days, weeks, and months following the revelation that Lawson was Billy Poe, Abraham had noticeably wrestled with his decision to remain a police officer and detective. On many occasions, he'd brought her into his wrestling. Why was he doing this job? Did it even matter when evil won so often? How, as a Christian man, was he supposed to forgive these people who were so deranged and immoral? Should he quit and find a new occupation before he turned into Detective Lawson—a good man whose heart had been seared by the darkness with which he interacted?

They were hard, vulnerable questions. They'd spent many walks together tackling the concepts of mercy, justice, and judgment. In all honesty, she had needed the conversations as much as he had. Her writing had exposed her to the darkness of the world. She'd not witnessed even a fraction of the depravity Abraham had seen as an officer of the law, but she'd condemned without a second thought those she'd deemed deserving.

Yes, their struggle was the same. As Christians, they were called to leave the judgment of others in God's hands while personally upholding justice and mercy. How did one balance their life with that? She still wasn't sure.

Her fingers were itching to pick up a pen and explore the idea through story. But how could she after all that had happened? She'd promised God she would walk away from writing, and so far, she'd stayed faithful to it. She glanced at the notebook lying on the corner of her desk. It was filled with random thoughts and story tidbits that wouldn't release her from their hold until they'd been committed to paper. It was both the bane and blessing of an author to be driven by story and characters that didn't really exist. She rubbed the two divots in her arm, reminders of that folly. Detective Darcy could never come into existence beyond the scribbles in that notebook.

Papa rapped on the doorframe. "Are you ready? The jury has made their decision."

While she would not be allowed in the gallery to hear the ruling, she'd promised Abraham she would be waiting outside for him when it was finished.

She and Papa made their way to the courthouse, where they chose an outdoor bench near the entrance. It was a sunny, temperate afternoon. Unless the weather took a sharp turn in the next week, a white

Christmas was unlikely. Less than a quarter hour passed before the doors pushed open and reporters raced to their offices to be the first to get the news printed in an extra or the evening post.

Mr. Clemens spotted her as he exited and redirected his steps. "He's been found guilty and sentenced to a hanging," he informed them quietly. "Not even his connections could save him this time. They were too afraid that anything less would lead to an actual riot."

How could she respond to that? There was no simple answer. She felt brokenhearted by the man's downfall and coming judgment. Glad that justice was being upheld. Guilty that her stories had pushed him into the insanity of Billy Poe.

Perhaps that last one most of all.

At her lack of a response, he drew a deep breath. "It's not your fault, you know." He looked away but kept speaking. "I hate that you wrote *Shadow in the Night*, and I initially blamed you for the deaths, but Lawson's decisions were his own. You didn't make them for him. If I no longer hold you responsible, then you shouldn't hold yourself responsible either."

Lydia wasn't sure what to make of his consolation. She was grateful, but it did seem odd coming from him—like she was missing an important piece of information.

He stood there, awkwardly silent, staring down the street but not appearing to see. Whatever thoughts had dragged his attention away, he shook them loose. When he turned her way, an energetic smile stretched across his face. "If you should ever decide to write again, Miss Pelton, stick to romances and happily-ever-afters."

"Life is more complicated than happily-ever-afters. I don't see myself writing ever again, but should I pick up the pen, I want to write about light, truth, and hope, even in the face of darkness, evil, and loss."

"Can there really be hope in the face of such darkness?"

"I believe so. If you want to know, look in your Bible. Jesus is Hope and Light. In Him, there is no darkness, and from Him, all darkness will flee."

"I'm a man of logic. You can believe what you want, but religion isn't for me. At any rate, I'm afraid I have a rather dark story to write for tonight's paper. Good day, Miss Pelton."

Mr. Clemens strode away, leaving behind a sorrow and compassion Lydia had never expected to feel for the reporter. Nothing she could say to him would change his mind, so she did the only thing she knew to do: pray.

Lord, may You get hold of his logical heart and show him how You are the Creator of logic and not confined by it. Help him to see there is no greater comfort than having You as we face the injustice and evil of this world.

"What did he want?" Abraham's gruff voice drew her attention. He stood with hands jammed in his pockets and his shoulders hunched, defeat marring his face. The poor man.

"He told us the verdict and ruling. I'm sorry, Abraham."

Papa stood to clasp Abraham's shoulder. "It's a hard profession we've chosen, but not everyone who chooses it turns into Lawson. We need good men like you to stay and minister to those who walk in the dark. Who knows? You could be the light that guides them to the path of change."

"That sounds rather utopian, sir."

"It's only utopian if you believe you can save everyone. Our job is to shine the light. People must choose for themselves whether to walk toward or away from it. We can't force them, but we can offer truth."

Abraham nodded. "Thank you for that perspective. I'll give it some thought and prayer."

"Good." Papa stepped back, rubbing his hands together. "Now, if you promise to behave with my daughter, I have some urgent Christmas shopping to complete without prying eyes." The meaningful look he sent Lydia only made her grin.

Just this morning, he'd found her snooping through Momma's hiding place for presents.

She plunked her hands on her hips in mock frustration. "What's the point of a mystery if you can't sniff out the clues?"

"Presents are surprises, not mysteries, dear."

"But there's more joy in the figuring out of a gift than the receiving of it."

"Are you saying that you'd rather guess what I have in this box than receive it?" Abraham pulled a small jewel box from his pocket.

Saucers could fit inside her eyes for as wide as they felt. Was he going to propose, right here in front of the courthouse, just after hearing Lawson's sentencing?

She didn't know whether to be thrilled or appalled.

"I'll take that as my cue to leave." Papa dipped his hat and strode away, a chuckle following in his wake.

She jumped for the box, but Abraham pulled it out of reach, a broad smile on his face.

"What's your guess as to what's in here?"

"It's a ring box!"

"It could be earrings."

It could, but he was having way too much fun for it to be something like that.

"You, Theresa, Nora, and Flossie have been sneaking around for weeks. It has to be a ring, and I expect a proposal with it as well."

"Oh, you do, do you?" He shook his head and lowered the box to within reach. "In that case, I suppose I have no choice but to follow through now, rather than with the surprise I had planned." He lowered to one knee and lifted the closed box. "Lydia Pelton, you would make me the happiest of men if you would do me the honor of agreeing to"—he opened the box, revealing a square piece of confectionery—"eat this piece of chocolate."

"Abraham!" She swatted his arm and, at the same time, nabbed the chocolate. "You're such a scoundrel."

"But you had everything figured out. I couldn't very well give you what you wanted." He plucked the chocolate from her hands, split it, and popped one piece into his mouth, offering the other to her.

"So you *are* planning to propose." She tossed the chocolate into her mouth and gave him a saucy grin.

"Maybe. Maybe not." He kissed her cheek and slipped her arm around his. "Come, I've been at the courthouse since breakfast. I'm famished."

She shook her head. "All right, but since you've been such a scoundrel, you're getting your present now, and I'm going to tell you it's because I'm tired of you smelling like Florida Corpse Water."

He laughed as she thrust the wrapped cologne at his chest. "I suppose I had that one coming."

"Yes, you did."

They strolled to a restaurant far enough away from the courthouse to be free of the hungry crowd of trial observers. The food was delightful and the company even better. At the end of the meal, Abraham pulled a long rectangular box from his pocket and set it in front of her.

"It's still not a ring, but I've been praying about something regarding you, and something your father said the other day confirmed it. Maybe for both of us. Open it, then I'll explain."

She squinted suspiciously at him before flipping it open. A simple fountain pen lay atop a sheet with the verse 1 Peter 4:10 written beneath it. She read it aloud. "'As every man hath received the gift, even so minister the same one to another, as good stewards of the manifold grace of God.'"

Abraham took her hand in his. "God has given you a passion and a gift for writing. I don't think you should set it aside forever. Your writing is an opportunity to minister to others. You might have gone about it poorly in the past, but when God places a story that honors Him on your heart, I think you should write it."

She gaped at him. The story that wouldn't leave her alone? Was he really saying she should write it? Was God? Even after the heartache and terror her stories had wrought? "Do you really?"

"Yes. I've seen your longing as you scribble notes when you think no one is looking, and then your heartache as you set them aside." He lifted her hand and kissed it. "Write that story you've been trying so hard to deny. There is no need to write in secret anymore."

She bounced up from her chair and circled around to hug and kiss him. Who cared if it was an unseemly display of affection? The place was nearly deserted anyway.

He laughed and allowed her only a respectable peck. "If I'd known it would make you so happy, I would have given it to you in the privacy of your parlor. What do you say to a stop at the confectionery before heading home?"

"But I've already had chocolate."

"Half a piece, and are you actually going to turn down an opportunity for more?"

"No."

"Good."

The moment they entered the store, Lydia knew something was off, but she couldn't quite put her finger on it. Nothing about the small space looked amiss. The trays of chocolates were mostly picked over, but that was to be expected with it being minutes before closing time. The owner's face had lit up, and she'd perhaps seemed a little too excited to see them, but maybe she'd been lonely. Abraham and Lydia quickly made their selections, and the woman placed them into a box with a bow attached to the top.

Once Abraham paid, he handed Lydia the box. "Which one should we eat first?"

His twitching lips and failure to stay nonchalant immediately made her suspicious.

She pulled off the lid, and in the center of their eight pieces of chocolate was a gold band with a small garnet in it. In her periphery, Abraham dropped to one knee.

The triumph on his face at having caught her by surprise was clear. "Well, Lydia, this is the second time you've had me drop to one knee today, but this time, I'm asking the question I think—or at least hope—you were wanting to hear. Will you marry me?"

She laughed. She couldn't help it. The man had gone to such extreme lengths to twist her expectations.

"Did you have this planned the whole time?"

"Do you have an answer for me?"

"Of course, you daft man. Yes, I'll marry you."

"We've already got the details planned out. All we need is a date."
Theresa came out of the back room. Nora, Flossie, Papa, Momma,
Madelyn, Clara, Jake, and Abraham's parents trailed behind.

Evidently Abraham wasn't the only one capable of surprising her.
"How on earth did you all fit back there?"

"We didn't. It was awful," Madelyn complained. "Can you kiss
him so we can go home now?"

Abraham arched a brow at Lydia. "Should we, with such an audience?"

"Absolutely."

Abraham's arms wrapped around Lydia's waist as he leaned down
and gave her a kiss that made her weak-kneed and dizzy.

She lifted her feet, forcing Abraham to hold her up. "I believe
you've done it. You've finally knocked me off my feet."

Making it literal might have required a little dramatics on her
part, but what good was a whirlwind romance without a bit of theatrics? After all, he had to know what he'd gotten himself into: a lifetime of practicing kiss scenes for her next romance novels, featuring
none other than Detective Darcy.

ACKNOWLEDGMENTS

THIS STORY CAME ABOUT DURING one of the hardest years of my life, and it only happened because of some amazing people. There were days—let's be honest, months—when I didn't think I would ever finish writing it. All glory for its accomplishment goes to God. Thank You, Jesus, for faithfully seeing me through.

Thank you, Travis, for helping me to make Abraham better and for arranging ways for me to be able to write despite the chaos. Thank you to all of my family, who are constantly there for me, making time for my writing and cheering me on. Thank you to my fellow Mayhemmers for being my sanity and sounding board; the Historical Fiction Book Club for helping me work through the theme of justice; Crystal Caudill's Reading Friends Facebook group for your prayers, brainstorming, and support; Rob Fain for giving me a police officer's perspective; retired Chief Gene Ferrara of the Greater Cincinnati Police Museum for the tour and research information; Lieutenant Justin Peter of the Cincinnati Fire Department for your historical knowledge of firefighting; my beta readers; my supportive agent, Tamela Hancock Murray; my editors, Rachel Overton, Andrea Cox, Lindsay Danielson, and Brittany Stonestreet, who guided me in fixing this mess; and, of course, to Kregel who took another chance on me and has worked with me to make the story the best it can be.

Thank you, reader, for giving me the gift of your time. I pray you were as blessed by this story as I am by you.

DISCUSSION QUESTIONS

1. When did you first realize who the villain was? What clues led you to believe that person was guilty?
2. What were your favorite moments in the story?
3. Who was your favorite character? Why?
4. Are Lydia and Abraham a good match? Why or why not?
5. Abraham initially had an unfavorable opinion of dime novels, and many in society thought they should be banned altogether. Should some books be banned? Why or why not?
6. Abraham judged both Dupin's character and status as a Christian by the stories Dupin wrote. Do you think these things can be determined about an author by the content of their books? Why or why not?
7. What is justice? What does it look like?
8. Was it wrong for Lydia to take the stories of real criminals and rewrite them to fit her sense of justice? Why or why not?
9. When the government fails to enact justice (or what we view as justice), what do you think is a Christian's responsibility in how they respond?
10. What does it look like to live out the instruction in Micah 6:8, to "do justly, and to love mercy, and to walk humbly with thy God," in light of the brokenness and injustice in the world?

Author's Note

Dear Treasured Reader,

Thank you so much for taking the time to read my story. It is truly an honor to spend time with you, as I know there are so many other wonderful books you could have chosen to read. Your time is a gift, and I am more grateful to you than words can express. Know that you have been prayed for, and I welcome the opportunity to pray for you by name. I invite you to email me anytime at crystal@crystalcaudill.com and to join me on my writing journey by signing up for my newsletter at crystalcaudill.com. I pray monthly for my subscribers by name, and it would be an honor to add you to that list. If interested, you can check out the book club kits and other bonus materials on my website.

Once again, reader—*thank you* for the gift of your time. May your day be blessed and may you draw ever nearer to Christ.

Your fan,
Crystal

PS: You can scan this QR code to visit my website and sign up for my newsletter.

HISTORICAL NOTES

The Dime Novel

Were dime novels really so scandalous that the city would be lathered into an uproar at Lydia's writing them? When I started my research for dime novels, I felt they could not be that bad—and many of them weren't—but I was shocked at just *how* scandalous some of them were. Allan Pinkerton had one such detective story where he spoke very candidly about the sex–slave trade industry. While most dime novels were not so explicit, many pushed the boundaries of acceptability and would have flown in the face of the Gilded Age's view of a woman's innocence and piety.

Aside from the scandal of a woman reading—let alone writing—these novels, there were many in society who viewed detective novels as glamorizing crime and inciting the youth to criminal behavior. Dime novels were considered morally concerning and were vocally opposed. However, despite the outcry, dime novels of the romantic, western, and even crime varieties were wildly popular and, as a genre, sold hundreds of thousands of copies in their time.

Cincinnati Police History

During the 1870s and 1880s, the Cincinnati police department had a reputation for corruption, mostly due to the very political nature of how the police department was managed. With the exception of four brief periods between 1859 and 1886, full control of the police department—including hiring and firing—fell solely under the direction of the city's mayor. In 1886, the Civil Service Commission was established, bringing with it reform and shared responsibilities between the mayor and four commissioners of varying political parties. But the department's history wasn't all bad. Cincinnati was one of the first cities in the nation to adopt telephone communication for their police officers. Locked telegraph boxes were converted to telephones in 1879, making it easier for officers to regularly check in or call for backup while on duty. Despite the volatile political-climate challenges they faced, most Cincinnati police officers admirably served and protected their community.

Criminal Injustice

During the late nineteenth century, Cincinnati suffered from corruption and dysfunction, especially in the court system, and the entire city was growing weary of it. While researching for *Counterfeit Love*, I read about the 1884 riots, and the story spark for *Written in Secret* was ignited. On Christmas Eve 1883, William Kirk was bludgeoned and then strangled to death by two of his employees, William Berner and Joe Palmer. Both men confessed to the murder, but Palmer knew only he would hang, as Berner's people had money. Berner was tried first, and the entire city expected a hanging sentence. Instead of the jury ruling murder, however, they ruled manslaughter with a maximum twenty-year sentence. The judge was horrified, and the city was outraged. They believed the jury had been bought. A meeting was called in hopes of organizing a legitimate reform movement to restore order to the city, but instead, a lynch mob formed that quickly turned into three days of rioting. Exact numbers vary depending on the resource, but more than fifty people died, and hundreds were injured. Berner escaped safely to the state penitentiary to serve eleven years of his twenty-year sentence before being released for good behavior. As Palmer predicted, he was sentenced to death and hung in 1885. This trial was the final straw; many others like it had occurred for decades beforehand. While I used the background of this riot as the basis for Poe's almost victim, I changed the names so I could eventually set a story during the 1884 riots without interfering with history or my story world.

The Deer Creek Gang

The Deer Creek Gang really did exist and was just as nasty as described in the story. From about 1880 until 1885, this monstrous gang terrorized the streets freely and fearlessly. The outlaws almost always traveled in crowds of fifteen to forty, committed robberies nightly, held up anyone whose path they crossed, and regularly used their weapons for intimidating citizens, fighting each other, and harming anyone who dared stand up to them. The part of the city where the gang operated was the toughest of the police beats and was not a safe place to patrol. Officers traveled together in hopes of preserving their lives. Eventually, the police employed new tactics and over one hundred gang members were sent to the workhouse or penitentiary, while the rest were cowed.

Fire Grenades

Fire grenades were decorative glass bottles with bulbous bottoms and long necks. These beautiful vessels weren't for decoration though. They were filled with salt water or carbon tetrachloride. When deployed, the glass would shatter, and the contents would extinguish the fire. However, each held only about a pint of liquid. They were either suspended from the ceiling with special brackets so that the wax seal could melt and allow the liquid to pour out in a sprinkler-like fashion, or thrown at the intended target. Wondering "what if a fire grenade were filled with something flammable?" sparked my idea for Abraham's close-range experience.